"I never meant to fall in love with
well have tried to stop a tornado or a p
sealed our fate, when we saw each o
love began to grow, Jesse was all hea
waiting for a match."

Zee Mimms was just nineteen in 1864—the daughter of a stern Methodist minister in Missouri—when she fell in love with the handsome, dashing, and already notorious Jesse. He was barely more than a teenager himself, yet had ridden with William Quantrill's raiders during the Civil War.

"You'll marry a handsome young man," a palm reader had told her. "A man who will make you the envy of many."

"What else?" I asked.

She shook her head, avoiding my gaze. "Nothing else. I wish you every happiness."

"There was something else," I said. "You saw something that upset you. What is it?"

She pursed her lips. "I saw that it won't all be happiness for you," she said. "There will be . . . hard times."

Hard times were nothing new, but the way she said the words sent a cold shiver up my spine—the feeling my mother referred to as 'someone walking across your grave.' I wanted to ask for more details. What kind of hard times would these be? But I was a coward and kept silent.

Zee and Jesse's marriage proved the palmist right. Jesse was a dangerous puzzle: a loving husband and father who kept his "work" separate from his family, though Zee heard the lurid rumors of his career as a bank robber and worse. Still, she never gave up on him.

And he earned her love, time and again.

The Woman Who Loved

Jesse James

by

Cindi Myers

Bell Bridge Books

Bell Bridge Books
PO BOX 300921
Memphis, TN 38130
Print ISBN: 978-1-61194-082-4

Bell Bridge Books is an Imprint of BelleBooks, Inc.

Printed and bound in the United States of America.

We at BelleBooks enjoy hearing from readers.
Visit our websites – www.BelleBooks.com and www.BellBridgeBooks.com.

10 9 8 7 6 5 4 3 2 1

Cover design: Debra Dixon
Interior design: Hank Smith
Photo credits:
Cover art (manipulated) © Ateliersommerland | Dreamstime.com

:LWtw:01:

Dedication

For Jim, Always

Acknowledgments

I need to thank many people for their support in making this book come together. Colleen Collins, Emily McCaskle and Isabel Sharpe read early versions of the manuscript, and their comments were immensely helpful.

Thanks to the Duetters, the BGs and the Fairplay Secret Society for cheering me on and providing encouragement as I wrote. To the Hand Hotel and Mike Stone for the best writer's retreat ever.

And many thanks to Deborah Smith and Debra Dixon and everyone at BelleBooks and Bell Bridge Books for their enthusiasm for this project.

Finally, I couldn't have done this without the love and support of my husband, Jim. Love you.

—*Cindi Myers*

"There is a dash of tiger blood in the veins of all men; a latent disposition even in the bosom that is a stranger to nerve and daring, to admire those qualities in other men. And this penchant is always keener if there be a dash of sin in the deed to spice the enjoyment of its contemplation."
—*The Kansas City Times,* September 29, 1872

March, 1881

From the upstairs window of the house that was to have been our refuge, I stared down at the line of men with guns. That line of men on fine, fast horses, loaded rifles laid across their saddles, loaded pistols at their hips, had come to destroy everything I held most dear—to destroy me in the process.

I gripped the window sill with hands like ice, determined not to surrender to the terror that threatened to buckle my knees, and looked back over my shoulder at my children. They slept peacefully, sweet angels unaware of danger. I feared for them, of course, but that fear was a beast behind a locked door, contained for the moment.

The terror that threatened to overpower me was for their father, the man to whom I had linked my fate years before. My fear for him was a demon I wrestled daily, the distaff side to the love that bound us together.

I cast one more fond look on my sleeping children, then felt in the pocket of my dress for the pistol their father had given me so many years before. I had never fired the weapon at anything other than tin cans or old bottles, but I would use it now if I had to, to defend all I loved.

I shut the door softly behind me and started down the stairs. If this was the end, then I would stand with the man those gunmen had come for. I would stand with Jesse; my heart gave me no other choice.

Chapter One

I never meant to fall in love with Jesse James, but I might as well have tried to stop a tornado or a prairie fire. The summer that sealed our fate, when we saw each other with new eyes and our love began to grow, Jesse was all heat and light, and I was tinder waiting for a match.

But I wasn't thinking of Jesse that hot August day in the summer of 1864 when my oldest sister, Lucy, was married to Bowling Browder. I merely welcomed the distraction of a celebration after years of hardship before and during the war.

"I hear tell there's to be a band, with fiddles, *and* a flute player," my best friend, Esme Purlin, said. Clad only in shimmy and drawers in the stifling heat of my attic bedroom, hair twisted in dozens of rag curls all over her head, she waltzed across the floor, arms extended to grasp the hands of an invisible beau. The air was heavy with the scent of honeysuckle that trailed across the sloping tin roof below my window, sweet with the promise of honey from the bees that droned among the golden blossoms.

"And dancing," I said as I struggled to roll my own hair in the strips of rags I'd torn from a worn-out petticoat. "Lucy promised there'd be dancing."

"It's a shame *we* can't dance," Esme said, letting her arms fall to her sides. "It always looks like so much fun—though perhaps that's why Papa says it's sinful."

"I don't care if it's sinful or not," I said. "If someone asks me, I intend to dance." How many chances would I have to whirl around a dance floor in a man's arms?

Esme sucked in her breath. "Zee, you can't! What will people say? What will your *father* say?"

"If he sees me, he won't like it." My father, a Methodist minister, would be scandalized by even the thought of one of his daughters dancing. If caught, I would be punished, perhaps severely. Having sired eleven children, my father was not one to spare the rod. But even a caning seemed worth the opportunity to give free reign to my feelings.

Too often lately my life seemed a constant battle—the outer

meekness I was taught was proper for a Southern lady warring with an inner boldness out of all proportion with my upbringing as a pastor's daughter. Like the country itself, I was unsettled of late, and wondered if peace was truly possible, both for my nation and for myself.

"I'm looking forward to the cake," Esme said.

I couldn't remember the last time I'd eaten real sugar or light flour. The war had brought hard times here to Missouri, especially for Sesech families like ours. "But dancing's better than cake," I said. "Lucy said that after dark the Browders have ordered lanterns hung in the trees to light a dance floor. Which means there'll be lots of dark shadows for sneaking away and stealing kisses." I had never kissed a man, but I had thought of it often, and on a night when I anticipated such a rebellion as dancing adding kissing seemed scarcely to compound my sin.

Esme giggled. "Maybe the unfortunate Mr. Colquit will try to kiss you."

I made a face and knotted the last rag into place. "Mr. Colquit and his misfortunes would do best not to come near me." Anthony Colquit was a member of my father's congregation, a widower who, in addition to three unmanageable children, was possessed of a prominent mole on his left cheek. His wife had died of cholera the year before, leading my mother and the other women in our community to refer to him as "the unfortunate Mr. Colquit." Recently, he had indicated an interest in me, one which I had no intention of reciprocating.

Esme plopped onto my bed, making the ropes holding the mattress squeak. "He's not so bad," she said.

"I'm not interested in Mr. Colquit," I said.

"I'm not so sure either one of us can afford to be uninterested in any man who courts us," Esme said. "We're both of us already nineteen and it's not as if there are a great many young men available, what with the war and all. At least Mr. Colquit has a farm, and he's not so terribly old."

"He must be almost thirty!" I protested. But neither his age nor his mole nor his three terrible children were the chief reason I rejected the notion of Mr. Colquit as a husband. "I'm already a poor farmer's daughter. Why should I end up a poor farmer's wife?" And I didn't want to wed a man who sought a convenient mother for his children; I wanted a man who would love *me*—not for what I could do for him, but solely for who I was.

I searched in the drawer of the dressing table for the bit of red flannel I used to darken my lips, and the precious tin of rice powder, which I *would* wear to the wedding, even if my mother had forbade it. I avoided looking at my reflection in the spotted glass of the mirror. I was thin and pale, yet who of us wasn't after so many years of deprivation? "I'm tired of suffering and making do," I said. "I want someone who can offer me more in life."

"As if you're going to meet a man like that in Missouri."

"Mrs. Peabody says a woman should never sell herself short."

"My mother says Mrs. Peabody is no better than she should be."

"My mother says the same thing, but that doesn't mean Mrs. P. is wrong." Amanda Peabody lived alone in a little cabin a quarter mile from our farm. She said she was a widow, though some folks thought otherwise. And no one could deny that Sheriff T. Wayne Henry—a married man—spent a great deal of time at her place. The sheriff claimed Mrs. Peabody was only doing his ironing, which led to any number of ribald comments about what, exactly, was being ironed.

"I guess if anyone knows about a woman selling herself—short or otherwise—it would be her." Esme hooted with laughter, and fell back on the bed.

I scowled at her. "Mrs. Peabody is my friend, and I won't have you saying mean things about her. She's never been anything but nice to us whenever we've visited her."

"You're right," Esme said, staring up at the sloped ceiling. "I'm sorry. I'm just out of sorts, wishing I was the one getting married, and not your sister. With most of the young men off fighting the war and the ones left at home either old or crippled or Northern sympathizers—it makes me despair of ever finding a husband and having a family."

"The war can't last forever," I said. "When it's over our men will come home and they'll all be looking for wives. You'll have so many beaux you won't know what to do."

"I'll have to ask Mrs. Peabody what to do. She'll be able to tell me."

We were both laughing over this when my mother called up the stairs. "Sister! Esme! You girls come down here. I need you to take the punch over to the wedding."

Grumbling, we slipped on our wrappers and hurried down the stairs. We found my mother in the kitchen, stirring something on the stove with one hand and wiping jam from my little brother Henry's face with the other. A row of flatirons heated on the stove, bundles of dampened linens piled on the hearth.

"We can't go anywhere right now, Mama," I protested. "We just rolled our hair."

"Put on your bonnets and no one will see you. Your father's already loaded the cask of punch into the trap, but he and Joey had to leave to see about a cow down by the creek." Joey was the darky who worked for us part-time. We were too poor to afford even one slave, unlike the family my sister was marrying into. The Browders owned *seven* slaves, both field hands and household servants.

"Why do we have to take the punch now?" I asked. "The wedding's still hours away."

"It has to be put on ice to cool. Now go. All you have to do is drive over to the Browders and one of their men will unload it for you."

Esme opened her mouth to protest, but I tugged on her arm, silencing her. "We'll be happy to go, Mama," I said. "Let me run upstairs and fetch my bonnet."

I raced up the narrow flight of steps to my room, Esme at my heels. "What are you looking so cheerful about?" she asked. "It's hot as Hades outside and over a mile to the Browders's place. We'll melt."

"We can come back the long way by the creek, in the shade." I threw open the wardrobe and pulled out the dress I'd made special for the wedding. Or made-over, rather, from an old-fashioned ball gown Mrs. Peabody had given me. No one around here had seen new cloth since before the war.

"What are you doing?" Esme asked as I tugged off my wrapper and tied on the crinoline hoops necessary to make the wide skirts then in fashion fit correctly.

"Tighten my laces for me, won't you?" I asked, turning my back to her.

She did as I asked, pulling the laces to my corset tight and tying them in neat bows in the back. Then she helped me lift the dress over my head. Fashioned of blue and buff striped satin, it featured wide flared sleeves trimmed with flounces, a low, square neckline with more flounces, and a deep flounce around the hem. I had spent many an hour gathering all those ruffles and carefully attaching them to the dress, but I was proud of the results. I was sure I would be as fashionable as any young woman at the ball.

"On the way home from the Browders's we can stop by Mrs. Peabody's," I said as I smoothed my skirts over the hoops. "I want to show her my new dress."

"You can't go downstairs all dressed up," Esme said. "What will your mother say?"

"Nothing. She won't even notice." My mother was so distracted by the demands of running a large household that whole days passed without her looking directly at me.

"We'll get in trouble." Esme looked unsure.

"We'll ask her to read your tea leaves—to tell you about the man you'll marry."

Esme's expression brightened. "All right." She shed her wrapper and took her crinolines and gown from where she'd laid them out on the end of the bed. "Pull tight on my laces," she said. "This is last year's dress and it'll never fit, otherwise."

In record time we were dressed and down the stairs, our rag curls hidden by deep poke bonnets. Mama was busy in the kitchen; she didn't look up as we passed.

The sun beat down on the main road, baking us beneath the patched parasols we held over our heads. The horse moved at a plodding pace, puffs of dust as fine as face powder rising with the impact of each hoof. Esme and I held an old blanket over our laps in spite of the heat, to protect our skirts from the dirt.

The Browders's property was marked by a wooden fence, whitewashed each spring by a team of darkies. Horses grazed behind the fence, and beyond that stretched fields of corn and hemp that drooped in the heat.

I turned the trap in at the front gate, which stood open, its broad expanse decorated with wreaths of laurel and oak. An old darky near the front told me how to get to the kitchen, and I guided the horse to the open-sided cook house behind the main house. A trio of black women—two small and one very large—worked amid billows of steam from boiling pots and smoke from the pit fires where big joints of meat were roasting. I told the big woman I'd brought the punch and she ordered a younger man to unload it for me.

As soon as we were able, I turned the trap and left. "We should have asked to water the horse," Esme said. "And we could have asked for a glass of lemonade for ourselves." She fanned herself. "I'm parched."

"Mrs. Peabody will have lemonade." I slapped the reins across the horse's back, urging him into a trot. He could have all the water he wanted at Mrs. Peabody's.

"But she won't have ice," Esme whined. The Browders were the only ones in our neighborhood who were wealthy enough to afford to have ice shipped down the river and packed in sawdust all summer in a special ice house they'd had cut into the side of a hill.

I ignored her and turned the trap onto the shady creek road. I was thinking about what I'd said earlier to Esme—that Mrs. Peabody would read her tea leaves and tell her who she'd marry. I would ask Mrs. P. to read my leaves as well—to tell me of my future husband. Please God, let it not be the unfortunate Mr. Colquit, or any man of his ilk. Give me a man with some spark and sense of adventure. A man with ambitions that went beyond planting the next hemp crop.

Mrs. Peabody's cabin sat close to the road, with a small yard swept free of any greenery, behind a sagging wooden gate. I tied the horse to the gatepost and while Esme was pumping a bucket of water for him, Mrs. Peabody came out onto her porch. "Don't you girls look pretty," she said, with a Georgia accent as smooth and sweet as thick cream poured over ripe strawberries. She was dressed in a loose wrapper of faded pink cotton, a white lace cap pinned to her closely-cropped curls. "Come in out of this heat," she urged, and motioned us over to the porch swing in the shade of a wooden arbor onto which wild jasmine had been trained to grow. "Sit yourselves down and I'll fetch some refreshments," she said, clearly delighted to have our company.

Esme and I sat in the swing, arranging our skirts around us. It felt good to stop in the shade, and I even imagined a faint breeze stirring the jasmine.

Mrs. Peabody returned bearing a silver tray on which sat a cut-glass pitcher of some amber liquid. "Cool sassafras tea," she explained, filling three china cups. "Very refreshing on a hot day like this."

She served us, then sat back in a wicker rocker across from the swing. "Now let me look at you. Are these the dresses you're to wear to the wedding?"

"This is the one I made over from the gown you gave me," I said, fingering the striped satin.

She nodded. "And a fine job you did. It looks just like a picture from *Godey's*." She turned to Esme. "Did you make your dress as well? It's very pretty."

Esme blushed and smoothed the brown cotton figured with pink roses. "My mother made it," she said. "I don't sew as well as Zee."

Mrs. Peabody set her teacup on a small round table between us. "Tell me all about the wedding. I hear it's to be a grand affair."

"We delivered a keg of punch to the Browders's just now and they're fixing enough food to feed an army," Esme said.

"Likely they'll have enough guests to fit out their own regiment," Mrs. Peabody said. She leaned forward and spoke in a conspiratorial tone. "My friend, Mr. Henry, tells me you'll be having some very special guests at the wedding."

"Who?" I asked, confused. Why would Sheriff Henry know more about the wedding guests than we did?

"He's heard your cousins, Jesse and Frank James, plan to attend—they who've lately distinguished themselves with Bill Anderson's men."

"Frank and Jesse James?" Esme turned to me, eyes wide. "I'd forgotten they were your cousins. Are they really going to be there?"

I shrugged. "They might be. There's no reason they shouldn't." Though I was named after Jesse and Frank's mother Zerelda, their father, my mother's brother Robert James, had died many years previous. Zerelda had married a prosperous farmer, Ruben Samuel, and the family lived in Kearney, a two days' ride from our home in St Louis, so we didn't see them often.

"Those boys aren't very popular with the Yankees at present," Mrs. Peabody said. "Jesse in particular is said to have quite distinguished himself on their raids, inflicting heavy damage on the Union men."

"Jesse?" The last time I'd seen my cousin, he'd been a gangly fourteen-year old, a pale Mama's boy who had terrorized us girls by throwing mud balls at our skirts. I couldn't fit this image with that of an elite soldier.

"No doubt he's out for revenge," Esme said. "After the scandalous way the Northern Militiamen treated his mother and step-father."

"It was disgraceful, hauling a woman in her condition off to jail simply because she refused to tell what she didn't even know," Mrs. Peabody said.

"And poor Dr. Samuel almost *died* from their ill treatment of him," Esme said.

That spring, a group of militiamen had descended on my aunt and uncle's home and demanded to know the location of William Quantrill and his men. Though Jesse was still at home at the time, his brother Frank was said to be riding with the famous guerrilla. Zerelda and her husband, Dr. Samuel, refused to provide any information to men they viewed as their enemies, and for their trouble Dr. Samuel was beaten and hanged to within an inch of his life and Zerelda, pregnant with her sixth child, had been jailed for many miserable weeks. Shortly after this, Jesse had joined his older brother in riding with the bushwhackers, aligning himself with one of Quantrill's lieutenants, William "Bloody Bill" Anderson.

"He and Frank will have to watch themselves today," Mrs. Peabody said. "Lest some Northern sympathizer decide to try to make himself a hero and take them out."

I shivered at the idea. I might not care for Jesse and his brother much, but they were still my kin. "The Browders wouldn't invite any Yankees to the wedding," I said.

"A party that large, who's to tell?" She smoothed her skirts, then looked at us expectantly. "Now surely you girls didn't come all this way on a hot day to show me your dresses. What really brings you here?"

"We were hoping you'd read our tea leaves," Esme said. "And tell me who I'm to marry." She glanced at me. "Though my father says such things are tools of the devil."

"And who's to say the devil doesn't know the truth as well as the Lord, considering Satan was once said to be the highest angel?" Mrs. Peabody laughed at Esme's shocked expression. Then she turned to me. "What about you, Zee? Do you want to know what type of man you'll wed?"

I nodded. "Yes."

Mrs. Peabody rubbed her hands together. "It's too hot for brewing tea, so I'll read your palms instead. You first, Esme."

Esme hesitated, then thrust out her hand, as if she half-expected Mrs. P. to sever it at the wrist. Our hostess grasped Esme's arm and held it steady while she bent low over the palm.

"You will live a long life," Mrs. Peabody said, tracing the crease across the center of Esme's palm. With her forefinger, she followed another line. "You will marry a man with three children. A farmer, I think."

Esme's eyes widened. "That sounds like Mr. Colquit! Does my future husband have a mole?"

"A mole? I can't tell that. But he will treat you well and you will be happy and have . . ." She paused and studied Esme's palm again. "You'll have five children of your own."

"Five?" Esme grinned. "I hope you're right."

"My turn." I offered my hand. Mrs. Peabody took it, her skin cool and dry against my own, her fingers work-roughened and red as she traced the lines across my palm. Deep furrows marred her brow as she studied my hand for a long time, saying nothing.

Esme and I exchanged glances. "What is it?" I demanded. "What do you see?"

She hesitated. "You'll marry a handsome young man." She released my hand. "A man who will make you the envy of many."

"What else?" I asked.

She shook her head, avoiding my gaze. "Nothing else. I wish you every happiness."

"There was something else," I said. "You saw something that upset you. What is it?"

She pursed her lips. "I saw that it won't all be happiness for you," she said. "There will be . . . hard times."

Hard times were nothing new, but the way she said the words sent a cold shiver up my spine—the feeling my mother referred to as 'someone walking across your grave.' I wanted to ask for more details. What kind of hard times would these be? But I was a coward and kept silent.

Mrs. Peabody refilled our cups. "Enough of worrying about the future," she said. "Tell me what your mother is wearing to the wedding. And your sister."

"Mother is wearing the best dress she made before the war," I said. "Lavender checked taffeta with leg-o'-mutton sleeves. Lucy has a new dress—white cotton lawn worn over big hoops and trimmed in yards and yards of handmade lace."

"I heard the groom's friends talked about kidnapping the bride tonight and having a chivaree," Esme said.

"Bowling told them if they tried he'd shoot to kill." I shivered. "I don't know if he meant it, but my father spread the word he wouldn't stand for any trouble where his daughter is concerned."

"She'll have enough on her mind with the wedding night, without worrying about a bunch of drunken young men dragging her away from her new husband," Mrs. Peabody said.

"Is it so awful?" Esme asked. "The wedding night?"

Mrs. Peabody let out a bawdy laugh. "Who told you a wedding night is awful?"

Esme blushed. "I overheard my mother talking to my older sister, Liz, before she was married. Mother told her a lady doesn't enjoy lying with a man, but it's necessary in order to bear children, so the best thing to do is to submit quietly."

"That's the biggest bunch of horseshit I ever heard!"

The words were as shocking as the sentiment behind them. "My mother says men always enjoy marital relations more than women," I said. "That it's part of women's punishment for what happened in the Garden of Eden, when Eve tempted Adam."

"So Adam holds no blame for taking the apple from Eve?" Mrs.

Peabody waved away the notion, then leaned toward us and spoke in a confiding tone. "Believe me, girls. Women can enjoy sex every bit as much as men—provided they're with a man who knows what he's doing."

"But how would we know if the man knows what he's doing or not?" Esme protested.

"You know because you learn for yourself what pleases you and you inform him if he comes up lacking."

Esme and I exchanged glances again. We had eavesdropped on enough conversations among the older, married women to know that men had strong sexual urges. It was a wife's duty to satisfy these urges, but the closest I had ever heard any woman come to admitting to enjoying the marital bed was once when my Aunt Zerelda said her husband, Dr. Samuel, was 'considerate' of her feelings in this regard.

"Don't look so owl-eyed, both of you," Mrs. Peabody chided. "Don't tell me you've never touched yourself for pleasure."

Esme and I couldn't even look at each other now. Yes, I had touched myself. I had enjoyed discovering the changes in my body as I grew into my womanhood. And sometimes, on lonely nights in my rooms, the caressing and fondling of my own body had been a kind of comfort. But I would never admit such depravity to anyone else.

"It's all right if you have," Mrs. Peabody said cheerfully. "Everyone does. It's how we learn about our own bodies. And about the most pleasurable ways to be touched."

Cicadas hummed in the trees just beyond the porch. Or was that my own head, buzzing with this onslaught of dangerous ideas?

Esme looked as distressed as I felt. "Is it true what people say—that you and Mr. Henry are lovers?" she blurted.

Mrs. Peabody frowned at her. "My relationship with Mr. Henry is a private matter," she said.

"But he's a married man," Esme protested.

"A man whose wife is an invalid, whom it would be dishonorable for him to leave." She leaned toward us. "I don't expect either of you girls to understand this now, but I want you to listen to me and take what I have to say to heart. When you find a man you truly love, with both your body and your heart, you will be willing to endure a great deal of pain for those moments of pleasure. Not merely sexual pleasure, though that is not to be undervalued, but the pleasure of knowing that he loves you with the same intensity and passion."

Passion. The word and the sentiment it conveyed were as exotic as a rare orchid or a tropical bird. It was a word that hinted at sex and sin and emotions not kept demurely in check. The ideas made me shiver and started an ache deep inside me. *That* was the kind of man I wanted—not cool Mr. Colquit and his good manners, but a man of *passion.*

"Mr. Henry?" Esme's astonishment reminded me that the man to whom Mrs. Peabody was so devoted was not the sort to make my own heart beat faster. The sheriff was a stout, graying man who walked with a limp from a ball he had taken in the leg at Antietam.

Mrs. Peabody laughed again. "A man's looks and age have little to do with his skill at pleasing a woman," she said. She patted my knee. "Now that I've sufficiently shocked you, why don't you take off those bonnets and let me fix your hair? I have a new issue of *Godey's* that shows some very fetching styles."

The wedding of my sister Lucy to Mr. Bowling Browder was the social event of the year in our part of the county. Easily a hundred buggies, traps and saddle horses filled the pastures and lined the drive leading up to the Browders's house, a two-storied, white-washed manse with a broad front veranda.

Lucy looked happy and not at all nervous as she stood with her husband-to-be to say her vows. My father performed the ceremony on the top step of the verandah while friends and family looked on. Bowling stammered a little, but recovered enough to plant a not-so-chaste kiss on his new wife, while his friends whistled and cheered.

Afterwards, Esme and I joined the crowd making its way to the buffet spread beneath trees behind the house. Darkies in crisp white aprons delivered trays of smoked meats, pickled and fresh vegetables, fried chicken, baked beans, and steaming rolls. To finish, there was a huge white-frosted cake decorated with sugared flowers, its layers rising three feet above the table where it sat, watched over by a small black boy who kept away the flies with a palmetto fan.

Esme and I filled our plates and found a spot on a blanket beneath a spreading oak, from which vantage point we could observe the crowd. "There's Mr. Henry," Esme said, nodding toward a group of men who loitered near the cookhouse. The sheriff stood at their center, gleaming pistols just visible beneath his open coat. I studied his stout, stocky figure. This was Mrs. Peabody's skilled lover?

"He must be over thirty-five," Esme said. "Almost as old as my father."

"Mrs. Peabody must be at least that old," I said. Though I still couldn't imagine wanting to sleep with a man like Mr. Henry.

"Have you seen your cousins yet?" Esme asked.

"Frank and Jesse?" I shook my head. "No." Then again, would I even recognize the boys if I saw them again?

We were almost finished eating when Fanny and Rachel Grace, friends from school, joined us. "There's a group of young men here, recently returned from the war," Fanny said, her eyes shining.

"How many of them are there?" Esme's face brightened. Young men meant possible suitors.

"I heard half a dozen," Rachel said. "Though if any of them are worth knowing, I can't say."

"I say any eligible young man is worth knowing in these times." Fanny glared at her sister. Already twenty-two, she was in danger of being labeled an old maid, while Rachel was just eighteen.

"Or even an eligible older man," Esme said, giving me a knowing look. "If he's nice and can support a wife I wouldn't say no to him."

"Frank and Jesse James might be worth knowing," Rachel said. "I hear Jesse in particular is a handsome one."

"Are they here?" Esme asked.

"So I hear," Rachel said. "Though never having met them, I couldn't say."

"Frank and Jesse are Zee's cousins," Esme volunteered.

Fanny regarded me with renewed interest. "Then perhaps you'll introduce us."

"Perhaps." I stood and excused myself, pretending I had to visit the outhouse, when all I really wanted was to escape from the cloying desperation of these women who were so determined to snare a man at any cost.

Yes, I wanted a husband, and a home and children of my own. But our visit this afternoon with Mrs. Peabody had made me more certain than ever that I wanted to do more than settle for the first man who would ask me. I wanted the grand passion she'd spoken of—a man I could love with both my body and my heart, who would add color and adventure to my life, and not merely more drudgery.

Chapter Two

I slipped around the side of the house, toward a grove of trees along the edge of the back pasture, anxious to return to the relative coolness of the shade. I leaned against the gnarled trunk of an elm and squinted up at the pattern of light and shadow filtering through its slipper-shaped leaves. The hum of voices from the party seemed very far away, the indistinguishable conversations of a dream.

"Don't you think it's dangerous for a young lady to be wandering into the woods by herself?"

I gasped at the low, deep voice so close to my ear, and whirled to face the speaker. He laughed at my obvious discomposure, but swept off his hat and sketched a bow. "I didn't mean to startle you," he said.

"What did you expect, sneaking up on me that way?" I studied him through lowered lashes. More than the sudden fright made my heart race now. He was a handsome man, near my own age, with fine, sharp features, thick sandy hair and broad shoulders.

But his eyes were the feature that caught and held me. Eyes as blue as the summer sky, as full of light and heat. Eyes that looked directly into mine without flinching, seeing not just the picture I presented of myself as a nicely dressed young lady, but seeing *me*—the secret self few others bothered to notice.

"Cousin Zee, don't you recognize me?" he asked.

My gaze fell to the hat in his hand—a flat-brimmed felt pinned up on one side, of the type favored by Quantrill's guerrillas. "Jesse?" I gasped.

"At your service, ma'am." He sketched another bow, lithe and graceful in a black suit, gray-striped waistcoat and string tie.

"What are you doing hiding out here in the woods?" I demanded, drawing on anger to cover my confusion. I couldn't quite believe the dashing man before me was my whiny cousin Jesse.

"I might ask you the same question." He replaced the hat on his head and regarded me from beneath the rakish angle of the brim.

"I came for a breath of fresh air and the coolness of the shade," I said.

"I wanted a good look at the crowd before I ventured forth." He nodded toward the gathering. "Who's the stocky man with the frock coat and the pistols—standing by the punch keg?"

"That's Sheriff T. Wayne Henry. Why?"

"Is he Union or Secesh?"

"Southern. He fought at Antietam."

Jesse nodded. "Anyone here who might have Northern sympathies?"

"No. My family and the groom's are both firmly with the Confederacy."

"Then I suppose it's safe for me to join the party." But he made no move to leave.

"Is it true you're riding with Quantrill's men?" I asked.

"I have the honor of serving with Quantrill's lieutenants, Bill Anderson and Archie Clement, as we strive to further the Southern cause."

"Bloody Bill" and Archie Clement were well known to Missourians. Among Southern sympathizers they were revered for their success in wiping out whole groups of Union soldiers in daring raids on encampments and troop trains. Unlike the regular Army, the guerrillas were free to choose their own targets, and to attack and withdraw with lightning speed. That a not-yet seventeen-year old could distinguish himself in such a company of seasoned fighters spoke volumes about Jessie's abilities and made me see him in a new light.

I began to walk along the edge of the trees and Jesse fell into step beside me. "Are you really worried about Union soldiers disrupting the wedding party?" I asked.

"I'll leave and draw them away before I let that happen."

I stumbled on a fallen branch and he took my elbow to steady me, his hand remaining there for a heartbeat too long. I glanced up and found his eyes fixed on me with uncommon intensity. "What is it?" I asked, annoyed at being the object of such scrutiny.

"Last time I saw you, you were a skinny girl," he said. "You've grown into a fine woman."

My cheeks burned and I looked away, reminding myself that this was the boy who had ruined my skirt with mudballs, the one who had cried and run to his mother when I dared to retaliate by firing a rock at him.

But this was no boy standing beside me. Jesse's voice was the deep, rich tones of a man, and he had a man's build. A man's capable hands reached out and guided me over a second fallen branch, and this time they did not release me. He leaned close and I caught the smells of leather and gun oil that clung to him. "Did you truly not recognize me just now?" he asked.

"It's been a few years since we last met," I said. "I was thinking of you as a boy still."

"I've done and seen things no boy should do or see," he said solemnly.

A shout rose from among the wedding guests, distracting him. He looked across the clearing to where his brother Frank, who Jesse always called Buck, stood with a group of young men. The men were surrounded by a bevy of young women, including Rachel, Fanny and Esme. "I'd better join my friends," he said, releasing my arm. "Good afternoon, Cousin."

He nodded, then strode away. I stood as still and calm as the atmosphere on a sultry afternoon, nothing within me moving, though the air around me had the heavy, charged atmosphere of a storm about to break.

The handsome, young bushwhackers swept into the celebration like a cool mountain breeze, enlivening the party with a jolt of energy and daring. Women circled them like butterflies around blossoms and the men obliged by flattering and flirting, paying court to each young miss with equal fervor. Darkness fell and lamps were lit and hung in the trees and from the eaves of buildings, and large canvas sheets were spread on the ground for dancing.

The band began a lively reel and the young men and women paired off. I was more than pleased when one of the bushwhackers, a handsome young man named Cole Younger, bowed before me. "May I have the pleasure of a dance?" he asked.

On trembling legs, I stood and put my hand in his. "Certainly," I said.

Though forbidden to dance, Esme and I had practiced the steps of the waltz and the quadrille in my attic bedroom, humming to ourselves as we turned, twirled, and promenaded. We were determined to be as accomplished as the young women in the novels, also forbidden, that we read in secret—hours spent in the seclusion of the woods behind my house, huddled over the pages of *Pride and Prejudice*, *Wuthering Heights* and other romantic tales.

But dancing with a man would be a different thing altogether, and I prayed I would not disgrace myself in this, my maiden public effort.

"Zerelda! What do you think you're doing?"

I froze as my father's voice cut through the hum of conversation and whirl of music. Cole released my hand as if singed, and turned to face my father. "Sir," he said, with a stiff bow.

Father ignored him and turned to me. "Zerelda, what are you doing?" he demanded again.

I held my head high, and willed my voice not to shake. "Mr. Younger has done me the honor of asking me to dance," I said.

Father turned to Cole. "I am sorry if my daughter has misled you," he said. "But she does not dance."

"The fault is entirely mine, sir." He flashed me a look full of sympathy, bowed, and melted into the crowd.

Father turned to me once more. "Zerelda," he began.

"I don't see what harm there is in dancing at my sister's wedding," I protested. "What sin can happen here in the open, with so many people watching?" *And what is so wrong with a little sin if it makes me feel more alive?* I thought, but did not dare say the words out loud.

"You know that not all sin is evident for all to see." He took my arm in his and began to lead me away from the edge of the dance floor. "We must also be concerned about the sin within our hearts."

If my father only knew the things I had thought and felt and longed for, he would no doubt judge my heart black with sin. Yet better black than empty of any true emotion or feeling.

He patted my hand. "I know it is hard for you, dear," he said. "The war has deprived you of so many little pleasures. But there are still many things for you to enjoy. Go and sit with your friends and enjoy their company. And no more talk of dancing or other unseemly behavior."

"Yes, Papa." I allowed him to lead me to a chair with the other unattached young women. While their conversations flowed around me like the twitters of a flock of birds, I searched the crowd until I found the one young man who did not participate in the revelry. Jesse sat on the sidelines, in a group of older men, their faces somber as they talked of the war, of depredations visited upon friends and relatives, and of the success of the guerrillas.

I finally broke from the group of young people and edged to the outermost rim of this circle of Jesse's admirers, darkness concealing me from my mother and father, who wouldn't hold with their unmarried daughter associating with so many men who were strangers to me.

One of the other men, a Mr. Cleveland, had taken up the tale of Jesse's exploits: "The reins in his teeth, a pistol in each hand, Jesse charged into that camp, guns blazing," he related to an avid group of listeners. "Those Yankees must have thought the devil himself was riding them down. They fired, but none of them even grazed him."

The image of Jesse as avenging warrior stirred me. I watched his face as the flickering lantern light highlighted the fine bones of his cheeks and hard line of his jaw. Too many men who had returned from the fighting had a hollowed-out look, as if the rigors of battle had drained their very souls. Yet Jesse radiated health and vitality. Where others bore the weary air of defeat and failure, Jesse held the promise of a bright future.

"The Yankees are scared of us, boys," he said. "I've seen it in their eyes when we charge them. They turn tail and run at the first sight of us. It's only because there are more of them than us that they've lasted this long. The South has better men in a single county than the whole of the Northern Army, I'm convinced." His voice rang with conviction, and I saw many an older man nod his head in agreement.

Then I noticed I wasn't the only female in the group. I spotted Esme and Rachel across from me at the edge of the circle of lantern light. Fanny was a little farther away, watching Jesse with all the avarice of a cat who has cornered a mouse.

I looked away from her, and at that moment, Jesse raised his head and his eyes met mine. He rose. "If you'll excuse me, ladies. Gentlemen." He nodded and crossed the circle of admirers at an angle that would take him away from me, and disappeared into the darkness.

I didn't hesitate to go after him. I moved carefully, on the very edge of the lantern light, making sure I was unnoticed. I met Jesse near the elm where we'd first encountered one another that afternoon. The band struck up a mournful rendition of *Lorena*, the sweet, soulful notes soaring over the shuffling of feet on the canvas and the muted conversation of the crowd. "Why aren't you dancing?" Jesse asked, before I could speak to him.

"You know the answer to that."

"Dancing is an invention of the devil," he said, in perfect imitation of my father delivering a sermon.

I laughed at his apt impression, and he caught my hand in his. "I've noticed that the devil has cornered the market on interesting amusements," he said. He removed his hat and hung it on the lowest branch of the tree, then offered me his arm. "Will you walk with me?"

I slipped my hand into the crook his elbow, surprised by the iron hardness of his muscles, aware of a growing tension within my own body. I thought of the devil and his amusements, and wondered at Jesse's own devilment, and how he seemed to speak to every contrariness in my own soul.

"Where will you go from here?" I asked as we strolled just outside the line where light met darkness.

"Wherever I'm commanded to go. It may be a good while before I return."

"Do you think the war will be over soon?"

"The formal battles may end soon. Conditions are bad all over, but especially in the South, and people and politicians are crying for an end to the fighting. But a treaty won't end this fight. As long as the North insists on trampling the rights of Southerners, men like me will keep fighting."

"I want the fighting to end," I said. "I want life to get back to normal, to be able to buy coffee and sugar and cloth again."

He patted my hand. "It's natural for women to want such things. Men have to be more contrary."

"Then you want to fight?"

"I can't explain the feeling a good fight gives me. In the midst of battle, every sense is more keen. I feel so powerful, as if a force greater than myself is guiding my horse and firing my pistols." He stopped and faced me, grasping me by the shoulders. "I believe God made each of us for a purpose in this life and fighting for the South is my purpose."

"And what is my purpose?" I asked.

"Perhaps your purpose is to wait. To support the fighters."

Then he pulled me close and kissed me, his lips firm and sure against mine. I cried out, but not in protest. Though I had never been kissed by a man before, I had never wanted anything more. I leaned toward him, pressing my body to his, feeling the hard wall of his chest, his strong arms enfolding me.

He tasted of the whiskey I knew the men had passed amongst them in a flask, and smelled of leather and gun oil and the faint tang of sweat. The stubble of his beard scraped the side of my face, and the callouses of his hands caught on the silk of my dress. Every softness in me was answered by a hardness in him, everything familiar transformed in his embrace.

I never wanted the moment to end, but of course it must. He released me and stepped back, his breathing uneven, his voice rough. "I have to go now," he said. He retraced our steps to the elm tree, where he retrieved his hat and replaced it on his head. Then he slipped into the darkness once more.

I waited until even the echo of his footsteps had faded, unsure if I could walk on legs that felt made of jelly. I thought of what Jesse had said about going into battle and feeling as if something larger than himself had taken over. That's what I'd felt when he had kissed me—as if someone other than me was kissing him back, pulling him close, behaving so wantonly. So *honestly*. That woman—that other me—had shaken off the bonds of demure Southern womanhood and surrendered to what she wanted. I had wanted Jesse, but now he was gone. Who knew when I'd see him again, or how much I would suffer until then?

Esme married Anthony Colquit on a bright September morning scarcely a month after my sister's wedding. At her request, he had grown a beard, which did a fair job of camouflaging his mole, but only served to make him look older than his years, owing to the fact that it was heavily streaked with gray. Esme professed not to mind and indeed, she looked happy as she stood in the parlor of her family's home to say her vows. I stood up with her and wished her well, while the three Colquit children looked on with the expression of generals plotting disaster.

As happy as I was for Esme's marriage, the loss of the company of her and my sister in the same month filled me with restlessness. Everyone was moving forward with their lives while I was plagued by uncertainty about the future. The bleak picture of myself as an old maid, spending my life by the side of my aging mother, seemed a very real and unsettling prospect. My two older sisters were married, my five older brothers either away fighting or established on their own, as my younger brothers Thomas and Henry eventually would be. And as pretty and lively as my younger sister Sallie was, I had no doubt she would marry well. I might one day soon be the only one of my siblings left at home.

For now, I welcomed the chance to run errands, escaping for at least a little while the house that might very well be my tomb. Even a trip to the general store for a packet of pins offered the opportunity to hear news and gossip, or glimpse a stranger passing through. If the storekeeper's wife, Mrs. Riker, looked down on me, what did I care? Any chance to tweak her nose was a welcome diversion.

Mrs. Riker was absent from the store the October Saturday I next heard news of Jesse. Mother had sent me to the store for a tin of saleratus and a bottle of bluing, but I was making the errand last as long as possible, lingering amongst the sewing notions, examining cards of buttons, when a man burst into the store.

"Word just come from Centralia!" he shouted. "Bloody Bill's done wiped out a hoard of Union soldiers."

I froze at the mention of Bloody Bill. "Was Jesse James with him?" The words were out of my mouth before I could stop them.

But the man gave no sign that he thought my question unusual. "The James boys was with him, I hear," he said. "Right there at the front lines. Bloody Bill had some eighty men with him. They cut the Northern Missouri rail lines and cleared the Yankees out of Boone County, then wiped out a bunch of bluecoats just returned from the Battle of Atlanta. Word is more than a hundred and fifty of the Yankees was slain in a fierce battle."

Word of what came to be known as the Centralia Massacre soon spread. It was all anyone talked of and many of their tales featured Jesse, who was lauded as a particular hero of the day, though so many versions of the action circulated I could never be sure what, exactly, had happened.

But I pictured Jesse as Mr. Cleveland had described him, riding into battle with the reins of his horse gripped in his teeth, a loaded pistol in each hand, putting the fear of the devil into his enemies. In my mind, he was no devil, and certainly no mere man, but an angel—not the ethereal, meek harp players in the paintings in my father's big Bible, but a powerful, beautiful, fearful being wielding a gun instead of a sword.

In less fanciful moments I knew Jesse was mortal, and subject to the same injuries as other men. In the days after that first announcement of the massacre, I combed what papers reached us, searching for mention of his name and news of his safety, but found nothing to ease my mind or satisfy my curiosity.

Finally, I resorted to asking my mother. "Have you heard from Aunt Zerelda if Frank and Jesse are safe?" I asked one evening while I struggled to darn a pair of black stockings that had already been mended so often there was more darn than sock.

"As far as I know, they're fine," Mother said. "Zerelda is very proud of them and talks of their heroism to everyone."

To say that Aunt Zerelda was proud of her sons was an understatement indeed. From the time they were small she had praised her boys as the most handsome, the brightest and the best sons a woman could want. Any schoolmaster who dared to try to correct the James boys knew he would face a tongue-lashing or worse from Zerelda. Six feet tall with shoulders as broad as any man's and a tongue twice as sharp, she reduced many a man to trembling, and the neighborhood girls had learned not to bat their eyes at Frank or Jesse, or risk Zerelda's wrath.

"I'm glad to hear they're safe," I said, setting aside my darning, too weak with relief to focus on my work.

"I worry that Zerelda boasts too much," Mother said. "She's never been one to act meekly, but now is not the time to be so outspoken against the North. I heard just last week of a young boy being dragged through the streets of Quincy and beaten for stating a wish for the South to win the war."

"Surely Aunt Zerelda's suffering in jail has made her more circumspect," I said.

My mother laughed. "My sister-in-law is not one to hold her tongue. If anything, jailing her made her more outspoken than ever. She'll never cease to champion the cause of the South—or to sing the praises of her sons."

I didn't say, but I couldn't see that championing 'the cause' was doing much for us. The sympathies of the entire state seemed to be shifting to the North, leaving those of us who clung to loyalty to the South isolated and in desperate straits. With so many men fighting, women had to work in the fields. Slaves were abandoning their masters and many farms fell into disrepair. My father preached about the darkness before the dawn, but I saw no sign of light.

In late October, Major Price's troops were defeated in the Battle of Westport and Confederate forces were driven from Missouri. Three days later, a Union Scout named Samuel Cox captured and murdered Bloody Bill. The rest of the guerrillas, including Jesse, were said to be on the run.

That winter was the hardest we'd yet endured, with no word from Frank or Jesse and no sign of the war's end. We ate a wild turkey my father shot for Christmas dinner. It was the first fresh meat we'd had in months. I made a duster out of the feathers and presented it to my mother, who gave me a pair of stockings she'd knit out of a vest of hers she'd unraveled.

In January, word came down that Aunt Zerelda had been banished from the state, forbidden to live here on pain of death. She was staying in Nebraska with friends, and sent frequent letters declaring her hatred of the Northerners who would persecute an innocent woman so. My mother read the letters, then burned them in the stove, unwilling for their venomous words to taint our family by association.

In April, the final blow came. General Lee surrendered at Appomattox Courthouse. The Confederacy was dissolved and everyone was required to swear an oath of allegiance to the Union.

Many did so gladly, anxious for peace and hopeful for a return to the prosperity we had known before the war. But our oaths were not enough for the federal troops who now descended upon our part of the state. These men went out of their way to take offense and to mete out punishment. It was as if the victor in a horse race had turned around and trampled the loser.

Still, I was naïve enough to believe those I loved would be safe. My father had an excellent reputation as a man of God, and my mother was known for helping anyone who needed nursing or a hot meal, or assistance of any kind. I was no longer allowed to come and go as I pleased, without my father or brothers accompanying me. I chafed at these restrictions, but I recognized their sense. The Union men were a rough lot, and not to be trusted.

But all my innocence was shattered on the day in May when my younger brother, Thomas, raced into the house, face flushed and eyes wide with excitement. "The militia men have taken Mrs. Peabody!" he shouted.

I almost dropped the kettle of blackberries I'd just removed from the stove. "Taken her? Taken her where?" I asked.

"It happened last night." Thomas snatched a blackberry from a bowl on the table and popped it into his mouth. At eighteen, he was a charmer who could talk himself out of almost any trouble, and he was a favorite of my mother. "I heard folks talking about it in town just now."

"Who took her?" I asked. "And where did they take her?"

"Some militiamen put her on a boat early this morning. Folks said they'd bloodied her nose and she was wearing nothing but her shimmy and a petticoat. They hung a sign around her neck that said "Confederate Whore." He glanced at Mother, ready to dodge any blows she might mete out for using such language.

But Mother was too distressed over his news to scold him. "Where was the Sheriff while all this was happening?" she asked, her expression grim.

Thomas shrugged. "I guess he wasn't there."

With trembling hands, I stripped off my apron and flung it to the floor. "I have to go see," I said.

"Sister, no!"

But I ignored my mother's words, running out of the house and down the road toward Mrs. Peabody's cabin. Tears blinded me as I ran, the horror of my friend's disgrace filling my head.

Ever since President Lincoln's assassination the month before, times had been hard as ever on anyone who formerly sided with the South. Groups of men—former Union soldiers and militiamen—had taken it upon themselves to punish those they deemed not sufficiently loyal to the Union. But why would they attack a defenseless woman who had never harmed a soul?

By the time I reached the cabin my side ached and my hair had come undone. Before I even entered the yard I saw that the jasmine arbor had been pulled from the porch, and the front door hung loose from its hinges. I heard footsteps pounding behind me and turned to see Thomas. "I figured I'd better come with you," he said.

I nodded, grateful for his company in the eerie silence of this once-familiar cabin. Slowly, we walked up onto the porch and into the house. Broken pottery littered the front room, the remains of a tea set that had once held pride of place in a corner cupboard. Furniture was overturned, the drapes ripped from the windows. In the kitchen, sugar crunched under our feet and flour drifted over everything like lime dust.

Thomas stepped into the bedroom first, then blocked the doorway. "Don't go in there, Sister," he said. His face was pale, but he was doing his best to be manly.

I shoved him aside and stepped into a scene of more chaos. The bedclothes were dragged to the floor, the dressing table mirror shattered. The silver dresser set Mrs. Peabody had prized was gone, along with a blown-glass bird that had been a gift from Mr. Henry.

Only when I had absorbed these things did I recognize the other, more grisly evidence of what had happened here—the things Thomas had tried to keep me from seeing. Frayed rope hung from the four posts of the bed, knotted, then cut with a knife, as if someone had been tied there. Rusty stains flecked the linens of the bed, along with a single muddy print from a man's boot. I turned away, fresh sobs escaping as my imagination filled in the story behind these ugly details.

Thomas took my arm and led me back onto the porch. The swing had been chopped to splinters, so we sat side by side on the top step. He gave me his handkerchief and I struggled to control my sobs. "What else did people in town say happened?" I asked. "Tell me everything."

"There's nothing else to tell," he said. "They said she was put on the boat at dawn, so the militiamen must have come here some time during the night."

"Why wasn't Sheriff Henry here?" I wailed. "They wouldn't have dared do this if he'd been here to stop them."

"He didn't usually spend the night here," Thomas said. "Not all night, anyway." His cheeks burned. "Leastways, that's what I heard."

So Henry had been safe at home in his own bed while his lover was abused and driven out of town in disgrace. Mrs. Peabody had said the moments of pleasure she enjoyed were worth the moments of pain—but surely not this much pain.

"What did Henry do when he found out about this?" I asked.

"I don't guess he did anything. Nobody mentioned it."

If he loved her, why hadn't he gone after her? Why hadn't he raised a posse to hunt down the men who had done this? How could he claim to love her, yet do nothing to avenge her? Was his reputation worth more to him than the woman he loved?

The cruelty of the answer to that question showed me the kind of man he really was. No matter that he was the Sheriff and a veteran of the war; Henry had been weak. He'd professed to love Mrs. Peabody, but hadn't had the strength of his convictions to stand by her in her time of need.

While Mrs. Peabody had loved enough to give up whatever her life had been, to move here and live alone under the censure of her neighbors, Mr. Henry's feelings had not moved him to raise even a word of protest in her defense.

One night not too many weeks later, her old cabin burned to the ground. Six months later Mrs. Henry, who was apparently not so much of an invalid after all, gave birth to a son, named Thomas Wayne Henry, Jr.

And still I had no word from Jesse.

The summer dragged on long and hot. I vowed to no longer think of Jesse. What was he to me but a boy I had kissed once?

But Jesse was a man I could not ignore. Though I banished him from my thoughts during my waking hours, he visited my dreams—as an avenging angel robed in white, or a laughing man who lobbed dirt clods at my skirt, then caught me up in his arms and kissed me until I was breathless.

Then Jesse came back into my life, not as the avenging angel I'd dreamed of, but as a ghost of a man who frightened me more than anyone ever had.

Chapter Three

He arrived on the night train, born on a stretcher carried by his mother and his brother, Frank. Under cover of darkness, they brought him to our house, where they were met with many tears and cries of alarm.

Already in bed, I wrapped a shawl around my shoulders and raced down the stairs to discover the cause of such commotion. Then I saw Jesse laid out on the floor of the kitchen, swathed in blankets, his face pale as death, unmoving. I gasped, and stumbled back, into the arms of my Aunt Zerelda. "No need to take on," she said briskly. "Your cousin lives. Despite the graveness of his injuries, the Lord has spared him." There was a note of pride in her voice, as if she had personally charged the Lord with keeping her favorite son alive, and knew that even the Almighty would not dare cross her. "I've brought him here where he can safely mend."

"What makes you think he'll be safe here?" my mother asked. Her face was pinched, the lines on her pale forehead deeper as she struggled to face her sister-in-law's glare. "What if the soldiers followed you here?"

"No one followed me," Zerelda said. "And he'll be safe because I trust you to have sense enough not to tell anyone he's here. Carry him into the parlor," she barked at Frank. "And someone find him a bed."

Mother hesitated. I knew she didn't like Zerelda ordering her around, yet she wouldn't turn away a dying man. "Thomas, bring your bed down and set it up well away from the window," she ordered. "You can make a pallet on the floor until Jesse is well. Sister, tear some fresh bandages—but first, fetch me a good handful of rosemary from the garden. And strip as many leaves as you can carry from the black walnut tree and bring them to me."

With shaking hands I lit a lantern and carried it into the yard. The moon was a silver sliver overhead and the stars shown like shards of glass. Dew wet my bare feet and soaked the hem of my nightrail as I made my way to the garden. I'd forgotten to bring a knife, so I ripped handfuls of rosemary from the herb bed, filling the air with the sharp, astringent aroma. Then I hurried to the black walnut tree and filled my shawl with the long, narrow leaves.

I deposited the greenery in two bowls my mother had set out on the kitchen table, and covered them with boiling water from the kettle on the stove. The rosemary infusion would be used to clean the wound, then a poultice would be made from the black walnut to draw out infection. The herbs steeping, I raced to the parlor, where my brother and father were reassembling the bed. I joined my mother and Aunt Zerelda at Jessie's side. They had peeled back the blankets and unbuttoned his shirt to reveal a corset of blood-soaked bandages around his torso. I must have gasped, alerting the women to my presence, for my mother looked up and said, "Go away, Sister. We don't need you here."

"No. She should stay," Aunt Zerelda said. "She can help you nurse him. It's not safe for me to stay here and you'll need her help." She thrust a section of old sheet at me. "Start tearing bandages."

I bit at the linen to start a tear, then ripped a long strip of bandage, forcing my eyes to remain fixed on Jesse. The women gently cut away layers of linen, revealing an angry hole on the right side of his chest. He groaned and I flinched, at the same time rejoicing at this sign of life. "What happened?" I asked.

"He was shot through the lung by a Union Patrol," Zerelda said. "His friend, Archie Clement, cared for him and got word to me." She pointed to a second scar very close to the first. "This isn't the first time he's been wounded," she said. "He was shot last summer in a skirmish with the Missouri militia." Rather than expressing dismay at the injury to her son, Zerelda sounded pleased at this evidence of her son's bravery.

My mother laid a hand across Jesse's forehead. "His fever's high," she said.

"The train trip was hard on him." Zerelda discarded the last of the bloody bandages. "But he's strong. If he was going to die from this, he would have done so before now."

I could tell my mother didn't share Zerelda's optimism, but she kept silent. She went to the kitchen and returned with the steeping rosemary and clean rags, and began to swab Jesse's wound. He opened his eyes, their blue darkened almost to violet, but he gave so sign of recognition of any of us.

Aunt Zerelda stuffed the bloody bandages and Jesse's blood-stained shirt into the parlor stove and struck a match. They burned red and orange behind the isinglass stove door. Mother handed the bowl and rags to me. "Keep cleaning the wound while I make a poultice," she said.

I knelt beside the pallet, and gingerly touched the wet rag to the edge of the wound. Even through the cloth I could feel the heat radiating from Jesse. The smell of putrid flesh and fever-sweat overpowered even the camphor smell of the herb, and I swallowed hard, determined to keep control of my feelings.

The man who had kissed me last fall had been broad-chested and muscular. This Jesse was wasted away to skin and bones, the outline of each rib clearly visible beneath his blue-white skin. His chest scarcely moved with each shallow breath, and fresh blood bubbled from the wound with each swipe of my cloth.

My mother returned with the poultice and Aunt Zerelda moved from the fire to help with the job of bandaging it in place. The bed was together now, and I helped Thomas spread it with fresh sheets and blankets. Then the women sent the rest of us from the room while they bathed their patient and dressed him in a clean nightshirt of my father's.

When I returned, Jesse was in bed, covers pulled to his chin like a little boy tucked in for the night.

"Where's Frank?" Thomas asked.

"He left already," Zerelda said. She sat on the edge of the bed and sponged Jesse's face with cool water. "He couldn't risk being seen here. I have to go, too." With obvious reluctance, she stood. "Someone should stay with him tonight," she said. "To make sure he doesn't become delirious from the fever."

"I'll stay," I said. I knew I wouldn't sleep if I returned to my bed. And I welcomed the chance to be alone with Jesse, to discover if my feelings for him were merely fantasies engendered by a single kiss, or something more.

I was left with a single lamp burning low on a table by the parlor door and the admonition to wake my mother if Jesse took a turn for the worse. My father knelt beside the bed and said a long prayer for healing, to which we all echoed "Amen," then Aunt Zerelda vanished into the night after Thomas and the others trooped upstairs.

I pulled a chair close beside the sick bed and studied Jesse's face in the dim light. Several days' growth of sandy beard made him look older than he had before, or maybe it was the lines of pain around his eyes that added a maturity beyond his eighteen years. His hair had grown long in the months he'd been away, curling up at the collar, dark gold against the whiteness of the pillow case.

He slept poorly, each breath coming in an anguished gasp that made my throat ache. The fire had burned out and despite the summer's heat the room felt cold. I wrapped my shawl more tightly around my shoulders and drew my bare feet up under my nightrail, my eyes never leaving Jesse. I had never seen a person die before, and I was terrified he would be the first. How could I bear to lose him when I had only just begun to know him?

Yet how could a man live with such a wound?

For several hours nothing happened. Jesse slipped into a deeper sleep and I felt some of my tension ease. I even dozed, sitting up in my chair, but was awakened by a moaning and the rattle of the metal legs of the bed against the floor.

Jesse had thrown off the blankets, and thrashed about so wildly I feared he would fall out of bed and injure himself further. "Shhhh. Shhh." I rushed to his side, and pressed his shoulders against the mattress. He quieted some at my touch and stared at me with wide, uncomprehending eyes. "C . . . c . . . cold," he groaned, his jaw clenched against the shivers that rattled his frame.

I pulled the blankets over him once more, but still he shook. The fever burned and I tried to cool it with wet compresses. But any coolness they offered disappeared almost immediately. His body, so wracked with pain and loss of blood, shook uncontrollably, his teeth chattering.

Desperate to ease his suffering, I searched the room for more blankets, but there were none. I could start a fire in the stove, but I'd have to go outside to fetch wood, and I dared not leave him alone in his condition. I could fetch my mother, but again—how could I leave him?

I put a hand to his chest, trying to hold him still, and felt the dampness of fresh blood seeping through the bandage. If I couldn't keep him still and get him warm again I feared he would bleed to death, or the life left in him would simply burn up.

On winter nights when ice formed in the bowl on our dresser and the heat from the kitchen stove had no chance of warming our attic room, my sister Sallie and I would huddle together beneath the covers, drawing on each other's warmth until we were able to settle into sleep in each other's arms. What other way did I have to keep Jesse warm now?

Scarcely pausing to consider the audacity of what I was doing, I folded back the blankets and slipped into the narrow bed beside him. Pulling the covers over us both, I wrapped my arms and legs around him and held him close. His skin burned and he continued to shiver, but I closed my eyes and held on tightly, murmuring soothing nonsense beneath my breath.

After a very little while, he grew calmer. The tension drained from his muscles and his breathing became more shallow as he slipped back into sleep. I tried to leave him then, but he clung to me with a fierceness that belied his weakened condition. "Don't leave me," he whispered, a plea that held me as surely as his grasp.

I would have to extricate myself somehow before the rest of my family awoke, but for now I was content to stay with him. I rested my head in the hollow of his shoulder and listened to the reassuring beat of his heart. Anyone coming upon us might have assumed it was a commonplace matter for me to share a bed with a man I scarcely knew. How was it that I could be so at ease with Jesse, who was a stranger to me in spite of our family connection?

Yet for all our differences of gender and experience, I sensed in Jesse the same longing for adventure that stirred so often within me. As a man, he had found outlets for this spirit in war, while as an impoverished female, I was limited in my rebellions. Jesse had a wildness about him that drew me like a bee to honeysuckle.

I became aware of the heat of his body seeping into mine, and of the thin layers of cotton between the hard lines of his form and the soft curves of mine. I had younger brothers; I knew what men looked like below the waist. I had grown up on a farm, one of eleven children—the details of mating and procreation were no real mystery to me.

But lying so close beside a man, heat building within me that had nothing to do with fever, I was an adventurer into unknown territory. I craved Jesse's touch, yet if he was incapable of touching me, I could not help but touch him.

Hesitantly at first, then with increasing boldness, I skimmed my hand across his bandaged chest, down to the faintly ridged muscle of his stomach. I rested there a moment, feeling the rise and fall of his breathing, and the faint pulse beneath my fingers. Gaining courage, I moved my hand lower, across thighs hardened by hours on horseback.

Jesse stirred and mumbled words I couldn't understand. I stilled, heart pounding, scarcely daring to breathe. His arm reached around me, pulling me closer with surprising strength. My hand slipped, coming to rest between his thighs, finding evidence that in one respect at least, he was far from dead. I froze, appalled at what I had done, but powerless to undo it. I waited, feeling the heat and hardness of him, but he had lapsed into insensibility once more, his hold on me weakening.

Slowly, careful not to disturb him, I eased from his grasp and out from under the covers. He continued to sleep peacefully. I thought he was less warm than before, and a fine sheen of sweat dampened his forehead. I returned to my chair and tucked my feet up once more, arms wrapped around my knees, as if I might hold in the whirlwind of emotion that rocked me. I felt giddy at my own boldness, yet bereft with the knowledge that the pleasure had been one-sided. Jesse had not known I had lain with him. He would have no memory of my hands on his body. Would he even want me if he were in his right mind? Had that kiss in the trees months ago meant anything at all to him, or was it a mere diversion, one of dozens—even hundreds—of such kisses he had bestowed in his roaming across the country?

I wanted to believe in romantic notions of love and fate, but the South's defeat and Mrs. Peabody's banishment had stolen my trust in such fantasies. Jesse wasn't a character in a book or a hero in a song. He was a real flesh and blood man. But I believed him to be a man of conviction, a man who had stood strong in battle. Would he be true to me as well—the kind of man I could truly depend upon?

"Zee, is that really you?"

Two days after Jesse was brought to our house, he looked up at me with clear eyes and spoke with a voice grown raspy with disuse. "Yes, it's me," I said, smoothing the covers over him. "Your mother and Frank brought you to our house two nights ago."

"I don't remember . . . I don't remember much after that bullet tore into me." He wrinkled his brow, concentrating. "Archie was there."

"Yes. Your mother said he took care of you until she could get to you. How do you feel?"

"Weak as a baby."

"You should eat something. Mother made broth. We didn't have beef, but one of the neighbors brought some venison."

I started to rise, but he waved me back down. "Don't go yet. Stay and talk to me a minute. Who knows I'm here?"

"No one. My mother told people I was sick. I've been looking after you, so no one's seen me to know different."

"You're a better-looking nurse than Archie." He smiled, a look that made my stomach quiver. "How many days has it been?" he asked.

"You've been here two, but I don't know how long before that you were shot. What happened?"

"We rode right into a Union cavalry patrol. We were caught like a bear in a trap."

He tried to sit up, and I rushed to his side. "You shouldn't move," I cautioned. "You could start bleeding again."

His face had blanched with the effort, and I feared he might pass out again, but his grip on my arm was strong. "Prop me up, then. I think I could breathe better."

I did as he asked, bolstering him with pillows from the parlor sofa. He patted the bandages around his chest with one hand. "How bad's the damage?"

"The bullet left a good-sized hole. I imagine it bled a lot at first, and more after you were brought here, though it's mostly stopped now. The bullet's still in you. I guess the doctors thought it was too dangerous to try to take it out. You had a terrible fever and we feared infection, but that's come down considerably now." I swallowed hard, blinking at the tears that stung my eyes. "We were afraid you might die."

"I imagine I came close." He smiled at me, but his expression sobered when he saw the tears that threatened. "Hey, now, don't you cry over me. I'm going to be fine, thanks to your good care."

"I'll get the broth," I said, turning away. "You need to eat to keep up your strength." And I needed a moment to get away from him, to regain my composure.

He was still too weak to hold the spoon, so I fed him half a bowl of rich broth. "Ain't this a sorry state?" he said as I wiped his chin with a napkin. "A grown man reduced to being fed like a baby."

"You'll be stronger soon," I said.

"In the meantime, I can't complain about the company."

My mother and father came in to see how our patient was doing, and banished me while they bathed him and checked his dressing. I took the opportunity to change into a fresh dress and a new hair ribbon. If my job was to include providing entertainment for Jesse as well as nursing, then I needed to look my best.

He tired easily in those early days, but before the week was out he was able to sit up for longer periods, and to take a turn about the room, supported by my father or Thomas. By the next week, he refused to wear the borrowed nightshirt any longer and asked that his trousers and shirt be returned. The shirt had been burnt at the same time as his original bandages, but mother had cleaned and patched the trousers, and Thomas gave up one of his shirts to clothe his cousin.

Thus attired, Jesse was able to leave his bed to sit on the parlor sofa, though he was still too weak to move much further. In any case, he couldn't have gone far; Union militia were still active in the area, and not hesitant to punish their old enemies. Our family told no one of his presence with us; visitors were kept from the house by the convenient fiction that I was ill and not to be disturbed. Even Esme was turned away when she came to call, though I looked forward to the time when I could confide these adventures to her.

When we were able to get a newspaper, Jesse asked me to read it to him. "My eyes hurt when I read too long," he said. "And the sound of your voice is soothing."

So I read to him the news of the day: an account of James Butler "Wild Bill" Hickok's shootout with Davis Tutt, Jr. in Springfield; and discussions of the fight in Washington over whether or not to readmit Southern states to the Union.

When we tired of reading, we talked, and in those quiet conversations we learned to know each other better—our hopes and ambitions, our secret fears and dreams. I learned that Jesse idolized his father, who had died when Jesse was only three; that he loved peach pie more than any other food; and that he both revered and resented his brother Frank, who had been both his teacher and his tormentor since childhood.

He, in turn, discovered my tendency toward secret rebellion, such as hiding my mother's recipe box when I knew she was determined to make the molasses pie I loathed; and my love of romantic poetry.

In those hours of conversation or silent contemplation in one another's company we fell in love. If that first kiss beneath the elm tree had been the thunder clap that woke me to his presence, those hours in my parents' parlor were a drenching rain that soaked me with longing for him to never leave me. I blossomed in his attentions, as if something inside of me, long locked away, had been set free and allowed to grow with his encouragement. With Jesse I was no longer Sister, one of too many children in a poor preacher's family. I was Zee, the woman who had returned the light to Jesse's eyes, who had the power to make him well.

By his sixth week in our home, Jesse was much stronger. He ventured out of doors some, and even took short rides with Thomas, though he returned looking gray and in obvious pain. "He insisted on galloping," Thomas said, helping Jesse to his parlor bed once more.

"I'm not going to know what I can do unless I try," Jesse said through gritted teeth.

Despite mine and my mother's insistence that he rest, he prowled the house and grounds like a stallion intent on breaking out of its stall. He carried full feed buckets and lifted logs over his head until the muscles of his chest and arms strained the seams of his shirt.

He could have moved upstairs to share a room with Thomas, but his bed stayed in the parlor, pushed against one wall and piled during the day with his personal belongings: two pair of Colt's Navy revolvers, a Henry rifle in leather scabbard, leather saddlebags, brass spurs, the Bible which he read each morning, and a sheaf of maps rendered on oilcloth. They were military maps he'd taken from a Union soldier. I assumed he'd killed the man, but never asked. In the evenings when Jesse had exhausted himself, he reclined on the bed and studied the maps, tracing the hatch-marked lines of railroads and the broad meanderings of rivers and sinuous courses of roads.

"I can't bear being laid up here while there's so much work to be done," he complained one evening as I sat on the sofa across from him, embroidering a pillowslip. "If I could sit a horse I'd be out there now, helping in the fight."

I set aside the pillowslip—meant to be part of my trousseau, which, like every young woman of my age I had been working on since childhood—and turned my attention to Jesse. "What fight?" I asked.

"Just because the war's over doesn't mean the fighting's done," he said. "The North wants to take away everything—our farms and families and way of life. They've made us sign their oaths and give up our seats in the government and they expect us to lie down and take it. But we won't let them get away with it."

His eyes flashed and his voice rose in anger. I shivered, glad I wasn't on the receiving end of such ire. But it would be a long time before he was well enough to do any fighting, or to ride very far at all. Selfishly, I didn't mind that he was slow to mend. I enjoyed our time together and was loathe to see it end.

In August, a letter came from Aunt Zerelda, letting us know that she and Dr. Samuel had returned to their farm in Kearney. She ordered Jesse to join them. He read the letter through twice, then folded it and laid it on the table beside his cot in the parlor. "I don't see how I can go home for several weeks yet," he said.

"We're happy to have you stay as long as you like," I said.

"The time I'm with you passes pleasantly, anyway."

Our conversations continued, endless hours of words flowing effortlessly between us. Even Esme and I had not conversed so freely. We talked not about the war or his experiences with the guerrillas, but about ordinary things—the crops coming in, who was getting married or giving birth, who had died or moved away. We shared childhood memories, too. "Do you remember that time a few years back when we came to visit and I hid in the barn and launched dirt clods at you and your sisters when you walked past?" he asked.

I laughed. "I'd just been allowed to wear my hair up and I was trying to be such a lady, but all I really wanted to do was to chase you down and make you say 'uncle.' I thought you were the most horrid little boy."

"And I thought you were beautiful. Being horrible was the only way I knew to get your attention."

"Did you really think that?" I asked, shy in the face of such flattery.

"I did. I still do."

I wondered if he was thinking of kissing me again. I certainly wanted him to, but it was broad daylight and my mother and sisters were in the kitchen canning beans so there was no way we could risk it. But the way he looked at me, blue eyes as clear and deep as a mountain lake, was almost as good as a kiss, and had much the same effect, making me feel weak at the knees.

"You've had an effect on me, Zee, and that's no lie," he said. "Ever since I kissed you at Lucy's wedding, I've thought about you. I even dreamed you crawled into bed with me, here in this parlor. Does that shock you?"

My face burned, but I shook my head. "That was no dream," I said.

"No?"

"No." I lowered my voice, fearful of being overheard. "It was the first night you were here. You were suffering horribly from fever and chills. I was afraid you'd injure yourself if I didn't find some way to warm you."

He took my hand and squeezed it. "It was the best dream I've ever had. Would you consider doing it again, now that I'm sensible enough to enjoy it?"

I caught my breath, scarcely believing what he was asking.

He wrapped both his hands around mine. "I'd never ask you to do something you wouldn't enjoy, but I can't help thinking on these nights when I can't sleep for the pain, how nice it would be to have you with me."

"How could I manage it?" I asked. He no longer needed anyone to sit up with him nights.

"Sneak down here after the others are asleep."

I should have been appalled by the idea. Instead, I remembered how good it felt to be so close to him. "We might be caught."

"We won't be. Not once in all these nights has anyone come down to check on me, though many times I couldn't sleep and would have welcomed the company."

"All right. I'll try to slip down tonight." The thought of spending the night with him thrilled me as much as the idea of doing something so daring and outrageous.

I took extra carc washing before bed, and left my hair loose, then slipped under the covers to wait. I would have thought sleep would escape me, but I must have dozed, for when I woke moonlight streamed through my open window. The world was utterly silent; not even a cricket chirped. Careful not to wake Sallie, I crept to the window and peered out. No sign of sunrise on the horizon; morning was still hours away.

I moved down the stairs on tip-toe, scarcely putting my weight on the treads. I'd expected to have to make my way to the parlor in the dark, but a faint glow guided me, and I found that Jesse had left a lamp on the table by his bed, turned down low.

He waited to speak until I stood beside the cot. "I'd about given up on you," he said.

"What time is it?" I asked.

"My watch is there by the lamp." He rose up on one elbow and picked up the silver pocket watch and held it to the light. "It's just after one." He held back the covers. "We have plenty of time."

I slid in beside him and he pulled the covers over us and blew out the lamp. Darkness closed around us, shutting out the rest of the world and driving away some of my nervousness. The bed was narrow, and I had no choice but to lie pressed tight against him, but I made no protest. The sensation of his body pressed to mine thrilled me.

"This is better than any dream," he said, smoothing his hand down my back. "Thanks for coming down to keep me company."

I rested my head on his chest and closed my eyes. His heart beat strong and rapid as a military tattoo. "Do you often have trouble sleeping?" I asked.

"Often enough."

I put my hand over the bandages that covered his wound. "Are you in much pain?"

"It's not the pain in my chest that bothers me so much as the pain in my heart."

I rose up to study him, trying to fathom his meaning from the look in his eyes. But the darkness swallowed up his features. "I don't understand," I said. "What pain?"

"When I left home to ride with the bushwhackers, I never thought about the danger," he said. "I wanted adventure and glory, and for folks to be proud of me."

"We are proud of you," I said. "All of us."

He patted my shoulder. "That means a lot. We had a lot of scary times, but we believed in the cause, in fighting for the South. We believed we could make a difference and that made it worth it. Even if it meant doing things I never thought I'd do." His hand traced a path along my side, up and down. "Brutal, bloody things. Things I can't begin to tell you."

"Is it those memories that keep you awake?" I asked.

"Some, but it's not so much what I did as what was done to me." His hand stilled. "I left home a boy, believing nothing bad could ever happen to me, and I came home near a dead man. Knowing I almost died shook me to the core. It makes me wonder how much time any of us have left."

"But you didn't die. And you won't. Not for a long time."

"How can any of us say?"

The desolation in his voice distressed me. I searched for some way to comfort him. "At Lucy's wedding, you told me your destiny was to fight for the South," I reminded him. "Doesn't the fact that you survived prove God has more great things in store for you?"

"All I know is, I feel the need not to waste any time. I want to take advantage of every opportunity that comes my way—whether it's to right a wrong or to enjoy what time I can with you."

He pulled me to him and his mouth found mine. I responded as ardently as I knew how, pressing my lips to his with heated fervor, arching my body to him without shame. His hand on my hip steadied me, as his tongue urged my lips apart.

His kisses grew bolder, and I grew bolder still in my response. I opened my mouth to him and twined my tongue with his, reveling in the taste and feel of him. All my hours of fantasy were nothing compared to the reality of this moment. To have him here with me, solid flesh and blood, when he had so nearly died, was reason enough to abandon caution and enjoy these new sensations without thought to consequences.

He massaged my hip and I writhed against him shamelessly, feeling the hard length of him pressed against the juncture of my thighs. He clutched me fiercely and gave a muffled groan, then stilled, his breath coming in ragged gasps. I felt a warm wetness on the front of my gown and drew back in surprise.

"It's all right," he soothed, stroking my shoulder. "Being so near you was too much for me. I couldn't wait."

The realization of what had happened made me blush, but I had little time to ponder the situation. Jessie had pulled up the hem of my gown and gently parted my legs with his hand. His gentle caresses and skillful fondling sent a flood of sensations through me—heat and tension and longing. I wanted to pull away from his touch, yet at the same time I never wanted the contact to stop.

"Wh . . . what are you doing?" I whispered.

"I'm making you feel as good as you've made me feel." He bent his head and began to nuzzle at my breast. His tongue traced a circle around the tip, wetting the cloth, flicking back and forth against my painfully erect nipple. He moved to my other breast and I bit back a moan, and arched against his hand, which pressed me down firmly into the bed.

Just when I felt I could not bear the onslaught of sensation any longer, release came, sudden and sharp. I bucked against him and would have cried out, but his mouth covered my own, his tongue plunging between my teeth, silencing me.

He kept his hands on me, easing me back to myself, then holding me close. I clung to him, panting. The pleasure I'd occasionally found at my own hands was nothing compared to this.

He raised his head and looked at me in the dim light. "Are you okay?" he asked.

I nodded.

"Did you like that?"

I nodded again, unable to find words to express my feelings.

He chuckled. "Can't say I've ever rendered a woman speechless before." He kissed the top of my head. "Go on. You'd better get back to your own bed. Your pa will be coming down to start the cook fires before we know it."

I nodded and slipped from the cot and hurried back to my room. Upstairs, I changed out of the wet gown, stuffing it far back in the wardrobe to be retrieved for washing later. Sallie slept on, snoring softly. I crawled beneath the covers and stared at the ceiling, marveling at everything that had happened.

Chapter Four

"You're looking well this morning, Jessie," my mother said as she set a bowl of cornmeal porridge in front of him.

"I'm feeling much better, thank you," he said. When my mother turned toward the stove once more, he winked at me and I looked away, fearful my eyes would betray every emotion. Jessie did indeed look robust and well-rested this morning. He was no longer the wasted wraith who had been delivered to our door four months earlier, but a well-formed, handsome man who attracted the attention of any who saw him.

Jesse could not be in a room without being the center of attention. It wasn't anything he did, but a quality of his person that drew others to him. The brilliant blue eyes, the upward quirk of his mouth, the way his shock of sandy hair fell across his brow—all combined to attract the gaze of any who were near. His voice was deep, and soft with the cadences of the South, but everyone hung on his words. It was as if he'd cast a spell of enchantment over all of us, one we had no wish to break.

"You're not coming down with something, are you, Sister?" My mother set my own bowl in front of me and rested one hand on my shoulder. "You look a little peaked this morning."

"I . . . I didn't sleep well last night." I avoided meeting her gaze and I especially avoided looking at Jesse. It wasn't a lie; after I'd left Jessie I'd lain awake for a long time, trying to decide if what we'd done was horribly wrong or wonderfully right. My heart leaned toward right, but everything I'd been taught, as the daughter of a preacher, said I'd sinned and would likely burn in hell for it.

"I should probably apologize for disturbing your sleep last night, but I can't honestly say I regret it," Jesse said later, when he went with me to gather apples from trees on the far side of my father's property.

I said nothing, too unsure of my emotions to speak.

He took my arm and turned me toward him. "Come to me again tonight?" He traced the line of my jaw with his index finger, sending shivers down my spine.

"No, I can't," I turned my head away.

"Don't be afraid," he said. "You know I won't hurt you."

"I know, but . . . it's wrong, Jesse."

"What's wrong about two people who love each other being together?"

I raised my eyes to his, searching them to see if he meant the words. "I do love you, Zee," he said.

"I love you, too, Jesse."

"Then come to me tonight." He kissed my cheek. "I want to be with you."

"I want to be with you, too, but—"

"It's all right." His voice was soft, soothing, his hands stroking my back, heating my skin and sending fluttering sensations through me. "I'm not some man who's going to take advantage, then leave you. I want to marry you."

"Marry me?"

He nodded, his smiled dazzling. "I want you to be my wife."

"Oh, Jesse!" I threw my arms around him and he lifted me off the ground. I felt like shouting or weeping, but I did neither, merely clung to him, my heart pounding as if I'd just run across the fields.

Slowly, he eased me down until my feet touched the ground once more. "We can't tell anyone until I've broken the news to Mother," he said.

Aunt Zerelda. The name cast a dark cloud over my happiness. Though she and I had always gotten along, everyone knew she set great store by her oldest boys, Frank and Jesse. She had yet to think any woman was good enough for her sons. "What do you think she'll say about us getting married?" I asked.

"She'll be happy," he said. "She likes you, and she'll love any woman I love."

Jesse was used to being the center of his mother's world, so naturally he thought she'd be happy about anything that made him happy, but I wasn't so sure.

After Jesse's father, my Uncle Robert, had died in the California gold fields, when Jesse was only three, Aunt Zerelda had been left with nothing. Uncle Robert had no will; by law everything went to his children—Frank and Jesse and their younger sister, Susan. A local official was given control of the estate on behalf of the children and a neighbor, Mr. West, was given guardianship of the children. A widowed woman, even one of Zerelda's strong temperament, had no power, even over her own children. Determined to regain control of her life, Zerelda chose the only course open to her—marriage to a wealthy neighbor.

The marriage was only talked about in our family in hushed tones. What little I knew I'd picked up listening in on my mother and older women gossiping. It seems Aunt Zerelda's new husband, Mr. Simms, didn't care for children, and Jesse and his siblings continued to live with their guardian, Mr. West. Unable to bear being apart from her children, Zerelda left her husband after eight months and moved in with the Wests. Those must have been desperate times for her, and part of me couldn't blame her for clinging to her children so tightly after that.

But fortune smiled on Zerelda, in the form of Mr. Simms's death. He did have a will, and had left his estate to her. She had a little money now, and more determination than ever. She chose a better husband in Dr. Samuel, and had him made the children's guardian. She even had him sign a paper before their marriage that guaranteed that, in the event he preceded her in death, she would retain ownership of the farm and all his property. Never again would Aunt Zerelda be cut off from all that was rightfully hers.

I could admire all these things about her, while knowing she was just as unlikely to surrender control of Jesse. It didn't matter that he was a grown man who had fought in a bitter war and almost died; he was still her golden boy, and I was sure she wanted to be the only woman in his life. The question remained—would Jesse stand up to his mother and go against her wishes when it came to marrying me?

Most people looking at me would have said I was no match for Zerelda. Despite sharing the same name, we were physical opposites: she was taller than most men, and capable of striking a man down if he crossed her; I stood barely over five feet and made no claims to physical prowess of any kind. Zerelda was known for her scorching tongue. She was never reluctant to express her opinion on any matter and countless men lived in fear of her tirades. I was quiet and usually kept my opinions to myself.

Better women than I had made the mistake of turning their eyes toward Frank or Jesse and been driven away by Zerelda's sharp tongue. But loving Jesse had made me brave—brave enough to face even Aunt Zerelda's wrath. "I'll come to you tonight," I said, smiling up at him. "I want us to be together." That night, and forever.

Jesse and I spent many pleasurable nights together in the next weeks. As a lover, he could be both tender and fierce. I never knew which Jesse awaited me in the evenings when I slipped into his bed. His ever-changing nature fascinated and excited me.

I think my mother might have suspected what was going on between us. Not that we were sharing his bed; she would never had condoned such wantonness. But she saw that Jesse and I had developed an affection for one another.

"I think your cousin is the kind of man who could turn a young woman's head if she isn't careful," she said to me one afternoon as we worked in the kitchen. We were making pickles, and the air was full of the smell of vinegar and spices.

"What do you mean?" I asked, pretending not to understand.

"Jesse is younger than you," she said. "He's a long time from being ready to settle down, while you should already have a husband and family of your own."

"You're wrong," I said. "About Jesse, anyway. There's only two years' difference in our ages, and he's ready to settle down. In fact, he's asked me to marry him."

To my mother's credit, her hand didn't falter in lifting a heavy jar of pickles from the canner, but when the jar was safely on the table she turned and studied me, her eyes full of sadness. "I had hoped you'd find a husband among our neighbors," she said. "A stable man who could care for you."

"Jesse will take care of me."

"Jesse has a wildness in him I fear will never be tamed."

I stuck my chin in the air, defiant. "He's a good man, mother. He loves me and I love him."

She shook her head, perhaps seeing it was useless for her to argue. "Think about this, child. Marriage is for life. You don't want to make a mistake."

"Jesse and I will be happy," I said. "But please don't tell anyone yet. Jesse wants to wait until he's told his mother."

My mother's frown deepened. "Zerelda won't be pleased."

"She can't stop us," I said, with more bravado than I possessed.

"I hope you're right, child. Though I'm not sure even Jesse James can stand up to his mother."

In October, Zerelda sent word once more that she expected Jesse to come home. Frank had returned, and she wanted all her children around her. "I have to go," Jesse told me as we lay in each other's arms in a secluded copse where we'd been meeting. Wrapped in blankets against the chill of fall and hidden from the sight of others, I was drowsy and content until his words roused me. "I've intruded on your family's hospitality long enough," he continued, before I could protest. "I'm well enough now to ride, and there's work to do."

Remembering the tirades he'd made before against the men who now controlled Missouri, I suspected he wasn't referring to work to be done on the family farm, but I didn't press him. "You'll tell your mother about us?" I asked.

"I will." He squeezed my shoulder. "It will be all right, Zee. You'll see. I'll write to you soon."

The next day, I stood with the rest of my family and watched him ride away, my heart heavy. I would have been more sorrowful still if I had known then how long it would be before I'd see him again—and how much longer it would be before I would be his wife.

Two weeks passed before I heard from Jesse again. Every day I searched through our mail, longing for word from him, for reassurance that his love for me was real—that the passion we'd shared had not been my imagination.

I had begun to despair when my younger brother Thomas brought the letter from the post office, and waved it at me. "A letter for you from Cousin Jesse," he said grinning. He winked at Sallie. "Do you think it's a *love* note?"

"Give me that!" I snatched the letter from him, my heart pounding, my face heated.

"Open it," Sallie commanded. "We want to see what it says."

"No," I said. "It's private." I turned and ran all the way up the stairs and locked the door of my room behind me. Then I sat on the edge of the bed and slit the envelope with trembling fingers and eagerly withdrew the single sheet of paper.

Dear Zee,

I am on the mend, though still not as pert as I would like. Frank is home now and he and I have been keeping busy, doing what we can to help on the farm. You may have heard I was baptized recently. After coming so near death, I thought it only right to cleanse myself of my sins when I had the chance.

You'll be happy to know Mother took the news of our engagement well. She knows what a fine young woman you are and wishes us every

> *happiness. But she advises we wait to make our vows. We are young and with so much unrest, now is not the best time to start a life together. I think her advice is wise and we should not rush into marriage when there is no reason we shouldn't wait.*

Wait! I thought I knew my aunt well enough to know what was behind her supposed 'happiness' at the news of our engagement. She wouldn't risk Jesse's anger by forthrightly opposing the match. Instead, she'd counsel delay and hope that time and distance would accomplish what her opposition could not.

> *I hope this letter finds you well. I must go now to help Frank with the horses.*
> *Love, Jesse.*

I stared at the letter, my heart heavy as lead. This was the great declaration of love I had been waiting on? These were the words of undying passion I had longed for? That single word 'love' above his signature was a poor substitute for the sentiments I had imagined.

Where was the man who had swept me off my feet—and into his bed? I didn't see him on this page, in words he might have written to a casual acquaintance—or a maiden aunt!

Heart breaking, I refolded the page and returned it to the envelope, then hid it under a corner of my mattress, wondering if, in giving myself to Jesse, I had made a huge mistake.

I waited for Jesse to return for me. When he did not, I decided to go to him. In late January of 1866, I wrote to Aunt Zerelda, and told her I would like to pay a visit. I made no mention of my engagement to her son or of any other issue that might be likely to raise her ire. Instead, I flattered her with soft words and appealed to her sympathy. *I long to see you, dear Aunt, for whom I was named. I know you could teach so many things that as a woman I should know. My mother is so busy with the duties of running the boarding house that it would relieve her of a burden to have me stay with you for a few weeks.*

Whether it was flattery or persuasion on the part of Jesse, or merely Zerelda's decision that the best way to control an adversary was to keep them close, she replied within a few days, stating she would love to have me come to the family farm in Kearney, to stay as long as I wanted.

Jesse was not there when I arrived. Indeed, no one met me at the train station. I stood on the deserted platform and shivered in the Arctic wind for almost an hour before, half-frozen, I left my trunk on the platform, and set out on foot. I didn't pass a single rider in the four miles to the Samuels' farm along a road rimed with frozen mud. By the time I reached the house my cheeks burned with the cold and I could no longer feel my toes.

The Samuels' farm was a prosperous looking place, with a white-washed board fence encircling the yard around a low-slung wooden house, also white-washed, and several out buildings. Empty fields flanked the long drive, last year's dried corn stalks rattling in the wind like dancing skeletons.

The first person I encountered was five-year old John Samuel, Jesse's little half-brother. "Hello," he greeted me from the branches of a coffee bean tree in front of the house. "Are you come to visit?"

"Yes, I am." I craned my head and just made out his overall-clad figure in the branches of the tree. "Where is your mother?"

"She's in the kitchen with Charlotte."

I went around back and found Aunt Zerelda in the kitchen with the family's Negro cook. The two women were scalding a pair of roosters, the pungent odor of singed feathers filling the air, more feathers spilling from a bucket by the back door.

"Hello, Aunt Zerelda," I said.

She looked up from the chicken. Zerelda would never be pretty—her features were too coarse, her expression too sour. But like her son, she had the kind of presence that drew the eye whenever she entered a room. Many people were afraid of her, though I was determined not to be.

"Zee!" She barked my name like an order. "You weren't supposed to be here until tomorrow."

"I'm sure I wrote I'd come today," I said.

The furrows on her brow deepened. "I'm sure you didn't. But seeing as you're here now, put on an apron and help with this chicken."

The hired man was sent to fetch my trunk from the station, and I rolled up my sleeves and went to work. We made dinner for eight that night: Zerelda and her husband, Doctor Reuben Samuel, the children Sarah and John, myself and three rough-looking men whose names I never learned.

The meal began with a long prayer, during which Dr. Samuel asked the Lord to bless not only the meal, but all those gathered around the table, and all those who fought for the cause of the glorious South. The wrath of the Lord was called down upon the enemies of the Rebel cause, and thanks were given for the return of the South to power, which we were sure was soon to come.

The others around the table responded to this sentiment with a hearty Amen, while I stared in wonder. Even the most ardent supporters of the Southern cause that I knew had given up hope with the Rebels' surrender at Appomattox. Only Aunt Zerelda and her tribe held out such fervent belief that the South would rise again.

The conversation that evening was about crops and livestock and the sad state into which the economy had fallen. No mention was made of Jesse and Frank or their whereabouts.

Jesse did not appear at breakfast the next morning, either. I was a little put out that he, of all people, was not here to welcome me. Wasn't he as anxious to see me as I was to be with him? Zerelda remained silent on the subject, though she must have known I was curious. I debated waiting her out, but my longing to know won out over any desire to best her. "Where are Jesse and Frank?" I finally asked.

"Their whereabouts are none of your concern," she said. She set down her coffee cup with a loud thump. "When you've finished your breakfast, you can help me with the laundry."

I opened my mouth to protest, then shut it. If Zerelda was going to work, I couldn't very well sit idle. I'd prove to her I could do my share, and give her no excuse to dismiss me as lazy or incapable.

Zerelda built a fire under the wash pot in the back yard. The incessant wind whipped the smoke into my eyes and fought to drag the wet laundry from my arms as I carried the piles of sheets and shirts from boiler to scrub pail and back again. The harsh lye soap made my fingers burn and the icy weather made the rest of me numb. Zerelda ignored me as we worked, except to bark orders to stoke the fire or stir the pot or to drape an armload of heavy wet sheets across a row of privet to dry. She deflected my attempts at conversation and refused to talk at all about Jesse or Frank.

The next day was devoted to scrubbing floors and polishing silver. Still no sign of Jesse or Frank. As I crawled into bed that evening I decided that Zerelda had determined to work me until I cried Uncle and returned home. But I was as least as stubborn as my namesake, and determined to stick it out.

And I definitely would not go home before I saw Jesse and spoke to him. What did he mean, staying away when he must have known I'd come to be with him? Were all his words of love merely empty boasting, good only as long as I remained a two days' journey from him?

So I mended blankets and cleaned stoves, peeled potatoes and blacked boots and every other job Zerelda assigned me without complaint. I was stirring a stinking vat of soap over a smoking fire in the back yard on the afternoon of my fourth day with Aunt Zerelda when Jesse came striding across the yard toward me. I peered at him through the smoke, unsure if the man I saw was real or merely a phantom born of my intense longing for him.

Then he was at my side, flesh and blood and blue eyes that burned into me. "Zee, what are you doing here?" he asked.

"I've come for a visit. Didn't your mother tell you?" I searched his face for some sign that he was glad to see me. But all I could find there was fatigue and a wariness I hadn't known in him before. His clothes were wrinkled and dirty, his trouser legs and boots caked with mud. Dark half-moons hung beneath his eyes, and several days' growth of beard roughened his jaw. "Where have you been?" I asked. "What have you been doing?"

He shook his head. "It doesn't matter." He turned from me, headed toward the house.

"Jesse, aren't you glad to see me?" I asked, hating the plaintive sound of my voice, but unable to keep the words back.

He stopped, and that was enough to give me the courage to go to him and put my hand on his shoulder. "Of course I'm glad to see you, Zee," he said, and covered my hand with one of his. The heat of his touch sent a shudder through me, burning away my resentment and fear.

"Then show me," I said, and leaned close to kiss him on the lips.

"Zee, no, not here." He gently held me away from him.

I laughed at this sudden show of propriety. "Jesse, we're engaged," I said. "There's no reason we shouldn't greet each other with a kiss."

"We'll talk later," he said, and released me and headed for the house once more.

I stared after him, and I might have hurled the soap paddle at him, if I'd had any confidence that I could hit him with it. I wanted to shout that this was not the welcome I'd expected. This was not the greeting of lovers who had too long been apart. But Jesse had already disappeared into the house, leaving me to silently fume.

Frank returned later that afternoon, and Zerelda and I spent the rest of the afternoon in the kitchen with Charlotte, preparing a feast for the prodigals. At dinner the two men ate with the silent concentration of the starving and exhausted. No questions were asked and no explanation was made for the brothers' absence.

I wanted more than anything to go to Jesse's bed that night, to hold him close and be held, to whisper plans for our future and hear once more the promises we had made during his weeks at my family's home. But Jesse shared a room with Frank and their brother John, while I slept with his sisters Susan and Fanny. We had no opportunity to be alone at night, and I saw little of Jesse the next day. I began to suspect he was avoiding me. My heart broke as my anger increased. I told myself I should take the next train home, and never speak to him again.

But I stayed, unable to tear myself from him. I wouldn't leave until he'd told me to my face that he no longer loved me.

That evening, all of us sat in the parlor after supper. Beneath the large Rebel flag that decorated one wall, the men read while Zerelda and I sewed, though I was having trouble staying awake after a day spent cleaning the Samuels's attic. Dr. Samuel folded back the paper and cleared his throat. "It says here a group of masked bandits robbed the Clay County Savings Association over in Liberty—in broad daylight," he said. "They made off with over $58,000."

"That's a lot of money," John said.

"Not that the bank will miss it," Jesse said.

Something in his tone made me turn to him, so that I caught the sharp look Frank sent him. Jesse's smile was almost a smirk, the expression of a boy who has pulled a good prank.

"What else does the paper say?" Frank asked.

"It says the men were described as bushwhackers." He paused, silently scanning the columns of newsprint. "Among the men present, several have been identified as Jim and Bill Wilkerson, Frank Gregg, and Archie Clement."

"Well, what do you know about that?" Jesse drawled, and smiled a lazy, satisfied smile that sent a chill up my back. All those men were friends of Jesse and Frank, men they'd served with during the war.

"A young man was killed," Dr. Samuels continued. "Name of George Wyman, eighteen years old. The bank's offering a five thousand dollar reward for apprehension of the criminals, and the governor has sent a platoon of militiamen to track them down."

"A whole platoon," Jesse said. "After a few masked men that everybody seems to have identified in spite of their masks."

"Shut up, Jesse," Frank said, but there was no heat in his words. He rose and stretched. "I think I'll go out and check on the horses."

"I'll come with you," Jesse said.

In my family, we all knew that when a man said he was going out to check on the horses, he really intended to take a few drinks from a bottle of whiskey tucked behind the feed barrel in the barn. But Frank wasn't known as a drinking man, so I suspected he wanted a word with Jesse alone. A word about the bank robbery? Had the James brothers been among those masked bandits?

The next morning I found Jesse in the barn, currying a horse. "Jesse," I said as I approached the stall. "We need to talk."

He glanced up at me, before returning his attention to the horse. "What about?"

"I've been here a week now and we've scarcely been alone ten minutes," I said. "I came here to see you, yet I feel as if you've been avoiding me."

"I haven't been avoiding you, Zee. I've just had things to do."

"What kind of things?"

He moved around to the other side of the horse, his back to me now, and made no answer.

"Jesse, did you and Frank have anything to do with that bank robbery over in Liberty?" I asked. "Is that where you've been?"

"I can't answer that, Zee."

"What do you mean, you can't answer it? Why not?"

"Because it's not an answer you need to know."

"Who are you to decide what I need to know?" I drew nearer, facing him over the back of the horse. I grabbed the wrist that held the curry-comb, forcing him to look at me. "Jesse, I'm going to be your wife. Don't you think I need to know what you're up to?"

His expression softened. He set aside the brush and twined his fingers in mine. "I won't tell you anything that might hurt you," he said. "Let's just say what I'm doing involves a certain amount of danger, and I won't have you exposed to that." He squeezed my hand. "You mean too much to me to ever see you hurt."

His words cooled my anger, and reminded me of all the reasons I loved him. I stood on tiptoe and leaned toward him, eager for his kiss, but just then the barn door opened, and Frank stepped inside. He looked at us for a long moment, with the sad, solemn expression he almost always wore. "Mama's looking for you, Zee," he said after a moment.

"She probably has more work for me to do," I said. But I let go of Jesse's hand and set my feet firmly on the ground once more.

Hard work and agreeableness had done nothing to win over my disagreeable aunt, so the next day I took off my apron, set aside my scrub brush and went to face both my affianced and his mother.

"Did you finish scrubbing the floors?" Zerelda asked when I found her and Jesse seated by the fire in the front room.

"No, I did not." I sat on the sofa beside Jesse.

"Zee's been working mighty hard," Jesse said. "I think she deserves a rest."

Zerelda ignored this attempt to keep the peace. "Why didn't you finish?" she asked.

"Because I'm not your slave," I said, willing my voice not to tremble in the face of her formidable stare. I raised my chin higher and clenched my hands at my sides to keep them from trembling. "I didn't come here to do all your chores. I came to visit so that you and I could get to know each other better, seeing as how Jesse and I are to be married."

Beside me, Jesse sat up straighter. Now would he come to my defense? Or would he protest and say he'd never intended to marry me at all?

Zerelda never flinched. "You said in your letter you wanted to learn what I had to teach you," she said. "That means the proper way to run a house."

"I already know how to run a house," I said. "And I know how to cook and sew and make herbal remedies and dance a quadrille for that matter."

"You obviously don't know how to keep a civil tongue in your head," she snapped. "And you don't know the first thing about looking after my son."

"That's for your son to say, not you."

"I'm sure Zee can take care of me fine," Jesse said, with maddening calmness. "When the time comes."

But when would that time be? This was not the declaration of undying love I had longed for. I felt as if the breath had been knocked from me. Somehow I managed to stand. Unable to face Zerelda's smug expression, I turned and ran from the room.

Blinded by tears, I raced up the stairs and pulled my trunk from beneath the bed. I shoved dresses, shawls and underthings into it, with no thought for order. If I had to drag the thing all the way to the train station myself I would, so anxious was I to be on the next train out of this God-forsaken place.

"Zee, what are you doing?"

Jesse's words only added to my pain. I gripped the edges of the trunk, gathering my strength. "I'm leaving," I said. "It's obvious I'm not wanted here."

"I want you, Zee."

"You have an odd way of showing it."

Then he was kneeling beside me, gripping my shoulders. "I'm sorry, Zee," he said, his voice soft and low, each word an arrow piercing my defenses. "I know you've had a poor reception here. I've been too preoccupied with other matters, though that's no excuse for the way you've been treated." He rubbed his hands up and down my arms, as if trying to warm me after a chill. "It was only today that I noticed how hard Mother was working you, and I meant to speak to her about it—truly I did."

"What's been so on your mind you'd ignore me?" I asked, bitterness still tainting my words.

"It doesn't matter, Zee. It's in the past now. All that matters now is that we're together. I promise to make it up to you."

He kissed the back of my neck, and I leaned against him, feeling myself weaken. Determined to remain strong, I shifted until I was facing him, and searched his eyes. "Do you really intend to marry me?" I asked. "Or did you only say that to get me into your bed?

The color in his cheeks heightened, as if I'd slapped him. "They weren't empty words," he said. "I love you, Zee. I want you to be my wife."

"When?"

"Now isn't the time."

"Then when will be the time? If you're waiting for your mother to give us her blessing, you'll be waiting a good, long time. And I won't wait with you."

"This has nothing to do with my mother. I can't marry you now because it isn't safe." His voice was firm, his gaze intent, silently pleading for me to understand. "I won't put you in harm's way," he said. "Even if that means postponing being with you."

"I hate being apart from you," I said. "I'm so lonely without you."

"I know." He touched my cheek, the tips of his fingers rough. "It scares me sometimes, how much I want you. How much I *need* you. It feels like a weakness to say as much, but it's the truth."

If I hadn't already been kneeling, my knees might have buckled with the force of this sentiment. "I don't care if it's dangerous," I said. "I want to be with you."

"Soon." He kissed the corner of my mouth. "As soon as I'm sure I can protect you." Then his lips fully covered mine, his arms encircling me, sealing the promise.

Once more all the reasons I shouldn't pledge myself to him faded in the heat and light of Jesse himself. Any conflict with his mother or strife with my own family seemed insignificant compared to the love Jesse offered. He wanted to protect me. To cherish me. I had spent my life wanting to be thought of as special, hoping to earn the regard Jesse had given so freely.

Chapter Five

The bank in Liberty offered a $5000 reward for apprehension of any of the suspected robbers. The thought of a price on Jesse's head chilled me—how many men in these desperate times would sell their souls for less? But the worst blow came in December, when Archie Clement, Jesse's friend and mentor, was assassinated while drinking with a friend in a saloon—a friend who might have easily been Jesse.

I was frantic when I heard the news, and sent a telegram to Jesse, begging for word that he was safe. He sent a three word reply: *All is well.* Tears ran down my face as I stared at the words. How could anything ever be well again as long as there were men out there who wanted Jesse dead?

And as long as the danger existed, we were not free to marry. I understood the danger was real. I believed Jesse when he said he only wanted to protect me. But as the months passed I began to despair that we would ever wed.

"I'll be twenty-two soon," I confided to Esme one afternoon as we sat sewing in her front parlor. "How long does he expect me to wait?"

Esme was only three months older than I, but already she was expecting her second child, and she had become a true mother to Mr. Colquit's children. Under her care the three had been transformed from wild creatures to respectable young persons. "Why should you wait for him at all?" she asked, her gaze focused on the tiny rows of stitching on the infant's surplice she was sewing. "I'm sure there are any number of men who would be happy to make you their wife. Mr. Colquit has friends . . ."

"No!" I struggled to temper my strident protest. "Thank you, Esme, but I don't want another man. Jesse is the one I love."

"It's one thing to love a man, quite another to marry him," Esme said. "Jesse doesn't strike me as good husband material. He's too wild and always in trouble. Even now, he has to constantly be looking over his shoulder for some enemy or other he made in his bushwhacking days. His past sins prevent him from taking the oath. He'll never be allowed to vote or hold a local office. He'll never be thought of as respectable."

The Iron-Clad Oath, as it was also known, required every man to swear that he had not committed any of a list of eighty-six 'acts of rebellion' against the United States, up to and including expressing sympathy for the Rebel cause. Under those conditions, no one we knew could have truthfully taken the oath, but most people looked the other way and swore to it anyway. Jesse, who was well-known to have fought for the guerrillas, could use no such fiction to clear his name.

"As long as I respect him, I don't care what anyone else thinks," I said. I stabbed the needle into the cotton tea towel I was embroidering, crying out as I pricked my finger beneath the cloth. I sucked on the throbbing digit while Esme shook her head—not over my clumsiness but my short-sightedness when it came to Jesse.

"You deserve a better life," she said. "A man with a steady job who'll provide you with a good home."

"I love Jesse," I said again, as if that explained everything. But for me, it did. I had waited years to find a man who would stir me the way Jesse did. I knew everyone around us expected my devotion to him would fade, but the months apart only strengthened my feelings. With Jesse, I was more alive than I had ever been. Who would willingly give that up?

"Love isn't enough to make a good marriage," Esme said. "In fact, it isn't even necessary. Respect and a shared outlook and goals are much more important."

Esme had not loved Mr. Colquit when they wed; she had made it clear she favored his suit because he was a good provider and could give her what she wanted—a house of her own and children. I had to admit she seemed happy in her marriage, and evidence of her compatibility with her husband was swelling in her womb. Was she so content now because she had grown to love Mr. Colquit—or because she had decided she did not need love?

But I did need love—and Jesse was the man to whom I'd given my heart. I believed he needed me as much as I needed him. His words said he loved me, but his actions made me doubt. If he truly loved me, wouldn't he want to be with me regardless of the risk?

My father died in April, 1869, aged sixty-four, leaving my mother to manage family affairs with the help of my oldest brother, Robert. The summer of 1869 I turned twenty-four. Though my mother declared me a great help to her in running the household, only Sallie, Henry and I were still left at home, and Sallie was engaged to be married the following spring. I was acutely aware that I was another mouth to feed and another body to clothe in a household that was now without my father's income. The girls I had grown up with were almost all married, managing households of their own, while I continued to wait.

Jesse sent me a birthday present of a fine carved cameo set in a gold frame, but I didn't see him again until early December.

On a pitch-black night I was pulled from sleep to instant wakefulness by the knowledge that something was out of place. I lay scarcely breathing, senses straining. Then I heard the rattle of gravel against my bedroom window. Careful not to disturb Sallie, I slipped from beneath the covers and crept to the window. As I watched, a shadow separated itself from other shadows, taking the shape of a broad-shouldered man in a long riding coat.

My heart beat faster and I shoved up the sash and leaned out. "Zee!" The voice was soft. Deep, and there was no mistaking its owner.

"Jesse!"

"Come down to the barn."

Without waiting for an answer, he turned and strode away. I closed the window and flew from the room. Out the door and across the ground I ran, frost stinging my bare feet and ankles, an icy wind whipping my gown, but I scarcely noticed.

The barn was warm with the scent of horses and sweet hay. Jesse had lit a lantern and hung it from a beam in the center of the room. He stood in the halo of the light, his coat and hat discarded. He wore a pair of striped trousers tucked into tall boots, and a dark shirt with deep breast pockets—a guerrilla shirt, we called them, the pockets designed to hold shot and cartridges within easy reach. His hair was shorter than when I'd seen him last, and he'd grown a neat beard, which made him look older and a little forbidding.

"It's good to see you, Zee," he said. His voice rumbled through me, making me tremble. "What are you doing running out without even a shawl? You're shaking like leaf." He held out his arms. "Come here and let me warm you."

I have no memory of going to him, but I was suddenly in his embrace. "I've missed you, Zee," he said, his nose buried in my hair. "I hope you've missed me."

I wanted to berate him for staying away so long, to chastise him for all the worry I'd endured. But when I opened my mouth to speak, all that came out was, "Oh, Jesse."

His kiss silenced anything else I might have said. It was an urgent, seeking kiss that said more than any words could how hungry he was for me.

One look from him stripped away all caution and any check on my impulses. I threw my arms around him and pulled his head down to mine, opening my mouth to him and reveling in the feel of my breasts pressed against the unyielding wall of his chest.

He took me standing, my back pressed against the rough boards of a stall, his gun belt still slung about his hips. It was a wild, frantic coupling, energetic and exhilarating. He sank into me with a fierceness that stole my breath, thrusting hard, driving me back against the wood. But for all his force, he touched me with skill, his hands and mouth knowing just how to bring me the most pleasure. I bit his shoulder to keep from crying out as my climax shook me, and this seemed to fuel his passion. He groaned out his own release, and crushed me to him, his face buried in my hair once more.

It was a long while before our breathing returned to normal. When he finally withdrew, he kept a steadying hold on me. "I didn't hurt you, did I?" he asked, studying my face.

I shook my head. "Why did you stay away so long?" I asked.

He released me and stepped back, buttoning up his pants and straightening his gun belt. Then he took a handkerchief from his pocket and handed it to me. "You might want this to, um, freshen up."

I laughed out loud. After what had just passed between us, such delicacy seemed out of place. But I turned my back to him to clean myself. "Where have you been?" I asked when I was finished, facing him once more.

"I wanted to see you, Zee," he said. "But it hasn't been safe. There are men watching my every move."

"What men?"

"Lawmen. Bank officials. Militiamen who think every former bushwhacker is up to no good."

"Has it really been that bad?" I asked.

"It has, Zee. That's why I've stayed away. I didn't want anybody following me here. I didn't want to put you and your family in danger."

"No one followed you tonight?"

"No. I'm certain of it." He walked over to a stall and for the first time I became aware of the horse there—a beautiful bay mare wearing a gleaming saddle. Jesse collected fine horses the way some men collect wine. At Jesse's approach the mare looked over her shoulder and blew out a breath. He ran a gentling hand along her flank, which rippled at his touch. "I brought you something," he said, and opened the saddlebag.

He handed me something bundled in a gray bandana. I unfolded the cloth to reveal a gold and ruby broach, and a necklace with diamonds and pearls. They glinted in the lamplight, impossibly beautiful. "Jesse!" I gasped. "Where did you get these?"

"It doesn't matter. You keep them. You can wear them at our wedding."

The mention of a wedding brought sudden tears of happiness to my eyes. "When can we get married?" I asked.

"As soon as things calm down a little. The government will have better things to do before long than harass a bunch of bushwhackers."

I ran my fingers across the jewels. Never had I imagined owning anything so fine. "Thank you," I said. "They're beautiful."

"Put them some place safe and don't tell anybody where you got them," he said.

I didn't question the need for secrecy. Already I'd accepted that part of being with Jesse was learning to keep confidences. Neither did I ask him where he'd been or what he'd been doing. I told myself his activities when we were apart didn't concern me. Maybe I was afraid to know anything that might tarnish the image I'd built of him as the daring war hero, the reckless champion of the South, and the fearless young Rebel.

He led the mare from the stall and to my dismay, I realized he was preparing to leave. "You can't go!" I protested. "You just got here."

"I can't stay." He shoved against the horse's side and tightened the saddle girth.

"Then let me come with you." It was an absurd suggestion; I knew it as soon as the words escaped my mouth. But thankfully, Jesse didn't ridicule me. "I wish you could come with me," he said. "But not yet." He motioned me to him. "Come give me one more kiss, then you'll need to douse the lamp."

The kiss was all too brief, then he swung up into the saddle. I did as he asked and blew out the lamp, then felt my way to the barn doors and swung one side open.

I felt more than saw him ride past me, a large shadow dissolving into darker shadows as he moved out of the yard and into the surrounding woods. I stood there a long time, eyes straining into the darkness, ears alert to the last rustle of a shod hoof in dry leaves or the scrape of a branch against a canvas coat. Only when all was silence did I realize I was shivering with cold.

I might have believed I dreamt the entire encounter, if not for the sticky dampness between my legs, and the square of white linen in my hands. In my room I unfolded the handkerchief and studied it, my eyes fixing on the neatly embroidered letters in one corner: JWJ. Jesse Woodson James. A name the whole world would know before long.

It seemed I had hardly laid my head upon the pillow that night before my mother was shaking me awake. "Sister, you and Sallie need to dress and come downstairs right away."

"Why? What time is it?" Sallie rubbed at her eyes and tried to burrow back underneath the covers.

My mother showed no mercy. She jerked the blankets from the bed. "There are two sheriff's deputies downstairs. They say if we don't answer their questions, they'll have us all arrested."

This news shocked me to instant wakefulness. "What do they want to question us about? We haven't done anything wrong."

Mother was pale. "They're looking for Jesse and Frank, and they seem to think we know something." She gave me a hard look, but I glanced away, willing myself not to react, though I felt as if a vise had tightened around my chest, cutting off my breath.

"Hurry and get dressed," Mother said. "They say they'll come up and drag you out of bed if you don't, and I wouldn't put it past them."

She left and Sallie and I hastily pulled on petticoats and dresses and pinned up our braids. I studied my reflection in the dressing table mirror. My face was pale as milk, and bluish half circles shadowed my eyes. I thought I looked as sick and scared as I felt, but prayed the sheriff's deputies would accept this as the normal reaction of any properly bred young lady suddenly accosted by gunmen.

We found the entire household gathered in the kitchen, watched over by two men. I'd expected a pair of burly gunslingers strung about with cartridge belts. Instead, these were two very ordinary looking men dressed in black business suits and modest bowler hats. They might have been a pair of bankers, if not for the gun belts that showed in their open jackets.

"If you young ladies will have a seat at the table with the rest of your family, we have some questions to ask you," the older of the two men, who sported a walrus mustache and long sideburns, said.

I sat next to my mother, across from my eldest brother, Robert. His hair was uncombed and he needed a shave. I thought he looked particularly forbidding as he scowled at the two strangers, but they ignored him.

"Two days ago, a bank was robbed in Gallatin," the man with the walrus mustache continued. "Two men, whom we have reason to believe were Alexander Franklin and Jesse Woodson James, held up the Davies County Savings Association. They murdered a man in cold blood before riding away."

An icy chill swept over me at his words. *Murder.* Jesse is not a murderer! I wanted to protest, but I managed to keep silent.

"What makes you think these men are Frank and Jesse?" Robert demanded.

"People in town who know the James brothers identified them as the robbers," Walrus Mustache said. "And one of them was forced to abandon his horse—a fine bay mare widely known to have belonged to Jesse James. That same night, another mare disappeared from a barn near Gallatin. We suspect Jesse took it to replace the mount he'd lost."

My heart lurched, but I somehow managed to swallow my gasp. I sat on my hands, and forced myself to keep quiet.

"Any fool can steal a horse," Robert said.

"As you say." The younger deputy spoke at last, a severe, dark man with sallow skin and sunken eyes. "We tracked that horse into your barn."

Robert laughed at this. "There are no strange horses in my barn," he said. "But you're welcome to take a look."

"We already checked." The older detective resumed the conversation. "We believe the horse was there—along with the man who stole it, and that he left very early this morning."

"We've had no visitors for several days," my mother said, truly perplexed. "We haven't seen Jesse in almost a year, and Frank in more than two years."

"We understand Jesse writes regularly to your daughter." Walrus Mustache fixed a baleful eye on me.

"Jesse writes to lots of people," I said, meeting his gaze with a cold look of my own, though beneath the table I clasped my hands tightly together to keep them from trembling.

"People in town say you and Jesse are engaged to be married." The younger deputy pushed himself away from the wall and came to stand beside his partner. Though they were on the far side of the table, it felt as if they loomed over me. It took all the strength I could muster to keep from shrinking away from them.

"Jesse and I have an understanding," I said.

"So it wouldn't be unreasonable to think he came to see you last night, to say hello, and perhaps to give you some money or other things to hide for him."

I thought of the jewelry Jesse had pressed into my hand. But he hadn't asked me to hide it; it had been a gift. "I haven't seen him," I lied.

The younger man scowled, though the older one's expression remained bland. "I imagine for a young girl such as yourself, a man like Jesse seems a romantic figure," he said. "Handsome, well-spoken, inclined to dramatic gestures. If he rode into the yard after midnight, dressed in a dashing suit, astride a fine horse, it would be only natural if your head was turned, and your judgment swayed temporarily." He planted both hands on the table and leaned toward me. "But now, in the light of day, now that you've had time to think, you can see such midnight assignations are the practice of a man with things to hide. A man who is guilty of a crime. Asking you to keep his secrets implicates you in the crime as well."

"What are you saying?" my mother asked. "She already told you she doesn't know anything. My daughter does not lie."

"I think your daughter does," the younger deputy said. "I think she knows quite a bit about Jesse James, and if she's smart, she'll share that knowledge with us."

"I don't have anything to tell you," I said, and pressed my lips tightly shut. I knew nothing about Jesse's activities before last night. I didn't know whether he was guilty of the things these men accused him of or not. But I knew that admitting he'd been to see me, no matter how innocent his reasons for doing so, would put him and the rest of my family in danger.

"If you don't tell us, and we find out for sure he was here, things will go badly for you," the younger man said. "You could be jailed as an accessory to his crimes."

Walrus Mustache studied me for a long moment, his expression almost kindly. "You appear to me to be a well-bred, genteel young lady," he said.

I sat up straighter, as if to confirm just how well-bred and ladylike I could be.

"If you were my daughter, I would hate to see you involved with a ruffian like Jesse James," he continued. "Maybe he's persuaded you he's a Rebel fighting for a cause. A good guy doing noble deeds. But you need to realize he's none of that. He's a common thief, and a murderer. In broad daylight, he put a gun to the head of an innocent, unarmed man—a respectable father with a wife and children—and pulled the trigger. Then he rode away, leaving the man to bleed to death."

Beside me, my mother gasped, and Sallie began to softly cry. I felt sick to my stomach, and chilled to the marrow. The image he painted was horrible, but his words were mere words to me. I couldn't imagine Jesse—gentle, jovial, loving Jesse—committing such horrific violence. Some part of me accepted he had killed men in the war; killing was a part of war. But I imagined the men he had killed had been faceless enemies who were trying to kill him as well. Only a monster would do what the detective had described, and I knew Jesse was no monster.

"You can say anything you like," I said. "But it won't change how I feel about Jesse. You've made up your mind as to his character, but I've known him practically all my life. I know the real Jesse, and he wouldn't do the things you've described."

The two lawmen exchange glances. "Maybe we should arrest her," the younger one said.

Robert rose. "That's enough," he said. "You won't arrest anyone without proof and a warrant. Some horse tracks that you *say* lead to my barn aren't proof of anything. The fact that my sister and Jesse James have exchanged a few letters isn't proof of anything either. You're grasping at straws, trying to build a case out of nothing, and I think it's time for you to leave."

The younger man opened his mouth as if to argue, but the older one nodded and replaced his hat on his head. "All right," he said. "We'll leave. For now." He glanced at me. "You think about what I said, young lady. The people we love are seldom as good and perfect as we'd like them to be. I think Jesse James has misled you badly as to his character and I'd hate to see you hurt because of it."

When the deputies were gone, everyone turned to look at me. "You want to tell us what that was all about?" Robert asked.

"How should I know?" I got up and filled the kettle and set it on the stove.

"They said they tracked that horse here," Robert said. "*Did* Jesse come by here last night after we all went to bed?"

"No!" I kept my back to them, afraid they'd read the truth in my eyes.

"If they'd had any real proof, they would have produced it," Thomas said. "They're probably going around to all Jesse and Frank's friends and relatives and fishing for anything that might implicate them in a crime."

"They won't find anything," Robert said. "Even if people know anything, they won't tell any lawmen. No matter what Frank and Jesse have done, they're seen as heroes by a lot of folks."

"Heroes?" I turned to him, puzzled. "Because of their service in the war?"

"That, and because they've taken a stand against the Reconstructionists and the Northern-run banks and railroads who've made it hard for ordinary people—especially former Secesh families—to get ahead," Robert said. "One of the reasons the bushwhackers have gotten away with their crimes so far is that people have been willing to cover for them." He gave me a hard look, as if accusing me of doing some covering of my own. I looked away.

"Why pick on Jesse and Frank at all?" Sallie asked.

"Because they've been a thorn in the side of the folks in power around here since during the war," Robert said.

My mother had remained silent all this time, but when I turned from the stove I found her eyes fixed on me. "I want you to write to Jesse and tell him you won't see him anymore," she said.

"No!" Tears stung my eyes at the very thought. "I can't believe you'd even ask that. You've known Jesse since he was born—are you going to condemn him now on the say-so of two detectives who want to make him and his brother scapegoats?"

"Whether Jesse did this or not, he's a man who was born looking for trouble," she said. "I don't like to see you involved in any of it."

"You're wrong," I said. "Jesse is a good man. You'll see."

My attitude was defiant, but inside, I was terrified—both for Jesse and for myself. I thought I knew him almost as well as I knew myself, but now doubts crowded up against my faith. Could he have really murdered a man in cold blood, as the detectives had charged?

I wanted to write to him, demanding to know the truth. But I feared the detectives might intercept the mail and anything I said might incriminate Jesse, whether he was guilty or not.

So I bided my time, determined to question him at the first opportunity.

Over the next few weeks, the newspapers were filled with news of the robbery in Gallatin. The suddenness and violence of the crime and the death of the cashier, one John Sheets, left the country in shock. The end of the war was supposed to mean an end to the violence in our state, but our reprieve had been short-lived. Perhaps there were those who would not accept that the war had ended and there were no more battles to be fought. Or maybe men who for so many years had lived with daily fighting and bloodshed could not give up the habit so easily.

Several former bushwhackers were arrested for the crime; two were lynched by an angry mob in Warrensburg, who stormed the jail where they were held and hung them from a nearby tree. Like Archie Clement, these men were afforded no trial or chance to argue their innocence. The very fact that they had once been bushwhackers—that they had once fought for the safety of some of the very men who now condemned them, albeit on the losing side of the battle—was enough to earn them a death sentence. That Jesse could easily have been one of the two made me sick with fear.

A week after the visit from the deputies, my mother sent me to the general store for thread and a bottle of the molasses and lemon cough syrup the store's owner, Mr. Riker, mixed for his customers. The cough syrup contained a number of 'special' ingredients Mr. Riker refused to reveal to anyone, and was considered the most effective remedy for any kind of catarrh.

Unfortunately, Mr. Riker was out when I called at the store. In his place behind the front counter stood his wife, a pinched-faced woman who looked at everyone as if she'd just heard something bad about them. She collected gossip the way some people collect stamps, delighting in taking out each choice bit of news and showing it off to whoever would listen.

"I see the sheriff hasn't been back to arrest you yet," she said by way of greeting when I approached the counter.

"I've done nothing to be arrested *for*," I said, and immediately regretted the words. Mrs. Riker took any sort of denial as sure proof of guilt.

"Associating with that thief and murderer, Jesse James, is reason enough in my book," she said. "No telling what awful secrets about him you're keeping from the authorities. If I was your mother, I'd lock you in your room until you'd gotten over this nonsensical infatuation with that demon in pants."

If you were my mother, I'd poke out my eardrums to keep from having to listen to you, I thought. "Mother would like a bottle of Mr. Riker's cough remedy," I said, as sweet as pie. Nothing infuriated Mrs. Riker more than people who wouldn't rise to her bait.

"I'll have to get it in the back," she complained.

"I don't mind waiting."

She made a hrrmphing sound, then darted into the back room. I wandered over to the thread and selected a spool of brown cotton, then studied an attractive display of hat pins. They were the large, ornate kind, easily ten inches long, with colored crystals at the ends, and fancy gold-colored finials. The kind I'd always wanted, but could never afford.

I glanced toward the front counter. Mrs. Riker was taking her time back there. She was probably brewing a cup of tea and laughing to herself about keeping me waiting.

I looked at the hat pins again. After all the abuse I'd taken from that woman, she owed me something. A fancy hat pin wouldn't even the score, but it would help. Heart pounding, I snatched a gold and blue one from the pin cushion in which they were displayed, then searched for somewhere to hide it. The dress I wore had no pockets, and the pin would never fit in my reticule.

"I didn't have one of the regular blue bottles, so I put it in a canning jar. Don't suppose it makes any difference, anyway." Mrs. Riker's voice grew louder as she neared the front of the store once more.

Hastily, I jammed the pin in my hat, narrowly missing my scalp. I hurried to the front counter and thrust the spool of thread at the old woman. "I'll take this, too."

"I suppose you want me to put it on your bill," she grumbled.

"Yes, thank you."

I waited as she pulled out an oversized, cardboard-backed ledged and flipped through the pages, searching for our family name. She never even looked at me. I held my head up, silently daring her to notice me—and my new hat pin.

"What are you looking so smug about?" Mrs. Riker glared at me.

"It's a beautiful day," I said. "Why shouldn't I be happy?" I scarcely breathed. Any moment now, she'd notice the pin. She'd scream that I was a thief. I'd make some excuse about having tried the pin and forgotten it was there, but she'd be sure to tell the story to everyone she knew, further harming my already damaged reputation.

She grumbled something under her breath, but her eyes never lifted above the level of my chin. I gathered up my purchases. "You have a wonderful day," I said.

I resisted the urge to run out of the building, but I couldn't keep the satisfied smile from my face. I knew I ought to feel guilty about stealing the hat pin; instead I felt as giddy as the time Esme and I had sampled too much of her uncle's homemade elderberry wine.

Was this what Jesse felt when he'd robbed those banks? This elation? This *power?* I hugged my arms to my chest and practically skipped along.

My euphoria lasted until I entered my mother's kitchen. She turned from the stove and with one look knew something was up. She scrutinized me, her gaze fixing on the hat pin. "Where did you get that hat pin?" she asked.

I had the decency to blush, but having already sinned in stealing the pin, I saw no reason not to add to my transgressions with a lie. "Jesse gave it to me," I said. "The last time he visited."

"I haven't seen you wear it before," she said.

"No. I've been saving it for a special occasion."

The lines along either side of her mouth deepened. "There's nothing special about today."

"It's a beautiful day, though. Isn't that special enough?" I turned and glided from the room. I promised myself I wouldn't make a habit of taking things that weren't mine, but I wasn't sorry I'd indulged the whim this once. Whatever happened to me for the rest of my life, I would never forget this wonderful feeling of power and freedom.

Chapter Six

Then Jesse was with us again, riding in just after dark one evening, looking handsome in a gentleman's frock coat and tall black boots. He brought presents for everyone—a watch for Robert, a brooch for my mother, coins and candy for the younger children. We didn't question where he'd gotten the money for such gifts; the James-Samuel household had always been much better off than our branch of the family. And Jesse certainly didn't behave like a man running from the law.

He suggested a walk and I readily agreed. I suspected he wanted a chance to return to the barn or some other secluded spot, but I was more interested in talking than lovemaking.

"Two sheriff's deputies came to the house the morning after you were here last," I said when we were out of earshot of the others.

"I heard," he said. "Who were they?"

"If they told their names, I never heard it. One was young and dark, with sallow skin. The other was older, with a walrus moustache and long sideburns."

He nodded. "What did you tell them?"

"I told them you hadn't been here. That I hadn't seen you in months."

He patted my arm. "Good girl."

I pulled from his grasp and turned to look into his eyes. "I lied for you, Jesse," I said. "But now I want you to tell me the truth. Did you do the things they say you've done? Did you rob that bank and murder that cashier?"

He dropped his chin, staring at the dirt between the toes of his boots. "Would it make a difference in your feelings if I did or didn't?"

My stomach clenched. "How can I know until you tell me?"

"I have to know, Zee. Do you love me, or just some idea of me? Are you in love with the preacher's son or the heroic war veteran or the rogue outlaw? Or are you in love with me—*all* of me, good and bad?"

The disappointment in his eyes tore at me. "I love you, Jesse." My voice caught and I swallowed hard. "Of course I do."

"Then it shouldn't make any difference what I do apart from you. As long as I'm loving and faithful to you—as long as I always do right by you—nothing else should matter."

"What are you saying? That you're guilty?"

He compressed his lips into a hard line. "I have good reasons for everything I've done. I'm asking you to trust that. It's better for everyone if you don't know what I do. That way you'll never be able to give away information to the wrong people. If you don't know where I'm at or what I'm up to, you won't have any reason to worry."

"I always worry about you when we're apart. Not knowing won't change that."

"You never know. You might worry more if you knew the details."

"I don't understand. If you love me, you ought to be able to tell me anything."

"It's because I love you that I *don't* tell you." He pulled me close. "When we're married, it will be my job to protect you. That's a job I intend to take seriously."

"We're not married yet."

"As good as, in my eyes, and I won't shirk my responsibility."

His words sent a shiver down my spine. I thought of Mrs. Peabody, who'd been left alone to her horrible fate. No matter how much time he spent apart from me, I believed Jesse *would* always protect me. He wasn't a weak man, like Sheriff Henry had proved to be, and his love wasn't false. I knew this in my heart as surely as I knew my own name.

How could any woman walk away from a man like that?

Still, I was wounded that he wouldn't confide in me. "You're saying you won't tell me anything."

"Only what you need to know."

I wanted to protest that it wasn't fair that he got to decide what I needed or not, but he was kissing my throat, his hands stroking my breasts, and I lost all will to argue.

But it wasn't Jesse's touch that persuaded me so much as my own heart. I'd made my decision when I'd lied to the deputies and to my family. With those few words, I'd crossed a line; it was too late now to go back.

I loved Jesse because of who he was and in spite of it. If he had a dark side to his character, it was no darker than the shadows within my own soul. I had been raised to be a good girl, a genteel lady who would never do wrong. But the mold had always chafed. Unlike Jesse, I couldn't ride with a guerrilla band or pull a gun on those who tried to confine me to a role I didn't want. I was limited to smaller rebellions; loving Jesse was one of those, one I refused to ever give up.

I wanted to believe that the danger to Jesse would soon pass and it would finally be safe for us to marry. But Jesse himself dashed these hopes, as his every action seemed designed to increase his peril. June 3, 1871, Jesse and Frank, Cole Younger and Clel Miller robbed the bank in Corydon, Iowa. Or at least, this is what the papers claimed.

I cut out the articles about the robberies and added them to the scrapbook I had begun keeping shortly after the end of the war. I no longer asked Jesse about the accusations against him. I doubted he would admit to anything, and living with uncertainty was better than having him admit to things I knew were wrong. If he denied them, I would have to wrestle with the question of whether or not he lied to me. I didn't want to believe he'd do so, but I knew he had a glib tongue, and plenty of reason not to admit the truth about such serious crimes.

In April of 1872, a bank in Columbia, Kentucky was robbed. The same group of bandits was suspected of holding up the ticket office of the Industrial Exposition in Kansas City in September of that same year. The newspapers viewed these crimes with varying degrees of admiration. Even the harshest spoke of the daring of the robberies, and the coolness with which they were executed. Others cited these exploits as blows for the common man against the big businessmen who controlled the banks.

In May of 1873, Jesse, Frank, and others were accused of robbing the Ste. Genevieve, Missouri Savings Association. In July of that year, they turned their attention to railroads; more specifically, the express company cars which carried the payrolls for factories, mines, stockyards and other businesses. Six men, supposedly including Jesse and Frank, boarded the Rock Island train outside of Council Bluffs, Iowa, emptied the safe, and escaped.

In January 1874, Jesse, Frank, Arthur McCoy and Cole and Bob Younger were implicated in the hold-up of a stagecoach near Hot Springs, Arkansas. In February, they were the prime suspects in the robbery of a train at Gad's Hill, Missouri.

Once more the press was captivated by the daring of such an action, while I could only clip the newspaper reports and marvel at the contrast between the sometimes brash, sometimes brooding young man who was my lover and the larger-than-life vigilante celebrated in print.

Each time the robbers struck they left behind empty safes and cash drawers. On the Gad's Hill train, there was a new touch—a press release describing the robbery in glowing detail. The robbers were clearly thumbing their noses at the authorities, and more than one small shopkeeper or struggling farmer cheered them on.

I think it was at this point that I began to accept that Jesse was involved in these robberies. The press release was exactly the sort of eloquent, flamboyant gesture he loved. I tried not to think too much about the nature of his crimes—the people who had died, and those who had lost valuables. I turned my mind instead to what little good I could see in these exploits. The banks, express companies and railroads held a lot of power in the new economy that rose after the Civil War—power Jesse and his friends seemed determined to take back. I told myself this was a good thing, and shoved aside all dark thoughts to the contrary.

As the charges against Jesse and Frank mounted and rumors about them persisted, my family and friends pressured me to break our engagement. My mother and Esme tried to interest me in eligible men in our neighborhood. When I'd protested that I was already promised, my mother shook her head. "Jesse isn't the kind of man a respectable woman should associate with," she said.

But maybe I'm tired of being respectable, I thought. *Is it so wrong that Jesse excites me as much for the danger and excitement he brings to my life as for the love he's promised me?*

I had lived a life of virtuous self-denial. I didn't dance because my parents didn't approve—though I longed to twirl across the dance floor in time to beautiful music. I surrendered the last piece of cake when my older brother wanted it, even though the cake was my favorite—because I had been taught that men were to be given precedence in all things. I patched old dresses instead of making new ones because the money was needed to buy shoes for my younger siblings, or a coat for my father—though I dampened the pages of fashion magazines with my tears, mourning my lack of finery.

But I would not deny myself Jesse. In my own household, I was just another child in a family of too many, not even addressed by my own name. But when Jesse looked at me, I felt like the most important woman in the world. No other person had ever made me feel that way, and it wasn't something I could afford to give up.

"There's no sense you wasting your best years waiting for him," Esme chided. She was pregnant again; the knowledge making me feel emptier still. She and I had been bosom friends since girlhood, and I wanted her, of all people, to understand how I felt.

"Jesse needs me," I said.

"Every man needs a good wife," she said. "There are plenty of men here who would welcome your attentions."

"Jesse doesn't merely need a wife," I said. "He needs *me*." I was a refuge from the violence and danger with which he'd surrounded himself, the keeper of his secrets, the soother of his soul. I was sure no other person could comfort him as I could, and I knew no other man would ever see me as Jesse did.

But I would not sit and wait forever. I searched for a way to force Jesse's hand, and end this impasse between us.

All of Jesse's success, and both the acclaim and censure it had brought him, had made him famous. While a single man could afford to be reckless, a husband and father had to take more care. I reasoned that marrying me might induce Jesse to settle down and exercise more caution; it might even save his life.

So I sat down and wrote Jesse a letter. I told him he had to come see me, that I had news that couldn't be delivered in a letter. I knew his first assumption would be that I was pregnant. How quickly he answered me—and if he answered me at all—would be the first test of his feelings toward me. If he'd only been leading me on all these years I'd know soon enough.

But Jesse didn't disappoint me. Scarcely four days after I sent my letter to his mother's house, he rode up on a chestnut mare. Another in Jesse's growing collection of fine horseflesh, the mare had a black mane and tail, and warm brown eyes that watched him adoringly as he strode across the yard to meet me.

"You're looking well, Zee," he said, studying my face intently. "Your letter made me fear you were indisposed."

I almost laughed at this choice of words, but decided to pity him and put him out of his misery. Out of one misery, that is, and perhaps into another. "Come sit with me on the porch," I said, leading the way to the wooden swing that hung there.

He took a seat beside me, hat in hand. He wore a black wool frock coat and hat, with a paisley silk vest and a black silk cravat. He looked like a man on the way to an important meeting—or a funeral. His sandy hair was slicked back with pomade and his face was clean shaven. He was the kind of man any woman would have noticed, but the blue eyes and the sly curl of his lips made him a man they remembered. I often thought if women had clerked in the banks and express companies of the day the lawmen would have collected better descriptions of the bandits, and Jesse might not have run free so long.

"What did you want to talk to me about?" he asked, settling his hat on one knee, his eyes searching my face.

"We've been engaged nine years," I said. "It's past time we marry. Either you set the date today, or I won't see you any more."

I had my doubts whether I could keep this pledge, though if it took finding another man to wed, I would do it. I would not see thirty without a ring on my finger.

I was prepared to argue my case. To berate him for leading me on. But my carefully rehearsed words were unneeded.

To my amazement, Jesse gave in without a protest. "You're right, Zee," he said. "It's high time we married."

"Do you mean that?" I asked, still wary of his sincerity.

"I do." He took my hand in his. "You've waited for me so patiently all these years. I'm tired of us being apart. I want us to be husband and wife, as soon as possible."

"No more delays?"

"No more," he said. "I know you think I've been purposely putting you off all this time, but I've lived a rough life, and I didn't want to put you through that. Now I know I'll never have real peace until you're with me every day. I need you, Zee. "

With those few words, my torment ended, and my heart melted. Jesse was not a man who needed anyone. He chafed at any restraint or dependence, but now he had willingly surrendered to me. "I'll be a good wife to you, Jesse," I promised. "I'll make us a good home."

"I'll make sure you never lack for anything with me," he promised. "I'll always take care of you."

My mother was not happy with my announcement that Jesse and I were finally to wed, but she saw the futility of trying to change my mind. My brother Robert gave his blessing, perhaps happy to transfer the responsibility for me and my upkeep to another man.

Now came the challenge of finding someone to conduct the marriage ceremony and a place to hold the nuptials. I asked my uncle, Reverend William James, to perform the service, but he refused. "I won't see you wed to a man with so much blood on his hands," he told me, his face somber as a funeral.

"You're wrong!" I protested. "Jesse hasn't done half the things people say he has. He's a good man. He'll be good to me."

Still, Uncle William refused to budge, until Jesse himself went to him and swore his innocence. Jesse's charm and sincerity softened even the hard heart of our uncle, and he agreed to perform the ceremony.

My sister Lucy and her husband, Bowling Browder, had moved to Kearney by this time, and it was decided we should hold the wedding at their house. On April 24, 1874, I stood with Lucy and Esme in my sister's bedroom and prepared to say my vows.

I stared at my unnaturally pale face in the mirror over my sister's dresser and pinched my cheeks, hard, trying to bring some color to them. "Maybe I should use some rouge," I ventured.

"Don't be silly," Esme said. "You look beautiful. That dress is very becoming."

My wedding gown was made of pale blue silk, with a demi-train draped over a full bustle. I smoothed the skirts and the crinoline beneath rustled like dry leaves. "I've waited so long for this day, I can scarcely believe it's here," I said.

"You weren't the only one who had doubts." Lucy handed me a bouquet of jonquils from her garden that she'd tied up in white ribbon. "More than once I feared Jesse was leading you on."

"Jesse never led me on." My family and friends could think what they would about him, but I knew his intentions toward me had always been the best.

A knock on the door interrupted us. Thinking it was Uncle William, I hurried to answer it. But instead of my uncle, I came face to face with Aunt Zerelda.

Jesse's mother regarded me with the air of someone observing a bug from great height. "Are you happy now that you've gotten your way?" she asked.

"I'm very happy to be marrying Jesse," I said, refusing to let her cow me, though beneath my full skirts my knees shook. "Jesse's very happy too."

She blew the breath out her nose, like a bull snorting before a charge. "Jesse needs a wife like a bucket needs a hole. And he especially doesn't need a penniless spinster like you."

"I'm exactly the woman Jesse needs," I said. "He doesn't care about money, only that together we'll be happy, whether you wish it or not."

Her face reddened, only the muscles at her jaw showing white. "Don't do this," she said.

"Jesse and I are going to marry," I said. "I'm going to bear his name and live with him as his wife. You can either welcome me to the family, or risk losing him altogether."

"Jesse is my *son*. Marrying you doesn't change that."

"And he's going to be my *husband*. Even the Bible says a man shall forsake his parents and cleave to his wife. If you make Jesse choose, do you want to take a chance on the choice he'll make?"

Zerelda squared her shoulders. "I wouldn't dream of not welcoming Jesse's wife into our family," she said stiffly. Then her eyes met mine, their blue as cold as steel. "But if you do anything to make him unhappy—ever—you'll have me to answer to."

I nodded, afraid my voice would shake if I tried to do more. Zerelda loved Jesse and I loved Jesse—but she and I would never love each other. We could only circle warily, two dogs in possession of the same bone.

Uncle William appeared in the hallway behind Zerelda. "Ladies, the guests are all here," he said. "Are you almost ready?"

"We're ready," Lucy called.

The three of us made our way down the hall to the front parlor, where Jesse stood with Frank and Bowling Browder. Robert waited to give me away. My mother and younger sisters sat in chairs on one side of the room, while Zerelda and Doctor Samuel and Jesse's younger siblings filled the chairs on the other side of the room.

I thought for a moment of Lucy's grand wedding, and felt a pang of regret for the modesty of my own celebration. But a larger gathering had been out of the question. "It's impossible to keep a large party like that a secret," Jesse had pointed out. "The Pinkertons and their like would be sure to take advantage of the occasion to make a raid."

The last thing I wanted on my wedding day was for the groom and his best man to be arrested, so I'd readily agreed to this smaller celebration with guests who could all be trusted to keep their mouths shut about what was happening here today.

Jesse looked as handsome as ever in a black wool morning coat and brocade vest, his face solemn, his blue eyes shining when he looked into mine.

Esme leaned close. "Is Jesse wearing a *gun* beneath his coat?" she whispered.

My gaze shifted to Jesse's side, and the disconcerting bulge of a gun belt at his hip. Frank, who stood up with him, was also armed. "I imagine a number of the men in the room have weapons," I said. I wouldn't have been surprised to learn that Zerelda carried a gun somewhere on her ample person.

"It seems sacrilegious for him to say his vows while armed," Esme said.

"I'm used to Jesse wearing a gun," I said. "He almost doesn't seem properly dressed without one." Other men might go about unarmed, but Jesse wasn't like other men. His gun marked him as different from them—dangerous and daring. The knowledge sent a thrill through me.

"All right, let's begin." Uncle William arranged us at the front of the room, Jesse and I together in the center, our attendants around us. "Dearly beloved, we are gathered here in the sight of God and these witnesses . . ." Uncle William's voice rose above us, rich and deep. My heart pounded wildly and I struggled to breathe. All the nervousness and excitement that had been building for years was pent up inside me, and I feared at any moment I might burst forth in either tears or shouts of joy.

But I held my composure and repeated my vows, my eyes fixed on Jesse, who looked as calm as a summer pond.

We'd gotten as far as 'in sickness and in health' when my young nephew, Robert Browder, burst into the room. He'd been stationed in the front yard to keep watch for suspicious characters. "Two men coming!" he shouted. "Strangers. They're headed right this way."

Before I could utter a sound, Jesse and Frank whipped out pistols and raced to the door. Some guests dove for cover, but most, like me, stared at the curious spectacle of half a dozen grown men peering around the doorframe and from behind the front curtains at the two men walking down the street.

I told myself I should be afraid, but fascination and frustration beat out fear. Knowing Jesse was marrying me under threat of danger somehow made his vows to 'love, honor and cherish' all the more precious. And the incident confirmed my hope that I was not binding myself to a life of dull drudgery, but one of excitement and adventure, with a man who would be sure to never bore me.

"Those aren't strangers," Bowling declared, hauling his son up by the collar. "That's Mike and Author Delwood. They live two houses down and wouldn't harm a flea."

Looking sheepish, everyone holstered their weapons and filed back into the parlor. Uncle William mopped his forehead with a handkerchief. "Shall we start over?" he asked.

"Can't we pick up where you left off?" I asked. I was afraid if we had to start over every time something spooked the crowd I might have to wait another nine years to be married.

The ceremony concluded and we invited everyone into the dining room for refreshments. As soon as I had cut the cake, Esme spirited me away into a side bedroom. "I have something important to tell you," she whispered.

I thought maybe she was going to announce that she was pregnant again. Instead, she took my hand in hers and squeezed. "I just wanted you to know that Mrs. Peabody was right."

"Mrs. Peabody?" I couldn't think of my missing friend without a pain. "What was she right about?"

Esme's cheeks turned a rosy pink. "She was right when she said the wedding night could be most pleasurable—for the man *and* the woman."

I didn't bother telling Esme I knew what a pleasure it could be. But I was grateful that Jesse and I would now be able to make love in a bed, and not have to worry about who knew what we were up to. "Thank you, Esme," I said. "That's good to know and relieves my mind greatly."

Jesse and I spent our wedding night in St. Louis, at the Lindell Hotel, registered under the name of Mr. and Mrs. G. W. Howard. After a pleasant dinner in the hotel dining room (where Jesse sat with his back against a wall, facing the doorway so that he could observe everyone who entered) we retired to our room. I was surprised to find that I was suddenly nervous. The brief encounters we'd stolen under cover of darkness hadn't prepared me for the prospect of an entire evening with Jesse—with the lights on if we so desired.

Jesse locked the door, then turned the gas lamp down low. "You look beautiful, Zee," he said, moving toward me. "I'm a lucky man."

"I'm glad we can finally be together," I said.

"Me, too." He leaned down and I thought he would kiss me, but instead, he began to take the pins from my hair. "I want to take my time with you tonight," he said. "To get to know you all over again."

Despite the years we'd known each other, that night really was like the first time. We undressed each other slowly, fumbling with buttons like children tearing at the wrappings of a long-awaited gift. I traced my finger down the twin indentations from the bullet wounds in his chest. "Do they still hurt?" I asked.

"Sometimes." He dismissed the idea with a shrug.

We crawled into bed and he pulled me into my arms. "I've missed you, Zee," he said—words he said every time he came to me after months apart, but this time they rang with a deeper emotion, the relief of a man who is well and truly home.

The hotel bed was broad and wide, with a feather mattress and linen as white and soft as clouds. When Jesse laid me back on it I felt almost as if I was floating, and when he sank into me I came back to earth with the exultant knowledge that this was not a dream or a fantasy. Jesse was mine and he would be for the rest of our lives.

Afterwards, we lay in each other's arms. I thought Jesse was asleep, until he broke the silence. "We'll make a good home together," he said. "We'll have a family, maybe even put in a few crops. It'll be a real home."

"I'd like that," I said.

His voice was wistful. I realized how lonely he must have been, hunted like an animal, always on his guard. Even now his pistols hung on the end of the bed, with another on the table beside his head, within reach if he should need it.

I tried to put these things from my mind as I lay in the shelter of his arms. The outside world didn't matter now. Nothing was as important as the fact that I was finally Mrs. Jesse James.

From St Louis, we traveled to Galveston, Texas. Jesse delighted in showing me around the bustling port city that had once been home to the pirate Jean Lafitte. The flamboyant privateer fascinated Jesse, and he listened eagerly to tales of buried treasure with which saloon owners and local venders entertained tourists such as ourselves. I'm sure that in another time or place, Jesse would have been a pirate, way-laying the rich government ships the way he now way-laid the trains.

And I would have been his lady, arrayed in jewels and gold—the bounty from his sea raids. I admit the idea appealed to me. After a lifetime of self-denial, I was ready for a little indulgence.

For the most part, Jesse and I indulged ourselves in each other's company—hours of lovemaking, getting to know every inch of each other's body as we had not had the leisure for before. He told me I was beautiful. He thought I was smart. He made me feel special in the magical way he always had.

We strolled the boardwalk by the ocean, past grand hotels that looked like castles. We ate salt-water taffy and ices purchased from carts along the shore, and took off our shoes and splashed in the warm ocean. In the evenings, we dined by candlelight on fresh fish, exotic fruits and wines imported on that day's steamers, then retired to our opulently-furnished room to make love until we fell asleep, exhausted, in each other's arms.

Far from the familiar faces and climes of Missouri, and the accompanying political tensions, Jesse was a new man. Rather than being a notorious outlaw or a dangerous criminal with a price on his head, he was simply another young, handsome tourist on his honeymoon. Even the gun belt strapped about his hips beneath his finely-cut suit coat was not out of place here, as every other man seemed to go about armed in this country not so long removed from the frontier.

Of course, Jesse was not a complete stranger to Texas, and friends and acquaintances found their way to him. One of these was the journalist, John Newman Edwards. A distinguished, sad-eyed man with a drooping moustache, Major Edwards had served with General Shelby in the war. He had championed Jesse in his newspaper, *The Kansas City Times*, since before the Gallatin Bank robbery in 1869, and was considered one of the James brothers' staunchest allies. "It is a delight to meet you, Mrs. James," he said, bowing low over my hand when we were introduced. "You are every bit as lovely as Jesse has led me to believe."

Jesse delighted in reading Edwards' praise of him. Each morning before breakfast he would buy whatever papers were available and read them while he enjoyed his coffee, porridge and toast. When we were alone, he would read his favorite parts aloud. "Don't he make me sound grand?" he'd say, with a boyish grin.

It was John Edwards, writing under the name of Ranger, who broke the news of our marriage to the world in an article in the *St. Louis Dispatch.* The article was full of errors intended to throw off any officer of the law who might be on Jesse's trail. By the time it was published, we had left Galveston and were in Sherman, staying with Jesse's sister Susie and her husband, Allen Parmer, a former bushwhacker.

I saved the article in my scrapbook. It is one of my favorites, if only because of these words, which I have underlined. Jesse told the reporter, *"Through good and evil report, and notwithstanding the lies that had been told upon me and the crimes laid at my door, her devotion to me has never wavered for a moment. You can say that both of us married for love, and that there cannot be any sort of doubt about our marriage being a happy one."* My most fervent wish was for those words to be true.

Chapter Seven

Our time in Sherman was some of the happiest of our lives together. I was full of hope for the new life Jesse and I were beginning together. This would be a fresh start for both of us. I loved Susie like my own sister, and Allen was as pleasant a man as I had ever met. He and Jesse spent hours riding, exploring the local countryside while Susie and I visited. Occasionally, the men traveled out of town for a few days, scouting for farm land Jesse might purchase, or horses to add to Allen's stables.

Upon their return from one of these trips, Jesse decided I should learn to shoot a gun. "Every woman should know how to defend herself," he asserted when we gathered for breakfast one morning.

"Oh, I don't know about that," I demurred. "Why would I ever need a gun when you're around?"

"Sometimes I'll have to be away, and I don't want to leave you defenseless."

"I'm a little afraid of guns," I said. "It seems to me accidents are always happening with them." Jesse himself was proof of that; the tip of the middle finger of his left hand had been shot off by a pistol that misfired during his bushwhacker days. He did his best to hide the deformity, and hated for anyone to mention it.

"There's nothing to be afraid of if you're careful." He nodded across the table to his sister. "Susie has known how to shoot since she was a slip of a girl."

Susan nodded. "Mother made us learn, in case we needed to defend ourselves against Yankees."

I could well imagine Zerelda drilling her family with pistol and rifle—a general preparing her troops for attack against her hated enemy, exhorting them to fight for the glory of the South.

Feeling I had little choice in the matter, I relented. After breakfast the four of us—Susan, Allen, Jesse and I—trooped out to the prairie behind their house. Jesse produced a small nickel-plated gun with a dark wood grip. "We'll start with this little .22 revolver," he said. "It's big enough to do real damage and more accurate than the pocket derringers ladies often use—but not so big you'll hurt yourself firing it."

The gun was heavier than I'd expected, the grip cool and smooth in my hand. Jesse showed me how to load and unload the weapon, and made me practice over and over, cautioning me to keep the barrel aimed firmly at the ground.

When he felt I was proficient at this task, he had Allen set up a bottle on a tree stump some distance away and invited me to aim at it.

I proved a miserable shot. In six tries I never even hit the stump. The acrid stench of burnt gunpowder stung my eyes and my arm and wrist hurt from the kick of the weapon.

"You have to accommodate for the recoil," Jesse said. He moved behind me, wrapping his arms about me and steadying the pistol with his own hands around mine. I enjoyed the physical closeness, even if I wasn't deriving much pleasure from the rest of the lesson.

"Now, fix your eye on your target," he said. "And bring the pistol up, in line with your vision. Don't move your eyes to the gun—bring the gun up to where your eyes are aiming. Then, when your target's in sight, squeeze the trigger slowly but firmly, bracing your arm to hold the gun steady." He demonstrated, his finger over mine on the trigger guard. Though he was left-handed and I favored my right hand, he was able to shoot well enough from the right side to shatter the bottle into sparkling bits.

"Now you try," he said, releasing his hold on me and stepping back.

I waited while Allen walked out and set up a second bottle, then squinted toward it, trying to remember everything he had told me. I focused on the bottle, raised the gun slowly, then braced the gun with two hands and fired. I jumped and squealed as the bottle exploded.

"That's it, sweetheart." Jesse clapped me on the back and kissed my cheek. "Now you're getting the hang of it."

We spent the rest of the afternoon shooting, and I began to see the fun of it. My everyday accomplishments had been limited to neatly ironed shirts or a well-cooked dinner; there was something very satisfying and empowering about firing a weapon and seeing the object I'd been aiming at destroyed. I didn't think of myself as a destructive person, but I appreciated the immediacy and permanency of the result.

The men took turns testing their marksmanship, shooting lines of bottles at various distances, or tossing them into the air and shattering them before they hit the ground. Susan proved adept at firing even Allen's heavy Navy Colt, and I began to feel more comfortable with my little revolver.

By the time we retired to the house once more my arms and shoulders ached, and the smell of burnt cordite clung to my clothes and hair. "I feel better now," Jesse said as we washed up in our bedroom. "I like knowing you could defend yourself if you had to."

"I hope I never have to," I said. I shook a generous dose of dusting powder into my hair and began to brush it through, hoping to remove or at least tame the gunpowder smell.

"Better to be prepared." He sat on the end of the bed and watched me brush out my hair. "It's no secret I've made enemies, Zee. You know that."

"I know." I did my best to put from my mind all the people who wanted Jesse locked behind bars, or worse. Pretending they didn't exist was the only way to get through each day without going crazy with worry.

"I'll do my best to see that they never bother you," he said. "But if they should try, I want you to be able to defend yourself."

I nodded. "I appreciate it, Jesse. I really do."

"Besides," He smiled. "I've been thinking we might go down to Veracruz. I hear they have big snakes down there in the cane fields. You might need to shoot one."

"Veracruz?" I turned to face him. "Really?"

He shrugged. "Allen and I have been talking about it. He knows some people down there. The land is cheap and great for ranching. And the weather is temperate, being right on the ocean."

"That might be nice," I said. Though I hated the thought of leaving the rest of my family behind, I knew in Mexico Jesse would be beyond the reach of United States law, away from Pinkertons and the ever-more-vengeful Missouri government and banks and express companies. All those forces had pursued him for years, and kept us apart. Life without them would be a new beginning. And I liked the idea of shooting snakes better than shooting people.

A few days later, Susan and I were invited to a tea hosted by the Ladies' Mission Society at the local Methodist church. Susan introduced me as her sister-in-law, Mrs. Howard, visiting from Tennessee. The hostess of the tea, a sweet-faced matron named Maddie Westfall, greeted me warmly. "We're so glad to have you with us," she said, leading us to one of several white-clothed tables set for six. "Allow me to introduce my sister, Corrine Gates, visiting from Austin with her little girl. Corrine, this is Mrs. Howard and Mrs. Parmer."

"You must call us Susan and Zee," Susan said as we took our seats. "I was in Austin last winter and thought it was a beautiful city."

"It is, but I'm thinking of relocating here to Sherman," Corinne said. "I'd like to be closer to my sister, and I think it would be a safer place to raise my daughter."

"Corinne had quite a frightening experience on the trip to see me," Maddie said, when we were all settled around the table and tea was poured.

"More exciting than frightening, to tell the truth," Corinne said, her brown eyes sparkling. "Our stagecoach was way-laid by highwaymen!"

"Oh no!" The fifth woman at our table, a very young blonde whose last name was Addison, gasped. "You must have been terrified."

"I was very frightened at first," Corinne said. "But they were really most gentlemanly and polite." She grinned. "And the taller of the two was quite handsome, with sandy hair and the most brilliant blue eyes."

I carefully set my cup back in its saucer and folded my hands in my lap. "Do you know who it was?" I asked, my voice surprisingly calm, though my heart raced.

"No, but certain things he said and did make me wonder if it wasn't Jesse James himself."

This announcement caused considerable excitement at the table. I caught Susan's eye and she gave a little shake of her head, as if to warn me to keep silent. But I needed no warning.

"He was definitely a Southerner," Corinne continued. "He addressed me as 'Ma'am' and told my little girl she didn't have anything to be afraid of. Then he held out a wheat sack and asked us all to please hand over our valuables. I was third in line, and I somehow found the boldness to speak to him. I told him he struck me as too much of a gentleman to rob a poor soldier's widow of all she possessed."

"I still can't believe you had the nerve to speak up that way," Maddie said. "He might have shot you dead."

"He didn't strike me as that kind of man," Corinne said. "When I said I was a soldier's widow, he looked downright sympathetic. He asked where my husband had served. I told him my Henry fought with Hood's Texas Brigade. He was killed at Second Manassas."

We all murmured our sympathies, which she accepted with a gracious nod. "The response of the handsome robber was remarkable," she said. "I swear there were tears in his eyes as he returned my purse to me. Then he pressed a ten-dollar gold piece into my daughter's hand."

"What about the rest of the people on the stage?" Mrs. Addison asked.

"They were all men, and the two robbers relieved them of all their valuables. One of the men had a little silver revolver with mahogany grips that the handsome bandit seemed especially pleased with. The owner said he'd bought it as a gift for his wife and pleaded for its return, but the bandit refused. He tucked the pistol in his coat, then doffed his hat and bid us all good day, and mounted up and rode away. It was the most remarkable thing I've ever experienced."

"What makes you think the robber was Jesse James?" Susan asked.

"Oh, because he was such a gentleman. And because he was so moved by the news of my husband's service in the war, and because of the gold piece he gave my daughter. Everyone knows Jesse James has great sympathy for the South and its soldiers, and a generosity toward the common people."

"Those men were probably common people and he didn't have any compunction about robbing them," Maddie said.

"Well, yes, but I'm sure they could afford the loss better than I could." A wistful smile lingered on Corinne's lips. "I shall never forget those blue eyes and that handsome face as long as I live."

Susan and I exchanged glances again. I hoped I looked calmer than I felt. Fortunately, the conversation at our table ceased as the afternoon's speaker rose to begin her address. We all bowed our heads for the invocation, but my mind wasn't on the prayer or the talk that followed. I was thinking of Jesse, and how pleased he'd been when he'd presented me with the little revolver, as if he'd chosen it especially for me.

The robbery itself didn't upset me as much as perhaps it should have; I had had years to grow accustomed to the stories of Jesse's exploits. Yes, robbery was a sin, and against the law. But Jesse operated by his own code, one that I had come to accept as my own: his enemies were the Northern businessmen and politicians who oppressed the South. They had made the lives of our family and friends miserable for so long. Was it so wrong to demand justice from them now?

I was more distressed by the realization of how naïve I'd been to hope that marriage to me would make Jesse leave his life of crime. 'Settling down' obviously didn't mean the same thing to Jesse as it did to me. I should have realized as much when he insisted I learn to shoot in order to protect myself 'while he was away.' I thought he meant away visiting his mother or attending a horse or cattle auction. He meant away robbing stage coaches or banks.

No more mention of Corinne's handsome outlaw was made for the rest of the afternoon. Susan and I walked home in silence, where we found Allen and Jesse playing cards in the kitchen. "How was the tea?" Allen asked.

"Interesting." Susan sat across from him. "Maddie Westfall's sister is visiting from Austin. She's thinking about moving here."

"What do I care about Maddie Westfall or her sister?" Allen asked.

"You should care," Susan said. "The sister—Corinne Gates—was on a stagecoach that was robbed on her way here. She was very much taken with one of the bandits—a handsome man with sandy hair and very blue eyes, and courtly Southern manners."

We all looked at Jesse, who returned our stare, his expression grim. "What do you mean, 'taken' with him?"

"She said she would never forget him as long as she lived," I said. "And she's sure the man who robbed the stage was none other than Jesse James himself."

Jesse relaxed his shoulders, though I sensed he did so with effort. "Imagine that—somebody going around impersonating me."

"This robber stole a little silver pistol from one of the passengers," Susan said. "A gift the man had bought for his wife."

"I take it this Mrs. Gates is sharing this story with a lot of people?" Allen asked.

"With everyone she knows," Susan said. "I'd say it was the high point of her summer."

No one said anything else for many minutes. The only sound was a fly buzzing in the window. The heat pressed in on us like a heavy blanket, and I felt the first twinges of a headache.

Jesse's chair scraped back from the table. "I'm going to check on the horses," he said.

"I'll go with you." Allen rose also.

When the men were gone, Susan came and put her hand on my shoulder. "Don't worry, Zee," she said. "Jesse knows what he's doing. It'll be all right."

I nodded. Of course he did. And I thought I'd known what I was doing when I married him. I'd never truly considered the reality of pledging my life to a man to whom ordinary rules and expectations didn't apply. I wasn't disappointed, exactly—more surprised to find all the assumptions I'd so naïvely made about our future stripped away.

But I would adjust. I loved Jesse, as much for his uniqueness as for anything else. He was a man like no other—tough, yet caring, a criminal who was also an idealist, a man capable of great violence and great tenderness. I would prepare myself to live a life with him that resembled nothing I could have ever imagined.

The next morning, Jesse announced that we were returning to Missouri. That afternoon, we boarded the train, headed not for Veracruz or any other exotic location, but for the place we both knew best. We were going home.

Frank met us at the station upon our return. Dressed in a new suit of brown wool, he paced the platform while we waited for our trunks to be unloaded from the baggage car, jingling change in his pocket, tugging at his lapels, adjusting and re-adjusting his hat.

"Buck, what's got into you?" Jesse finally demanded. "You're jumpy as a cat."

"There's someone I want you to meet," Frank said, addressing not his brother, but me.

"Oh?" I glanced at Jesse. He shrugged. "Who is that?" I asked.

"Her name's Annie. Annie Ralston." To my amazement, Frank blushed a deep red. "Well, Annie James now."

Jesse gaped at his older brother. "Buck, you old son of a gun!" He slapped Frank on the back. "Do you mean to tell me you've gone and gotten hitched?"

Frank looked sheepish. "I've known her a while now. She's a good woman—a real lady."

Though Frank was normally gruff and reserved, he looked almost boyish as he talked about his new wife. The change delighted me. "I can't wait to meet her," I said. "We'll have the two of you to dinner as soon as we're settled."

Frank drove us to a little house Jesse had rented before the wedding. "If you don't like it, we can find someplace else," Jesse said as we toured the rooms.

"No, it's fine." I turned to face him. "Wherever I am with you is perfect."

He drew me into his arms and kissed me, the faded wallpaper and crooked floors of the house receding in the warmth of that embrace. When we finally parted, he smiled down at me. "Do you think Buck was jealous of our happiness, so he decided to find a wife of his own?"

"He said he'd known her a while." I tried to imagine what sort of woman would be drawn to the stern, studious elder James brother. "We must have them to dinner soon, so we can meet her."

"I'll bet she's not as pretty as you," Jesse said.

I tried to hide my pleasure at this praise. "It's not a competition," I scolded. "She's family now, so we must welcome her regardless of her looks or temperament. As long as she makes Frank happy, that's all that matters."

The following Friday evening, I prepared to greet my new sister-in-law. In the days since learning of Frank's marriage, I had formed half a dozen different pictures in my mind of what Annie James would be like. I had settled on the image of an older woman, close to Frank's age. She would be practical, sturdy and solemn, like Frank himself.

So I was not prepared when he escorted an elegant young beauty into my front parlor that evening. Easily ten years Frank's junior—eight years younger than me—Annie Ralston James resembled a music-box figurine, with porcelain skin, spun-gold hair and violet eyes. She spoke in a low, refined voice and moved with the grace of a dancer. "How very nice to meet you," she said formally, and took my hand in a fleeting, cool embrace.

Over a supper of ham and corn pudding and beaten biscuits, Frank gave her history, while Annie looked on, the hint of a smile on her petal-pink lips. It was not the worshipful smile of a naïve girl, but the self-congratulatory look of a woman who is sure she has won a valuable prize.

"Annie was a schoolteacher," Frank said, a note of pride in his voice. He himself was something of a scholar, and had intended to go on to university before the war interfered. A prodigious reader, he was fond of Shakespeare, and often quoted from the Bard's plays. "She was educated at the Independence Female College. Her father is Judge Sam Ralston. They have a big farm in Independence."

I had never met a woman who had been to college before. Most of the teachers I had known had barely completed eleven grades before sitting for their teacher's certificate, which was issued by the county. If her father was a judge and owned a large farm, that meant Annie came from money, though one look at her would have told me that. So how had she ever become involved with the notorious outlaw, Frank James? Did she even know how Frank earned his living?

After supper, the men retired to the front porch to smoke cigars, while Annie and I cleared the dishes. I wondered if she had grown up with servants to do such menial chores, and if she expected as much from Frank. But she didn't hesitate to tie on an apron and join me at the sink.

"How did you and Frank meet?" I asked as I filled a dishpan with hot water.

"We met at a horse race." She scraped leftovers into the slop bucket.

"A horse race?" I couldn't completely hide my astonishment. Race tracks were not places generally frequented by genteel young ladies from good families.

"Yes. I enjoy the races, whenever I can attend."

Jesse and Frank were both wild for horse racing. They regularly entered their own horses and bet on others, losing prodigious amounts of money in the space of an afternoon.

"You must have made an impression, if you could distract Frank from a horse race," I said.

"Actually, I scolded him because he was blocking my view of the track."

I studied her more closely, trying to imagine this delicate creature berating a man said to be one of the most feared in the state. "How old were you?"

"I was seventeen." She picked up a cup towel and prepared to dry the dishes. "All I knew was a man in a big hat was blocking my view of the horses in a race on which I'd placed a wager. I told him he either had to remove his hat or his person—I didn't care which."

I laughed. "What did he do?"

"He told me if I wanted to see I should come stand beside him instead of behind him. So I did."

"And that was it?"

"After the race—which my horse won and his did not—he asked permission to call on me."

"And now you're married." I plunged my hands into the hot, soapy water and began to wash the dishes.

"Now we're married. But if my father had had his way, we wouldn't be. When he learned the man coming to court me was the notorious Frank James, he ordered him to never come near me again."

I smiled in sympathy. "He didn't know he might as well tell the sun not to rise as to tell one of the James brothers not to do something."

"I think Frank might have respected my father's wishes if I'd agreed," she said. "But I didn't."

"Why didn't you?" I asked. "I mean, you scarcely knew him."

She was silent for a moment, the only sound the squeak of linen against a china cup as she dried it. "When my father looked at Frank, he saw a man who had broken the law," she said finally. "A man who had killed other men. I saw a quiet, modest man with a keen intelligence. A man who respected the strength of my own mind and will."

"Yes." I nodded. Maybe because they had been raised by such a strong, forceful woman, both Jesse and his brother did not dismiss women as readily as some of their contemporaries. "Sometimes I read the newspaper descriptions of Jesse and it's as if I'm reading about a stranger," I said. "He's been described as 'ruthless' and 'blood-thirsty' and I think this can't be the same man who stays up all night, babying a sick horse, or the man who plays tag in the pasture with his younger half-brothers and sisters. The man they write about isn't the one who sends me beautifully composed letters, or brushes out my hair for me at night."

"I wonder." Annie's hands stilled, the cup towel dangling idly from her fingers. "Does love cause us to judge them differently, or is love a lens through which we see them more clearly?"

"Maybe it's a little of both," I said. Impulsively, I reached out and squeezed her hand. "I'm glad Frank married you. It's good to have someone close who understands."

She nodded. "I'm hopeful now that they have families and responsibilities, Frank and his brother will settle down and not be so restless and on the lookout for trouble."

My heart went out to her. Hadn't I so recently shared those same hopes? "I don't think marriage is enough to change a man," I said. "They are what they are, and we must accept that."

She nodded. "I expect it won't be easy at times, but I'm determined to stand by him." A smile tugged at the corners of her mouth. "I've made the biggest wager of my life and I don't intend to lose."

Marriage to Jesse introduced me to a new world—I took on not only the new roles of wife and mistress of my own household, but I became a part of the universe over which the James brothers ruled, a world in which finances were determined by whatever they could take, people were judged by which side of the war they had supported and notoriety was welcomed as equally as it was feared. While Jesse loved being famous, Frank preferred the anonymity that was vital to their continued survival. Yet, in the state of Missouri at least, the name James had a power that guaranteed the brothers a measure of safety against those who pursued them, an invincibility that kept us balanced between caution and recklessness.

Jesse's friends and allies became my friends as well. Among my favorites was Clel Miller, who had ridden alongside Jesse and Frank during the war. He was an affable man with sleepy brown eyes and hair that curled around his head like a halo. I also welcomed Cole Younger, the man who had asked me to dance at my sister Lucy's wedding. Cole was a frequent visitor to our home, along with his brothers, John, Jim and Bob. The men spent many an evening in our parlor or on the front porch, smoking and talking of their days riding with Bloody Bill. Often Annie was there as well. She and I sewed or drank tea in the kitchen and talked into the night. Even now I look back on those companionable evenings fondly. This was the contented life I'd imagined during those years when I'd waited for Jesse.

As the sons of a Baptist preacher, Frank and Jesse seldom drank, and Jesse was so indisposed to use profanity that he had earned the nickname 'Dingus' when he rode with the bushwhackers, after a made-up word he had used as a curse.

So I was startled one evening to hear Jesse's voice coming from our parlor, raised in anger. "God dammit, Buck, what's wrong with you? Don't you see what an opportunity this is?"

"An opportunity to get killed," Frank answered. "It's too reckless."

"That's why we're the only ones who could pull it off. It's reckless and daring, and profitable."

"I worry about you, Dingus. You're starting to believe your own press."

Annie was not with me that night, so I retreated to the kitchen alone and shut my ears to their discussion. The harsh words disturbed me, and every sense told me danger was near. I told myself everything would be fine. I didn't want to know the details of Jesse's activities, at least before they happened.

Two days later Jesse kissed me good-bye. "Buck and I are going to take a little ride, maybe pay a visit to Mama for a few days," he said.

I frowned. "You're going to see your mother?"

"We may stop off a few other places while we're away, but we'll be sure to stop in at the farm for a few days. I'll tell Ma you said hello."

"Yes, do." No doubt, Zerelda would have a few choice words to say to her son about his wife. I wondered if she'd met Annie yet. Did she approve of her rich, educated blonde daughter-in-law any more than she had of me, her poor, dark namesake?

"You'll be all right here?" Jesse asked.

I nodded. "Of course. But I'll miss you. Hurry home."

"I will, Sweetheart. I'm always anxious to get home to you."

Being alone in the little house felt strange after so many weeks in which Jesse and I had been virtually inseparable. Annie must have felt the same, for she came and asked if she could spend the night. "I don't like being at our place by myself," she confessed. "Besides, I hope with you for company I'll worry less."

"Why are you worried?" I asked. I wasn't enamored of the idea of Jesse leaving me alone to call on his mother, but she was, after all, his mother, and it was to be expected that a dutiful son like Jesse would visit her.

"You don't really believe they took this trip just because they missed their mother, do you?" Annie asked.

I flinched at the scorn in her voice. "What else would they be doing?" I asked.

Annie took both my hands in hers and looked me in the eye. "Zee, you do know what Jesse does for a living, don't you?" she asked.

I jerked out of her grasp. "Of course I know. I'm not some naïve child."

"I didn't mean to offend you," she said. "Jesse's so protective of you I thought he might have managed to keep the true nature of his activities from you."

"Jesse and I don't have secrets like that," I said. "I know what he's done, though we don't talk about it." I hesitated, then added, "Does Frank talk to you about his work?"

She shook her head. "No. But I keep informed as best I can. I listen to things he says, make note of people he talks to. That way I'm never completely in the dark."

"You *spy* on your husband?" I stared at her.

She shrugged. "I don't think of it as spying. I learn what I need to know."

"The less I know the better," I said. "I can't worry about what I don't know about."

I could tell by her disapproving look that Annie didn't think much of this philosophy. "Then I suppose you don't want to know where they went tonight," she said.

"They *said* they were going to see their mother."

"Oh, I expect they'll get there eventually, but first they're going to rob a bank. Or a train. Or maybe something else. That part I didn't hear."

"How do you know this?" I asked, astonished.

"I overheard Frank tell Jesse they'd need provisions for several days ride, and for Jesse to bring his maps."

"That doesn't mean they're planning a robbery."

Her violet eyes bore into me. "They both lost a lot of money at the track last week, and the rent on our houses is due at the end of the month. They have to get money from somewhere."

I shifted in my seat. "That doesn't bother you?" I asked. "That they rob other people to support us?"

She shrugged. "The men in charge of the banks and railroads took plenty from all of us during the war, and after, too. My father lost almost everything. I don't feel much pity for them."

I nodded. She made Frank and Jesse's wrongdoing sound so logical—something anyone with sense would do if they had the nerve. When she explained things this way, it didn't sound so much like sin—no more than my having sex with Jesse before we married had been a sin, at least—I'd been taught it was wrong, but since nothing bad had come of our actions, I told myself it wasn't the sort of thing that put my soul in any real danger.

We learned soon enough that Annie's prediction had been right: two days after they left us Jesse, Frank, and a third man (some say Cole Younger, some his brother Jim, and some their friend Arthur McCoy) waylaid a horse-drawn omnibus outside of Lexington, Missouri, ordered the passengers to disembark, then robbed them.

This proved a fine entertainment for folks from Lexington, who gathered on a bluff above town and watched the scene unfold. Amazingly enough, no lawmen were dispatched to stop the robbery-in-progress, and the three bandits rode away. No one was injured, and even the victims, though mourning the loss of their possessions, commented on the dash and gallantry of the robbers.

The audacity of the robbery, carried out in front of such a large audience, captured the imagination of newspapers around the country. *The Lexington Caucasian* reported: "The whole proceeding was conducted in the coolest and most gentlemanly manner possible . . . Prof. Allen doubtless expresses the sentiments of the victims when he tells us that he is exceedingly glad, as he had to be robbed, that it was done by first class artists, by men of national reputation."

The authorities, however, were not so impressed at being made to look the fool. Lieutenant Governor Johnson sent St. Louis police officers in pursuit of the James brothers. They were at their mothers' farm by this time, protected by the loyalty of friends and neighbors, and by Zerelda's assertions in letters to journalists across the state that her boys were innocent of any wrongdoing—and any man who said otherwise would have to answer to her.

Thus was established a pattern for our married life those first few years. Frank and Jesse made frequent trips out of town. I no longer pretended these expeditions were entirely innocent, but unlike Annie, I had no desire to know the details of their activities until both men were home safe. Jesse handed over money and jewelry to me with the polite fiction that he'd been lucky at the track, or had made a profit on the sale of a horse. I thanked him and enjoyed spending his largesse, and refused to think at all of where the money had come from, or about the danger we all might be in.

The year ended with the hold-up of the Kansas Pacific Railroad in December, near Muncie, Kansas. The bandits blocked the tracks with old railroad ties, then signaled the train to stop well shy of this barrier. They robbed the Wells Fargo Express safe of $30,000.

This robbery led the governor of Kansas, Wells Fargo, and the Kansas Pacific Railroad to offer rewards for the capture of the robbers, said to be Frank and Jesse James, Cole and Bob Younger, and several others. When I read this in the papers, a chill swept over me. Times in Missouri were still hard, and while the threats of lawmen had no power to make Jesse's friends or neighbors betray him, money had a different kind of power I wasn't sure everyone could resist.

Jesse came into the room just then. "What's the matter, Zee?" he asked. "You're pale as a ghost."

"What's this about a reward?" I asked. "For 'the capture of Jesse or Frank James, Cole or Bob Younger.'" I read.

"Idle posturing." He waved away the words as if swatting a fly. "The railroads are furious we've taken back a little of their greedy gains. The local folks are cheering us on."

"But a reward . . ."

Jesse took the paper from me and pulled me close. "It doesn't mean anything," he said. "Nobody would have the nerve to ever collect it. They know they'd have to answer to us if they did. And no one wants to cross the James or Younger brothers." He kissed the end of my nose. "You don't have to worry about a thing. Let's just be happy and enjoy our first Christmas as man and wife."

He began to unbutton my dress, distracting me from thoughts of newspapers and rewards and danger of any kind. I saw through his manipulation, but I didn't care. I didn't want to think about these things, as if ignoring them would somehow keep us safe.

We celebrated Christmas with Frank and Annie, with a goose Annie prepared, which was over-cooked, but none of us mentioned it. We attended church together that evening, where we sang hymns and celebrated Christ's birth day.

I had another reason for great happiness at this time. After so many years of hoping, I was finally expecting a child. Jesse was beside himself with joy at the news. When I told him, he waltzed me around the room, then immediately insisted I sit down with my feet up, lest I grow too tired.

I laughed at his concern, but I wasn't without fears of my own. I was constantly sick to my stomach, unable to keep anything down. Jesse, worried that I would fall seriously ill while he was out and about during the day, paced the floor of our bedroom one evening in early January, fretting. I had spent most of the day in bed, too weak to even drag myself to the kitchen to make a cup of tea.

"Maybe you should go to your mother's for a while," he said. "So she can look after you."

"I don't want to leave you," I protested. "Besides, Mother is too busy running her boarding house. The last thing she needs is someone else to look after." At my mother's house, I wouldn't be the cherished prodigal daughter returning home to be lovingly pampered. I'd merely be Sister, another mouth to feed and body to house and child to claim another fraction of my mother's scarce attention.

"Then we should both go to my mother's. She and Charlotte can look after you well enough."

I shuddered at the thought of facing my mother-in-law while my emotions and my body were in such turmoil. "Your mother doesn't even like me," I said. "Why would she want to look after me now?"

"She's mellowed a great deal since the wedding," he said. "Now that she's grown used to the idea of you as my wife. And she's excited about a new grandchild."

Still, I resisted the idea, until I became so weak I fainted, and came close to falling down the front steps. The incident terrified both me and Jesse, and he insisted I go to his mother.

I didn't have the strength to resist. "Promise me you'll join me there as soon as possible," I said before I boarded the train.

"I promise." He kissed my cheek. "Just remember," he said. "You're my wife and you're going to be the mother of my child. Nothing Ma says can change that."

His words gave me strength. Zerelda might not like me, but she could never take Jesse away from me now. Whatever battles she sought to wage didn't matter, because we both knew she had already lost the war.

Jesse's stepfather, Reuben, met me with the wagon and drove me to the farm. He was a docile, agreeable man, considered somewhat 'simple' since his near-death at the hands of Union militia during the war. His placidness suited Zerelda, allowing her to take command of the household without having to pretend to defer to him.

Zerelda greeted me stiffly but not unkindly when we arrived at the farm. "You're looking well, Zee," she said. "At least we know you come from good stock, and shouldn't have too much trouble bearing children." Zerelda herself had borne eight children by now. In addition to Jesse, Frank and their sister Susan from her first marriage, there had been another son, Robert, who died in infancy. With Reuben, she had Sarah, John Thomas, Fannie and the youngest, Archie.

Charlotte made more of a fuss over me. "You sit right down by the fire and put your feet up to keep them from swelling," she said. "And I'll bring you a warm tonic to settle your stomach and strengthen your blood."

In addition to Zerelda, Reuben, the four younger children and Charlotte, the household included two more black servants—eighteen-year-old Ambrose and six-year-old Perry. Clel Miller was also a frequent visitor, often staying for dinner. Clel could always make me laugh with his stories and jokes.

As much as I'd dreaded this visit, I found myself enjoying it. I began to feel better, too. Charlotte and Zerelda prescribed soothing herbal teas for my nausea and cooked rich puddings and eggnogs to build my strength. The children vied to wait on me, and delighted in entertaining me with songs and skits.

Jesse joined us after a week, his arrival charging the atmosphere in the house with a contagious joy. He loved the farm where he had grown up, and he delighted in being with his younger half-brothers and sisters—fifteen year-old Sarah, thirteen-year-old John, ten-year-old Fannie and especially eight-year-old Archie. Named after Jesse's friend Archie Clement, the baby of the family was a particular favorite.

Surrounded by the love of family, I could never remember being happier. When one is in the midst of it, happiness seems the strongest emotion imaginable, something so big and powerful nothing could defeat it. Yet it is the most fragile thing, like a dream made of spun sugar. In an instant it can shatter, destroyed by unimaginable fear and cruelty. In a single instance, so much is lost, and no matter how hard we try, we are never able to abandon ourselves to that joy again.

Chapter Eight

January 25, 1874, fell on a Sunday. After church we settled into a pleasant day of visiting and socializing. Frank rode over, though due to the threat of snow, Annie remained behind in Kansas City. Clel Miller came to visit. If the men were worried about recent rumors that the governor had joined forces with the Pinkertons in pursuit of them, they gave no sign of it.

Sarah, John and Fannie were excited about a party that evening at a neighbor's house. Archie, too young for the party, cried at being left behind, but Zerelda dressed him in the new suit he had received that Christmas and made a fuss over him, and Jesse promised to take him into Kearney soon and buy him a present.

We had a hearty dinner, with good food and good company. Afterwards, Jesse, Frank and Clel took their leave. Jesse caught me as I made my way down the hallway from the kitchen to the parlor. He wrapped his arms around me and gave me a long kiss. "You look beautiful tonight, Zee," he whispered.

"You should stay home tonight," I said, caressing his throat. "We can go to bed early." Marriage had earned us a bed to ourselves in one of the tiny attic rooms, a step up from sharing quarters with Jesse's half-brothers and sisters.

"I'd like that." He kissed my cheek. "But I promised Buck and Clel I'd ride out with them. On the way over here this morning, Buck heard there were a couple of strangers in the area, asking a lot of nosy questions. It's made him nervous as a cat and he won't give any of us peace until we check it out."

This news made my stomach knot, but I had learned not to allow my fear to show. "Be careful," I said, the caution and blessing uttered by every mother and wife since Eve. If only words had the power to keep our loved ones safe.

After the men left, the rest of us sat in the parlor, talking and watching the fire in the stove until the children returned from their party. Zerelda and Reuben and the children all bedded down in the large front room, near the fire, while I retired upstairs. Still exhausted in those early days of my pregnancy, I slept the sleep of the dead.

I awoke after midnight, to screams and wailing and the smell of smoke. At first I thought I was dreaming, and I struggled against the heavy lethargy of deep sleep.

The hollow ring of gunfire brought me to my senses, and my heart pounded as if trying to escape my chest. Fumbling for my wrapper in the darkness, I stumbled downstairs and into a scene out of my worst nightmares:

Charlotte, John and Perry were clustered around a bloody figure in front of the fireplace. With a sickening jolt, I realized the body was that of little Archie, drenched in blood, his face almost unrecognizable in its anguish.

I heard a deep moan from the other side of the room and turned to see Dr. Samuel tending to his wife. Zerelda's eyes were closed, though her mouth was open, moaning in pain. She, too, was drenched in blood, but clearly alive. Ambrose, blood running from his scalp, struggled to carry the woman, who was half again his size, to her bed. A veil of gray smoke filled the room and the stench of blood and ash and charred flesh made my stomach roil.

But I didn't have time to think of myself. I rushed to help. Ambrose, Dr. Samuel and I managed to get Zerelda to her bed on the other side of the room. Her right arm dangled limp, and she was in and out of consciousness. The sight of my mother-in-law, a giant of a woman in both size and spirit, reduced to such a state shook me almost as much as the reality of Archie's injuries.

But I had no time to mourn these shocks. I left Fanny to tend to her mother and turned my attention to Archie. As I approached, Charlotte's eyes caught mine and she sadly shook her head. "He's hurt mortal bad," she said, and pulled a blanket up to his chin.

I began to cry, sobs tearing at my body. John, at thirteen already taller than me, put his arm around me and tried to comfort me. I had a sudden image of him eight years previous, little older than Archie, greeting me from the branches of the coffee bean tree. That he would try so hard now to be a man in the midst of so much suffering among those he loved made me weep all the more.

After seeing his wife safely in bed and determining there was nothing more he could do for his son, Reuben had run out into the yard and shouted for help. Neighbors, having heard the shouts, gunshots and commotion, began to arrive. Doctors were sent for, blankets were fetched. Someone wrapped me in one and ushered me to a chair in the corner, where I was given a cup of strong tea and a hot brick was placed beneath my feet. "What happened?" I asked, over and over, but it would be the next day before I was able to piece the whole story together:

Shortly after midnight, Ambrose, who had been sleeping in the kitchen with the other servants, woke to the sound of voices just outside the house. He smelled smoke, and got up and looked out the window and saw the shadows of men moving about. Before he could sound the alarm, the window shattered.

At first, Ambrose thought someone had fired into the house. Then he saw a large metal ball rolling about the kitchen floor.

By this time, the noise had awakened Reuben and Zerelda. Flames licked from beneath the wallboard of the house. Reuben tore at the burning wood, trying to put out the fire, while Zerelda ran into the kitchen. She found the metal ball, which was also burning now, and tried to kick it out the door, but it proved too heavy. Reuben rushed in and scooped up the burning ball and carried it to the fireplace in the front room. Zerelda and the servants beat at the burning siding with quilts and succeeded in smothering most of the flames.

By this time, everyone in the house was awake but me. The children gathered with their parents and servants around the fireplace, wondering what to do next. They sensed there were still people outside of the house, but they didn't know how many, or if they were heavily armed. They were debating what to do when the metal ball in the fireplace exploded.

Fragments on the bomb struck Reuben and Ambrose in the head, but the glancing blows only momentarily stunned them. A larger chunk caught Zerelda in the arm, and she collapsed, screaming.

But it was Archie, standing closest to the fireplace, who bore the brunt of the explosion. Burning metal fragments ripped through his little body. He lingered for several hours, but from the first, there was little hope.

After the neighbors began to arrive, Archie was carried to Zerelda's bed so that she could say good-bye. I had always thought her a strong woman, hard even, and fearless. But that night I saw a different side of her, as vulnerable as any mother could be. Her face was a mask of grief as she stroked Archie's hair and cradled his limp body. "I thought it would be Frank or Jesse I would have to lose first," she whispered, her eyes blurred with tears. "I know the risks they take and I was prepared to accept their fate. But Archie . . ." She kissed her son's forehead and rested her cheek against his. "My baby. He never did anything to hurt anybody. Why should he be taken from me?"

Archie died before dawn and as the sun rose I clutched Zerelda's left hand as Dr. Allen from Liberty, Missouri amputated her right arm just below the elbow. Zerelda held me in an iron grip, but made no sound as the doctor sawed off her arm, nor would she accept the whisky offered as the only anesthesia. When the Justice of the Peace convened a coroner's jury in the front room that evening to determine the events of the night before, Zerelda was able to give a clear, dignified testimony despite what must have been terrible pain, both mentally and physically.

My respect for her grew tenfold that night, and I wished for even a fraction of her strength to deal with the ordeal ahead.

A sheriff's posse arrived the next day, as Ambrose and Reuben worked to replace the burnt siding on the house and repair the broken window. Archie was to be buried the following morning; I helped Charlotte prepare his body, combing his hair and dressing him in the little suit of Confederate gray that had so delighted him two nights before.

I thought the posse had set out in pursuit of the fiends who had murdered a little boy and maimed his mother, but as I listened at the door while they addressed Reuben, I realized to my horror that they were intent on tracking Jesse and Frank. I bit my finger to keep from crying out as they informed Reuben that they had posted guards all around the farm, so that no one could leave or arrive without their notice. They demanded the right to search the house, then, not waiting for permission, pushed past the men and came inside.

The sight of the little body stretched out on the kitchen table stopped them momentarily. Avoiding our eyes, the three who had been designated to search quickly removed their caps and bowed their heads. "What do you mean, intruding like this on a house of grief?" I demanded.

"Who are you?" one of the men asked.

I drew myself up to my full height. "I am Mrs. Jesse James," I said.

"Then I am very sorry for you, ma'am." He replaced the hat on his head and moved past me, into the front room.

Even after the posse left us, we could have no peace. Strangers and inquisitive neighbors gathered in the yard and along the road. Annie took the train from Kansas City the morning of the funeral. She hired a driver to bring her from the station and threatened those who blocked her way with an iron-tipped parasol if they didn't let her pass.

"Have you heard from Frank?" a tearful Zerelda asked when Annie stopped beside her bed to offer her sympathies.

Annie shook her head. "I don't expect he or Jesse will risk communicating with us as long as they know we're being watched."

Somehow, we got through the funeral, watched over by the government's guards and the curious crowd. Afterwards, I took to my bed, sick with grief and worry over Jesse. Every hour a new rumor reached our ears, along with sensational newspaper stories. Some reported that Jesse, Frank, and Zerelda James had all been killed in the raid. Others said the house had been burned to the ground. I began to see the unreliability of the press to ever get at the real story.

Gradually, however, more of the truth came to light. In the middle of the night, a group of Pinkerton agents had surrounded the Samuels' house and set fire to the siding, then launched the little bomb through the window. One agent claimed they had only intended to illuminate the interior of the house so they could see who was inside, but others argued their intention from the first had been to maim and kill, to exact revenge for the death of one of their colleagues at the hands of the James brothers the previous year.

While the governor and the Pinkertons and their posses might have hoped to arouse public sentiment against the notorious outlaws, the brutality of their actions only garnered more support for the James family. Papers as far away as New York wrote about the affair, calling it shocking, and a great tragedy.

The attackers were quickly identified as Pinkerton detectives from Chicago. That men in the employ of the government had committed such atrocities particularly upset the public, and newspapers around the country talked of the persecution of the James brothers. People chose up sides on the issue, largely along Union and Southern lines, and some people talked as if this one horrible act would be enough to start the Civil War all over again.

I devoted my days to nursing Zerelda. She and I were united in our fears for her sons. Every morning as I changed the dressing on her arm, she asked me, "Have we any word from Frank and Jesse?"

"No." I shook my head and avoided looking into her eyes, fearful of giving way to tears in front of this woman who never wept.

"If anything had happened to them, we would have heard by now," she said.

"Yes. I imagine you're right."

"They're too clever to ever be caught," she continued. "No one can outsmart the James boys."

I wish I had her confidence in Jesse and Frank's invincibility. To the rest of the world—and to Zerelda, too—they were larger-than-life figures. But I had nursed Jesse's wounds and knew the narrowness of some of their escapes. I knew how vulnerable they could be, and that knowledge weighed heavy on me during those long, empty days.

We had no word at all until John Newman Edwards visited the second week in February. "I'm sorry we must meet again under such dire circumstances," he said as he bowed low over my hand.

"Have you seen Jesse recently?" I asked. "Have you talked to him?"

"I have not seen him, but we have been in communication. I promised him I would personally visit to assure that you and the rest of his family are all right."

"I'll never be all right again," Zerelda moaned. "Not without my dear Archie, never mind my arm."

"A great loss indeed," Edwards said gravely. "Jesse is quite upset about it, and if it were in his power to seek revenge on those who have caused you such pain, he would do so, as Odysseus avenged the suitors' depredations on Penelope."

I stared at him, uncertain whether to be awed or amused by this man who spoke as floridly as he wrote.

"That's all well and good, but is there anything you or other members of the press can do to make the Pinkertons and sheriffs and other lawmen leave us alone?" Annie asked. "I can't go into town to shop for a yard of ribbon without being followed by some armed man on horseback."

"That is another reason for my visit, dear lady," Edwards said. "Shall we sit and converse?"

We sat, and Charlotte served coffee and cake while Edwards shared his news. "Certain sympathetic lawmakers, sensitive to the public outcry against the persecution of your family, intend to propose legislation granting amnesty to Jesse and Frank for all previous trespasses," he said.

"Amnesty?" Zerelda asked. "Does that mean they'll be declared innocent?"

"It means it will be as if the events never took place," Edwards explained. "They will be wiped from the record."

"And they'd be allowed to return home, unmolested?" Annie asked.

"On the contrary, they would be welcomed home as heroes," Edwards declared. "They could resume life as law-abiding citizens, with the full voting rights that have been denied to them thus far."

"Praise be to God!" Zerelda declared. "My boys have been

persecuted too long."

I bowed my head, hiding my expression from the others. The promise of amnesty was an exciting one, but after so many years of taking what he wanted from those he considered his enemies, would Jesse be content to live as a farmer again?

For the next month and a half, the debate raged in the Missouri legislature. Were the James brothers persecuted heroes or ruthless outlaws? Did they steal because the draconian laws of the time gave them no other choice, or because they lacked consideration for their fellow man?

In the end, the bill was defeated, by the narrowest of margins. Lawmen continued to haunt the road in front of the Samuels' farm, though they knew better than to venture down the driveway. Ambrose and others had been posted along the property line, with orders to shoot to kill any trespassers.

Jesse did manage to slip through the woods to see us a few times, arriving in the dark of night and leaving well before morning. His brother's death and mother's maiming hit him hard, etching new lines of pain on his face. Not even joy over the growth of the baby within me could wipe out the sadness that was now always present in his eyes.

If Frank and Jesse felt any guilt for not having been at the farmhouse to protect their loved ones that night, or for having drawn their enemies to the house in the first place, they never indicated such to me. But they wasted no time exacting revenge on any they thought had aided the attackers. When neighboring farmer Daniel Askew, who was known to have provided a base of operations for the Pinkertons, was gunned down at his home, there was little doubt who was responsible for the slaying. Samuel Hardwick, another neighbor who had helped the Pinkertons, had sense enough to leave town before the James brothers came to call.

Eventually, things calmed down. More pressing matters drew the lawmen away. Zerelda recovered her strength and Jesse was able to return home once more. Life began to seem more normal—or as normal as it can ever be for a man with a price on his head and the people who love him.

"I've been thinking," Jesse said at breakfast one morning late that spring, when we had returned to our home in St. Louis. "We should move."

"This house is a little small," I said. "Especially with a baby on the way."

"Yes. We need a bigger place." He stirred sugar into his coffee. "What would you think about moving to Tennessee?"

"Tennessee? You want to leave Missouri?" Jesse was a Missouri man born and bred.

"I think it'd be good to get away for a while," he said.

"I agree." The spoon rattled against the cup as I stirred my tea. Too many people here knew what Jesse looked like and where he lived. As hard as it might be to live among strangers, I believed it would be safer.

And after so many months at his mother's farm, I was weary of the constant press of other people around us. I longed to have Jesse to myself for a while, as lover and husband and confidant—the two of us, safe in our own little world.

"Then we'll do it." He smiled at me across the table. "I'll find us the perfect place."

In June, we moved to a house in Edgefield, near Nashville. "You'll have to get used to hearing me addressed as Mr. Howard," he told me. "John Davis Howard. Whatever you do, don't call me Jesse."

This decision startled me, and made my stomach clench. The danger must be greater than I'd feared, if Jesse felt compelled to take an alias. "All right. What if I call you Dave?" John was his brother's name, as well as my brother's and my brother-in-law's.

"Dave." He tried the name out. "All right. What should I call you?"

I giggled at the idea of being anything but 'Zee' or 'Sister.'

"Come on," he chided. "If I'm to have another name, so must you."

"When I was a little girl, I always wished my name was Josie," I said.

"Josie." He tried the name out on his tongue. "I think I could grow to like it. Then Josie you'll be."

Jesse—Dave—told our new neighbors that he was a wheat speculator, which explained both his long periods of inactivity, and his travels, as he still spent time away from home, visiting his mother and old friends.

For the first time in my life, I was free to spend as much money as I wanted. Though I was careful not to be too extravagant, I bought some fine furnishings for our new home, including a lovely cradle for our soon-to-be-born baby. Not having any faith in the safety of banks, Jesse kept cash hidden around the house, along with jewelry worth thousands of dollars. No mention was ever made of where the money came from. I knew, but chose not to dwell on it. In those moments when guilt over our sins plagued me, I told myself the money had been taken from those who deserved to lose it. And I reveled in the knowledge that because of Jesse, I would never want for anything again.

Sadly, as much money as Jesse made, we never kept it for long. Jesse let cash run through his fingers like water. He wagered freely on horse races and in faro games, losing thousands of dollars at a time, but never distressed about it.

We were friendly with our neighbors, but not overly so. We had to always be on our guard not to give away our true identities; I lived in fear that I would call Jesse by his real name. For his part, Jesse usually referred to me as 'dear' or 'sweetheart.'

On nights when Jesse was not out riding or gambling, he stayed at home and we sat together in the parlor. I read to him from popular novels of the day—we enjoyed *The Adventures of Tom Sawyer* and *Around the World in Eighty Days*. While I read, he would sometimes rub my feet, his big hands tenderly caressing my arches and toes, and soothing my swollen ankles. We talked about our baby, and what we would name it—after Jesse if it was a boy, and either Mary or Susan if a girl.

I went into labor in the early hours of August 31. I lay staring at the ceiling between waves of pain, determined not to wake Jesse until I had to. As any woman does, I had both dreaded and looked forward to this moment. I couldn't wait to welcome my child into my arms, but so many things could go wrong for both the baby and me in the complications of labor and delivery. In between my contractions, I prayed fervently that everything would go well.

Never a sound sleeper, Jesse soon sat bolt upright in bed, one hand instinctively reaching for the pistol kept ready on the bedside table before he even opened his eyes. "It's all right," I reassured him.

He laid the gun aside and shifted to look at me. "Are you all right?" he asked.

I managed a shaky smile. "I'm fine. I think our child has decided it's time he made his entrance into the world."

Jesse's face paled as the knowledge hit him, then he threw back the covers and began pulling on his trousers. "I'll ride into town for the doctor," he said.

"No. Don't leave me!" Alarmed, I shoved myself into a sitting position.

"I'll stop and ask a neighbor woman to come sit with you." He was already putting on his boots and reaching for his gun belt.

"Can't you stay with me?"

"If I do that, who's going to deliver this baby?"

"Can't you do it? You've delivered foals before and it can't be so very different."

He'd gone all white again, and I feared for a moment he might fall over in a faint. The idea that Jesse James, fearless outlaw and reputed killer, would collapse at the idea of delivering a baby struck me as funny, and I began to giggle, until another powerful contraction cut off the sound.

My bitten-off cry of pain sent Jesse into action once more. "I won't be gone long," he said. "I'll send the neighbor woman over."

"Jesse no! I'm afraid in the midst of the pain I might say something to give you away." I lived with the fear that something I did might one day lead to Jesse's downfall. I had made a solemn vow that outside the confines of our bedroom I would address him only as Dave or Mr. Howard, and so far I had been able to keep this promise. But in the throes of childbirth, who knew what I might say?

I could see that Jesse was torn. More than anything, he wanted to be away from my pain. But he hadn't remained a free man for so many years by taking unnecessary risks. He set aside the gun belt and began rolling up his sleeves. "All right. But if anything goes the least bit wrong, I'm off for the doctor."

I knew my husband to be a brave man, but the bravest I had ever known him was that night, when he sat on the side of our bed and held my hand as I fought the waves of pain. He never flinched when I cried out, though his face paled and sweat bloomed on his forehead. He wiped my forehead and gave me sips of water, encouraging me as I labored to bring our son into the world. I found all the encouragement I needed in his eyes; when Jesse looked at me, I believed I could do anything.

Jesse Edwards James entered the world around noon, cradled in his father's hands. Hands more accustomed to holding a gun or a horse's reins cut the cord and bathed the newborn, then tenderly bathed me as well. Exhausted, but happy, I cradled our child to my breast and fell into a deep, satisfied sleep.

We named the baby Jesse Edwards for his father and for the newspaperman John Newman Edwards, who had done so much to champion and defend Jesse. But officially he would be known as Tim Howard. I'll admit I cried a little over that—that my son couldn't even be addressed by his real name. But everything we did was necessary to protect Jesse, and to protect us as well. Jesse didn't want the horror that had visited his mother and her family to come home to us as well.

Jesse was as proud a father as anyone ever knew. He delighted in showing off his son, proudly carrying him to church on Sunday, or on shopping trips downtown. In the evenings, he would rock the baby while I cooked supper, sometimes crooning off-key lullabies that made me laugh.

But I sensed a growing restlessness in Jesse as well. Never had he spent so many weeks at home, idle. Each day he read the papers, and where once they had been filled with stories both praising and reviling the James gang, now weeks went by with scarcely a mention. Though Jesse could not risk being recognized in public, he missed being talked about by strangers. He had not lived in true anonymity since before his seventeenth birthday and the absence of a spotlight now gnawed at him.

I think the worst moment for him was in early September, when the papers were filled with news of the robbery of the Bank of Huntington in Huntington, West Virginia. Four men entered the bank in the afternoon and took off with $10,000. There was much speculation that one of the robbers was Cole Younger and another Frank James. The other two bandits—Tom McDaniel and Thomas Webb, both acquaintances of Frank and Jesse and the Youngers—were eventually captured, though they refused to give the names of the accomplices.

Seeing other men hailed for this daring crime—one of them his own brother—Jesse fumed. "A year from now, the public will forget Jesse James even exists," he said one morning over breakfast, slapping the latest paper down in disgust.

I thought this wouldn't be such a bad thing, but I knew enough to hold my tongue. "No one will ever forget Jesse James," I said placidly. "Would you like more coffee?"

Annie and Frank came to visit soon after that, bringing gifts for the baby and their warm congratulations. I was thrilled to see Annie again, having missed the company of another woman. I was wary of getting too close to our new neighbors, who could know me only as Josie Howard. With Annie I could let my guard down and be Zee again.

Soon, men began gathering at our house. Most were familiar faces, such as the Younger brothers, minus John, who had been killed in a gun battle two years previous. Our old friend Clel Miller was there, along with Bill Chadwell and Charlie Pitts. They poured over maps and railroad timetables while Annie and I served coffee and cake. Annie and I exchanged wary glances, but we kept whatever fears we shared to ourselves. This was the lot our men had chosen, a path we'd known about when we took our vows to stand by them, for better or for worse.

Much as I feared for Jesse's life and worried about the justness of his actions, I knew in my heart that if he had been a different kind of man I would not have loved him so well. I couldn't have given my heart to a dull, law-abiding farmer the way I had given it to Jesse. His danger and daring drew me as much as his strong arms and piercing blue eyes. It was as if the flaw in me needed the flawed part of him to make me complete.

On June 25, 1876, General George Armstrong Custer and his Seventh Cavalry were slain in the Battle of Little Big Horn. Jesse read and re-read the accounts of the slaughter, impressed by the magnitude of the defeat, though he had no soft feelings for the Union Army.

After all these years, Jesse still saw himself as a soldier, though his was a cause many had long abandoned. He had held on so long I think he felt the cause *was* him—if he let go of it now, what would be left of him?

In early July, he kissed me goodbye and he and Frank left for a visit to their mother. Though Zerelda and I had grown closer after Archie's death and her long recovery from the injuries she suffered that same night, we still were prone to clash, so I was happy enough to use the difficulty of traveling with an infant as an excuse to remain behind.

Content to tend my house and care for the baby, I gave little thought to Jesse's activities in Missouri, until a bold headline caught my eye as I waited in the store one day for a few small purchases. "Frank and Jesse James strike again!" the large black letter shouted.

With trembling hands, I picked up the broad sheet and added it to my purchases. As soon as I was out the door, I walked around to the side and sat on a bench. With the baby cradled to my shoulder, I held the paper with my free hand and read the account of the robbery of an express train at a place called Rocky Cut, Missouri.

The tale was the stuff of fiction: masked robbers silhouetted in the glare of the train's headlight cutting through the black of night. The ghostly figures waving a red lantern as a signal for the engineer to stop. With the echo of the squealing brakes still reverberating in the night, the men overran the train and applied themselves to the two safes in the express car. The newspaper reported they had stolen over $18,000. "The two daring leaders of the gang were none other than the notorious Frank and Jesse James."

I read the account with a measure of doubt. The papers had gotten many things wrong before. But whether or not they were guilty, lawmen were once more determined to find and arrest Jesse and his brother. All that evening I sat by the front window and rocked my baby and watched the road for my husband's return, or for signs of any strangers who might have figured out that Mr. Davis Howard was not who he seemed to be.

Jesse returned a few days later, saying nothing about his activities while he was away, though he brought a jar of pickles and a pail of lard from his mother, and greetings from the rest of the family.

The newspapers soon lost interest in news of the robbers, their headlines given over instead to the upcoming presidential election in which Democrat Samuel Tilden faced off against Republican Rutherford B. Hayes. Sentiment ran both for and against Tilden among our intensely Democratic families and friends. Jesse followed the campaign closely in the papers, and sat up nights in our parlor, debating politics with Frank and Clel Miller and others who stopped by.

Just when I had begun to think things had settled down, the papers reported that a man named Hobbs Kerry had been arrested near St. Louis. The name meant nothing to me, but when Jesse read the news, he blanched white, then red. I half-rose from my chair, afraid he was ill. "What is it?" I asked. "What's wrong?"

"The St. Louis police have arrested Hobbs Kerry," he said. "He's offered to give them the name of every man involved in that Missouri Pacific train robbery last month."

I sat down again, my legs too weak to support me. I didn't have to ask if Jesse's would be one of the names Kerry would give the police. And if he gave the police a name, he might very well give a description, too, one good enough for their police artists to draw a likeness of Jesse. I smoothed my napkin across my lap and tried to remain calm. "Has Mr. Kerry been to our home?" I asked. I couldn't always keep track of the men who visited Jesse.

"No." He folded his napkin and laid it beside his plate. "I hear Baltimore is very nice this time of year," he said. "I've been thinking we should go there."

The following day, we loaded a hired wagon with most of our household goods and moved to Baltimore. Before we left, Jesse dyed his hair dark brown and began to grow out his beard. He bought a top hat, a long frock coat, and a silver-head cane. The effect was of an older, dignified man. I admit it was a good disguise, but I couldn't help miss the handsome young adventurer who had swept me off my feet.

I had never seen this side of Jesse before. In the days that followed, he was often angry and impatient. He no longer slept, but prowled the house at night like a restless animal. He talked of revenge on all who had wronged him—Detective Allan Pinkerton; Archie Clement's killer, Bacon Montgomery; Missouri Governor Hardin, and others.

When we made love in those dark days it was like lying with a stranger. Gone was the smiling, light-hearted man who had teased and tempted me, replaced by a more solemn, intense partner who approached lovemaking with a kind of desperation, seeking release from whatever demons tortured him.

I had first come to Jesse as a naïve girl. Now I played the part of willing courtesan, eager to provide the release he sought, more aware than ever of my own needs and desires. If he wanted to take me in total darkness or with every lamp blazing, from behind as I stood washing dishes or three times in one night I was a compliant, even eager partner. With his body joined to mine I was sure I would find the key to the secrets that tortured him. As the person who loved him most and knew him best of any on this earth, why shouldn't I be the means of his salvation as well, and thus of my own?

Chapter Nine

I have never been to Northfield, Minnesota, but for me it will always be a cursed place. I picture a cold, windswept town set on a plain as level as a brick, the sky flush against the horizon like a flat blue wall. To me, it is as desolate and embittered as any battlefield, and if I had the power to damn a place, then I would rain curses down on its streets and buildings.

I will never know what attracted Jesse to Northfield. Some speculated he was there to strike a blow for the South, by destroying the bank that was partly owned by former Mississippi Governor Adelbert Ames. Part of the Reconstruction government that sought to crush the South after the war, Ames was despised by all true Southern patriots.

Some speculate the James and Younger gang sought to prove to the world that their influence extended far beyond Missouri—that they were a national band to be reckoned with.

Others believe they chose Northfield because they thought it would be easier to get away with a crime in an area where they were not widely known.

Whatever their reasoning, they arrived in Northfield in late August and early September. I know that Jesse was away from home for several weeks during that time, while I passed long days and lonelier nights with only baby Tim—little Jesse—for company.

In fact, I had no inkling that anything out-of-the-ordinary had happened until the morning of September 14. I had just sat down to a pile of mending when a knock at the door made me jump. Josie Howard didn't have many visitors and living with Jesse had made me suspicious of strangers. I tip-toed to the front window and looked out. But only a small boy waited on the stoop, a folded piece of paper in his hand.

My curiosity further piqued, I opened the door to him. "Telegraph for Mrs. J. D. Howard," he said.

"I'm Mrs. Howard." The lie came easily from my lips now, scarcely seeming like a lie. If Jesse had taken the name of Howard I, as his wife, had naturally taken it also. I accepted the folded piece of paper and tipped the child a penny, then closed the door and opened the note right away, not even waiting to sit down.

> *Looking forward to your visit today. Will meet the 8 o'clock train.*
> *—Fannie*

I puzzled over this strange message. The only Fannie I knew was Jesse's younger half-sister, but she had never written to me before, much less sent a cable, and had no reason to do so now. And I had made no plans to visit anyone today, much less by train.

Something in my brain clicked as I read the missive yet again. I felt weak, and groped for a chair, lowering myself into it. I did know another Fannie. Fannie Woodson was the name Annie James used when she and Frank traveled. She must have sent this cable. And she wasn't referring to a planned journey, but one that I must make. She had something to tell me and couldn't risk traveling here to do so. I must go to her to receive the news.

I clutched my stomach, ill. Had something happened to Jesse? I struggled to breathe, unable to imagine living without Jesse in my world.

Then the baby began to cry, and the blackness around me receded. I mustn't panic yet. I had a child to care for, and travel plans to make. I hurried to Tim's crib and gathered him close, soothing him, then rushed to the desk in the front room and found a train time table. A train left in two hours that would deliver me to Kearney by eight o'clock.

I hastily packed a carpetbag with a change of clothes for myself and supplies for the baby. The bag contained a false bottom Jesse had fashioned for it and into this I secreted several hundred dollars in cash and as much gold and diamond jewelry as would fit. Then I tied on my bonnet, settled the baby on my shoulder, and walked next door to our neighbors, Dr. and Mrs. Vertrees. "My sister has taken ill and I must go to her at once," I said. "Mr. Howard is away on business and isn't expected back for several days. Would you mind watching the house for us and seeing to the horses?" As usual, Jesse had two very fine horses in the barn behind the house, mounts easily worth $150 each.

"I'm so sorry about your sister," Mrs. Vertrees said, her kind face creased with concern. "I do hope it's not serious."

"I hope so, too," I said, not bothering to hide my distress. "The telegram didn't say, only that I must come at once." I was sure they would have seen the boy deliver the telegram to my door earlier, so nothing I said would arouse their suspicion.

"Don't worry about the house or the horses," Dr. Vertrees said.

"We'll look after them until you return."

"Thank you," I said. "Thank you so much." I turned to begin the walk to the station, but Mrs. Vertrees called after me. "Mrs. Howard, let Dr. Vertrees take you the station in our buggy. It's much too far for you to walk, carrying your bag and your baby."

I gratefully accepted his offer and fifteen minutes later he handed me down in front of the train station. "Would you like me to wait with you?" he asked solicitously.

"No, thank you. You've already been so kind. I'll be fine." I picked up my bag and hurried away before he could protest. I didn't want him to know my destination. When I bought my ticket, I purposely paid the fare all the way to Omaha, though I would be getting off in Kearney.

The baby was fussy, and I spent much of the journey trying to quiet him. The constant rumble of the wheels on the track made my head ache. The first class coach being full, I was forced to ride second class, and smoke and cinders blew in almost constantly through the open windows, leaving me coated with grit.

Between Nashville and Centralia, I shared seats with a woman slightly younger than myself who was traveling to her parents' home with a boy of about eight and a girl who was about three. "My husband's in the bar car," she said as she settled herself and the children in the seat. "He says the only way he can cope with my family is to drink heavily."

"Oh. I'm sorry to hear that," I said, uncertain how to respond to such a frank confession.

She laughed. "To tell you the truth, I don't blame him. They can be a trial. But my sister's getting married this weekend, and I won't miss that. She and her husband-to-be, at least, are sane enough."

Her son, who had the seat beside me, knelt to look out the window. "Pull your head back in the car this instance," his mother ordered. "You'll get all covered with ash."

"I'm watching for bandits," he said.

"For bandits?" his mother asked. "Why would you be watching for them?"

"I want to meet Jesse James," the boy said, his face glowing with excitement. "I think it would beat all if he was to rob this train."

"Don't be ridiculous," his mother said. "A man like that would as soon shoot you as look at you. If you ever did meet him, you'd do best to stay out of his way. Now sit properly in your seat."

I bit my lip, fighting the urge to defend Jesse. The ruthless killer sometimes portrayed in the papers had no relation to the man I knew.

My Jesse was kind and fond of a good joke. He wasn't perfect by any stretch of the imagination—he was vain about his looks, stubborn and inclined to impatience. But those were faults shared by many; they certainly didn't make him evil.

"I read in the paper that Jesse James held up a train and when he found out a widow woman who was on the train didn't have any money to give him, he took a five dollar gold piece from a banker on the train and give it to the widow," the boy said. "Do you think if I told Jesse I didn't have any money to give him, he'd give *me* a five dollar gold piece?"

"He might if you told him your parents had abandoned you," his mother said. "Which might very well happen if you don't settle down and behave yourself."

"I'll sit down." The boy sat properly in the seat, but he seemed to think he'd found an interested audience in me. "Did you know that Jesse James is missing a finger?" he asked me. "Got shot off by Pinkerton agents in a gun battle." He aimed an imaginary pistol and fired. "It was just Jesse and Frank, against a whole passel of Pinkertons, but they got away, leaving a bunch of the Pinkertons dead."

I didn't know whether to be amused or horrified by this tale. "How do you know so much about Jesse James?" I asked.

"I read everything I can find about him, and I hear stories folks tell. I think he's just about the most interesting person I ever heard of."

"Yes, he does sound interesting."

"He's left-handed, just like me." The boy fired the imaginary gun again. "He lives in a big cave up in the mountains that he's outfitted with all kinds of fancy furniture and rugs and stuff—like a real house. Only it's back where nobody can ever find it. And when he brings people to visit, he blindfolds them first so they can't tell anybody else where it is."

Thank goodness the real Jesse didn't live in a cave. I'd never liked dark, small places.

"As you can see, George has a very vivid imagination," the young woman said. "I'm hoping he'll put it to good use and become a writer someday."

"A writer?" George looked horrified. "I'm going to be a desperado, just like Jesse James."

George and his family got off the train at Centralia, so I didn't get to hear anymore of his fantastical stories about Jesse James. Without this distraction, my mind fixed once more on all the possible bad news Annie might have for me. I tried to convince myself it had nothing to do with Jesse, but unlike George, my imagination wasn't fertile enough to think of any other reason Annie might have summoned me.

By the time I arrived in Kearney, I was trembling with fatigue, worn out from hours spent staring out the train window, imagining every possible terrible scenario. When I saw Annie waiting on the platform, I hurried to her and collapsed into her arms, choking back sobs. "Shhh, Shhhh. It's all right." She patted my shoulder and set me upright once more, then handed me her handkerchief and took the baby from me. "Where's your bag? Ambrose is waiting with the wagon."

We retrieved my bag and rode in silence to the Samuels's farm. I followed Annie's example and assumed a pleasant expression, nodding to those who greeted us as we passed. I tried to read some clue as to her news on her face, but her expression was as serene as ever, though I detected an extra tightness around her mouth and tension in her shoulders.

Zerelda rose to meet us when we stepped into the front room of her home. Though she had been scarcely recovered from her accident when I saw her last, I was shocked by the change in her. She had aged beyond her years, heavy lines from her mouth to her chin and creasing her forehead, her once-dark hair turned the powdery gray of galvanized nails. The right sleeve of her dress was pinned up, a grim reminder of the tragedy that had taken place in this very room.

Yet these changes did not diminish her. If anything, she was more forbidding than ever, a woman who had no reason to compromise.

"It's a grim business, Zee," were her first words to me as I untied my bonnet.

I froze and sent a questioning look to Annie. "I haven't told her anything yet, Mother," Annie said. She spread a blanket on the floor and put the baby on it. He giggled, happy to crawl about at our feet, free of his bundling after the long train ride.

"What is there to tell?" I sat beside her and looked at Zerelda expectantly, my hands clenched in my lap, fingernails digging into my palms.

"There's been a robbery, of a bank in Minnesota." She fitted a pair of wire-rimmed spectacles to her face and picked up a newspaper from a stack on a table at her elbow.

"As far as we know, Frank and Jesse are alive and free," Annie hastened to reassure me. "But we don't know where they are, and whether or not they are injured."

"I'll tell her." Zerelda silenced Annie, then began to read from the paper: "The brave citizens of Northfield, Minnesota faced down the worst of banditry today, as a group of armed men attempted to rob the Northfield National Bank . . ."

The words began to run together as I listened. The details were too frightening to fully absorb, but I was able to put together the story:

A group of armed men had converged upon the town of Northfield, Minnesota on the afternoon of September 7. They rode fine horses and were dressed in long, linen dusters and battered hats. Three of the men entered the Northfield National Bank. They demanded the cashier, a man named Joseph Heywood, open the safe. When he refused, one of the robbers shot him. But in the scuffle, one of the bank employees escaped and sounded the alarm.

The citizens of Northfield responded quickly, descending upon the bank and firing at the bandits who waited outside. The robbers returned their fire and soon the street was a chaos of burnt-powder smoke and dust, men shouting, horses whinnying, and the constant ping and whine of bullets flying. The bandits—who later proved to be Cole, Jim and Bob Younger and Bill Chadwell, raced their horses up and down the street, shouting and shooting, driving people back inside.

Clel Miller was the first of the band to die, shot from his horse in front of a hotel. I thought of the sweet-faced man who had entertained me with funny stories and couldn't believe he was gone.

Cole was shot, but managed to stay on his horse. Bill Chadwell was the next to fall. The Younger brothers continued to try to hold off the crowd, waiting for their three compatriots to exit the bank. But the crowd of citizens massed against them was growing larger and bolder. Cornered, Cole dismounted and made his way to the door of the bank. "The game is up!" he shouted. "We are beaten!"

The papers did not identify the men inside the bank, but we women knew well enough that two of them must be Frank and Jesse. The third man would later be identified as Charlie Pitts.

The robbers fled Northfield, leaving behind the bodies of Miller and Chadwell. In addition to Mr. Heywood the cashier, at least one other townsperson also lay dead. Every able man had ridden out in a hunt for the bandits, and in the week since the robbery hundreds of volunteers had converged on the area to search house to house and field to field for the James and Younger boys.

I sat in stunned silence for a long moment after Zerelda had finished reading the accounts. Annie took my hand in hers and squeezed it. "I didn't think you should be alone when you heard the news," she said.

I nodded. What torture it would have been to read the news accounts alone in Baltimore and not be able to share my fears with anyone.

"And I didn't want you going into hysterics and saying more than you should to the wrong people," Zerelda countered.

As if I hadn't been born with sense. "Has there been no word from them?" I asked Annie.

"No good or bad news," Zerelda said. "Some of these stories . . ." She indicated the pile of papers on the table, "declare some of the men are badly wounded. Others tell of stolen horses and encounters with desperate, armed men. But we all know what fantasies these reporters will create and call news."

I nodded, recalling the wild tales that had circulated after the bombing of this house. "What do we do now?" I asked.

"We wait," Zerelda said. "If I were a young man, I'd mount a horse and ride off to find them, but I'm not and I can't, so we're forced to wait. But my boys will come home. A little dust-up like this won't stop a James. They won't let me down."

Let *her* down? As if she was the only one who mattered to her sons. "If there's any way possible, Jesse will come home to *me* and to his son," I said. "He won't forsake his family."

Zerelda's lips thinned, and two spots of color formed high on her cheeks. "*I* am Jesse's family," she said.

"Arguing won't bring them home," Annie said. "All we can do is pray." She squeezed my hand again. "We pray for their safety."

Never had days stretched so long as the ones that passed during that dreadful time. We were certain the house was watched, though unlike the lawmen who had converged on us after the Pinkerton bombing, the current deputies were more circumspect. We knew Jesse and Frank wouldn't risk returning to the house unless they were certain they could slip in safely. Meanwhile, Ambrose and Reuben made regular rides into the countryside under cover of darkness, visiting places they thought Jesse and Frank might hide, but never finding any signs they had been there. Meals were tense interludes during which we picked at our food and shared theories about where the men might be now and what they were doing.

This home, which had once been so forbidding and unwelcoming to me, now became my refuge. Here were people who shared my misery, who understood my longing, who needed my company as much as I needed theirs. In our love and longing for the safety of the same men,

Zerelda and Annie and I drew closer. In praying and waiting and hoping we became a team—a family unlike any I had ever known.

I seldom ventured far from the farm, but one afternoon not long after I'd arrived, Annie needed some oil of cloves to soothe a toothache. Ambrose and Reuben were busy with a cow who was having a difficult birth. Annie agreed to watch Tim for me if I would go into town for the clove oil.

I was just leaving the pharmacy with my purchase when a tall, dark-haired man blocked my passage along the boardwalk. "Excuse me, ma'am," he said, removing a light tan Stetson. "Are you Mrs. James?"

I looked him in the eye, but didn't answer. To locals, it was no secret that I'd married Jesse James, but this man was a stranger to me. He was handsome, clean-shaven with eyes so brown they were almost black. But he wore a silver star over the left breast pocket of his shirt, and for me that definitely detracted from his looks. "Please move aside and let me pass," I said.

"I realize we haven't been introduced, but a couple of people pointed you out to me and indicated you are Jesse James's wife."

Still, I said nothing. If he knew the truth, he had no need for me to confirm it.

"I must say, it surprised me at first," he said. "When they pointed you out, I mean. I'd heard Jesse was married, but I wasn't expecting his wife would be such a lady. And such a pretty one."

If he expected me to soften at his compliments, he was doomed to disappointment. "I really must go," I said, and tried to move past him.

But the walkway was narrow, and he deftly moved to block my passage around him. "I just wanted to ask you one question," he said. "Why would a pretty, respectable woman such as yourself even want to associate with a man like Jesse James?"

I should have kept silent and not let him bait me, but the implication that Jesse was some kind of monster who didn't deserve a woman such as myself angered me. "Have you ever met Jesse James?" I asked. "Do you know him?"

"No ma'am. But I know what he's done, and it's not the work of a good man."

"You know stories," I said. "Things others say about him, but you don't know Jesse. He's as good a husband and father, as true a son and loyal a friend as any you'll ever meet. He's generous and loving and nothing like the criminal who's been portrayed in some papers."

The deputy's frown deepened, furrows forming on his forehead and either side of his mouth. I'd thought him handsome, but I didn't think that anymore. "What do you say to the charge that he murdered innocent people?" he asked.

"You wear a gun, sir. Have you never killed anyone with it?"

My question seemed to startle him. He blinked. "Only when I had to, ma'am."

"And yet no one calls you a murderer."

"I'm sworn to uphold the law, not break it."

"Laws are made for the advantage of those in power to oppress those without power." It was something I had heard Frank say one time. I didn't really believe it. Without laws, some people might feel free to kill anyone they disagreed with. But it sounded like a good argument to hurl back at this nosy lawman. "And now I really *do* have to go," I insisted, and shoved past him. Let him come after me if he felt he must, but I wouldn't stand there and let him interrogate me any longer.

I was out of breath by the time I reached the outskirts of town, having walked as fast as I was able away from the lawman. I slowed and massaged the stitch in my side, and looked back over my shoulder. The road was empty, and I breathed a shaky sigh of relief.

But the encounter with the lawman continued to haunt me. No doubt he had intended eventually to question me as to my knowledge of Jesse's activities or whereabouts. That didn't upset me as much as his judgment of Jesse did. What was it about Jesse that caused strangers to choose their preferred version of him? Some, like the boy on the train, saw him as a hero, while men like the deputy painted him as the worst sort of demon. The press didn't help with their sensationalist reports of every rumor surrounding the James brothers. The president himself didn't garner so much coverage in the papers, at least in Missouri.

Whatever the reason for the public's views of Jesse, I hated to see him so misjudged. The man I knew was neither devil nor angel. He was a special man, to be certain, but the qualities that endeared him to me were apparently hidden to most others. I knew Jesse's kindness and caring, and his deep, abiding love for me. I saw the vulnerability of the boy he had been and the man he was. I had seen the strength of his convictions and felt the depth of his sorrow at the loss of his brother and the injury to his mother. I knew the gentleness with which he held his child, and the passion with which he expressed his love for me.

Jesse had made me the woman I was today. If not for him, I would be some unhappy farmer's wife, condemned to always struggle to reconcile the dutiful role society had dictated for me and the private rebellions of my heart. Only with Jesse was I free to be myself, rebellions and sins and all. He loved me despite of and because of my flaws and foibles, and understood me as no one else ever could.

Those of us who lived now at the Samuels' farm carried out a daily ritual. Ambrose rose early and rode into town to meet the first train, and collected as many different newspapers as were available. We would begin reading them over breakfast and continue through the morning, drinking cup and after cup of milky coffee and sweet herb tea and debating the merits of this story or that.

"This story says two boys were plowing a field when six men in rubber coats accosted them." Annie indicated an article in the paper she was reading one morning. "The men took the horses at gunpoint, and forced the boys to guide them into the woods. They said one of the men was heavily bandaged and feverish."

"This story says three hundred men have rallied to the pursuit." I scanned another article. "It also says it's rained every day since the bank robbery." I closed my eyes, swallowing tears as I thought of Jesse, cold and hungry and possibly hurt, slogging through rain. He wasn't in the woods of Missouri or Kansas, territory he knew well, but in a strange northern land far from home, with hundreds of men pursuing him, like hounds determined to run a fox to ground.

Later reports that reached our ears indicated the six outlaws were on foot, having abandoned their horses. Zerelda scoffed at this idea. "My boys would never walk when they could ride!"

The men were said to be hungry, stealing food to survive—cabbages and corn from fields they passed through, and the occasional chicken. I could scarcely force food down my own throat as I thought of Jesse starving in some field somewhere.

September 21, when I had been at the Samuels' farm for a week, two weeks after the raid on the Northfield bank, lawmen cornered Cole, Bob and Jim Younger and Charlie Pitts in a farmer's field near Madelia, Minnesota. In the gun battle that followed, Pitts was killed and the three Youngers badly wounded. Out of options, the Youngers surrendered and were hauled off to jail.

I read this account with my heart in my throat, then looked across the breakfast table at my fellow sufferers. I knew we were all thinking the same thing, but Zerelda was the only one brave enough to say it out loud. "Where are Frank and Jesse?" She pounded the table with her fist, making the silverware jump. "What has become of my boys?"

We sent Ambrose to the depot for papers twice a day now. The reporters fell silent on the subject of Frank and Jesse, but we had an answer soon enough. Two days after the news broke of the capture of the Youngers, a posse approached the farm, calling for the surrender of Frank and Jesse. They were answered with a hail of bullets, and forced to withdraw. But the encounter made Zerelda almost giddy. "If they're looking for them here, that means they haven't found them elsewhere," she crowed.

The law was still hunting Jesse and Frank, but they had no proof to tie them to any crime. When Cole Younger was asked to reveal the identity of his two accomplices, his answer was a note, handed to his jailers. *Be true to your friends if the Heavens fall.*

I thought of the handsome young man who had asked me to dance that long-ago day at my sister's wedding, and sent up a prayer for his protection. I had not fallen in love with Cole, but the man I did love couldn't have asked for a better friend, and I hoped Cole wouldn't suffer too much because of that friendship.

If it is possible to live on hope alone, then that is what I did in those two weeks with the other women at the farmhouse. And I think it must be some of what kept Jesse going across hundreds of miles of hostile territory. The hope of warmth and food and safety. The hope of seeing home and family once more.

Only later did we learn that, having separated from the rest of the group, Frank and Jesse stole a pair of horses from a farmer's barn. They found kind folks who fed them and gave them a change of clothes. They forded rivers, crossed fields, and rode by moonlight to avoid discovery. They made it to Dakota Territory, then on to Iowa, and finally to Missouri.

They returned to the farm late one night at the end of the month. The pickets the Samuels had posted spotted them first, and sent word to the house. Perry, now seven, was sent to wake me, though he didn't tell me why. Pulling on a dress, I hurried into the front room, where a sight from my dreams—or my nightmares—greeted me.

Frank sat on the settee, his coat off, his trousers sliced open to the knee, revealing an ugly wound, which Dr. Samuel knelt before him to dress. Annie sat beside him, holding his hand and stroking his arm.

Jesse sprawled in a chair nearby, as filthy and thin as his brother, but seemingly unharmed. He looked up when I entered, and smiled broadly, though the happiness in that smile didn't reach all the way to his eyes. His gaze as it met mine spoke of weariness and unutterable suffering.

I ran to him and collapsed onto the floor beside him, throwing my arms around him. He was painfully thin, and filthy, his hair matted, his beard a thick tangle. I was reminded of the boy who had been brought to my parents' parlor all those years ago. He had not been expected to live then, and he had. He had not been expected to escape Northfield, either, yet he had. He was beaten, but not defeated, bent but not broken.

"God, I'm so glad you're safe," I murmured, my face pressed against his shoulder.

"I'm safe," he said, his hand caressing mine. "Did you ever doubt I'd find a way to make it home to you?"

"All I want is a meal and a bath and bed, in that order," Frank rasped. Annie smiled at his outburst, and smoothed his matted hair.

Zerelda moved from son to son, reassuring herself more than them with her ministrations. She barked orders to Ambrose and Charlotte, to haul water and stoke fires, to fry steak and potatoes and bake cornbread and pies. The prodigals had returned and we all must celebrate.

And celebrate we did. In the wee hours of the morning we drank and ate and praised the Lord for the return of those we loved. Later, Ambrose filled a zinc tub with hot water from the stove. Frank bathed first, then another tub was drawn and it was Jesse's turn. I waited anxiously outside the door, ready if he should need anything, but after some initial splashing, the room fell silent.

Alarmed, I rushed into the room, only to find that Jesse had fallen asleep, head lolling, one hand clutching the side of the tub, the other resting on the butt of the pistol in the chair beside him.

Even in sleep, he couldn't give up his vigilance. All the soap and hot water in the world would never remove that taint of violence.

Jesse slept for the better part of two days, scarcely even rolling over in bed, his face slack with exhaustion. When he woke, we made love with all the fervor and gratitude of two people resurrected from the dead. Afterwards, he trimmed his beard and combed his hair and dressed in a clean shirt and trousers. He admired himself in the washstand mirror, then went into the kitchen and kissed his mother and Annie, and even kissed Charlotte, waltzing her around the room until she shrieked in protest.

"They thought they had us trapped," he boasted. "But there hasn't been a trap set that could hold the James brothers."

Frank, always prone to moroseness, looked more downcast than ever. "We were lucky," he said. "But it seems to me our luck has about run out."

Jesse studied his brother, then drew up a chair beside Frank, who sat with his injured leg propped on a stool in front of him. "We had a close one," Jesse admitted. "But we made it through and we'll make it through again."

Frank looked at him, sad-eyed as a hound dog. The back door opened and Ambrose appeared, his arms full of newspapers, and we began the afternoon ritual.

The news was grim. Pictures of the dead Clel Miller, Bill Chadwell and Charlie Pitts dominated the front pages of almost every paper. I wanted to look away, but my eyes remained riveted to the staring eyes and blood-streaked bodies of men who had dined at my table and thanked me politely for the meal. Even in death, Clel still smiled sweetly, while Bill and Charlie looked surprised at their fate.

"It says here the James brothers are thought to be hiding out in Mexico." Jesse guffawed at the idea.

"This paper says they've gone west, to live with a tribe of Sioux Indians, where they've married squaws and have a pack of half-breed children." Annie regarded her husband over the top of the paper. "If you did that, you'd have more than some measly sheriff's posse to worry about."

"The question is, where do we go now?" Jesse asked.

"Away," Frank said. "Away from the heat."

"Can't none of these people say for certain we were at that bank," Jesse said.

"Haven't you figured out by now it doesn't always matter what proof the law has as much as what they think they know?" Frank's stool clattered back as he rose, clutching the back of the chair for support. "You can do what you want," he said. "But I'm going away."

Jesse's eyes met mine across the table. For as long as I had known him, he had always followed after Frank, from the days of toddling across the yard, trying to keep up with his brother, to the night he rode after him to join the bushwhackers. They were a team, "The James Brothers," or "The James Boys" or "Frank and Jesse James." One name didn't sound right without the other.

Jesse leaned across the table and took my hand. "What do you say,

Mrs. Howard?" he asked. "Shall we try our hand at respectable living?"

"I think we should, Mr. Howard," I said. I held my breath as I waited for his answer. I wanted Jesse to be happy, but I also wanted him alive, and it seemed Frank's idea to go away for a while—perhaps forever—was the best way to keep us all safe and happy.

He rubbed the side of his leg, his lower lip stuck out in contemplation. "We'll do it, Zee," he said finally. "It's time I put aside my wild ways and became a responsible citizen."

Frank snorted and mumbled under his breath about "impossibilities," but Jesse ignored him. He swept aside a stack of papers to clear a space in front of him on the table. "Charlotte, is there any more of that peach pie?" he asked. "Seems I have some catching up to do."

Chapter Ten

In October, the five of us—Jesse, Frank, Annie, our son Jesse Edwards and I—returned to Tennessee, to Nashville. Jesse and I rented a house in town and established ourselves as J.D. and Josie Howard. Frank leased a nearby farm and styled himself B.J. Woodson and his wife, Fannie.

I would have thought it wise to keep our distance from our neighbors lest, in getting to know us better, they became suspicious as to our true identities. But that wasn't Jesse's way. He enjoyed the company and conversation of others and even a simple errand to buy a set of shoelaces could turn into an hour-long expedition as he stopped to converse with the shopkeeper and other customers. People liked Jesse—men responded to his intelligent conversation and firm handshake, while women were ever susceptible to his winning smile and piercing blue eyes.

We had scarcely been in Tennessee a week before we were invited to dinner at the home of Mr. and Mrs. Waymon Endicott. Mrs. Endicott even offered the services of her housekeeper to look after Tim while we were dining. Jesse happily accepted.

"How is it you know Mr. Endicott?" I asked as we dressed for dinner.

"We met downtown, at Scott's Saloon." Jesse lifted his chin and tightened the knot on his tie.

"What kind of work does he do?" I asked.

"I'm not sure. Something that allows him the leisure to hang around at the saloon, debating politics."

Of course. Politics was a favorite subject of Jesse's. He followed every election passionately. I sometimes wonder how different things might have been for us if his voting rights and the ability to run for office had not been stripped from him after the war. He resented this disenfranchisement more deeply than most people knew.

We walked to dinner, since the Endicotts lived only three blocks from the house Jesse had rented for us. The housekeeper, Mrs. Boston, met us at the door of the attractive brick manse, and ushered us into a pleasant parlor before carrying Tim up to the nursery where the Endicotts' twin two-year old daughters waited.

Mrs. Endicott was a petite beauty with spun-gold hair and friendly gray eyes. She greeted me warmly. "You must call me Francis," she urged.

"Then you must call me Josie," I said.

She led me to the sofa, while Jesse took a chair opposite Mr. Endicott by the fireplace. "I hope you're enjoying your new home in Tennessee," Francis said.

"Yes, it's very nice to be here," I said.

"Where are you from originally?" she asked.

"Kentucky." This was the fiction Jesse and I had agreed on.

"I have a sister in Logan County," Francis said.

"I never had the pleasure of visiting that part of the state," I said. Though I knew Logan County was the location of Russellville, the site of one of Jesse's early robberies. I quickly sought to steer the conversation away from the minefield of our made-up past. "How long have you and Mr. Endicott lived in Nashville?" I asked.

"Four years now. He was sheriff in Chattanooga before taking the job here."

I caught my breath, sure I had blanched. "Y . . . your husband is the sheriff?" I stammered. "I didn't know." The room suddenly seemed very small and stifling. I avoided looking at Jesse, afraid I might give away my mounting panic.

"It's always a pleasure to meet an officer of the law," Jesse said heartily.

A Negro maid in a white apron appeared in the doorway. "Dinner is ready, Mrs. Endicott," she said.

Francis rose and led the way into the dining room. Jesse gave my arm a reassuring squeeze, but I took no comfort from the gesture.

The dining room was elegantly appointed, with Hepplewhite furniture and a crystal chandelier. Either the office of Sheriff of Davidson County paid very well, or one or both of the Endicotts had brought money to the marriage.

We sat down to a first course of cucumber soup. I forced myself to eat, not tasting the food. Was our host even now studying Jesse, comparing him to descriptions circulated on the posters which offered a reward for his capture?

"Do you find much crime to keep you busy here?"

I stared at Jesse. He seemed completely relaxed, smiling at Endicott as he awaited the answer to his question.

"Enough," Endicott said. "Tennessee hasn't had the trouble some other places have with bandits, but we're always on our guard."

"Yes, I imagine you have to be," Jesse said. "I'm really amazed at the audacity of some of these robbers, operating in broad daylight, then slipping past dozens of pursuers to escape."

"They've done that in Missouri," Endicott said. "Where they had sympathizers to hide them or cover their tracks. They haven't had such luck elsewhere. Look at that fiasco up in Northfield, Minnesota with the Younger brothers."

Jesse nodded solemnly. "Yes. But the law caught all those bandits, didn't they?"

"They were caught, but it took a lot longer—and cost a lot more in manpower and resources—than it should have."

"Except the James brothers. It seems no one can lay a hand on them."

"Their time will come," Endicott said. "They'll get cocky or careless and the law will be there to bring them to justice."

The maid cleared our soup bowls and delivered plates of Dover sole and new potatoes. "What do you think is the key to stopping these desperados?" Jesse asked.

If I'd been seated closer, and not been hampered by my skirts, I would have kicked him under the table. I couldn't believe he was deliberately keeping the subject on his own crimes. He clearly enjoyed leading the sheriff on.

"I believe more banks and express companies will begin stationing armed guards in their buildings and in the express cars on trains," Endicott said, warming to the subject. "I've also heard talk of alarm systems, and telegraph lines linked directly to the police. If enough of these thefts are stopped before they begin, and their perpetrators locked away, it will discourage the rest."

Jesse nodded. "You may be right. But I would think there'd be a danger of the robbers adapting their approaches to compensate for the law's moves. Perhaps they'd strike at night, when the guards weren't around. Or have an accomplice hire on as an employee of the bank or express company."

"These men don't strike me as intelligent enough for that," Endicott said dismissively. "Most of them are a bunch of ex-bushwhackers—country boys and farmers who don't have the education and skills to do anything else. No bank is going to hire someone like that."

"I suppose you're right," Jesse said, his expression as solemn as a deacon's.

"What kind of work do you do, Mr. Howard?" Francis asked. Perhaps she was also eager to steer the conversation away from criminal activity.

"I'm a commodities buyer. Wheat and corn mostly."

"I thought you might be a sporting man," Endicott said, using the polite euphemism for a professional gambler. "I understand you and your brother-in-law are good customers of the local faro and pinochle parlors."

My heart hammered wildly and I put my hands in my lap to hide their shaking, but Jesse only laughed. "You've been checking up on me," he said.

"I hope you're not offended. It's part of my job."

"I'm sure Waymon investigated *my* background before he started courting me," Francis said. "He has an insatiable curiosity about people."

I pushed the fish around on my plate, unable to eat another bite. What else had Sheriff Endicott learned about Jesse and Frank? Had inviting us to dinner been a ruse to lead us on—a plan to trap Jesse so that Endicott could arrest him and claim the reward?

"Do you trade horses, too, or just grain?" Endicott asked. "That was a fine looking mare you were riding the other day."

This seemingly innocent query did nothing to calm my nerves. It was well known that Jesse and Frank always rode the finest mounts.

"I like a good horse," Jesse said. "I've been thinking of investing in some racing stock—Kentucky thoroughbreds."

"My father trained race horses for a time when I was small," Endicott said. "I had aspirations to be a jockey, until I grew too tall."

"I saw some quarter horses down in Texas who ran a fine race, but I like a longer contest myself," Jesse said.

Then they were off, talking pedigrees and handicaps, long and short odds, two-year-olds and studs and half a dozen other terms I couldn't understand. I began to feel a bit easier, though I could never completely relax, one ear always tuned for any hint of danger.

Despite my best efforts to hide my uneasiness, Francis noticed. She took me aside after supper. "Are you anxious about your baby?" she asked. "I promise you, he's all right with Mrs. Boston. My girls adore her."

"I am a little uneasy," I admitted, relieved to find this excuse to explain behavior that might have struck anyone as odd. "This is the first time I've been parted from him for even a few hours."

"Why don't we go up and check on him?" She took my arm in hers. "I'd love for you to meet my girls."

Tim slept peacefully in a bassinet while the twins played on a rug under the watchful eye of Mrs. Boston. The girls, both blondes like their mother, toddled to us, clamoring for Francis's attention. For a little while I let myself forget the tension downstairs as we played with the children and talked about teething and diapers and the concerns of young motherhood.

"I don't know what I'd do without Mrs. Boston to help me," Mrs. Francis said, turning the girls back over to the housekeeper's care. "Waymon's work demands such long hours, he's not often able to help, though he delights in spending time with them when he can."

"I imagine a lawman's schedule is unpredictable," I said.

"The irregular hours would be easier to accept if not for the danger inherent in the position," she said. "I'm proud of him, of course, but I worry. You can't know what it's like to watch the man you love leave the house every morning with a loaded gun strapped to his hip, not knowing if he'll come home alive in the evening."

"I can't imagine," I lied, though wasn't that my reality as well? Every time Jesse left on one of his 'business trips,' I never knew if I would see him alive again. And even a simple errand to the store was fraught with the danger of discovery. I felt empathy for Francis Endicott, even though, in different circumstances, our husbands might have faced off, each intent on killing the other.

Downstairs, we found the men standing on either side of the fireplace, smoking cigars. "I couldn't help but notice the injury to your finger," Endicott said, nodding to Jesse's left hand. "How did that come about?"

Jesse's face reddened and he immediately shoved his hand into his pocket. I held my breath, frozen halfway across the floor. Silence stretched taut, broken only by the over-loud ticking of the mantel clock. I stared at the pocket into which Jesse had shoved his hand. I knew it contained a derringer, as he never went anywhere unarmed. Would he mistake Endicott's question for accusation, and draw the weapon?

Then Jesse's shoulder's relaxed, and a rueful smile stretched his lips. "Youthful stupidity," he said. "I spent some time with a cousin down in Texas, thought I might become a cowboy. Decided to try roping steers, the way the *vaqueros* do. I managed to get a loop on one, but when I went to dally the rope around the saddle horn, I got my finger hung up in it. The steer gave a yank and it pulled the end of the finger clean off."

He told the story with such conviction, *I* almost believed it. I made my way to a chair and sank into it, my eyes still fixed on him.

"I'm kind of self-conscious about it," he continued. "I try to hide it from people's notice."

"That's certainly understandable," Francis said. She gave her husband a scolding look.

We made small talk a while longer, until I stifled a yawn. Once more, Francis came to my rescue. "Josie looks worn out," she said. "We shouldn't have kept you so late."

I was exhausted from the tension of the evening, but I managed a sincere smile. "Not at all," I said. "I've enjoyed your company. Dinner was delicious. Thank you so much for your hospitality." In another time, under other circumstances, Francis and I might have become good friends.

We collected a sleeping Tim, then walked home, Jesse cradling the baby, my arm tucked in the crook of his.

I waited until we were safely in the house and Tim was tucked into his crib before I turned on Jesse. "Did you know Mr. Endicott was a Sheriff when you accepted his invitation?" I asked.

"I had no idea." He crossed to the dresser and began removing his cufflinks.

"Then why did you insist on baiting him that way?"

He loosened his collar and began to unknot his tie. "Baiting him? What do you mean?"

"Deliberately turning the conversation to talk of bandits and bank robbery. Were you trying to raise his suspicions?"

"He wasn't the least suspicious. You heard him—he thinks bandits are dumb yokels. I'm just a gambler posing as a grain merchant."

"But he's not a dumb yokel, either. How long do you think it will be before he notices that you ride fine horses, the way the outlaw Jesse James does? And you're missing part of a finger, the way Jesse James is said to? He doesn't strike me as the type who'll stop asking questions."

"Don't worry, sweetheart." He kissed my cheek and patted my shoulder. "I'll take care of it."

I slept poorly that night, but the next day Jesse did indeed 'take care of it.' He left the house before dawn and returned a few hours later with a hired wagon and news that we were relocating to the other side of the county.

"Don't you think that will make Sheriff Endicott even more suspicious?" I asked, alarmed.

"What's to be suspicious about? People move all the time. We'll put the word out among our neighbors that we found a house we like much better."

"Then Endicott will simply track us to the new house. You heard what his wife said—he has an insatiable curiosity."

"I'll tell everyone we went back to Kentucky to be near family. Your mother was ill, so we had to leave suddenly."

"I think we should stay here." Too often in the past few years we'd relocated. Each place held the illusion of safety, yet each time that peace had been short-lived. Rashly packing up and fleeing each time we began to feel wary seemed pointless to me. And I hated the thought of moving again after only a few weeks in our little house.

"I won't take the chance of Endicott finding out who I really am," Jesse said. "I can't very well go straight if people like him keep trying to drag me back into my old life."

"You're really serious about staying honest this time, aren't you?" I searched his face, trying to gauge the depth of his conviction. I'd wanted to believe him before, but Jesse had talked of going straight as far back as our honeymoon.

"I'm serious," he said, his expression determined. "I'll do whatever I have to, to stay out of trouble, including packing up and moving out of harm's way."

So that afternoon, we loaded a hired wagon and moved to the other side of the county. Sheriff Endicott would find our little house empty the next time he rode by. If he questioned our neighbors or clerks in the stores we had frequented, they would all share that we were headed back to Kentucky, to help care for an ill relative. The Sheriff would never see Dave Howard in the pinochle parlors or saloons of this neighborhood again.

Their narrow escape from Northfield had done what the pursuit of lawmen like Sheriff Endicott had not, and transformed the James brothers into law-abiding citizens—solid members of the community who took their civic duties seriously. As J.T. Howard and B.J. Woodson, Jesse and Frank registered to vote and cast their ballots for the popular Democratic candidate, Samuel J. Tilden. Tilden won the popular vote but the Republicans and their candidate, Rutherford B. Hayes, refused to concede the election.

Allegations flew about misprinted ballots and illegal votes. There were even disputes about who had the authority to count the votes. Weeks after the election the matter of our future president was still undecided.

Perhaps it was frustration with this outcome that led Jesse to seek diversion. One afternoon in mid November, he strode into the kitchen, where I was rolling out noodles. "Pack your best dresses, sweetheart," he said. "I've just bought two tickets to Philadelphia."

"Philadelphia?" I wiped my hands on my apron. "What are you talking about?"

"The Centennial Exhibition," he said. "It's almost over and I don't think we should miss the chance to go."

The hundredth anniversary of America's independence from England was being celebrated that year at Fairmont Park in Philadelphia, Pennsylvania. The papers regularly carried reports from the Exhibition and Jesse and I read them with interest, but I had never dreamed we would be able to attend. In truth, Mr. and Mrs. Jesse James could never have attended—but Mr. and Mrs. Howard could. "Are you serious?" I asked. "We're really going?"

"Yes, and we leave tomorrow morning, so you'd better get busy deciding what to wear. Pack a bag for Tim, too. Fanny and Buck are going to look after him while we're gone."

I faltered a little at this announcement. I had never been parted from my son for more than a few hours since he'd been born. Jesse rightly interpreted the stricken look on my face. "He'll be much happier here with his aunt and uncle than traveling with us," he said. "He's too young to enjoy the exhibits and you'd wear yourself out looking after him." He took me by the elbows and pulled me close. "Besides, don't you think it would be nice to go away for a while, just the two of us?" He nuzzled my cheek and my last bit of reluctance drained away.

"That would be wonderful, dear," I said. With Jesse's travels, moving and caring for the baby, we hadn't spent very much time alone. I missed the closeness we'd once enjoyed.

Living so quietly and apart for so long, I was unprepared for the bustle and energy and sheer *busyness* of the Exhibition. The official title was the "International Exhibition of Arts, Manufactures and Products of the Soil and Mine." Even that lofty name couldn't convey the scope and beauty of the place. I'm sure from the first day I went about with my mouth gaping open at all the sights and sounds. Jesse laughed at my astonishment, but I knew he was amazed, too, though more circumspect in showing it.

We secured a suite of rooms at the Trans-Continental Hotel, at the very gates of Fairmont Park. The entry lobby stole my breath, with its gilt chandeliers and thick carpet that muffled the sound of even Jesse's booted feet as he strode to the registration desk. I sat in a plush armchair and waited while he checked us in, observing him as one might observe a stranger: here was a tall, broad-shouldered man in a finely cut suit, polished boots and an obviously expensive beaver hat. He spoke in a soft Southern accent, assiduously polite, but with the attitude of a man who is used to giving orders and being obeyed. As he crossed the lobby, more than one head—both male and female—turned to watch him pass. He touched the tips of his fingers to his hat brim and nodded to one matron who crossed his path and she blushed like a school girl and almost collided with a potted palm tree. I smiled to myself, knowing the effect those dazzling blue eyes could have on a woman. The desk clerk hurried to greet him, all smiles. "We're delighted to have you with us, Mr. Howard," he said as Jesse signed the register.

We rode to our rooms on the second floor in a hydraulic elevator paneled in dark wood and lit with a gas jet. "Have you visited the Centennial Exhibition?" Jesse asked the elevator attendant, a middle-aged man who walked with a limp.

"The wife and I have been there three times," the man boasted. "I'm going to be sad to see it go." The Exhibition was scheduled to close at the end of the month, after reigning over the city since May. "It's one of the marvels of our age."

More gas jets illuminated our rooms, which looked out over Elm Avenue and the Centennial Grounds. The apartment was a wonder of high ceilings, gold damask draperies and red and gold carpets. Taps dispensed hot and cold running water into a porcelain tub in the bathroom and there was a separate water closet. French doors opened onto a balcony above Elm Street, and tall windows let in light and air.

"What should we do first?" I asked, turning from the window when the bellman had collected his tip and departed.

Jesse grinned. "I can think of something." He locked the door, then unfastened his gun belts and laid them on the dresser.

"You can't wear those guns to the Exhibition," I said, pretending to ignore his advance toward me. "They'll attract attention from the Centennial Guards." The St. Louis paper had published a picture of the

Guards—ranks of blue-suited policeman charged with keeping order at the Exhibition.

"I won't wear the gun belts," he said. "But I won't go unarmed, either."

"Of course not." I had never known him to be without a weapon close at hand. Even at church on Sundays, he kept a pistol tucked into his boot and another under his coat, at the small of his back.

"We don't have to talk about that now," he said, slipping his hands beneath my elbows and gently urging my crossed arms apart. "It's so good to finally get you alone."

I pretended to resist, but not for long. He planted kisses all along my jaw and down the column of my neck, sending little sparks of sensation through me.

"What if I said I was tired from the trip, and wanted to rest?" I teased him.

"I'd say I think lying down on the bed is a good idea." He bent and scooped me into his arms.

I squealed as he carried me to the bed, and beat on his shoulders, laughing as he dropped me onto the feather mattress. He fell down beside me and nudged me onto my side, my back to him. "You can't take a nap all trussed up like this," he said. "Let me undo these buttons and loosen your corset."

With deft fingers, he undid the row of pearl buttons down the back of the dress, untied the sash and pushed the cloth back over my shoulders. Then he reached around to my front, unhooked my corset and worked it from around me.

Cool air flooded across my thin lawn camisole, and I breathed deeply for the first time in hours. Jesse dropped the corset beside the bed and caressed my sides, his hands running over the wrinkled cloth of the camisole, around and up to cup my breasts. "How you stand to wear that thing I'll never know," he said, and dragged his thumbs across nipples that had risen to meet his touch.

I rolled back toward him and tugged at his tie. "If you're going to take a nap with me, you ought to get more comfortable, too," I said.

He sat up and began working at the knot of the tie. "So you still think we're going to take a nap?"

"Eventually," I said with a coy look.

While he stripped off tie and vest, boots and braces, I unfastened the buttons of my boots and kicked them off, then untied and stepped out of the caged crinoline and bustle and the dress itself, leaving me in stockings, garters, drawers and camisole. I propped one foot on a chair by the bed and started to unroll one stocking, when Jesse's voice stopped me. "Don't," he said. He came around the bed to me. "I want to do it. It's just like unwrapping a pretty package."

So I stood and let him undress me, only a little self-conscious about breasts that weren't as firm and round as they'd once been, skin no longer as smooth and unmarked by the signs of child birth. If Jesse noticed any of these flaws, he never said, instead lavishing attention on me with eyes and hands and mouth. "Sometimes I think I'm the luckiest man on earth, to have you as my wife," he said.

I swallowed a knot in my throat and looked away, blinking hard, struck by the understanding that he really meant the words.

Naked at last, I crawled backwards into the bed. Jesse stripped off his trousers, shirt, wool vest and underpants and joined me beneath the sheets. Sun streamed across the room from a window beside the bed, and the rattle of carriage wheels and the shouts of drivers drifted up from the street below. "It feels odd, being in bed in the middle of the day," I said.

"No one knows we're here." He kissed my shoulder and smoothed his hand around the curve of my hip.

"Y . . . you don't think anyone will hear, do you?"

I felt his mouth curve in a smile. "What if they do? We're a man and wife." He moved his mouth to the top of my breast. "Nothing we do here is illegal or immoral." He sucked my nipple into his mouth and I gasped and closed my eyes, surrendering to the pleasure of the moment. Jesse knew my body so well, but today he seemed determined to learn it anew. He took his time exploring every inch of my torso, touching and tasting, gauging my response.

All the tension and worry of the preceding months and weeks melted away in those moments. There were no lawmen hunting Jesse, no angry mobs intent on lynching him, no aliases to remember or lies to keep straight. We were simply a man and a woman in love, taking pleasure in being together.

I ran my hand up and down his back, reveling in the solid reality of him. He was still thin from his ordeal after Northfield, but there was nothing weak about him, the muscles hard beneath taut flesh. He wore a full beard these days, and I liked the way it felt against my bare skin, soft as washed linen, yet tantalizingly masculine.

We came together with heat and fervor, joyous and playful, without the guilt we'd fought as children or the weight of our responsibilities as adults to hamper our pleasure. I shrieked my delight as my climax overtook me, unmindful of being overheard by strangers in neighboring rooms. Jesse shouted his own satisfaction, and we grinned at each other and laughed, collapsing into each other's arms, still locked together, "two become one" in a way that felt new and whole all over again.

We slept the rest of the afternoon, then changed and went downstairs and around the corner to a restaurant where we dined on broiled steaks and creamed potatoes and delicate white cake with strawberries. Jesse insisted on taking me to an opulent gambling hall, where I sipped mint tea and watched while he played faro. He won and called me his good luck charm. When we returned to the hotel, we made love again, and I fell asleep smiling.

Chapter Eleven

The next morning we were at the gates of Fairmont Park by ten o'clock. Jesse paid our admission of fifty cents each, and bought a guidebook for twenty-five cents. The day was clear and sunny, not too cold, and visitors crowded the lavishly landscaped grounds. I held tightly to Jesse's arm for fear of being separated in the crush of people.

If he was nervous about the crowd, he gave no sign of it, but strode forward with confidence, his alert eyes taking in every detail. His ability to be as at home here as in the Missouri countryside impressed me. Then again, he had always been a person who made a stronger impression on his surroundings than he allowed his surroundings to make on him. Whether conversing with a small town shopkeeper or making his way through a crowded city, Jesse commanded attention and respect.

The park had been transformed into a magical city within the city, with its own police force, water works and transportation system. Over 200 buildings representing various industries and nations were arranged over 285 acres of wooded parkland. A narrow-gauge railway encircled the grounds, while overhead, a monorail zipped between stations within the park.

Our first stop was the Machinery Building, to see the giant Corliss Steam Engine we had heard so much about. This wonder rose forty feet over us, the enormous flywheel spinning at a dizzying rate. It provided power for almost every other machine at the fair, and required only a single man to keep it going—and he seemed to spend all his time sitting in a chair on the machine's platform, reading a newspaper.

"It's amazing," I said, craning my neck to see the top of the behemoth. "It says here in the guidebook that this machine can do work formerly accomplished by dozens of men laboring over boilers and burners."

"I wonder what all of those men are doing now?" Jesse asked.

"Maybe they have jobs building new machines like this one," I said.

"Come on," Jesse took my arm. "I want to see Mr. Bell's new speaking phone."

We made our way to the exhibit for Mr. Alexander Graham Bell's telephone. "With this astounding invention, a person can be standing in one location and converse with a person hundreds of miles away," a handsome young man in a blue suit informed the crowd. He picked up the bellflower-shaped earpiece and spoke into the speaking tube. "Hello? Would you please connect me to Mr. Bell's laboratory in Menlo Park, New Jersey?"

A moment later, a thin voice sounded from the phone. "Mr. Bell's laboratory."

"How do we know that's really Alexander Bell?" a man in the back of the crowd demanded.

"You can believe me or not, sir," the young man replied. "But one day, everyone will have one of these in their home. You'll be able to call your mother across the country or your wife from across town."

"What if I don't want to talk to either of them?" the man retorted, and was awarded with a laugh.

"The telephone is important not just as a matter of convenience," the young man continued. "It will be an invaluable aid to law enforcement agencies and fire departments everywhere. One phone call will send fire brigades rushing to stamp out a blaze before it becomes an inferno. And robberies will be reported before the outlaws responsible have reached the edge of town."

Jesse turned away, frowning.

"What's wrong?" I asked as we moved away from the exhibit.

"You heard the man. An instrument like that will make it harder to slip past the sheriff's deputies and police. It looks simple enough even the most incompetent bank employee could use it."

I squeezed his arm, but said nothing. I didn't want to think about bank robberies or lawmen or any of those things ever again. Mr. Howard was an honest citizen, who raced horses and speculated on wheat and corn and never did anything to put himself and his family in danger.

That morning, we also saw the Remington Typographic Machine, which printed words on paper at the touch of a button, and a working ten-foot long model of a steamship produced by the Hamburg-American Packet Company. We listened to mechanical canaries sing as sweetly as any live bird, and enjoyed a concert played on a Steinway Grand piano.

We lunched at the Restaurant of the South, on black-eyed peas that were over-cooked and greens that weren't cooked enough. "About what I expected of Southern food cooked by Yankees," Jesse said.

"Never mind," I said. "Let's buy ice cream from one of the booths

I saw near the fountain."

We found the ice cream vendor and purchased two dishes. "This may be the best ice cream I've ever eaten," I said as we strolled around the massive Bartholdi Fountain.

"It's pretty good," Jesse agreed. "What should we do now?"

"There's so much to see, it's a little overwhelming," I said. "But my feet are tired."

"Then madam, you should rest." He took my arm and steered me down the walkway.

"I won't ride in one of those wheeled chairs," I protested. "I refuse to be pushed around like an invalid." The Fair offered wheeled chairs for rent for those who didn't want to walk the long distances required to see everything.

Jesse didn't lead me to the chair rentals, but to the depot for the West End Railway, a narrow-gauge train that circumnavigated the park. From our car we had a wonderful view of all the buildings, from the Japanese temple to the Moorish Hall that housed the agricultural exhibit. "No express car on this train," Jesse observed. "Though I wonder how they transport the payroll, and all the money from the various exhibits."

I nudged him with my elbow. "What do you care?" I asked. "You're here on *vacation*."

He laughed, and I was happy his good mood returned. We left the train at Machinery Hall, and proceeded to an exhibit of 14-inch and 10-inch guns manufactured by the Krupp Company of Germany. My head could have fit inside the barrel of the first gun, and the ball it fired was the size of an apple. "I don't like it," Jesse said, backing away from the weapon as if he expected it to swing around at any moment and fix on him. "A bullet in a pistol or rifle kills one man at a time. A weapon like this could take out a dozen in one blow."

"This is the future of war," a stern-looking man with a thick accent informed him.

"Then I don't like your picture of the future," Jesse barked.

From here we moved to a display that cheered him some: Tiffany and Company Jewelers had a booth filled with glittering diamonds, shining platinum and gleaming gold. Jesse studied a case full of men's signet rings and women's wedding bands. A gentleman in formal dress, noticing our interest, approached. "All of the items on display are for sale," he said. "If you would like to examine something more closely, I could open the case for you."

Jesse studied the case a moment longer, then glanced at the armed guards stationed nearby. "No thanks," he said. "I don't see anything here that's worth my time."

We ate supper at a café near the fairgrounds, and returned to the hotel, where Jesse spent several hours in the billiard room while I wrote letters to "Ben and Fanny" and to Zerelda.

We had saved the foreign exhibits for the following day. We marveled at the Egyptian mummy and carved ivory from China, and stood amazed in front of a four-thousand-pound block of silver from Mexico. "I'd have hated to be in charge of getting that thing here," Jesse observed.

We admired stacks of coffee bricks from Liberia, and an intricately carved vase from Japan that towered over both of us.

"We should travel more," Jesse declared. "Maybe take a ship overseas and tour Europe."

"I might like that," I said. "As long as Tim could go with us."

"I wonder what Buck would think of the idea? I bet they've never heard of bank robbers over in France and Italy."

Though I wanted to believe he meant he and Frank could easily go unrecognized in Europe, I half feared he was toying with the idea of introducing the rest of the world to the James brothers' brand of outlawry.

I stifled a sigh. No matter how much I wanted to believe that here, in this crowd of people, Jesse was like any other tourist, I knew that was impossible. Jesse James, by any name, would never be ordinary. Outside forces and his very nature had shaped a man who saw the world from a different point of view from the rest of us.

And wasn't that one of the reasons I loved him—because he wasn't an ordinary man? As his wife, I could imagine myself exceptional also, if only by association.

"What's that over there?" I directed his attention to a line of people stretching out from an exhibit near the fountain.

"It looks like a giant hand," he said.

It was indeed a hand, holding a torch, attached to a giant arm. A sign explained this would one day be part of a gigantic statue, depicting Lady Liberty, that would be erected in the harbor of New York City, a gift to the United States from France.

We paid fifty cents to climb up the inside of the massive arm. Emerging on the balcony around the torch, we could see far across the fairgrounds, past the elevated railway and the turrets of the British Building, all the way to the spire of Independence Hall.

"Can you imagine how inspiring it will be for new arrivals to our country to see that statue representing Liberty, greeting them in the harbor?" I asked as we walked away from the exhibit.

"Liberty for those with the right political views, at least," Jesse said.

I ignored his cynicism. "Let's visit the Government Building next," I said.

"You know I have no great fondness for the U.S. Government," he said.

"We've come all this way to the Fair," I said. "We should see it all."

He relented, and we made our way to one of the largest and most impressive buildings at the Exhibition. Built in the shape of a cross, the U.S. Government Building boasted seven divisions representing the Army, Navy, Post Office, U.S. Treasury, the Agricultural Bureau, the Department of the Interior and the collections of the Smithsonian Institution.

I knew we'd made the right decision when one of the first things to catch our eye inside the building was the exhibits of American firearms by the Colt, Remington, and Smith and Wesson companies. Jesse was like a child in a candy store, wandering from station to station, admiring intricate revolvers and repeaters, guns with carved ivory handles and engraved silver barrels. He discussed distance and trajectory, firepower and reloading speed in the tones of an expert, and soon had an admiring crowd of men gathered around him. He liked nothing better, and entertained them for as long as he was able, until one of the Centennial Guards approached—probably because he was interested in the discussion as well—but Jesse quickly cut off his speech and excused himself from the building.

We returned to the hotel early that evening, and had supper in the restaurant on the first floor, dining on fresh oysters and roast beef, with lemon ices for dessert. Jesse talked of going out and gambling, but I persuaded him to return to the room with me. I intended to take advantage of our time alone—and that large feather bed—as much as possible.

Our third and last day at the fair, we toured the portions of the Exhibition halls we had not yet seen, including the rest of the U.S. Government Building. In the Agricultural Hall, we sampled bread baked using Rumsford yeast powder and bought chocolates made right there on the spot by another machine. We gaped at a stuffed polar bear, snow white and rising ten feet high, with paws the size of skillets and a head as broad as a man's chest; and marveled at a stuffed walrus, fifteen feet long, ivory tusks curving up like scimitars.

We ate sugared popcorn and drank soda water purchased from carts along the walkways, and sampled the free ice water from the Sons of Temperance Fountain. In the Horticultural Building, we marveled at tropical fruits and plants of every description. "Technology will soon allow us to grow fresh fruit and vegetables indoors, year-round," a guide told us.

"Imagine that," I said as we emerged from the building. "Anytime you want a banana, you could pick one from your own horticultural building."

"I don't know that food grown indoors like that is right," Jesse said. "The Garden of Eden wasn't under a glass dome, was it? Seems to me if the Lord had wanted us to eat bananas everywhere in the world anytime, he would have put them there for us."

At first I thought he might be joshing. Jesse had a sly sense of humor. But his expression was serious.

Several newspapers had presses on the Exhibition grounds and printed special editions that were available for sale and posted for display each day. Jesse and I had perused these each day of our visit, stopping to read stories about the increasingly contentious presidential election.

After lunch at the American Restaurant, we walked over to read the day's papers. Six feet from the display, we froze, our eyes fixed on the headline: *Younger Brothers Sentenced to Life in Prison.* Below were the pictures of Cole, Bob and Jim, taken at the time of their capture. Wounded and exhausted, they scarcely looked like the friends I knew.

Jesse's hand tightened on mine, and I thought we might turn away. But he straightened his shoulders and held up his head. "They didn't waste any time with the verdict in that trial," he said, perhaps for the benefit of those around us.

We walked slowly to the display and read the story. The Youngers had readily admitted their role in the Northfield Bank robbery, professing their guilt and their deep regret for their actions. None could be tied to the murder of the cashier, Heywood, since they were all reported to have been outside of the bank at the time. For this they were all spared the hangman's noose and sentenced to life in prison in Stillwater, Minnesota.

The paper reported their sentences might have been lightened further if they had been willing to reveal the identity of the other two robbers—the ones who had escaped. These men were widely thought to be the notorious Frank and Jesse James, and authorities were certain one of them was responsible for Joseph Heywood's death. But to the dismay of prosecutors, the Younger brothers refused to betray their friends, even at thc cost of their own liberty.

"God bless them all," I murmured, my face pressed against Jesse's coat. I put Mr. Heywood and the question of who had murdered him out of my mind. I cared only that Jesse was safe. Our home and family and the life that meant everything to me was secure.

"Yes." He bowed his head, as if struggling to collect himself. "And damn every man who has acted against them."

After that, the fair lost some of its luster for us. Instead of fascinating marvels, I now saw only how quickly the world was changing around us. New technology and an uncertain future were rapidly replacing all that was familiar and comfortable to me. What would become of us in a world full of labor-saving devices, instant communication and more and more power in the hands of manufacturers and moguls?

We turned back toward our hotel. I struggled to distract our thoughts from the Youngers' fate. "We saw so many marvels this week," I said. "It's hard to take it all in."

"Things are changing too fast." Jesse let out a sigh. "Telephones and giant guns—and giant polar bears. I don't know if I can keep up." Gone was the cheerful, energetic man who had entered the city with me, replaced by this sad, brooding specimen, shoulders slumped with the burdens of the world.

Tired from the week's exertions, I fell asleep early that evening. But I woke once in the wee hours to the smell of cigar smoke. Sitting up in bed, I saw Jesse silhouetted in a rocking chair by the window. The tip of his cigar glowed like a single angry red eye, and the lights of the city shimmered through the wavy glass behind him. "Is something wrong?" I asked.

He didn't turn from the window. "It's all right, sweetheart," he said. "Go back to sleep. Everything will be all right in the morning."

I thought of our time at the fair like a dream, one I wished could go on forever. If only I could hold onto those moments, to keep on sleeping, and never awake.

But real life must always intrude. On January 31st a special commission formed by Congress awarded the election to Rutherford B. Hayes. Jesse was incensed. He ranted and paced about the house until I told him I had a headache and couldn't bear anymore. A few moments later I heard him out back, firing off his pistols at cans he'd set up on a fence post.

In early April, Zerelda sent word that she intended to travel to Nashville on the train. If it wasn't safe for her sons to visit her, she would come to them. Reuben and her other children would remain behind to look after the farm.

She arrived on a warm spring day, with two large trunks and three carpetbags, her massive form swathed in the black silk and bombazine she'd worn since Archie's death. An artfully arranged shawl hid the fact of her missing arm, and an elaborately feathered hat drew attention away from her hawk nose and stern visage.

"Careful with those trunks," she barked at the Negroes hired to transport her luggage. "If I find anything broken, I'll hold you responsible."

Luggage seen to, she turned to survey her offspring and their spouses. "Well, *Dave*," she said, holding out her hand. "You're looking better than the last time I saw you."

"I'm well, Mother." Jesse embraced her. "How are you?"

"It's very dull around home," she said. "The newspapers are hardly worth reading these days, with no mention of the James boys in far too long. The sheriff's deputies have even stopped hanging around our front gate, and no reporter has called in weeks."

How that must have distressed her—Zerelda liked few things better than being interviewed by a reporter. I turned away to hide my smile.

She turned to Frank and Annie. "Hello, Fannie. And how is that man you married?" She sent a sly look to Frank.

"I'm very well, Mother Howard." Frank smirked, enjoying the charade that Zerelda was not his mother, but his mother-in-law. By choosing different surnames for their aliases, Frank and Jesse had assured they couldn't pass themselves off as brothers. Yet their obvious closeness spoke of a family relation, so they had decided that Annie would pose as Jesse's sister. She didn't look very much like Jesse, but then, neither did Frank.

Though Frank's farmhouse was larger, Zerelda had insisted on staying at our house. "I want to spend time with my grandson," she said, and I didn't dare argue. Despite the closeness we'd developed over the years, she still intimidated me.

Whether speaking to a newspaper reporter, lawman or daughter-in-law, Zerelda was not one to mince words. And we soon discovered her purpose in coming to Tennessee was not so much to see her children and grandchild, but to persuade her boys to return to live closer to home.

"It's not right for you girls to be holding Frank and Jesse back this way," she announced as she and Annie and I sat sewing in my front room the afternoon of her arrival.

"Holding them back?" Annie asked. She was generally less intimidated by Zerelda than I was, perhaps because she hadn't grown up with stories of the older woman's fierceness.

"You may think you're protecting them by convincing them to move here, so far from their home and family," Zerelda said. "But in reality, you are keeping them from their true purpose."

"I scarcely think it's holding a man back to encourage him to stay safe and alive," Annie said.

"They managed to stay safe enough before you came along," Zerelda said tartly. "Now you've exiled them here to this place where they don't know anyone and have no useful work to do."

"Frank enjoys his work now, and he enjoys not having to look over his shoulder every second of the day as well," Annie said.

I couldn't let Annie make her argument alone. "Don't you think almost dying at Northfield might have had more to do with Jesse and Frank's decision to leave Missouri than anything Annie or I said or did?" I asked.

"My boys have been in scrapes before. They never worried about it until you two came along and saddled them with responsibilities."

Responsibilities that included the grandson she so doted on, I might have pointed out, but I held my tongue. I'd seen Zerelda's grief over the loss of Archie, and part of me understood a mother's wish to keep all her children close.

"They aren't boys anymore," Annie said, her eyes flashing, her voice crisp with anger. "They're men. And yes, they have responsibilities. Ones they gladly chose."

Zerelda never flinched. "They've spent their whole lives fighting for the cause," she said. "I taught them there is nothing more worthy than the task of making sure the South's grievances are heard. Now you've forced them to abandon that."

I'd heard plenty of stories about Zerelda preaching the gospel of Southern superiority. In her household, the bushwhackers her sons fought with weren't merely heroes, they were next to gods. Her daughter, Fannie, bore the middle name Quantrill after the guerrilla William Quantrill, and her youngest son had been named for Jesse's mentor, Archie Clement. The Confederate flag was still proudly displayed in her home, and no prayer was said without mention of the need for the Lord to avenge the downtrodden South.

I'd never questioned her fervor, accepting it as one of the quirks of her personality, like her decision to wear black and to keep her empty sleeve pinned up as a badge of honor, rather than accept the prosthesis some had offered. But was she so blinded by devotion that she'd sacrifice her own sons' lives for an ideal that didn't even exist anymore?

"There is no cause left," I said. "The Confederacy is gone and can't rise again."

She stared at me, horrified, as if I'd suddenly announced I no longer believed in God. I think even Annie was stunned that I'd uttered such blasphemy.

I struggled to contain my emotions—fury that Zerelda would value anything more than the life of her sons, and despair that we should even be having this conversation. "Jesse and Frank are in Tennessee right now because that's where they want to be," I forged on. "Not because of anything I or Annie said or did."

Zerelda set her mouth in a hard line. "They belong in Missouri," she said. "They belong home."

"Then you should talk to them about it, not us." Annie punctuated her statement by stabbing her needle into the shirt she was mending.

"I most certainly will," Zerelda huffed.

But if she said anything to Frank or Jesse, they chose to ignore her pleas. A few days later, she boarded the train for the return trip, and no mention was made of the four of us following.

Chapter Twelve

Summer began on a better note, when Annie shared the news that she was expecting her first child. Before the month of June was out, I was sure I was pregnant as well. The news cheered Jesse, and he and Frank reveled in the role of proud papas-to-be, while Annie and I sewed baby clothes and contemplated names for our new children. Unlike my previous confinement, this time I experienced little of the nausea and weakness that had so plagued me with my first child, though Jesse teased me about my ravenous appetite.

I barely had time to celebrate this joy when I received word that my mother was gravely ill. Jesse didn't feel it would be safe for him to return to Missouri at this time, so Tim and I took the train at once to Kansas City, to the boarding house my mother ran with the help of my oldest brother, Robert.

The rest of my brothers and sisters were already there, seated in the parlor like people already in mourning. "I'm glad you could come, Sister," Sallie said, taking my bonnet and coat while my sister Lucy's daughter, Nannie, tended to Tim.

"How is she?" I asked, glancing toward the stairs that led to the upper floors, and mother's room.

"Not well," Sallie said. "The doctor says it's only a matter of days."

I tip-toed up the stairs and peeked into the room where Mother lay. Robert's wife, Nancy, rose from a chair beside the bed and smiled wanly. "I'm glad you're here," she said. "She's been asking about you."

"Sister!" Mother's voice was weak, but clear.

"It's good to see you, Mama." I took the chair Nancy had vacated and cradled my mother's hand in mine. Her bones felt fine and brittle as a bird's, the skin like dry, wrinkled silk stretched over them. "How are you feeling?"

"When the pain gets too bad, the doctor gives me morphine." She managed a weak smile. "To think I'd become a drug addict at my age."

I couldn't laugh at her little joke, but I tried to focus on brighter things. "I have some good news," I said. "I'm expecting another baby."

"A baby. That's wonderful. What does Jesse say?"

"Oh, he's beside himself. You know how much he loves children."

"Did he come with you?"

"No. We didn't think it would be safe."

Her expression sobered. "What is he doing with himself these days? I haven't seen anything in the paper."

"He's racing horses and buying and selling wheat and corn. Everything perfectly honest and legal," I said. I didn't mention the gambling. Mama wouldn't approve and really, neither did I. But I suppose every man must have some vice, and at least I could be reasonably sure this one wouldn't get Jesse killed.

"And my little grandson? How is he?"

"Not so little anymore. And talking up a storm. I'll bring him up to see you later. I think he's in the kitchen with Nannie right now. She's probably feeding him sweets."

"You do that, dear." Her eyes drifted shut and her grip on my hand lessened.

Nancy came to stand beside me. "She tires easily and spends a lot of time sleeping," she whispered. "She'll rest easier now that she's seen you."

Downstairs again, my brothers and sisters crowded around me.

"Where is Jesse?" one asked.

"What is he doing with himself these days?

"How is Frank?"

"Is it true they've gone straight?"

"How long is that likely to last?"

My sister Catherine listened to the barrage of questions and my answers, her expression growing increasingly distressed. "I thinks it's disgraceful Sister has to live so far away," she said. "And under an assumed name, like a fugitive."

"What else do you expect me to do?" I asked. "My husband is there and I must be with him." And Jesse *was* a fugitive, with a price on his head. The reward made everyone who knew him suspect, even members of our family. Worse than the threat of prison time was the very real danger that his enemies wouldn't wait for a fair trial, but would lynch him on the spot. My throat ached at the very idea.

"You could leave him," Catherine said. "You've no reason to stay with a criminal."

"Jesse is my husband and the father of my children and I won't have you talk that way about him," I snapped.

"What else do you call a man who kills innocent people and steals from them?" she taunted.

I looked to my other siblings and their husbands and wives, hoping someone would rise to Jesse's defense. But they avoided my gaze. "You all know Jesse," I said. "He's your cousin. He isn't the monster the papers make him out to be. He's as kind and gentle as ever."

"I doubt the widows of the men he killed think so," Catherine said.

"That's enough, Catherine." Robert stood and brought the subject to a close. The last few years had aged him; his hair had grown gray and new lines etched his face. I was struck by how much he resembled our father. "Now isn't the time for arguments like this," he said. "Sister is here for the same reason as the rest of us—to say good-bye to our mother. Nothing else is important."

I gave him a grateful smile, and turned my back on Catherine. I told myself grief for our mother had brought out this meanness, but that didn't lessen the pain of her words. I couldn't deny that Jesse had killed men. I'd always told myself they were men who had given him no other option—that they would have taken his life if he hadn't stopped them.

But had the bank president in Gallatin and the cashier in Northfield been a real threat to him? Of course, who was to say Jesse had even fired the fatal shots? It was easier to imagine someone else—even Frank, who was known to have a sharp temper when riled—killing someone than Jesse. Jesse knew the Bible better than I did, had more patience with Tim than I did, never failed to kiss me good-bye before leaving the house, and kissed me hello upon every return, even if he'd only walked to town to buy a paper. How could the ruthless killer I read about in the papers, and the tender husband and father I saw at home, be the same man? Had love blinded me to this other side of Jesse? Or was he better than most at keeping the two sides of his nature segregated?

Did everyone possess a light and dark nature? Did I?

My instinct was to deny such a charge, but looking back over my life, I saw evidence that refuted my denial: I was an obedient, dutiful daughter, yet I had defied society's conventions and my family to be with Jesse. I was an honest Christian woman, yet I had not hesitated to move to another city and live under an assumed name.

I told myself I had no choice; a wife must follow her husband. But I was not a slave to Jesse. I could have refused to join him and found safe haven with my family.

I had followed him willingly. Gladly. I welcomed the excitement of becoming a different person. I savored the sting of danger that heightened my senses and made me feel more alive.

Love sealed me to Jesse, but something within me—the darker nature I had not admitted to before—had drawn me to him in the first place and made me a willing partner in the life he offered.

My mother died on the morning of July 23, 1877, slipping quietly away from a morphine-induced slumber. My Uncle William James, the same who had joined Jesse and me in marriage, came over from Kearney to conduct the funeral, and my niece, Nannie, sang *Amazing Grace* in a voice so sweet and pure I felt I was in the presence of an angel.

After the graveside service, the mourners gathered at Robert's house to offer their condolences over plates of fried chicken and baked ham and coconut cake. I had little appetite, but made a show of eating to keep the older neighbor ladies from fussing.

Esme was there, with Mr. Colquit, whom I'd once thought of as unfortunate, but whom I now saw as a man who'd been blessed with a good wife and seven beautiful children. The older ones from his first marriage had turned into fine young gentlemen, and from the looks of things, Esme was expecting again. She had the kind of life she had often talked of when we were girls.

"I'm so sorry for your loss," she said, pulling me close in a hug. "Your mother was a dear woman, and I know you're going to miss her."

I nodded, and tried to swallow past the tightness in my throat. "She always thought a great deal of you," I said.

"Walk with me?" Esme hooked her arm in mine, and led me toward the back door.

Outside, the air surrounded us like a heavy quilt, hot and stifling. We headed for a grove of trees at the edge of the property, which offered the only shade and the faint promise of coolness. "How are you, really?" Esme asked.

"I'm doing well," I said. "Looking forward to the new baby."

"I miss having you close," Esme said. "You were like a sister to me."

"I miss you, too, but you know you can write to me any time."

The faint lines around her mouth tightened, making her look older than her years. "It's not the same, Zee. Not when I can't even call you by your real name."

"It's just a name. It doesn't change who I am."

"But you have changed. Jesse's changed you."

"No more than marriage ever changes a person," I protested. "No more than Mr. Colquit has changed you."

She shook her head. "If anything, *I've* changed him. Since our marriage he dresses better and his manners have improved. He respects me and honors me by seeking my advice." She lowered her voice, as if someone might overhear us even at this distance from the house. "He tells me all the time that I'm smarter than him, and I never disabuse him of the notion."

"And you think Jesse doesn't honor and respect me?"

"All I know is that marriage always changes one partner more than the other. When I met Tony, he wasn't the perfect husband for me, but I've made him into a man who more closely fits that ideal."

"I saw no need to change Jesse," I said. "I love him the way he is."

Esme continued to look unhappy. "When we were girls, you were always so much more daring and outspoken than I," she said. "I admired that spirit in you, even if sometimes you made me afraid. What happened to that brave girl?"

"I don't know what you're talking about," I said. "Don't you think living with a man who's wanted by the law, living under a name not my own, is daring enough?"

"I never thought you'd let yourself get caught in such an impossible situation," she said. "I always thought you, of all women, had the power to make a man behave as he ought."

"Are you suggesting I'm responsible for Jesse's behavior?" I asked. The idea was so absurd I wanted to laugh, but the mirth remained locked in my chest.

"A woman is supposed to have a civilizing influence on a man," she said.

"First of all, Jesse is living an honest life now in Tennessee," I said. "He's turned his back on crime."

"Then why do you have to hide and pretend to be someone you're not?"

"Because there are people out there who want Jesse dead. Men who would hang him before he ever received a fair trial. Men who would shoot him in order to collect the reward money."

Esme looked doubtful. "There ought to be some way for you to live as an honest woman again."

"I am an honest woman!" I struggled to rein in my emotions. "And secondly, I wouldn't want to live with a man who was so weak he would change on my say-so. Your husband may wear the shirts you pick for him and do the things you tell him, but Jesse has a mind of his own about such things and I'm glad of it. I want a man I can depend on, not another child to look after."

Esme flushed. "I can't believe you'd say such mean things to me," she said. "We were so dear to one another once; now I feel as if I hardly know you." Not waiting for an answer, she turned and hurried back to the house.

I sagged against the trunk of a tree and closed my eyes, the buzz of cicadas in the afternoon heat melding with the hum of conversation from the funeral guests. To think I had looked forward to the comfort of family and friends in this time of loss. But apparently it was easier for them to judge me than to try to understand me. They saw only the external trappings of my life with a man who was more myth than human to many. They imagined themselves pulled from their staid, safe existence and thrust into a life of uncertainty and half-truths and were sure they would not endure it.

They didn't see the other side of that picture. My life was never boring, and Jesse was never dull or predictable. The name others used to address me didn't matter to me, anymore than the address at which I lived. Jesse had given me the freedom to experiment with my life. I could be as ordinary as a housewife one day and as exotic as a concubine the next. If I made a mistake, we could pack up and move on, change our names, write a new story for our lives and try again.

What I found fascinating, they only feared. Their refusal to understand frustrated me, but I knew better than to try to make them see things my way. They could judge me as they wished. I knew the value of what I had, and I could never happily return to their brand of boring, conventional life again.

February 6, 1878, Frank and Annie's son, Robert Franklin James, was born. Annie told me later that Frank, a man not given over to displays of emotion, wept when the nurse placed his son in his arms.

We had had a bitterly cold winter, and ice and snow kept me confined to the house after Christmas, so I was unable to visit my new nephew and his parents, but Jesse rode over and reported the boy and his mother were both doing well. "Buck is strutting around like a rooster," he said, laughing. "If anyone would let him, he'd talk for hours about how perfect his son is."

"Of course he's perfect," I said. "All babies are perfect."

"And they grow up to be perfect little boys." Jesse pulled Tim into his lap and gave him his watch fob to examine. "It's only when they grow to be men that they mess things up."

I gave him a sharp look. Did he feel he'd 'messed things up?' "We have a good life," I said. "I'm happy."

He nodded, though his expression remained somber. "That's good, sweetheart. I always wanted you to be happy."

"I want you to be happy, too," I said. "Is something wrong?"

He began weaving the watch chain through his fingers for Tim's amusement. "I'll be happy when the baby is safely here," he said.

I hoped our new child would be a cure for Jesse's melancholy, but how long would that happiness last? Jesse was never satisfied staying in one place or doing one thing for long. I sometimes wondered if having been thrust into battle so young—having grown to manhood as part of the guerrillas, who roamed the countryside for months at a time, and who spent each day in chaos of their own creation—hadn't shaped Jesse in ways that could never be undone. He was always restless, always craving excitement, always searching for something I couldn't name.

I had not expected to deliver until mid-April, but recently I had grown alarmingly huge, and I began to feel I'd calculated wrong. On the morning of February 27, I recognized the signs of labor. I was more comfortable in my role as Mrs. Howard now, less fearful of uttering anything that might reveal my husband's identity, so when I felt it was time I sent Jesse to fetch the doctor.

At first, things progressed normally. The labor pains came in waves, but I did my best to bear them. Jesse had retreated to the barn with Tim, telling him they must wash and groom the horses, so I felt free to cry out against the pain that tore through me.

Whereas my first child had been delivered with seeming ease, this second baby seemed determined to remain in the womb. Dr. Montgomery, the first to attend me, became more and more concerned as the hours passed. He conducted an examination, then he left the room to consult with Jesse.

Soon my husband was at my side. By this time I was almost too weary and pain-wracked to open my eyes, but I looked up at Jesse when he said my name. "What is it?" I asked.

He held my hand, his fingers ice cold. "The doctor says the baby is turned wrong," he said. "He wants to call in a colleague who's had more experience with these things. I'm going to fetch him now."

"All right." I swallowed hard, trying to find courage where I felt there was none. "I'm sure it will be fine."

"I'm taking Tim with me. I'll drop him off with Buck and Fannie."

I mustered the strength to squeeze his hand. "Maybe the baby will be here by the time you get back," I said.

But it would be many hours before my baby would be born, hours in which Jesse would wear a path in the dirt of the barn floor, pacing back and forth in anguish, littering the ground with the butts of smoked cigars.

On the afternoon of February 28, after almost twenty-four hours at my side, Dr. Gould delivered a baby boy, followed a few minutes later by a second son.

I knew none of this for several days, slipping into unconsciousness after the second baby's birth. The doctors were forced to turn their attention from my sickly infants to me, as I began hemorrhaging dangerously.

When I next awoke, the room was dark and quiet, no sound but the ragged sough of my own breath. I blinked into the darkness, trying to focus, unsure of where I was or what had happened.

Then a shadowy figure emerged from the darkness at the end of my bed. "Child, how are you feeling?" my mother asked.

She was just as I remembered her, in an old-fashioned white lace cap and a gray dress with a white fichu. She came and stood beside me, smiling down on me with such sweetness tears pricked my eyes.

"Where's Jesse?" I asked, my voice barely a whisper.

Mother's smile vanished and she shook her head.

I tried to sit up, but an incredible lethargy paralyzed me. "Where's Jesse?" I asked again. I had to see my husband. I had to hold his hand and know that he was all right.

My mother's eyes filled with sadness, and she shook her head once more. "I never should have let you marry him," she said.

"I love him," I protested. "I want to see him."

"Jesse has a wildness in him that can't be tamed," she said, repeating the warning she'd given when she'd first discovered my love for Jesse. "He is plagued with a restlessness even your love can't overcome."

You're wrong, I wanted to tell her, but I no longer had the strength to speak. I closed my eyes, thinking to rest a bit and muster the strength to get out of bed and go in search of Jesse, but almost as soon as my eyelids shut I succumbed to blackness.

When I woke again, Jesse was there, slumped forward in a chair beside the bed, his fingers twined in mine, forehead pressed to the blankets beside me. "Jesse?" I rasped. I licked cracked lips and tried again. "Jesse!"

He raised his head and stared at me with reddened eyes. His hair was uncombed, his shirt wrinkled. "Oh, Zee," he said, and kissed my hand. "Thank God."

His obvious distress upset me. "How long have I been sleeping?" I asked.

"Two days." Tears streamed from his eyes. "Zee, I'm so sorry."

"Sorry about what?" Then full wakefulness returned, and with it the memory of my protracted labor. "The baby?" I asked.

"They're gone." He bowed his head. "Both of them. They were just too weak, the doctors said."

"Both of them? I don't understand—" I tried to sit up, but he hastened to urge me back against the pillows.

"Don't excite yourself," he said. "You need to get your strength back." He kissed my cheek and smoothed my hair. "I'll get Fanny."

A moment later, Annie came in. Her face was pinched and pale, but her grip was firm as she squeezed my hand. "It's good to see you awake," she said. "We've been very worried about you."

"What happened?" I asked. "Jesse said there were two babies?"

She nodded, and bent over me, smoothing the blankets. "You had twins. Little boys we named Gould and Montgomery." She paused and caught my eye. "I hope that's all right. Jesse said you didn't have anything picked out, and he was too distraught to think of anything, so I chose the names of the doctors who attended you."

"Gould and Montgomery." I tested the names on my tongue. "Yes, those are good names." Tears stung my eyes as I struggled to accept the reality of two babies, dead before I had a chance to know them. "Can I see them?" I asked.

"Oh, sweetie. We had the funeral yesterday, not knowing when you'd be well enough to attend." She squeezed my hand. "We had a photographer take a picture, and I saved you little locks of hair. And I dressed them myself. They looked like little angels. We buried them together, in the same coffin, since we didn't think it was right to separate them."

I nodded, crying now, too weak to fight the tears. Annie sat on the side of the bed and pulled me close. "I'm sorry as can be about this," she said. "I can't even imagine how much it hurts. But you mustn't distress yourself too much. You need to save your strength and concentrate on getting well. Tim and Jesse need you."

I lay back on the pillow, trying to pull myself together. "How is Jesse?" I asked. "He looked worn out."

"He's spent every minute with you," she said. "He took losing the babies hard, but when the doctors said we might lose you, too, he was wild with grief. He threatened to shoot them if they let anything happen to you. Frank had to drag him from the room and calm him down."

"Oh my God." I put a hand to my mouth. "What did the doctors do?"

"Frank convinced them it was just grief talking, and then Jesse apologized. That and the gold he paid them went a long way toward easing their suspicions." She patted my hand. "I never saw a man so torn apart," she said. "If you had died, I think we might have lost him, too."

"He would have pulled himself together for Tim," I protested. "Jesse is a strong man."

"Yes, he's a strong man. And he can be a hard one, too. But for all that, he has a weakness where it comes to you, Zee."

Annie and Frank moved in with us for a while, to help look after me and Tim and Jesse. I think having his brother around helped Jesse. Frank would take him for long rides and let him talk—about regrets of the past and wild plans for the future. More even than I, Frank knew his brother—knew his mind and his heart and how to handle him. Though many in the press and public saw handsome, outgoing Jesse as the leader of their gang, ahead of his more taciturn, morose older brother, those of us within the family knew how much Jesse looked up to Frank. Where Jesse was volatile and quick to air his emotions, Frank plotted strategy, though when riled he had a fearsome temper. Whenever he spoke in anger, people were sure to listen, and to shrink back in fear. Frank was the only person Jesse ever deferred to, and Frank was the one most able to offer him comfort now.

Frank and Annie stayed with us a month, while I slowly regained my strength. When they left us, the house echoed with their absence, and an emptiness that should have been filled with crying babies and all the bustle and joy of caring for them.

Jesse wrapped his grief around him like bandages holding closed a dire wound. He no longer slept the night, but prowled the house and yard, a restless wraith. Gray began to show amid the sandy hair of his sideburns and new lines fanned out from his eyes, which burned with a private pain.

I woke one night to a steady squeaking noise I couldn't identity. I rose and wrapped myself in a shawl and followed the sound to the front porch, where Jesse sat in our old hickory rocker. The stub of a candle burned at his feet, casting orange light up onto his face, and the face of our son, Jesse Edwards, known as Tim. The boy was sleeping, wrapped snug in a patchwork quilt my sister Sallie had made out of the scraps of old shirts and dresses, cut into triangles and sewn together in a pinwheel pattern. As Jesse rocked, the pinwheels moved in and out of the light, their bright colors muted to duns and grays.

Jesse had both arms wrapped around the sleeping child, his cheek pressed against the top of Tim's head, sandy whiskers to sandy curls. His eyes were closed and he made no noise, but tears glinted in the hollows beneath his eyes and caught in his beard, like bits of sleet snared in brush.

Pain tore anew at my heart as I watched this tableau of sorrow. I had been raised to have faith in a good and just God, and had turned to Him time and again in times of trouble, and found comfort there. But there was no comfort for me now. Where was the justice in the death of two helpless infants? Where was the goodness in visiting such tragedy on a man who had forsaken his sins and was trying his best to live a good and honest life?

I turned away, and crept back to my bed and my own tears. I wondered if we would ever be allowed to be happy again. The very idea of happiness seemed a phantasm.

Tim kept us from slipping further into the darkness of our sorrow and grief, and it was Tim who pulled us together. He was growing fast, a solemn, bright boy who was his father's shadow. Man and boy worked together each morning and evening to care for the horses. Jesse patiently showed Tim how to clean hooves and curry manes. When they were done, he would set the boy in the saddle and lead him at a slow walk around the paddock.

He took Tim with him to town to run errands, and set him up beside him at lunch counters and in pinochle parlors and introduced him solemnly, "This is my son, Tim. He's a big help to me."

With Tim, some of the heaviness lifted from Jesse's walk, and the old light returned to his blue eyes. Tim loved to be read to, and while I prepared breakfast each morning, Jesse would read aloud from the newspaper to both of us.

The papers were filled these days with stories about an outlaw in California who called himself Black Bart. He chiefly robbed stagecoaches, and left behind poems boasting of his deeds. He fascinated Tim, who every day pleaded, "Read me a story about Black Bart."

Jesse grudgingly read about the robber described as the most dashing, daring and chivalrous of robbers, known for his gracious manner and sense of humor. "He has taken to leaving poems at the scene of his crimes," Jesse read one morning. "One of which is quoted here.

> *"Here I lay me down to sleep To wait the coming morrow, Perhaps success, perhaps defeat, And everlasting sorrow. Let come what will, I'll try it on, My condition can't be worse; And if there's money in that box 'Tis munny in my purse."*
>
> *Black Bart, PO8*

Jesse slapped the paper down in disgust. "Of all the hogwash," he said.

"Why do you say that, Papa?" Tim asked.

"I say it because this Black Bart character is just a small-time, penny-ante thief compared to a real outlaw like Jesse James."

"Who is Jesse James?" Tim asked.

Jesse smiled. "A writer named John Newman Edwards said that Jesse James was 'diabolically daring and had a contempt of fear.' And that 'all the annals of romantic crime' could 'furnish no parallel' to Jesse's exploits."

"What happened to Jesse James, Papa?" Tim asked.

Jesse stroked his beard and looked thoughtful. "No one knows, son. He's disappeared. But they're all wondering. And the lawmen are still looking for him. But they'll never catch him."

"Why won't they catch him?"

I stilled, waiting for the answer as well.

"Because Jesse James will never be taken alive," Jesse said.

I shuddered at these words, and looked down at my plate. "Eat your breakfast, Tim," I said. "Dear, your coffee's getting cold."

While Frank was content to farm and hire himself out as a wagon driver and general roustabout, Jesse looked to make his living in easier ways. "I always figured a man was better off using his brains instead of his brawn to get by," he said.

So he increased his activities speculating in wheat and corn. "What exactly *is* speculating?" I asked him once.

"I buy grain in the field now at one price, speculating that the price will go up when it's harvested in the fall," he explained. "In the fall, I sell the crop for more than I paid—or rather, I sell my interest in the crop—and pocket the profit."

"So it's another form of gambling," I said. Jesse's chief flaw was a love of any wager, to the point of recklessness. He regularly indulged in the more common pursuits of betting on cards and horse races, but he would also wager on the arrival time of a train or the amount of weight a draft horse could pull. When he won, he celebrated by placing another bet, and when he lost, he increased his wagers in hopes of gaining back the money he'd already spent.

"Speculating is a legitimate business," he said. "Though it has a few things in common with gambling. Which makes it perfect for someone like me."

Then Jesse argued with a man named Steve Johnson over money Jesse felt was owed him from the sale of a corn crop. Jesse's pen practically scorched the page as he sent several scathing letters demanding payment, all of which were ignored.

"I'm going to sue," he declared. "We'll see how Johnson feels when he's hauled into court."

"Jesse, are you sure about this?" I asked, alarmed. "Hiring a lawyer? Facing a judge? What if someone recognizes you?"

"Why should they see me as anyone but J.D. Howard? It's not as if any of those reward proclamations circulating about have my picture on them. If anything, this will help establish me as a legitimate businessman."

"What if you run into Sheriff Endicott?"

"What if I do? I'll greet him like an old friend."

"An old friend who disappeared overnight. Don't you think he'll find that suspicious?"

"People move all the time for one reason or another. I'll explain that your mother was ill and we had to rush to see her."

Jesse! It's not right for you to use my mother as an alibi when she isn't even here to give her approval or not."

"Then I'll use my mother. It doesn't matter. Everything will be fine. You'll see."

Over the next few months, letters and accusations flew back and forth between Jesse and Mr. Johnson and the various lawyers on either side of the argument. The trial was finally set for June, and Jesse and Frank prepared themselves. Frank, as B.J. Woodson, had agreed to testify in Jesse's defense. Annie and I fretted, but were ignored.

Then, a letter arrived from Jesse's lawyer, telling him that the case had come before the judge on May 30th, and because Mr. Howard was not present, the ruling had gone in favor of Mr. Johnson. He would not be required to pay anything to Jesse.

Apparently the letter informing Jesse of the change of date for the trial had gone astray.

The failure hit Jesse hard. "I was robbed," he declared. "As surely as if Johnson stuck a gun to my head."

"It's a legal robbery," Frank said. "The court ruled against you, so there's nothing you can do now."

"I could go over there and threaten to kill Johnson if he doesn't return my money," Jesse said.

"Then you'd end up in jail for sure, and probably hanged," Frank said. "And once the authorities started digging around in your business, they'd likely find out about me and arrest me as well. So if you've got any sense left in your head at all, you'll forget about it and get on with your life."

Jesse was smart enough to acknowledge the wisdom of his brother's advice, but accepting this loss was a bitter pill that didn't go down easily. He'd struck back at every other failure in his life. When Union militia attacked his family, he fought back by joining the bushwhackers and wreaking havoc. When the Union used his past to deny him his full citizenship rights, he retaliated by robbing banks and trains controlled by Union businessmen. Even Northfield, a grand failure for the James/Younger gang, had been a kind of personal triumph for Jesse and Frank. They'd made it safely home against impossible odds, and thumbed their noses once more at the many lawmen who pursued them.

The loss of $56 to Mr. Johnson was a less-public failure, but one that stung more than most. Jesse had tried by honest means to earn his living and provide for his family and ended up at the mercy of the law he had spent so much of his life flaunting. More than the loss of money, the blow to his pride cut deep.

He was no longer Jesse James, the famous outlaw, fleeing in a hail of bullets and living to fight another day, but Dave Howard, ordinary citizen, whose downfall was scarcely worth a mention in the local paper—a man who tomorrow would be remembered by no one.

Chapter Thirteen

In July, I turned 33 years old, though I felt years older. Jesse presented me with a narrow-brimmed felt hat, trimmed with a cockade of feathers, and a pair of yellow kid gloves. "Happy birthday, sweetheart," he said, and kissed my cheek.

I found and held his gaze. "Thank you, dear, but the very best gift you could give me requires no money or wrappings."

"Oh?" He cocked one eyebrow in amusement. "And what would that be?"

"It would be for you to come to my bed tonight and make love to me."

His cheeks pinked. "After your ordeal this winter, I'm not sure that's wise."

"I'm all well now, Jesse. And I miss you." I grasped both his lapels and pulled him close. "I want to be a wife to you again."

He smoothed his hands down my arms. "I've missed you, too," he said. "But maybe you ought not risk having another baby. After I almost lost you . . ."

"Hush." I covered his mouth with my fingers. "There's no reason to think another baby would endanger me again. Or that I couldn't have other healthy children. What happened was horrible, but it doesn't have to happen again."

His face twisted, as if in pain. "I just don't know if we should risk it."

"Don't make me beg, Jesse." My voice trembled, and I feared I might ruin the moment by suddenly bursting into tears. I slid my hands beneath his coat, across his broad chest, down toward a stomach that showed no sign of a paunch. With no hesitation or shame, I moved my hands lower, to his trousers, beneath the gun belt slung there, under the waistband of his drawers. I brushed the tip of his erection, and a thrill raced through me at this evidence of his desire for me.

He grasped my wrist and pulled my hand away. "I can't hardly think when you do that."

"You don't need to think," I said. "Just act." I stood on tiptoe and whispered in his ear. "It will be all right, I promise."

If Tim wondered why we insisted he go to bed early that night, he made no protest. He'd had a busy afternoon, accompanying Jesse to the barber and the bootblack, then taking a long ride into the countryside. I wasn't sure if Jesse was trying to tire the boy out or work off his own frustration, but never mind. The result was the same: Tim was asleep within minutes of saying his prayers and crawling under the covers, and Jesse and I retired to our bedroom and shut the door.

We moved tentatively together, almost like strangers, each fearful of giving offense. Jesse's hands shook as he unfastened my gown, and in my hurried clumsiness I tore a button from his trousers. He turned the lamp low and we crawled beneath the sheets, and for a long moment merely held each other, catching our breaths, letting some of the urgency recede, enjoying the feel of being in each other's arms once more.

Jesse was usually the impatient one when it came to our lovemaking, but this night he waited for me to make the first overture. I began to kiss his neck, tasting the salt of his sweat and the sweetness of the talcum powder the barber had used. I traced my tongue along the hollow of his collar bone, and down to the twin indentations on his chest, where bullets had long ago marked him, one still buried within his body.

He smoothed his hands down my back, and twined his fingers in my hair as I continued to map his body with my mouth, laying a trail down his ribs and along the ridged muscle of his abdomen, delving into the indentation of his navel.

Before I could go further, he grasped my arms and dragged me up his body, silencing my half-hearted protests with a long, quenching kiss. I clung to him, savoring the return of a passion I'd feared lost.

His hands roamed my body, soothing and stroking, tracing each curve and hollow as if reassuring himself everything was as he remembered. He cupped my bottom, then gently squeezed, his smile as wicked and devilish as any he had flashed at me in his younger years. "Are you ready to go for a ride, sweetheart?" he asked.

"I'll ride with you anywhere, darling. You know that."

Then he lifted my hips until I was straddling him, his erection hard against my entrance. "You set the pace," he said. "I don't want to hurt you."

"You won't hurt me," I said, and proved it by spearing myself over him. The sensation of him inside me after so many months' absence was enough to bring joyful tears to my eyes. I tightened around him and was rewarded by the dazed look that came over him, and the smile that curved his lips.

Then I began to move, rising above him, then sinking into him once more. He grasped my hips and fixed his gaze on my face, his blue eyes almost violet in the dim light. I began to feel a little self-conscious, with him watching me so intently, and closed my own eyes in order to shut out his stare.

He moved his hands to my breasts, hefting them in his palms, toying with the nipples. Any semblance of self-control I had left vanished with these movements, and I came with a loud cry.

Jesse grasped my hips firmly, and began to thrust more strongly beneath me. I realized he must have been waiting for me, and it made me wonder how he'd dealt with his needs in the months we'd been apart.

But these thoughts vanished as his climax shuddered through us both. He bucked hard beneath me, and I tightened my thighs around him to keep from being thrown off the bed. Then he wrapped his arms around me and pulled me close, crushing me against his chest until I could scarcely breathe. "God, Zee, I've missed you," he whispered, his voice roughened, as if by tears. "I've been so alone without you."

I had scarcely left his side in all these bitter months, but I knew exactly what he meant. Grief and pain had wrapped us each in dark cloaks, shutting out each other and everyone else. Not even our love for each other had been able to penetrate those veils. But tonight I felt them rip asunder. Jesse had come back to me, and I would never let him leave me again.

By November I was certain I was pregnant again. My joy was restrained by fear, and I saw the same uncertainty in Jesse's eyes. While I dealt with my doubts by praying and endeavoring to focus on each positive sign of a normal pregnancy, Jesse coped by ignoring my condition altogether. He never spoke of the baby or my approaching confinement, and went about his business as if nothing at all had changed.

During this time, he spent much of his time at tracks around the country, indulging his passion for horse racing. He owned several racehorses either outright or in part, and they had won races at Hot Springs, Arkansas; Monegaw Springs, Missouri; Saratoga Spring, New York; and Long Branch, New Jersey. He and Frank regularly visited with breeders in Kentucky and Virginia, appraising new stock.

Newspaper reports about the James Gang often commented on the horses they rode. The fine thoroughbreds stood out amongst the work-worn nags and plow-horses more commonly seen. The sheriff's deputies and civilian posses who pursued the gang after a robbery were never able to keep up with Jesse and his men's swifter mounts.

Jesse talked about his horses the way some men talked about their children, going on at length about the merits of Tadpole or Jim Malone or Jim Scott—all horses he had raced at one time or another.

Several years earlier, he had acquired a new favorite, a black gelding named Skyrocket. The horse was a frequent winner at the track. When he retired from racing, Jesse brought Skyrocket home to our stables and made him a favorite saddle horse. He fed the horse treats of apples or carrots and groomed him until he shone. I chalked up this attachment as proof of the softer side of my husband few people ever saw, but I wasn't prepared when he came home one day with a flat, paper-wrapped package under his arm. He kissed me on the cheek and deposited the package on the table.

"What's that?" I asked.

"Is it a present?" Tim asked hopefully.

"It's a painting I commissioned." Jesse took out a pocket knife and cut the twine that held the paper in place, then removed the wrappings to reveal an oil painting of a horse.

"It's Skyrocket!" Tim exclaimed.

Jesse held the painting at arm's length and admired it. A small brass plaque at the bottom identified the horse, shown in profile standing beneath a tree, as Skyrocket. "It looks just like him, doesn't it?" Jesse said.

"What are you going to do with it?" I asked.

"I thought I'd hang it in the front parlor. Tim, fetch me the hammer."

Tim retrieved the hammer from the back porch and followed his father into the front room. A few second later, I heard hammering.

I turned back to the bread I was kneading, relieved. I'd been half afraid Jesse would want to hang the picture in our bedroom. It was one thing to have a horse vying for my husband's attention during the day; I didn't welcome the same sort of competition at night.

Several weeks after the portrait of Skyrocket arrived, Jesse discovered my scrapbooks. Not that I had ever tried to hide them from him; he had seen me cut out articles from the papers many times, but I suppose he never gave any thought to what I did with them. And I'd never thought to show him the two volumes I'd collected before we were married—accounts of every crime attributed to him, as well as various re-tellings of his and his brother's other activities.

"What are these?" he asked, bringing the stack of books into the parlor, where I was sewing, and setting them on the table beside me.

"Those are my scrapbooks," I said, focusing on inserting tiny stitches into the hem of a receiving gown. Normally, the scrapbooks resided in the blanket chest at the end of our bed. "What were you looking for in the chest?"

"That bearskin coat I bought last winter. Have you seen it?"

"It's hanging in the closet in the children's room. What do you want with it in July?"

"I think I left some gold coins in the pocket." He pulled a chair up to the table and opened the first scrapbook. "What do you do with these?"

Evenings when he was away, I enjoyed turning through the pages, re-reading accounts of daring getaways and exciting exploits. Even the negative articles held a tone of admiration, while the most flattering portrayed Jesse as a hero of the common man, a kind of Robin Hood exacting revenge upon crooked railroads and banks.

"They're all articles about you." I continued to sew, but I watched him out of the corner of my eye. Would he be upset that I'd kept these things? By tacit agreement, we never talked of what he did while he was away from home.

Each time he returned, it was with a polite fiction. "I got a good price on a hundred bushels of wheat in St. Jo," he'd say. "I made a good profit." Or "I lucked onto a sale of cattle that netted me a good paycheck." Whether he thought I really believed these explanations for a new influx of cash into his pockets or he merely shared them as a way of keeping in practice, or in case someone overheard, I never knew.

His eyes scanned the articles. "All the annals of romantic crime furnish no parallel to the exploits of Missouri's bold rovers," he read, then chuckled. "John Edwards always had a way with words. The news business could use more like him."

He turned more pages, stopping now and again to read through a clipping. "He robs from the rich and gives to the poor," he read, then added, "Tell me what outlaw in his right mind would bother robbing from the poor?"

At last he came to a series of blank pages—the end of my collection. The last clipping was dated almost two years previous. He stared at it a long moment. "I guess everybody's forgotten about old Jesse James by now," he said, and closed the book.

I looked at him sharply, something in his tone putting me on guard. "Everyone but the police and Pinkertons and all the people who'd like to collect the reward money the government and railroads have offered," I said. "Those rewards still stand—that money is there waiting for someone to collect it."

He looked unconcerned. "The lawmen must be getting bored without the James brothers to chase after."

"Then let them stay bored," I said.

"Too much sedentary living isn't good for a man," he said. "It makes him feel old before his time."

I watched him walk away, a cold chill in the pit of my stomach. Yes, our life now was mundane in many respects. And I hated being so far from family and old friends. But as Mr. and Mrs. Howard we were safe. Though Jesse still slept with a loaded gun on the night stand, I had stopped feeling it was necessary. Money was scarce at times, but it seemed little enough to pay for peace of mind we hadn't known in years.

For a while my father had farmed, and he'd taught me about seeds. Some could be freely sewn in fresh-tilled ground and would sprout almost immediately. But others required scarring with a file or soaking with water before they would grow and bear their fruit.

Jesse was like those tougher seeds, unable to flourish if left undisturbed. He needed to be bruised and battered in order to really live. Fighting for him was as natural as breathing. I could only stand on the sidelines and watch, and pray that he wouldn't destroy himself, and me in the process.

June 17, 1879 Mary Susan James was born. Jesse was at a horse sale in Kentucky when I delivered. I think he planned the trip, knowing my time was near and unable to bear the thought of seeing me suffer as I had before. A neighbor stayed with me and looked after Tim until the doctor came, but my labor was uneventful. Mary was born healthy, wailing lustily and clawing at the air—her father's daughter, determined to seize all life had to offer.

When Jesse returned the next day, Tim greeted him at the door. "I have a new little sister," he said proudly.

"You do?" Jesse picked the boy up and balanced him on his hip. "Then we'd better go see her."

Jesse held his daughter as if she was fashioned of spun sugar, his eyes locked to hers, studying every detail of her tiny face. "She's beautiful," he said at last. He glanced at me. "She looks like her mother."

Mary had my dark hair and eyes, but her father's upturned nose and slightly cleft chin. "Now you have another woman in your life," I teased him.

He stroked her cheek with the tip of one finger. "Don't worry, little one," he whispered. "Your papa will always take care of you."

For the next few weeks, Jesse returned to the role of devoted family man. He spent hours with Tim, reading to him, or riding with the boy in front of him on the saddle. In the evening, he would rock Mary to sleep, then sit with her in his arms, studying her as if she was a rare treasure, memorizing every detail of the curve of her cheek or the tilt of her nose. When she woke in the night, he would get her and bring her to me so that she could nurse. There in the darkness, the two of us would talk as we hadn't since our courting days—of memories we shared, and of our hopes and dreams for the future. Our lives were so intertwined, it was difficult for me to remember a time when we had not been together, and impossible for me to picture a future without him.

"I've been thinking about going out West," he said one early morning when Mary had awakened us with her cries.

"Where out West?" I asked.

"Nebraska. Or maybe California. I hear there's lots of good country there. Places a man could live and not be bothered. The kind of place we could really start over."

"I'd like that," I said. "I hear there are places in California where you can pick an orange right off a tree. Wouldn't that be something?"

"I could raise horses and race them. Buck could go in with me and we'd train them. He's always had a good way with animals."

I began to picture this dream of our own family compound—a ranch somewhere green and open, with neatly-fenced pastures inhabited by handsome horses. The brothers would each have their own home, but they'd be close enough for frequent visiting. Our children would all grow up together.

And no one there would know or even suspect, that Mr. Howard and Mr. Woodson were anything but what they said they were—ranchers with a talent for turning out fast horses. After a while, people back East might even truly forget the James brothers, and they'd be able to stop looking over their shoulders.

To live a life as ordinary people do.

This last thought pulled me from my sleepy daze. Jesse might live a different life one day, but it would never be an ordinary one.

"Whatever you decide to do, you know I'll be there with you," I said. I yawned, my eyes drooping. "Will you take the baby back to her cradle now? She's asleep and I almost am."

He took Mary from me and I slid down under the covers. I was asleep before he returned to me, and I dreamt that night of wild horses racing across the open prairie. Horses that would never be caught or tamed.

But Jesse's contentment with domestic life was short-lived. By the end of July he had returned to his old habit of going for long rides in the countryside, sometimes staying out past dark, saying upon his return only that he had been thinking, and his thoughts came easier on horseback.

One night in August, I woke very late to the sounds of him fumbling around in the kitchen. He had set out earlier that night, intending to ride to the river and back "for some fresh air." Hours had passed since then. I'd finally given up waiting for him and retired to my bed. I didn't allow myself to worry about him; he had stayed out much longer than this before, and always returned eventually. Though he was reckless in some things, he never took chances that might lead to his discovery, and he would stay away for days if he even suspected someone he didn't trust might trail him back to the house.

So I was relieved when he finally returned this night. I thought the rain we'd had earlier had driven him home, and I lay back on the pillows, intending to scold him for going out in such uncertain weather. But he delayed so long coming to bed that I finally rose and went to greet him. I found him standing at the table with a bottle of morphine granules, trying to measure a spoonful into a glass, but his hands shook so badly he spilled more than he caught. "Darling, what is it? What's wrong?" I rushed to his side.

"Got c . . . caught in a storm over n . . . near the river." His teeth chattered like castanets and his face had a sickly pallor that showed even in the lamplight.

I took the morphine from him and measured a dose into the glass of water. He only took the drug when the pain from the old wounds in his chest plagued him. "Is it only your chest hurting, or is there more?" I asked.

"I'm just a little feverish." He took the glass in both hands and drank the contents in one long gulp, screwing up his face at the bitter taste. "I'll be better in the morning."

I put a hand to his forehead. "You're burning up!" I began tugging at his heavy overcoat. "Let's get you to bed right away."

Without protest, he let me lead him into our bedroom, where I helped him out of his sodden clothes and into clean underthings. He fell asleep before I even crawled in beside him, though he slept restlessly.

The next morning, he was not improved. Tim cried when I wouldn't let him in to see his father. "I want Daddy!" he wailed.

"Daddy is sick," I said. "He needs to rest."

As the day progressed, I grew more and more worried. Jesse drifted in and out of delirium. In one of his more lucid moments, I shared my fears. "I really think you need to see the doctor," I said.

He nodded. "Send for one."

His easy compliance frightened me even more than the fever and delirium. I flagged down a neighbor boy and paid him a nickel to fetch a physician, and quickly.

Dr. Hamilton arrived within the hour. A distinguished man with a neatly trimmed black beard, he listened while I described Jesse's symptoms. "Has he had spells like this before?" he asked.

"No. Nothing like this."

He went into the bedroom with Jesse, shutting the door and leaving me to fret on the other side. When he emerged a half hour later, he said, "Your husband tells me he's had malaria before, but it's been several years since his last attack."

"Malaria? Is that very serious?"

"It can be serious, but fortunately, your husband is strong and relatively healthy. I'll leave you some quinine to dose him with. In a few days he should recover his strength, but it's important for him to avoid chills."

"Of course. Will he be well then?"

"There is no cure for malaria. Once stricken, sufferers are always subject to further attacks. The best we can hope for is to ward off its return as long as possible, and to lessen the severity of each subsequent attack." He opened his bag and took out a blue glass bottle and began writing on the label. "While I was examining Mr. Howard, I noticed two old gunshot wounds in his chest," he said.

My heart stopped beating for a breath, then began to pound, but I did my best to hide my terror from the doctor. "He was injured in the war," I said.

The doctor nodded. "He probably picked up the malaria then, as well. Most of the sufferers I see spent time bivouacked in the swamps." He handed me the bottle and explained the dosing. "If he takes a turn for the worse, don't hesitate to send for me."

"Thank you, Doctor. Thank you so much." I escorted him to the door and watched him drive away, then went back inside and leaned against the wall, my head pressed to the cool plaster. I'd been sure for a moment that the doctor had recognized his patient as the famous outlaw, Jesse James. But the bullet wounds apparently had not overly alarmed him. What would he have thought if he'd realized the half-delirious man he treated had a loaded gun beneath his pillow?

The quinine did its job and within a week, Jesse was on his feet again. As was his custom, he spent large parts of the day among his many friends in town. He debated politics with his acquaintances at the local saloon and traded stories with Mr. Addleson, the druggist where he bought his cigars. "Addleson says he's going to find me a job," he reported one evening at supper, his eyes dancing with glee.

"A job?" I asked. "Does Mr. Addleson need help at his drugstore?"

"He asked what kind of work I did before coming here and I told him I was a railroad man." He laughed and speared another slice of ham onto his plate. "He said his brother-in-law works for the Rock Island line and he'd ask if they could get me on. Wouldn't that be grand? Me, working for the railroad?"

I shook my head at the joke. I doubted Jesse would ever get close enough to a real railroad man to let him get a look, but it was good to see him healthy and laughing again.

"Why didn't you tell me you had malaria?" I asked.

"I was hoping I was through with it. I hadn't had an attack in years."

"The doctor told me there is no cure."

Jesse shrugged. "I don't see any point in cataloguing one's weaknesses or flaws, or in borrowing trouble by talking about something that might never happen again. If I thought about it at all, I assumed we'd deal with it when and if we needed to."

I didn't like the idea that Jesse had kept something like this from me. In many ways we were so close, but perhaps that was only my illusion. I wondered what other secrets he held back from me.

We each choose how much of ourselves we expose to another. For every confidence we share, there may be a hundred held back. This mystery spices a relationship with the ever-present possibility of surprise. No matter how long Jesse and I knew each other, we would constantly be on a journey of discovery. A relationship so blessed would never grow stale. What we didn't know would keep our love alive as much as what we did know, and our lives together would always offer the promise of adventure.

Chapter Fourteen

In September, Jesse turned thirty-two years old. To celebrate, I cooked a special dinner and invited Frank and Annie to eat with us. I presented Jesse with a stickpin in the shape of a horse's head, which pleased him. Tim gave him a new blue bandana, and Jesse immediately fastened it around his neck, outlaw style. Tim crowed and clapped his hands at the sight.

Jesse's eyes met mine across the table, and he grinned the same charming smile that had swept me off my feet so many years before. I could picture so clearly how he must have looked, climbing onto a railroad car and striding down the aisle as all around him people cowered in fear. He'd been described as 'gracious,' 'fearless,' and 'congenial.' A man happy to be where he was. A man who enjoyed his work.

It was in those descriptions that I'd seen the Jesse I knew—the playful father and loving husband, and even the mischievous boy who had once hurled dirt clods at my skirt in order to command my attention. I'd seen less of that Jesse lately. Though he was still charming, it was a more calculated charm, measured out for the effect he desired. He still played with Tim, but often broke the play off suddenly, as if suddenly recollecting some weighty manner that demanded his attention.

And now a simple bandana had transformed him before my eyes, from staid citizen to daring rebel. I loved both men, but it was the rebel I'd fallen for first. It was good to see him again, however briefly.

That evening at dinner, Jesse wore a new suit—dark green pinstriped trousers with a green brocade vest and a jacket of the latest cut. He was always particular about his dress, and paid as much attention to fashion as any woman. Recently, he had begun dying his hair to cover the gray at the temples and combing it differently to disguise the thinning at the crown. In addition, he spent an hour almost every morning in the barn, working out with weighted dumbbells and performing various exercises. While other men his age grew flabby or fat, he retained the body of a young man. As I sat across from him in the dining room of our little house I felt a surge of pride and desire. My husband was a very handsome man indeed.

Frank, on the other hand, looked fifteen years older than Jesse, rather than four. The disappearance of most of the hair on top of his head had the unfortunate effect of making his large ears and nose even more prominent. Deep lines furrowed his face on either side of his mouth and across his forehead, and blue shadows smudged the skin beneath his eyes.

"You look downright sickly, Buck," Jesse said. "Are you all right?"

"Just a little tired from work." Frank helped himself to another slice of bread. In addition to raising corn and oats on his farm, he hired out as a wagon driver for a local lumber company. The two jobs made for long work days, a fact Jesse had complained about before, when his brother wasn't available to ride out into the county with him or to visit the racetrack or a local gambling parlor.

"There's easier ways to make a living," Jesse observed as he poured gravy over his roast beef.

"That's true." Frank's lips clamped shut and he said no more.

After dinner, Annie and I retreated to the kitchen to wash the dishes. Annie snapped open a dishtowel and glanced toward the front of the house, where the men had retired to smoke cigars on the porch. "If Frank ever goes back to being an outlaw, I'll leave him," she said.

"You don't mean that," I protested.

"I won't live like that anymore," she said, her jaw set. "And I won't have my children living that way, either."

This revelation startled me. "What would you do if you left him? Where would you go?"

"My father would take us in. And even if he didn't, I'd find some way to support us."

"You never left him before," I said, turning my attention to the dishes in the sink. "You married him knowing what he was. Why do you say you'd leave him now?"

"I have Rob to think about now. And times have changed. Robbing a bank or a train isn't a novelty anymore. People are on the lookout for robbers, and are more willing to fight back. You can't have forgotten what happened at Northfield." Her voice shook, and she paused and took a deep breath. "They've been lucky for so long, but I can't help thinking that can't last, and I don't want to be around to see it happen."

"I'd think being apart from him, not knowing, would be worse than being with him," I said. "At least if you were there, there might be something you could do."

"There won't be anything anyone can do if Jesse or Frank are caught," she said. "The men who are after the James Gang want them dead. Jesse and Frank have made an awful lot of lawmen and government officials look like fools. Those men's pride won't allow them to let Jesse and Frank live."

I braced myself against the sink, stomach roiling. "Don't say such things," I whispered.

"It's the truth and you know it." She picked up a fork and began polishing it.

I struggled to pull myself together. "Why did you even bring this up?" I asked. "Has Frank said anything about going back to that kind of life?"

"No. But I know he thinks about it. He's never had to work this hard before, and it's a constant struggle for money now, when it never was before."

I nodded. Jesse often complained of not having enough money. Whatever he'd made from the previous robberies had all been spent on expensive suits, presents for friends and family and wagering on cards and horses.

"I think he misses the excitement and danger," Annie continued. "He used to come home from his trips out of town so . . . exhilarated."

She was talking about Frank, but it could have been Jesse she described. My heart ached for him when I remembered the youthful enthusiasm with which he'd come to me in those years before we wed. He had aged in the last few years, grown somber and serious, as if a great weight pressed upon him.

"Even if everything you say is true, I still don't believe you'd leave him," I said. "I can't imagine ever leaving Jesse. It would be like cutting off my arm—or cutting out part of my heart."

She gave me a pitying look. "Loving someone doesn't mean you aren't a whole person apart from them."

"I know that." But I couldn't *feel* it. I couldn't imagine myself apart from Jesse.

I was sweeping the carpet in the front parlor mid-morning a few days later when a knock on the door startled me. I hid behind the curtains and peeked out at a thin-faced older man with a luxuriant moustache, and breathed a sigh of relief as I recognized our landlord, Mr. Twitchell. He knocked a second time and I whipped off my apron, smoothed my hair, and went to answer the door.

"Mr. Twitchell, please come in." I held the door open wide. "It's so nice to see you." My manner was all politeness, though my curiosity was aroused. Mr. Twitchell had never called on us since the day we moved into the house.

"Is Mr. Howard in?" he asked. His eyes scanned the front parlor, as if he expected to find Jesse hiding behind the sewing machine or the sofa.

"I'm afraid he's out. Won't you sit down? I could fix some tea or coffee . . ."

"This isn't a social call, Mrs. Howard. I'm here because your husband has not paid rent in almost two months."

I blinked, and felt the blood drain from my face. "I'm sure there must be some mistake . . ."

"There is no mistake. I'm owed thirty dollars for this month and last month." The curled-up tips of his moustache quivered with indignation. "If you'll give it to me now, you'll save us all a lot of trouble."

Except for a few stray coins squirreled away in my sewing box, there was no other money in the house. Certainly not thirty dollars. "Mr. Howard handles all our finances," I said stiffly. "I'll speak to him as soon as he comes home and I'm sure he'll get this straightened out."

"If he'd get a steady job, instead of spending his days in the gambling halls and saloons, I'm sure he'd have less trouble paying his rent."

My anger rose at this criticism of Jesse. "I'll tell my husband you called and I'm sure he'll get this taken care of," I said stiffly.

"He'd better. Tell him if I don't have the money by the end of next week, I'll begin legal proceedings." Mr. Twitchell set his hat squarely on his head and let himself out the front door.

He had been gone several minutes before I recovered from my shock enough to think of a reply. I wanted to defend Jesse. To assure Mr. Twitchell that my husband was a good provider and that the nonpayment of rent had been a mere oversight. Perhaps Mr. Twitchell was wrong. Jesse *had* paid the rent and the landlord had misplaced it, or recorded the transaction in the wrong column in some ledger.

But in my heart of hearts, I knew the rent had not been paid. Money had been scarce lately. Jesse never talked about it, but when I had asked him for money to buy new shoes for Tim, he had told me I must wait until a business deal he was involved in was completed. And the last time I'd visited the general store, the clerk had encouraged me to make a payment on the account 'as soon as possible' or more credit would not be extended. That episode had prompted me to hide the few pennies I could scrounge in the button jar in my sewing box.

When Jesse returned shortly before supper, I told him of Mr. Twitchell's visit. "Is it true you haven't paid the rent?" I asked.

"I've had more important things to see to," he said. "He'll have his money soon enough."

"He seemed very upset," I said. "He threatened 'legal proceedings.' Does that mean eviction?" I shuddered at the memory of other families I'd seen, with all their belongings piled at the curb, their shame made public.

"I'll take care of it," Jesse said, his expression grim.

I told myself I needn't worry. Jesse had always provided for us before; he would do so now. But in the back of my mind, I made lists of everything I might sell to come up with the necessary funds.

Jesse's response was to pack a bag the next morning. "Where are you going?" I asked as I watched him add a clean shirt and vest to the carpetbag he used for traveling.

"I thought I'd ride out to see my cousins, George and Wood Hite." He added two pairs of socks to the bag. "They owe me a little money. I think it's time I collected the debt."

I had never cared for the Hites: to me they were lazy, slovenly lay-abouts who took advantage of Jesse's good will. Younger than Jesse, they looked up to him, and in flusher times he never hesitated to give them cash when they needed it. I doubted they'd have any now to give him in return, but if anyone could get the money out of them, it would be Jesse. Though I hated for him to leave me, I was relieved that Jesse was doing something that would get us out of trouble with Mr. Twitchell and allow us to stay in our house.

Annie rode over the next morning, ostensibly to invite me and the children to stay with her and Frank while Jesse was away. I accepted her invitation, grateful for the company her family would provide mine, and also thinking this would make it more difficult for Mr. Twitchell to find me and harass me about the back rent.

But I soon learned hospitality wasn't the only reason for Annie's visit.

"Where has Jesse gone?" she asked as we sat on the back porch, sipping tea and watching the children play. The trees were just beginning to show gold and the air held the underlying chill of approaching winter.

"He went to visit his cousins, the Hites," I said.

Annie frowned into her teacup. "I never cared for that bunch. The old man's wife makes eyes at everything in trousers."

"It's just gossip." But I'd heard the rumors, too. Major Hite's second wife was young enough to be his daughter, and pretty in the way an over-blown rose or over-ripe peach can be pretty.

"I don't really care about her, one way or another," Annie said. "But before he left, Jesse stopped by the farm and he and Frank argued. Frank won't tell me what the argument was about."

"Well *I* certainly can't tell you." Maybe Jesse had tried to borrow money from his brother. But that didn't seem a likely source of an argument. I was sure Frank would have lent any money he had to help his brother.

"I think they argued because Jesse wants Frank to rob another bank or railroad with him and Frank refused," Annie said.

"Why would you think that? Why would Jesse want to do that?" But I knew one reason. Had Jesse seen a return to his old ways as the solution to our money problems? Was the story about collecting a debt from his cousins merely a ruse to calm my fears?

"Because Jesse isn't satisfied unless his name is in the papers," Annie said. "He'd grown used to being the center of attention and now that he isn't anymore, he can't stand it."

"That's not true," I protested. Jesse had as much vanity as the next man, but he was an adult with a family to look after—not the pouting child she apparently saw.

"It *is* true, Zee and you know it." Her voice became strident. "He went from being Zerelda's spoiled little boy to Bloody Bill Anderson and Archie Clement's protégée, to the most talked-about outlaw in the country. Never mind that Frank is the one who introduced him to Bloody Bill in the first place. That it was Frank who put up with Zerelda's harangues while she doted on Jesse. Frank planned their first robberies. His strategy is what made them successful. And Frank's the one who led them to safety after the disaster at Northfield."

I stared at her, amazed at this outpouring. Annie had never before given any indication she harbored all this ill-will toward my husband. I held up one hand to stop the flow of words. "Annie, are you saying you and Frank are *jealous* of Jesse? Because the reporters wrote about him more than they did Frank?"

She sat back in her chair, visibly gathering herself. "I'm trying to tell you that Frank made Jesse what he is today," she said calmly. "If he's thinking of trying to rob railroads and banks and stagecoaches again, without Frank along, then he'll never succeed. And if he thinks he can persuade Frank to join him again, I won't let that happen."

"I don't see how you're going to stop him. Or Frank." I was sure my brother-in-law loved his wife, but Frank had a mean temper when riled and I couldn't imagine he'd allow anyone—much less a woman who'd promised to honor and obey—to tell him what to do. "Even if this is true—what do you expect me to do about it?"

"You could look through Jesse's things, for some clue as to what his plans are."

"I could never do that!"

She gave me an appraising look. "You don't really believe Jesse has never lied to you, do you?" she asked.

"All I know is that *I've* never lied to him." I stood and collected our teacups. Hers was only half-empty, but I was more than ready for this conversation to end. "Maybe it would be better if the children and I stayed here while Jesse's away," I said.

"Don't be ridiculous. I already have the spare room ready for you. Frank will come by tonight with the wagon to fetch you." She followed me to the sink and laid a hand on my shoulder. "I'm sorry if I upset you, Zee," she said. "But we aren't naïve girls anymore. We have children to think about, as well as our own safety. Our men may be reckless, but we can't afford to be. And we can't afford to be ignorant of what they're up to, no matter how much they try to keep us in the dark."

I nodded, though I wasn't sure I entirely agreed with her. After my one and only interrogation by Pinkerton agents, Jesse had told me I was better off not knowing about his activities, and I had believed him. Ignorance freed me from worry and guilt and a host of other uncomfortable emotions.

After Annie left, I put the children down for a nap and retreated to the bedroom Jesse and I shared, thinking I might lie down for a while myself. But Annie's words had aroused my curiosity. The idea that Jesse's belongings might provide a clue to his thoughts and intentions wouldn't leave me.

Curiosity won out over guilt and I got up off the bed and went to the tall wooden wardrobe that sat in the corner. Opening the doors, I stared at the neat rows of finely tailored suits and starched shirts. I felt in the pockets of the bearskin coat and probed the lining of the suit jackets, but they yielded nothing beyond a silver cigar cutter, twenty-three cents in change and a postage stamp.

At the bottom of the wardrobe sat an old Army trunk. I knelt and dragged this out onto the floor. It was locked, but I knew where Jesse kept the key. I fetched it from the cracked shaving mug on top of the wardrobe and fit it to the lock.

The heavy aroma of unsmoked cigars, horehound candy and old newspapers wafted up from the trunk like the mist of a genie rising from a lamp. I shuffled through the contents. Jesse had his own stash of newspaper clippings, most of them written by John Newman Edwards, praising Jesse as a hero of the South. I smiled, imagining Jesse pouring over these homages.

Setting the papers aside, I explored further into the trunk. I pulled out a tiny brass replica of the Corliss Engine, which bore the legend, *Souvenir of the Centennial Exhibition.* Next was a gold pocket watch engraved with the name J. A. Burbank.

The next item of interest was a small cardboard folder. Opening it, I stared at a photograph of our twin sons, Gould and Montgomery. Side by side in a single cradle, dressed in white gowns, they appeared to be peacefully sleeping. But I knew when this photo was taken they were already dead.

My throat tightened and I swallowed hard against the knot of tears, as much for the dear departed infants themselves as for Jesse, who must have stared at this picture for a long time, wrestling with his private grief, before hiding it away among his other treasures.

At the very bottom of the trunk, tied up in ribbon, was a thick packet of letters—all the correspondence I'd sent to him during our long courtship. I raised the packet to my nose and sniffed the faint reminder of the rosewater I'd sprinkled on the pages—my girlish idea of the appropriate gesture for a love letter.

The knowledge that Jesse had kept these letters touched me, and brought a renewed rush of guilt over snooping into his private possessions this way. I shut the trunk and returned it to the back of the wardrobe.

My detective work had yielded little of interest, but this was reassuring. Instead of hidden jewels or bundles of cash, I'd discovered Jesse's true treasures. Instead of secret maps or outlines of nefarious plots, I'd found pictures of his children and love letters from his wife. Jesse knew what was important in his world. I would hold on to that knowledge, and keep the faith that he would do what was right for me and for our children.

Not long after the children and I moved in with Frank and Annie, I came down to breakfast one morning to find everyone in an uproar. "I knew your husband was up to no good and now he's proved it," Annie said as I passed her on my way to the breakfast table.

"I've met some fools in my time, but I believe none of them is a bigger damn fool than my brother," Frank said as I took my seat across from him. He handed me a copy of that morning's paper.

I stared at the headline "Train Robbery at Glendale by the Notorious Jesse James."

My heart felt made of lead. I stared at Frank. "Maybe they made some mistake?"

"Keep reading." He nodded to the paper. "There isn't much doubt it was Jesse."

The hold-up had all the earmarks of a Jesse James raid—signaling the train to stop, the robbers boarding the train and escorting the engineer and fireman away from the engine at gunpoint, then proceeding straight to the express car. The courtesy and bravado of the leader, described as 'handsome and without fear.' The departure of the robbers in a hail of gunfire, riding into the distance on "swift, handsome thoroughbreds."

Even this might not have convinced me, but Jesse had left no room for anyone to doubt that he was responsible for this crime. He'd left behind a press release identifying himself and the members of his gang—the James brothers, Jim Connors, Underwood, Jackson, Flinn and Jack Bishop.

"Who are these men—Jim Connors, Underwood, Jackson, Flinn and Jack Bishop?" I asked. "I don't recognize any of them."

"Aliases, I imagine," Frank said. "Damn fool."

Annie returned to the table and set a tureen of oatmeal down hard between us. "Why did he have to drag you into it?" She directed the question to Frank. "Now the police will think *both* the James brothers were involved, when you were here all the time."

"I imagine he wrote the note before he left here," Frank said. "When he thought he could talk me into going with him."

"So Jesse *did* try to convince you to join him," I said. "That's what you argued about."

Frank lifted the lid of the tureen and stared morosely at the glutinous gray contents. "I should have gone. Maybe I could have talked him out of taking such a crazy risk."

"You should have done no such thing," Annie said. "If he wants to get killed, he can leave you out of it."

I finished reading the newspaper account of the robbery while the two of them bickered. I began to feel better as I read. "It says here all the bandits got away. And no one on the train was killed."

"No one was killed *this time*," Annie said.

"Jesse's not stupid," Frank said. "But he thinks he's invincible." He spooned oatmeal into his bowl. "He's stirred up a hornet's nest with this robbery. The railroads have gotten complacent, thinking their troubles were over, that the James Gang was done for after that fiasco in Northfield. Now this has happened and I can guarantee they'll be out for blood."

I felt cold all over. For so long, we'd lived with the threat of discovery, but in the last few years that threat seemed to have waned. As Mr. and Mrs. Howard, we had a comfortable life. We were part of our community. We had friends and participated in our church—was having a few extra dollars in Jesse's pocket worth throwing all that away?

"I think I'll check on the children," I said, and excused myself from the table.

Tim was playing with Mary and Rob in the backyard, drawing the outline of a town in the dirt and parading little wooden soldiers and stick men through it while the babies clapped their hands and laughed at the entertainment. He glanced up as I approached. He had his father's clear blue eyes and upturned nose, and an innocence that made my breath catch in my throat.

"Is everything okay, Mama?" he asked.

"Yes, I'm fine."

"You look worried."

For his sake, I pasted on what I hoped was a comforting smile. "I was thinking we might go back to our house this afternoon," I said.

His eyes lit up. "Is Daddy coming home?"

"Soon, I hope," I said. I squatted beside him and watched as he galloped a wooden horse through the dirt streets of his town. "What are you doing?" I asked.

"I'm riding my race horse," he said. "Away from the bad men."

I put one hand over my eyes to hide the tears that overflowed. Was Jesse even now riding his racehorse away from bad men as I waited here, unable to do anything to help him?

The next afternoon I packed our things and Frank agreed to take us back to our little rented house. Since we'd heard the news of the Glendale train robbery, things had been tense between Annie and me, and I think Frank was grateful for a reprieve. "Annie will calm down in a few days and feel bad about some of the things she said," he told me as he carried my trunk into the house.

I nodded. "You and Annie have always been good friends to me," I said. "But it's only natural now that she's worried about her own family more than mine."

"You need anything, you send for me," he said. "And if you hear from Jesse, you let me know."

"I will. And I know you'll do the same." He nodded and started to leave, but I put a hand on his arm to stop him. "What did Jesse say to you when he came by your place before he left town?" I asked.

He shoved both hands into his back pockets. "He wanted me to go back to Missouri with him, to get up a gang and do another bank job, or clear out the express car of a train."

So Annie had guessed correctly. "What did you tell him?" I asked.

"I told him no. That things are too hot for us to risk getting caught."

"Because you and Jesse are too well known?"

"Because times are changing. When we first started out, nobody expected to be robbed. Half the time the guards didn't even have guns. You told somebody to open a safe and they did it. Now everybody's armed and everybody wants to be a hero." He spat in the dirt. "There's telephones to send word around the country faster than a horse can ride. Even the contents of the safes are different—it's all checks and bonds instead of greenbacks and bullion." His eyes took on a haunted look. "And most of the men we rode with—the bushwhackers who knew how to ride and shoot and find their way around rough country, men with grit and sense—they're all dead or in jail. Jesse and I are about all that's left."

I couldn't bear to look at him any longer, at his homely, sad face and world-weary eyes. There was no sign of the wild rebel in him now. I looked past him, toward the corral where Jesse's beloved Skyrocket and another horse, a bay named Kentucky, loafed. "I don't think Jesse can accept that the glory days are over," I said. "He wants things to be the way they were—all the excitement and the fame. And maybe the danger, too. I think . . . I think ordinary life is too tame for him. That he doesn't feel as alive if he's not risking something, whether it's money at the race track or his life robbing a train."

> *"I am one, my liege, whom the vile blows and buffets of the world hath so incensed that I am reckless what I do to spite the world."*

At my blank look, Frank smiled faintly. "Shakespeare, from *Macbeth*. Annie and I have been reading it in the evenings."

"So you think Jesse is spiting the world?"

"Maybe." He patted my shoulder. "Take care of yourself and the children, Zee. As for Jesse—maybe all any of us can do is pray for him. The rest is up to God and the government."

I didn't hear from Jesse for that week, or the next. I told myself he was laying low, avoiding the lawmen who were crawling the country, searching for him. We had experienced these separations before and Jesse always came home to me.

But doubt nibbled at me like ants. What if this time was different? What if Jesse, having tried the role of stable family man and found it wanting, had chosen the carefree life of the rebel instead?

Chapter Fifteen

Every day, I waited for Mr. Twitchell to knock on the door and demand his money, but thankfully, he stayed away. Perhaps other business had taken precedence, or he had learned Jesse was out of town and decided to put off bothering a woman and children alone. Whatever the reason, I was grateful for his neglect, and prayed Jesse would soon be home safely—and with the money we needed.

The weather that October was cool and dry. One morning when I went to visit the outhouse, frost sparkled on the grass. Winter would be here before we knew it.

But weather, like life itself, can take a sudden turn for the worse. One evening about suppertime, the air felt heavy and still. My head throbbed and the children whined and refused to eat the supper of corn chowder I'd prepared. Clouds obscured the setting sun and the sky turned the ugly purplish-yellow of a bruise.

I was standing at the sink, washing dishes, when suddenly a great crack of lightning rent the sky, surprising a cry from me. The bowl I was scouring slipped from my hand and rain began to fall in a gray curtain.

"Mommy! Mommy!" Tim ran to me and clung to my skirts. In her high chair, Mary began to wail. "I want Daddy!" Tim sobbed. "Why isn't Daddy here?"

I tried to comfort him, even as the hair on the back of my neck rose with each bolt that crackled across the sky and each cannon shot of thunder. The rain sounded like bullets hitting the tin roof. Tim covered his ears with his hands, and Mary began to wail louder. I picked her up to comfort her, and heard another noise above the sound of the storm, the sound of wood striking wood.

I peered out the window, narrowing my eyes to see through the curtain of rain. A flash of lightning illuminated a gaping black hole where the barn door should be. The door itself slammed back against the side of the barn with each gust of wind. If this kept up, it would be torn from its hinges. I thought of the horses—the most valuable property we owned. These weren't the placid nags of the local farmers, but fine Kentucky bloodstock, high strung and inclined to spook at any sudden noise. They must be going wild in this storm.

I returned Mary, who was still wailing, to her cradle. "Keep an eye on your sister," I told Tim. "I'm going out to the barn."

"Mama, no! Don't leave me." He followed me into the mud room, where I shoved my feet into a pair of Jesse's old boots and reached for his slicker that hung on a peg on the wall.

"I have to see to the horses," I said, tying a scarf tight beneath my chin. "You'll be fine until I get back. Stay away from the stove. Talk to your sister." Not giving my courage time to falter, I yanked open the back door and pushed into the teeth of a gale.

Rain lashed at my face like icy needles. I sucked in my breath and ducked my head, my feet sinking in mud as I fought my way toward the barn. The wind buffeted me, tearing at my too-big coat. Rain cascaded down my back, soaking me to the skin. My boots filled with water and my hair fell down over my eyes in a damp tangle, obscuring my vision. I shoved it beneath the scarf as best I could and bent nearly double, keeping on a crooked course toward the barn.

As I drew nearer the dark opening, I could hear the harsh thuds of the horses' hooves striking against the sides of their stalls, and the high-pitched neighing that rose to a frantic pitch.

I felt my way along the open door to the edge, and fought the wind to pull it closed. The constant beating back and forth had worn a rut in the dirt, which had turned to a mud dam. I kicked at this barrier, leveling it out so that I could drag the heavy wooden door over it. As I finally wrestled it closed, I heard the sound of shattering wood as one of the horses destroyed part of its stall.

I latched the door and tied the latch in place, then with numb, fumbling fingers managed to light a lamp. The scene the light illuminated made my stomach plummet. The bay, Kentucky, had kicked out two slats of its stall and was working on a third. Skyrocket had stopped kicking, but stood in the middle of his stall, wild-eyed and trembling.

I went to Skyrocket first, murmuring soothing nonsense. I found a blanket and threw it over his sweating back, then I leaned over the top of the stall and caught his bridle and fastened it to an iron ring in the barn wall. I thought this would hold him.

Skyrocket secured, I turned my attention to Kentucky. His constant high-pitched cries sawed at my nerves even as his wild movements terrified me. I wished I'd thought to bring a gun from the house. At least then if the bay lunged for me in a fit of wildness I could shoot him.

I'd hate to do it, though. He was a beautiful animal, and a valuable one, too. Jesse always said a good horse was better than money in the bank. He could always find a buyer for his horses when he tired of them and the best ones, like Skyrocket, were good money earners at the track. Kentucky had not been with us long enough to prove himself, but I knew Jesse had high hopes for him.

"It's all right, old boy," I said, the way I had heard Jesse talk to the horses. "I'm right here to take care of you. You don't have to worry about any—"

Thunder shook the air, drowning out my words, and sending the horse into a renewed frenzy. He kicked at the partition once more, sending the last of the wood flying, then lunged from the stall.

I dove out of the way, and cowered behind a feed barrel as the horse crashed around the small open area between the stalls. He pawed at the dirt, then struck at the door. But the wood there was stout oak, held with iron strap hinges. I felt confident it would hold. The question now was how could I keep Kentucky from hurting himself—or me?

He lashed out at the barrel behind which I'd taken shelter, rocking it, nicking his foot on the iron banding. The sight of crimson blood blossoming against his dark red hair galvanized me to action. I couldn't cower here all night; I had to act to save us both.

When the horse turned away from me, I darted from behind the barrel and grabbed up a coil of rope. I wished I knew how to lasso an animal, the way I'd heard cowboys did. But I knew my chances of tossing a loop of rope around the whirling, bucking horse were slim to none. I'd have to take a more direct approach.

"Kentucky, look at me!" I commanded, trying to make my voice deep and forceful.

The horse whirled and faced me and I lunged for it, reaching for the bridle. I caught at the ring there and held on with both hands, my arms and shoulders straining to control the rearing animal, dodging the slashing hooves. Its screams echoed off the barn walls, and thunder reverberated around us, even as lightning showed through cracks in the siding.

I dug my heels into the dirt, ignoring the pain in my hands and back. I reasoned as long as I held on, the horse would eventually tire. Harder to ignore was the terror that filled my stomach and clawed at my throat. I turned my face away from the animal's slashing hooves and prayed he wouldn't knock me down and trample me.

"Mama! Mama!" My blood turned to ice as I heard the cries from the other side of the barn door.

"Tim! Go back to the house!" I shouted.

"Mama, I want to be with you." The barn door rattled as Tim tugged at it. I had visions of him pulling it free, and the horse trampling him as it raced for freedom.

"Tim, go back to the house! This instant!"

"Mama, I'm scared!" he wailed. "I want Daddy!"

I wanted Jesse too. I wanted him here, taking care of his horse, and taking care of me. I wanted to be inside my house, snuggled in blankets before a warm fire. I wanted to sip a cup of tea while he brushed out my hair.

But all I had was a wild horse, a frightened child, and quickly failing strength. "Will you just calm down!" I shouted, addressing both Kentucky and Tim, and myself.

To my amazement, the horse stilled. It stared at me with one terrified eye, its sides heaving, body shuddering. I put one hand to its neck, and smoothed the velvety coat, now slick with sweat. "It's all right," I soothed. "Everything is going to be all right."

I led the now docile animal back to the damaged stall, and tied its halter to an iron ring in the wall. Then I rubbed it down with clean straw and covered it with a blanket. Weary beyond measure, I picked up the lamp, and slipped back into the storm.

Tim sat in a soggy heap in front of the door. I picked up him up and balanced him on one hip, then carried him and the lantern back to the house. Raindrops sizzled against the glass of the lamp chimney, but it didn't shatter, and by its wavering light I was able to avoid the worst of the puddles and make my way onto the porch, where I doused the flame and went into the house.

Mary had fallen asleep in her crib, and Tim was almost out in my arms, exhausted from his ordeal. I stripped off his wet clothes and mine, then dressed us both in flannel and carried him into bed with me. I was too jittery with adrenaline to sleep, but I welcomed the comfort of warm quilts. The worst of the storm had abated, the lightning and thunder passed, the rain a gentle wash against the windows. I lay back on the pillows, my sleeping son beside me, and thought, as I always did at this time of day, of Jesse. Where was he tonight? Was he warm and dry, in a house with friends or a hotel in some distant town? Or was he camped in the woods, soaked to the skin and missing home? In the time I'd known him, he'd certainly been in worse situations. He'd stared down death more times than I could count. He'd escaped so many times I'd grown to think of him as invincible. But on nights like this I was haunted by fear for him. Jesse James the outlaw was the stuff of legends, but Jesse James the man was after all a mortal. How much time did he have before his luck ran out?

I did my best to hide my worries from the children. Though Tim asked every morning if Daddy was coming home today, Jesse had left often in Tim's short life to attend horse races or visit friends, so this absence wasn't particularly upsetting to the boy.

A more pressing concern was my growing shortage of money. I was reluctant to ask Frank and Annie for help, though I know they would have offered. Instead, I accepted a neighbor's offer to buy Kentucky. The cut on the horse's leg had proved minor, and there was no other damage from those moments of terror in the barn. But the memory of how close I'd been to death beneath those slashing hooves left me with little love for the animal, and I was glad to get a good price for him.

I delivered the rent to Mr. Twitchell's office in person. He was clearly surprised to see me. "Mrs. Howard, I would have expected your husband to come to see me," he said, the implication clear that Jesse should be ashamed of letting a woman take care of his responsibilities.

"Mr. Howard had business out of town to see to," I said. "May I have a receipt, please?"

He wrote the receipt, and handed it to me, a sour expression on his face. "Tell your husband I won't tolerate him being late again," he said.

"He won't be." I planned to put aside most of the money I'd received for Kentucky to safeguard against future such embarrassments. Jesse might balk at this, but I was determined to stand my ground. As Annie had pointed out, I had children to think of now, not just myself. Though I would never leave Jesse, I would do my best to see that my children never suffered for that decision.

For the time being, we would be all right. Jesse would be home soon. For my own sake and the sake of my children, I couldn't afford to consider any other possibilities.

And then one day, Jesse was home. He came riding into the yard at sunset, on a chestnut mare I'd never seen before. He wore a fine new suit and his hair was freshly barbered. His smile made my heart leap in my chest. He reined in the horse, then swung down and swept little Mary into his arms, and gave Tim a big hug. Carrying Mary, Tim clinging to his side, he strode to me, eyes shining. "It's good to see you, sweetheart," he said, and gave me a long kiss that left me dizzy and grinning like a girl.

"It's good to see you," I echoed, stroking his hair, touching his shoulder, my hands reluctant to leave him.

Was this the same brooding, morose man who had left not a month ago? He looked five years younger, and more handsome than ever.

"Where have you been, Daddy?" Tim asked.

"Off getting presents for you." He handed Mary to me and returned to the horse. From the saddle bags he took his gifts—a rag baby for Mary and a mouth harp for Tim, who immediately blew a loud blast on his new toy.

Then Jesse turned to me. "And this is for you," he said, handing me a knotted blue silk handkerchief.

There was a hard lump in the middle of the handkerchief, and when I unknotted the ends, I saw a gold ring with a large diamond solitaire. "A ring as fine as the woman who wears it," he said, slipping the jewel onto my finger.

I held my hand out to admire it. The diamond sparkled in the fading sun. "It's beautiful," I said. I shifted my gaze from the ring to his blue eyes. "I'm so glad you're home. I've missed you."

"I've missed you, too." He slipped his arm around my shoulder and we started for the house, the children trailing after us.

Hours later, after the new horse—whose name was Cassidy—was stabled, dinner eaten and the dishes washed, and the children snug in their beds, each clutching the new toy Jesse had brought them, he and I retired to our bedroom. I had informed him of the sale of Kentucky and how I'd used some of the money to pay the back rent. "I'm sorry you had to do that," he said. "But I'm proud of you for handling things. I know I can always count on you."

His praise made me feel two inches taller, and more in love with him than ever.

In the bedroom, I started to pull the pins from my hair, but he stopped me. "Let me do that."

I sat on the end of the bed while he knelt behind me and unplaited the strands. Then he pulled a brush through the locks in long, soothing strokes. The temptation to close my eyes and bury all my worries and fears beneath a blanket of peace and contentment was almost overwhelming. But I knew problems that were buried had a tendency to grow ten-fold, so I forced myself to sit up straight and address Jesse in a voice that was clear yet casual. "I saw the story in the papers about the train robbery at Glendale," I said. "'We are the boys who are hard to handle.' What were you thinking?"

He chuckled. "How did you like that? I thought it was a nice touch. Just when the railroads had begun to get lazy, Jesse James is back to make them toe the line."

"Who was with you? I didn't recognize the names."

"Oh, just Clel Miller's little brother, Ed; my cousin Wood and some men they knew. Young fellows mostly. They grew up hearing stories of the James gang."

I imagined a group of young men, in awe of their idol, the notorious Jesse James. Jesse would thrive in their midst, with no one to contradict him and—unfortunately—no one to rein him in.

"Frank was talking the other day about the men you used to be friends with—your fellow bushwhackers," I said. "He said they're all dead or in jail now. Only the two of you are left."

He set the brush aside and sat facing me. "Buck needs to quit sitting at home, brooding, and come ride with me," he said. "One holdup would set him right." He reached up and unfastened the top button of my shirtwaist.

"Annie says she'll leave him if he goes back to being an outlaw," I said.

His hand stilled. "You wouldn't leave me, would you?" he asked.

The gruffness in his voice unnerved me. I covered his hand with mine. "No, Jesse. I could never leave you." I might as well have tried to cut out my heart and leave it behind.

He traced the curve of my jaw with the back of his hand. "My work takes me away sometimes, but I'll never leave you or forsake you," he said.

I closed my eyes as his lips covered mine, and let this promise vanquish my worries. I had no control over what Jesse did for a living, no power to stop those who hunted him, no way to predict the future. The only guarantee I had was this moment, and I'd be foolish not to take what enjoyment I could from it.

We made love with the urgency of any lovers long parted, yet for me, at least, every caress was tinged with melancholy. Jesse was energetic and eager, but I sensed desperation beneath his ardor, as if he too, was determined to grab hold of every sensation, while he still could.

Whatever ill will had existed between Jesse and Frank when Jesse had left town vanished upon his return. He had been home only three days when Jesse decided we should leave our little house and move in with Annie and Frank. "I'm going to be traveling more and I don't want you and the children to be alone," he said.

"Leave our home? Jesse, no!" We had lived here longer than any other place in our marriage. Our children had been born here. And two of them were buried here.

The two little graves in the back yard drew my gaze. From the kitchen window I could just make out the wooden cross that Jesse had carved and set up as a marker. I'd taken comfort from the knowledge that Gould and Montgomery were out there close, not alone or abandoned to neglect.

Jesse put his hand on my shoulder. "It will be all right, Zee," he said. "We can come back to visit, and when things are more settled—when we have a place of our own—we'll move them with us."

I bit my lip, holding back tears. I wanted to believe in a future in which we'd have a home of our own, and peace and safety at last, but I no longer trusted in such a fantasy. "I don't want to go," I whispered.

"I know." He bent and kissed the top of my head. "But it's for the best. I won't rest easy knowing you and the children are alone while I'm traveling."

I could have pointed out this hadn't particularly bothered him before, but perhaps his renewed criminal activities *had* made things more dangerous for us all. I didn't bother to ask where he was going, or to pretend I didn't know what he planned to do. "Why are you doing this?" I asked. "Why are you putting yourself—and us—in danger like this?"

"It's only for a little while longer." He dismissed my worries with a wave of his hand. "I just want to get a stake. Then we'll buy a farm out west somewhere, and start over. I'll raise racehorses and wheat."

The idea of Jesse as a contented wheat farmer on a western homestead seemed as impossible as my persuading him to give up the idea of any more robberies. He had started out holding up banks and railroads as an extension of his bushwhacking activities, a representative of those for whom the war hadn't ended. But somewhere between revenge and riches, his motives had changed. Now Jesse craved the excitement and danger every bit as much as he enjoyed the rustle of cash in his wallet.

We packed our belongings and moved to Frank and Annie's farm the next week, thereby avoiding having to pay another month's rent. I cried bitter tears as I looked back on Montgomery and Gould's little grave, craning my neck until even the tree that sheltered them had disappeared from sight. I couldn't shake the feeling that I was losing them all over again, and that no matter what Jesse said, we would never be back.

Either Frank had said something to Annie, or she had decided on her own to stop taking her worries over Frank's future out on me. She went out of her way to be pleasant to me and the children, and even managed a smile or two for Jesse. I had yet to meet a woman who was immune to Jesse's charms. The hardest female heart would melt in the heat of his brilliant blue eyes and roguish smile.

One morning in early November, we were all at breakfast when a telegram arrived. Annie accepted it from the delivery boy and brought it to Frank, a worried frown on her face.

We all watched as he unfolded the page. "It's from Mother," he said, then read, "George Shepherd says he killed Jesse near Short Creek. Marshall Liggett says it's true. What do you say?"

I stared at Jesse. "Do you know anything about this?" I asked.

He shook his head. "I haven't seen George in ten years or more." George Shepherd, a former bushwhacker, had ridden with Jesse and Frank in 1868 and '69. He was arrested and convicted of the robbery of a bank in Russellville, Kentucky, and spent time in jail.

Frank struck a match and lit one edge of the telegram and watched the flames consume the paper. "Prison must have done something to George's mind, to make him lie like that," he said.

"But why would Sheriff Liggett say it was true?" Annie asked.

"Maybe he wanted part of the reward money," Frank said.

A chill shuddered through me, and I hugged my arms across my chest. I hated being reminded of the bounty on Jesse's head.

Jesse didn't look very happy with this latest news, either, but he wasn't thinking of the reward money. "George and I used to be good friends," he said. "Even if you didn't like a man, if you served with him you would never betray him. What's the world coming to, when an old friend will betray a man, all for the sake of some cash and his name in the paper?" He stood and tossed his napkin on the table, then walked out of the room and out of the house.

I stared after him, my heart in my throat. Jesse had always been invincible—the man who could not be tamed, the robber who couldn't be caught. Even a rumor that he could be killed made my blood run cold.

Jesse and Frank decided they should visit Zerelda, both to calm her fears and to get a better feel for the climate in Missouri. Annie protested vehemently, but Frank ignored her, calmly packing his bags and then kissing her goodbye, as if she'd never said a word.

I kept my fears to myself and didn't waste my breath trying to change Jesse's mind, but I helped him comb black dye through his hair and beard and told myself that no one he knew back home would recognize him. He'd slip in and out of the state as he always did, invincible. Untouchable.

Safe.

While Annie paced and fretted and scoured the house from top to bottom, I coped with my worries by keeping busy away from the farm. I volunteered with my church to take meals and donated clothing to needy families. Visiting with these people took my mind off my own troubles.

One afternoon, Tim and Mary accompanied me to deliver soup and bread to a young woman in a poorer part of town whose husband has recently died, leaving her with three young children. While our children played, the woman and I sipped weak tea and discussed the recent cold weather and the best way to remove stains from a carpet. I thought of the long, cold winter ahead for this little family and wondered what would become of them. What would I do in a similar situation, left with two children to care for and no means to do so?

Distracted by such thoughts, I failed to watch where I was going when I left the woman's house. As I emerged from the narrow side street where the woman and her children lodged, I collided with a tall figure in an imposing feathered hat.

"Oh, pardon me." I backed away, red-faced and flustered. Staring down at the woman's feet, I saw the scuffed toes of boots peeking out from beneath a once-fancy but now faded and patched gown.

"It's quite all right, dear," came the answer in a soft, Southern accent. "I wasn't watching where I was going."

The voice took me back to summer afternoons sitting on a jasmine-shaded porch, sipping cool sassafras tea. A glance at the woman's face confirmed the accuracy of my memory. "Mrs. Peabody!" I gasped.

She blinked, then studied my face, frowning slightly. "My heavens, is that you, Zee?"

Even the surprise of seeing her didn't make me forget the need to protect my identity, "Everyone calls me Josie now," I said. "Josie

Howard."

She nodded. "You're married then, and these are your children?"

"Yes. This is Tim and Mary." The children stared up at her, wide-eyed and silent. On closer inspection, I could see that her bonnet, though elaborate, was several years out of fashion. The face beneath it had aged as well, in ways even the skillful application of powder and paint could not completely hide. The blue eyes that met mine were faded and shadowed with weariness. She quickly looked away.

"What fine children they are," she said, with an overly-bright smile on her rouged lips. "Who is your husband? I don't remember a Howard family in our old neighborhood."

"No, um, I met him later. At a wedding." Not entirely a lie, for it was at my sister Lucy's wedding that I'd first fallen in love with Jesse. "How are *you* doing? I had no idea you were in Nashville. How long have you been here?"

"A little while." She fidgeted with her beaded reticule. "I've lived several places since leaving Missouri."

The horror of the day she had left—or rather, been forced to leave—had stayed with me all these years. "I was so sorry to hear about that," I said. "It must have been so awful for you."

"It was." She lifted her chin, her mouth set in a determined line. "But I hardly ever think of it."

"It's so good to see you," I said. "I'd love to catch up. We should go somewhere for coffee or tea. Is there a place nearby?"

She was already backing away, shaking her head. "Oh no, that really wouldn't be wise. Besides, I have company coming soon. I really must go."

She seemed anxious to leave, so I didn't try to stop her. "All right," I said. "But I hope I'll see you again some time. I'm in the City Directory. My husband is J.T. Howard."

She gave a half-hearted wave, then turned into the side street I'd just exited. Seeing her now, older and dressed so shabbily, made my heart ache, and I turned away, blinking back tears. I picked up Mary, and took Tim's hand and started across the street.

"Mama, what's wrong with that man?" Tim tugged on my hand.

I looked back and saw an obviously drunken man accosting Mrs. Peabody. He leered at her and pinched her bottom. Outraged, I turned to come to my friend's aid, but something in Mrs. Peabody's attitude made me hesitate.

Instead of taking offense at the brute's effrontery, she merely gave a weary smile and took hold of his hand in hers. Together, they made their way to one in a row of narrow shacks that fronted the side street. The man's voice rose, his words slurred but audible. "I won't pay more than four bits," he said loudly. "Not for someone as old as you. Not more than four bits."

Mrs. Peabody shut the door of the shack behind them and I heard no more.

"What was wrong with that man?" Tim asked again.

"He'd had too much to drink," I said. "Come on, now. We need to get back to the house. Aunt Fannie won't like it if we're late for supper."

I walked automatically, finding my way by instinct, my thoughts awhirl, fighting physical illness over what I'd just witnessed. How had things come to this—Mrs. Peabody selling herself to drunks and worse for fifty cents? After losing Sheriff Henry had she given up on respectable men altogether?

Or had she been selling herself in one way or another all along and I had been too naïve to see it?

The meeting saddened me for days. As a girl I'd cherished my friendship with Mrs. Peabody, even looked up to her as a role model of a strong, independent woman. I'd been inspired by her talk of true love and I'd sworn to find a man for whom I could feel such devotion.

But love hadn't saved Mrs. Peabody. If anything, her devotion to Sheriff Henry had led to her downfall. He had repaid her faith in him with desertion.

Mrs. Peabody had been wrong about Sheriff Henry's feelings for her, and that misjudgment had cost her everything. If only she had put her faith in a better man. A true love would have stood by her and cared for her forever. A true love would never have left her so alone.

Chapter Sixteen

Jesse and Frank returned from Missouri before Christmas, unharmed and in good spirits. We celebrated the holidays together, but I missed having my own home. "Can't we have our own place again?" I asked one evening as we prepared to retire for the night. "It doesn't have to be big or fancy, but I miss having my own kitchen, and my own rooms to decorate as I see fit." Though Annie was gracious and had urged me to make myself at home, she was so particular about everything that I was afraid to so much as move a picture, much less rearrange anything in her kitchen.

"You're right, we need our own place." Jesse stretched out in the bed beside me, hands behind his head. "Living here, Buck expects me to help him plow the fields and scythe the corn. The disapproving looks he gives me when I won't are downright depressing."

I laughed. "Heaven forbid you actually labor for a living!"

He joined in my laughter. "Buck can sweat in the fields if he wants to, but I had my fill of that when I was a boy." He reached out and pulled me on top of him. "I was made for better things."

I wasn't sure I agreed that holding up banks and railroads were better things, but I saw no profit in pointing that out. Besides, his kisses quickly distracted me from thoughts of anything but divesting us both of our clothes as quickly as possible.

We moved a week or so later to a boarding house in Nashville, and then to a house in the nearby town of Edgefield—the same town we had lived in when we'd first come to Tennessee when Tim was a baby. Jesse continued to leave for a week or more at a time, ostensibly to visit his mother. Zerelda reportedly suffered from ill health and needed Jesse to assist her from time to time on the family farm. Though I still chafed at the hold Zerelda had over her sons, I kept my objections to myself, smart enough to know argument would only drive Jesse more toward her.

Besides, I knew visiting Zerelda was not the main point of these trips. My scrapbooks filled with clippings during the summer of 1880, recounting the robbery of a tourist stagecoach at Mammoth Cave,

Kentucky, and a store in Mercer, Kentucky.

Jesse returned from these Kentucky holdups in high spirits, loaded down with cash and accompanied by a dapper, brown-haired man named Dick Liddil. Mr. Liddil was well-spoken, flirtatious and charming, but he made me uneasy. From the conversations he and Jesse shared over cigars in the evenings, I gathered Dick had ridden with Quantrill's raiders. The two shared this history of guerrilla fighting for the South and a love of horse racing.

Upon Skylark's retirement from racing, Jesse had acquired part ownership, with his friend, Jonas Taylor, of a colt named Jim Malone, who was a frequent winner at the track.

"Jim Malone is racing next week at Burns Island," Jesse said one night at dinner. Burns Island was a track in Nashville. "I think we should all go and cheer him on. We'll invite Frank and Annie, too."

"What about the children?" I asked.

"That woman Annie hires to help her with housework sometimes keeps children, doesn't she? We can ask her."

"All right." I smiled at him. "We'll make a fun day of it."

All the arrangements were made and as the day drew nearer, my excitement grew. Jesse and I had not been anywhere together without the children since the Centennial Exhibition. My only disappointment was that Dick Liddil would be part of our group. Much as I tried, I couldn't shed my dislike of the man.

But I wouldn't let his presence spoil my fun. Annie and I had new dresses and bonnets, and Jesse hired a carriage to take us to the track. The weather was bright and crisp, the bunting draped across the grandstand fluttering in a soft breeze, sun sparkling on the little lake at the center of the track.

We trooped to the paddock to admire Jim Malone and wish his jockey luck. Annie, who knew about horses and racing, remarked on the competition, while I preferred to admire the other ladies' bonnets and dresses. The men escorted us to a box in the grandstand, then went to place their bets.

We had been seated only a short time when Annie nudged me in the side. "Who's that woman who is staring at us?" she asked, nodding toward the unshaded wooden bleachers to our left.

I followed her gaze and to my dismay, recognized Mrs. Peabody. She was with a different man this time, an older, foreign looking sort, in a rough coat and trousers. She wore the same bonnet I had seen before, but a different dress, of bright purple silk, very low cut. "Her name is

Mrs. Peabody," I said. "I knew her when I was a girl back in Missouri."

"Is that man her husband?"

"I don't think so." The man said something, then laughed, open-mouthed and braying. Mrs. Peabody's expression grew more pinched about the mouth. "She's fallen on hard times, I fear," I said.

"Try to ignore her," Annie advised. "I don't want them coming over here."

Ashamed as I was of the sentiment, I didn't want Mrs. Peabody and her companion coming over to us, either. I looked away, some of the brightness of the day dimmed.

Dick Liddil was the first of the men to return to our box. He carried a mug of beer and smelled as if he'd already had several. "Can I fetch you ladies some refreshment?" he asked.

"No thank you." Annie didn't wrinkle her nose, but I could tell she wanted to. She didn't like Dick any more than I did.

I searched for some safe topic of conversation. "I can't remember if you said or not, Mr. Liddil," I said. "Are you married?"

"Not exactly." He grinned, his teeth flashing white beneath his luxurious mustache.

"What do you mean 'not exactly'?" Annie asked. "You're either married or you aren't."

He scratched his head. "There's a woman in Missouri who calls herself my wife, and I live with her when I'm in the area, but we've never made it official or anything."

Annie sniffed and looked away. Dick continued to grin at me until I began to feel even more uncomfortable. I was relieved when Jesse and Frank returned. Frank stepped into the box and handed Annie the ticket for the bet he'd placed for her, but Jesse remained with his hand on the open door, looking around.

"Is something wrong?" Frank asked.

"I thought I saw someone I recognized." He squinted toward the bleachers.

"Who is it?" I asked.

He shook his head. "I thought it was a sheriff's deputy from Clay County, but I must have been mistaken."

Frank rose and stood beside his brother, joining him in staring toward the bleachers. Each man had a hand poised to reach for the guns they always wore. I looked away, shivering despite the warm sun. I was reminded of my wedding day, when the ceremony had been interrupted by the approach of two strangers on the street outside. Back then, the possibility of gunplay had been exciting, even amusing. But the novelty had worn off long ago—after Northfield, when the terrible dangers of Jesse's lifestyle had been driven home to me.

"Hello, there!" A portly, red-faced man approached the box. Grinning, he seized Jesse's hand. "I'll be hornswoggled, if it isn't Jesse. Jesse James." He turned to Frank. "And Frank! Amazing to see you both here, in the flesh."

Jesse pulled his hand from the man's grasp. "You are mistaken. My name is Howard. J.T. Howard. This is my brother-in-law, Mr. Woodson."

Frank scowled at the man, one hand tucked beneath his coat, I was sure resting on the butt of his pistol.

"Aww sure. I get it." The man winked. "Imagine, the famous James brothers, right here in Nashville."

"Do *you* live in Nashville now?" Frank asked.

"Oh no. I'm just visiting. A day at the races, you know."

"So are we," Frank said. "Just visiting."

The man turned to Jesse again. "You're not going to hold the place up are you, Jesse? Could you at least wait until after the fifth race pays out? I've got a tidy sum wagered on a horse in that race."

It was clear the man had had too much to drink. He spoke in the loud, overly enunciated tones of the inebriated, and his eyes held a glassy sheen.

Jesse gripped the man's shoulder. "I told you my name is Howard." His fingers dug into the man's shoulder, bunching his suit jacket, crumpling the man in pain.

"Let go of me!" The man squawked. "What are you doing?" His skin was the color of paste, sweat beading on his forehead.

"I'm teaching you a lesson." Jesse's face was impassive, but his eyes were icy with fury. The man sank to his knees, tears streaming down his cheeks.

I stared at Jesse, stunned by such cold cruelty in a man from whom I and my children had known nothing but kindness. "Dave, please," I protested.

Jesse glanced at me, then released his hold on the man, who fell forward into our box, clutching his shoulder. "I'll have you arrested!" the injured man wailed.

"Not if you know what's good for you." Jesse nudged the man with his boot. "Get up."

The man struggled to his feet, his eyes never leaving Jesse's face, fear sobering his expression.

Jesse took a gold coin from his pocket and pressed it into the man's hand. "Buy yourself a drink on Dave Howard," he said, as pleasantly as if he'd been treating a friend.

The man took the coin and backed away, out of the shadow of the grandstand. Then he turned and ran.

I looked around, expecting a crowd to have gathered, sure I would see a phalanx of police making their way toward us. Yet no one even looked our way. The exchange had taken less than a minute, and I realized now that Frank and Dick had positioned themselves to shield the scene from the rest of the crowd.

"Mr. Howard, don't you think that was a little excessive?" Annie asked, her voice frosty.

"I had to shut him up and I did." Jesse stepped into the box, pulling the door to behind him, and took his seat beside me.

"Who was that?" I asked.

"Never saw him before in my life," Frank said, sitting between Annie and Dick.

"You put the fear of God into him," Dick said. "That's the way to do it. Show 'em who's boss."

Jesse ignored this praise. "The race is about to start," he said, consulting his racing form. "I like a horse called Gussie's Gumption in this one. What do you think, Buck?"

"They're all two-year olds," Frank said. "I didn't see anything worth betting on."

Gussie's Gumption lost the bet, and fifty dollars for Jesse. He tore the losing ticket into tiny pieces and let them drift to the floor of the box, watching them fall with all the concentration of a child admiring his first snow.

Jim Malone raced in the second heat. Jesse, Frank, Dick and even Annie stood to cheer the horses around the track. I sat silent, unable to shake the haunting image of the portly man crumpled at Jesse's feet, and the impassive cruelty of my husband's actions. Always before, I had dismissed news accounts that portrayed Jesse as a heartless killer as over-dramatization by the press. The Jesse I knew was no more a killer than I was.

Tonight I had seen another side to my husband—a side that frightened and confused me.

Jim Malone won the race. Jesse was ebullient, slapping Frank on the back, then pulling me close and kissing my cheek. I smiled, feigning delight, but the day was ruined for me. Even the money Jesse won did little to ease my dismay.

I kept watching the crowd for the portly man, but saw him no more. Mrs. Peabody and her escort left soon after the second race, the man smiling smugly. Mrs. Peabody ducked her head as they passed our box.

We stayed for two more races after Jim Malone's win, but Jesse grew restless, rising from his seat and pacing our box. "There's no point staying here any longer," he said. "Let's go home."

Annie looked as if she wanted to argue, but Frank gave her a quelling look. "Yes, we'd better go," he said, and stood also.

Jesse sent Dick to fetch the hired carriage. We rode in silence to Frank and Annie's farm and collected the children, who were sugar-smeared and full of tales of helping Mrs. Morrison with her baking.

Dick hung around our house for half an hour or so, as if he expected to be invited to supper, but Jesse finally sent him on his way.

Later that evening, when the dishes were done and the children sent to bed, after Jesse had smoked the day's last cigar and helped me out of my corset and combed out my hair, I crawled into bed beside him and turned down the lamp. I lay on my back, staring into the darkness, the image of the lamp flame still glowing on my retinas. Beside me, Jesse rearranged his pillow and settled under the covers.

"Would you have killed that man today?" I asked.

"What man?"

I wouldn't believe he'd already forgotten; he was being contrary, a tendency I'd always disliked in him. "The man at the track. The one who recognized you and called you Jesse."

"He had enough sense to shut up before I killed him."

I rose up on one elbow and tried to see his face in the darkness; it was only a blur of darker shadows against shadows. "Are you saying you would have killed him if he hadn't stopped talking?"

"I would have done what I had to do."

The icy calm of his voice chilled me. "How could you kill a man merely for talking?" I asked, trying to see the reasoning behind such a judgment.

"It was his choice. I drew a line and he had to decide whether or not cross it."

"Who gave you the right to draw the line?"

"Life is all about drawing lines. Every day. Surviving is a matter of knowing when to draw them—and when to step across."

"So if a man crosses your line, you kill him?"

"He had a choice. He didn't have to step across."

"And you don't have to shoot him!"

"But I do."

"No you don't. Plenty of men go their whole lives never shooting anybody."

"Sure. Men who live soft, safe lives behind a desk or store counter. That's not the kind of life I live. But if I start living like a store clerk or an accountant or a man like that—if a man crosses my line, and I don't make him pay, then I might as well hang it up tomorrow, because I'll be dead or behind bars within the week."

I lay back on my pillow, ignoring the hot tears that spilled from my eyes, anger and fear churning my stomach. "Sometimes I wish you *were* a store clerk or accountant," I said.

"No you don't." He entwined his fingers in mine. "Because then I wouldn't be me. You love me as much for *what* I am as for *who* I am."

I wanted to pull my hand away, to deny this accusation. But I couldn't. I wouldn't. "How do you know that?" I asked.

"It's the way we're made." He raised my hand to his lips and kissed my knuckles. "There's a wildness in you that nobody but me sees—that part of you would never be happy with a clerk or an accountant. Just like I'd never be happy with a schoolteacher like Annie."

He rolled to me and gathered me close. I made no protest, but clung to him. "Jesse, I'm scared," I whispered.

He smoothed my hair and kissed my forehead. "Sometimes, I am too," he said. "But it always passes after a while. It will for you, too."

For the rest of the year, Jesse and Dick traveled back and forth between our house in Nashville and who knows where. I heard rumors of stagecoaches way-laid and stores robbed, but these were easy enough to discount. For years, the James Gang had been credited with every robbery between Tennessee and California. Apparently the disgrace of being taken advantage of by robbers was lessened if the culprits happened to be the notorious Jesse James and company.

I knew he spent some of this time at racetracks around the country, watching Jim Malone win purse after purse. The horse's victories thrilled me, not because I cared about horse racing, but because I thought the excitement of racing and the winnings he collected might encourage Jesse to set aside some of his more dangerous pursuits.

But at the end of the racing season, Jesse sold his interest in the horse. "I got a good profit for him," he explained when I questioned this decision.

"What will you do now?" I asked.

His smile gave me no comfort. "Oh, I expect I'll find something."

In January, Frank turned thirty-eight, and Annie invited us to dinner in his honor. Jesse presented his brother with a new Colt revolver in a handsome case, which seemed to please Frank, but made Annie frown. I knew if she had her way, Frank would never have cause to fire a gun again.

Talk at the dinner table was all politics. President Garfield, a Republican, had won the last election and would be sworn in in March. "Garfield seems more moderate than Grant or Hayes," Frank remarked as he helped himself to creamed potatoes.

"Who's president doesn't matter as much to me as the man in the governor's chair," Jesse said. "Crittenden may be a Democrat, but he's no friend of ours."

Governor Thomas T. Crittenden had taken the oath of office that week as governor of Missouri. Though we had lived in Tennessee for three years now, Missouri would always be home, and Jesse and Frank paid keen attention to politics there. Crittenden's election had animated Jesse as few politician's had done before.

"Did you read his inaugural address in the paper?" he asked Frank. "The old goat practically declared war on us and our supporters."

"Times have changed," Frank observed mildly. "People want to put the past behind them and focus on earning a good living for themselves and their families."

I wondered if Frank was talking about the citizens of Missouri—or about himself.

"Since when has any politician cared two cents for the common working man?" Jesse asked. "Old Crittenden's concerned about taking care of the rich bankers and railroad men who got him into office in the first place. It sticks in his craw that a handful of former guerrillas—men he fought against in the war—have those bankers and railroad men shaking in their boots."

"The governor of a state can marshal a lot of firepower behind him," Frank said. "If Crittenden really is declaring war on the James Gang, the smart thing to do might be to find another line of work."

"Better men than him have been after me for the past fifteen years and none of them have succeeded yet," Jesse said. "I'm not afraid of

Crittenden and any army he can muster."

"Maybe you ought to be," Annie said. She rose and began clearing the table. "No more talk of any of this. It's time to bring the children in so we can cut Frank's cake."

"Did you bake it yourself?" Frank grinned at her. Annie was not known for her skills in the kitchen.

"Mrs. Morrison baked it," Annie said. "And Rob helped put on the candles."

"All those candles are liable to attract the Fire Brigade," Jesse teased. I was happy to see Annie's remarks and his disagreement with Frank hadn't put him out of sorts.

As the children rushed in from the kitchen where they'd been eating, he gathered Tim and Mary into his lap. "Did you clean your plates?" he asked them. "And drink all your milk?"

"Yes, Papa." Tim put his arms around his father's neck and hugged him close. "For my next birthday, can I have a cake as big as Uncle Ben's?"

"Even bigger," Jesse said.

"With choc'late," Mary added.

"Yes, with chocolate." He smiled at them and my heart turned over, moved by love and fear. All I wanted was for all of us to be safe and healthy—for Governor Crittenden to forget Jesse existed, and for Jesse to stop fighting the banks and railroad and whatever demons stirred inside him.

In early March, Jesse left home again, saying he was going to visit his cousin, Wood Hite, in Kentucky. He returned only a few days later, in high spirits and riding a new bay gelding. He had plenty of money, both greenbacks and gold and silver coins. I could only guess how he'd acquired such a sum, though of course he kept to the fiction that he'd made the profit off the sale of commodities.

Dick Liddil was with him, his sly smile and overly-courteous manner fraying my nerves. "Can't you send him away?" I asked that first evening when we were alone.

"Dick's useful to me right now," Jesse said. "You can tolerate him for a few days."

Jesse was reluctant to even venture out of doors for the next few days, which confirmed my suspicions that the money was ill-gotten. He was waiting for the furor over the robbery to die down before he showed his face around town.

Saturday morning, he sent Dick to town to buy the latest papers. "There might be something in them for your scrapbooks," he told me, laughter in his blue eyes.

Dick returned within a half an hour, hurrying up the drive almost at a run, several papers tucked beneath his arm. His sallow complexion was pale, his eyes agitated. "Bad news," he said as he burst in the door. "Where's Jesse?"

"In our room." I followed Dick down the hall, to the bedroom where Jesse was polishing a pair of boots.

"Bill Ryan's been arrested," Dick announced, tossing the papers on the bed. "He's sitting in the jail right here in Nashville."

Jesse set aside the boot he'd been working on and picked up one of the papers.

"Right there." Dick pointed to a column of print. "Says he's been positively identified as one of the men who robbed the Muscle Shoals payroll last week."

I picked up another of the papers and scanned the front page until I found a similar article. "Three bandits relieved payroll supervisor Alexander G. Smith of $5,240.18 in gold and silver coin and greenbacks at gunpoint," I read. "The money was the payroll of workers on the Muscle Shoals canal project."

Jesse frowned at the article. "Somebody better let Buck know," he said.

"Let me know what?" I turned and saw Frank standing in the doorway, Tim holding on to his hand. "Nobody answered my knock, so Tim let me in," Frank said.

"Tim, go play with your sister," I said.

"I wanna stay with Uncle Ben and Papa," the boy whined.

"Go to your sister, Tim," Jesse said firmly.

When the child was gone, Frank stepped into the bedroom and closed the door. "I came as soon as I read the papers," he said.

"No need for alarm." Jesse tossed the paper aside. "Bill won't say anything."

"Can you be sure about that?" Frank asked. "He's not one of the men we rode with during the war. These young fellows don't have the same sense of loyalty."

"Bill won't talk," Jesse said, but there was little conviction in his voice.

"There's something else," Frank said. "Did you notice who made the arrest?"

"I didn't read that far," Jesse said.

"Justice W. L. Earthman." Frank's scowl deepened. "The same Bill Earthman who's spent the day at the track with Dave Howard and Ben Woodson on several occasions."

"How long do you think it's going to take him to make the connection between Mr. Howard and Jesse James?" Dick asked. "Especially if Bill starts talking?"

Jesse sucked in a deep breath. "We'd better leave," he said.

"The sooner the better," Frank said. "I've already got Annie packing."

"Leave?" I cried, alarmed. "Where will we go?"

"Back to Missouri," Jesse said. "I'll send you and the children ahead on the train. I'll meet up with you when I can."

"Missouri? Jesse, it isn't safe there."

"We'll be safer there, among country we know," Frank said. "There are still people there we can trust."

The brothers' quick agreement let me know they'd discussed this before. The James brothers hadn't escaped capture for so long by failing to plan ahead.

"Get the children and pack a trunk," Jesse said. "We'll send for what we can later."

I wanted to argue against such a hasty decision, but the grim look in Jesse's eyes silenced my protests. I hastened to pull our traveling trunks from the box room off the kitchen, mentally cataloguing the items we would have to take with us and those we would be forced to leave behind.

Frank returned to his home while Jesse and Dick readied the horses for travel and collected all the guns we owned and made sure they were loaded.

The children sensed the new tension in their parents; Mary began to cry for no reason, while Tim followed me from room to room, peppering me with questions. "Where are we going, Mama?" he asked. "Why are we going now?"

I made up answers I hoped would satisfy him, pretending we were going to visit relatives, and that our stay would be temporary.

But I had heard the determination in Jesse's voice when he'd cited Missouri as our destination. It was the place he always came back to, drawn there by friends as well as enemies. That the governor of the state himself had declared his determination to put an end to men like Jesse deterred my husband not one bit. We were going home, and I knew we were going there to stay.

Chapter Seventeen

But before Missouri, there was Kentucky. "You and the children can stay with my old friends, the Carters, and I'll join you in a few days," Jesse said. "We'll travel to Kansas City together."

"We can't just invite ourselves into someone's home," I said.

"The Carters won't ask questions," Jesse said. "They've known me and Frank for years."

"What about Frank and Annie?" I asked. "Where will they go?"

"Annie and Rob are going to her father's place. Frank's going to stay in Nashville a little while and wrap up our affairs there."

I didn't like the idea of being separated from Jesse at a time of such danger. And I didn't like the idea of staying with strangers. But I couldn't argue with Jesse's years of experience in staying one step ahead of the law, and I trusted him to keep us safe.

So the children and I took the train to Kentucky, where the Carters welcomed us with open arms. Jesse joined us a few days later. "Is everything all right?" I asked anxiously, as soon as he and I had a moment alone.

"Everything is fine," he assured me. "No one has any idea where we are. We'll rest up here a couple more days, then head to Missouri. We'll be fine."

After supper that night, Jesse pushed his chair back from the table. "Care for a hand of cards?" Mr. Carter asked.

"No gambling in my kitchen," Mrs. Carter said.

"I wouldn't want to violate the rules of the house," Jesse said, eyes twinkling. "What if instead of wagering for money, we teach you ladies to play?"

I laughed. "You want to teach me to play cards?"

"Faro." Jesse pulled a deck from the inside pocket of his coat. "You too, Liv. You never can tell when such knowledge might come in handy."

"You do say the most surprising things, Jesse" Mrs. Carter said. But she removed her apron and joined us at the table.

I watched with interest as Jesse explained the value of the various cards in the deck. Both our parents would have been shocked to see us: our Methodist forebears believed card-playing was every bit as sinful as dancing. But I'd long since ceased worrying about what such seemingly petty things could do to the health of my soul.

Jesse had just finished laying out the cards when the Carters' eldest son came to the door. "Dad? Can I talk to you for a minute?"

Jesse and Mr. Carter exchanged glances, then the older man slid his chair back and joined his son in the hallway. They conferred in hushed tones. My eyes met Jesse's. I could see that he, like I, was straining to hear their words, but I could make out nothing.

Mr. Carter returned to the room. "There might be trouble," he said.

Those words turned my heart to ice. My chair clattered to the floor as I shoved up from it. Jesse put a hand on my arm. "Stay here," he said. Then he drew his revolver and followed our friend into the front room.

I followed, moving quietly so that Jesse wouldn't hear and order me away. But I was determined to know what was going on. Jesse and Carter stood on either side of a large front window, guns raised, watching the road. Carter's son stood near the door in a similar pose.

"What is going on?" Carter's wife, Liv, spoke from behind me.

"The sheriff is out there with four other men on horseback," Carter said. "I suspect there are others hidden in the woods back there, maybe some circling around."

I swallowed hard and fought a wave of faintness. "Are we surrounded?" I asked, my voice thin and high-pitched.

Jesse spoke without looking at me. "We don't know. Right now they're not doing anything but sitting there and looking at the house."

"Maybe we should fire a shot to warn them off," Carter's son said. He was seventeen, a big, broad-shouldered young man with the beginnings of a moustache on his upper lip. His face was pale, but he wore a determined expression.

"No," his father said. "We'll wait. Force them to make the first move."

We remained frozen in place, a tense *tableaux vivant*. The only sound was the steady tick of the mantel clock as it counted off the seconds. I stared at the back of Jesse's head, wishing I had the power to see through his eyes what waited on the road in front of the house. He stood so still, seemingly calm, eyes fixed on the road, gun at the ready. Was he afraid of facing death, or did he cope by refusing to consider the possibility? Did he have a strategy for dealing with the situation, or would he react on instinct?

As if feeling my gaze on him, Jesse turned and looked at me. "Sweetheart, go upstairs and check on the children," he said. "Stay with them until I come for you."

I started to protest, but part of me very badly wanted to know that the children were okay. So I turned and raced up the stairs, pausing at the door of our room to catch my breath before I tip-toed inside.

The children were asleep, Mary on her side, one knee drawn up to her chin, the other leg stretched out. Tim lay beside her on his stomach, arms folded beneath him. I noticed how tall he was getting, the hem of his trousers up above his ankles.

I tucked the blanket around them and smoothed my hand down Tim's back, careful not to wake him. Then I went to the window and pushed the curtain aside a scant inch so I could look out.

The scene I saw chilled my blood. Five men on horseback, guns at the ready. They faced the house, expressions unreadable from this distance but their intent clear. I gripped the windowsill to keep from sinking to the floor, heart racing, every breath a tortured gasp. I had lost countless hours over the years in fear for Jesse's life, but that anxiety was a poor counterfeit of the terror that gripped me now. Those guns held the promise of real death—an end to the life I knew.

An end to the man I loved.

I glanced at the children again, at their sweet, innocent faces. I tried to remember a time when I had been so unaware of danger. It seemed another lifetime ago, in a different world.

I bent to kiss each sweet head then, one hand in my pocket, stroking the grip of the pistol Jesse had given me so long ago, I slipped out the door and down the stairs. If Jesse was to die tonight, then I would be with him. I would not let him leave without me there.

I stepped into a scene unchanged from moments before. Jesse and Carter still stood on either side of the window, Carter's son by the door, weapons drawn. Liv waited in the passage between living and dining room. I took up a post beside her. The minutes stretched on—five minutes, then ten. I wanted to scream or weep or do anything to find release. But like the others, I could only wait.

Then the three men drew away from the window and door at once. "They're leaving," Carter's son said. "Why the hell are they doing that?"

I rushed to Jesse, though I didn't touch him. I didn't want to hinder him if he should suddenly need both hands free to shoot. Instead, I looked past him out the window, at the billowing dust that was the only sign a group of riders had been there.

"Maybe they're going for reinforcements," Carter said.

"We'll leave now." Jesse holstered his gun.

"The first train you could catch doesn't leave the station until nine o'clock," Liv said. "What are you going to do with Zee and the children for the next seven hours?"

"We don't have to act hastily," Carter said. He turned to his son. "Go to town and see if you can find out what's going on."

"Be careful," his mother said.

The boy was already shrugging into his coat. "I won't let them see me," he said. "But I'll find out."

Jesse and I retreated up the stairs—I to check on the children, he to make sure our luggage was ready to go at a moment's notice. Carter had headed to the barn to saddle horses for all of us. The thought of fleeing cross-country with the children terrified me. "If I have to go, you and the children will stay here," Jesse said as he closed and locked our trunks.

I nodded, mute. I'd already decided that would be the safest course. "I'll meet up with you in Kansas City when I can," he said.

"I wonder why they left like that," I said.

We had our answer soon enough. Within the hour, young Carter had returned. He must have galloped his horse all the way from town, but he burst into the kitchen in high spirits. "They left because they're all cowards," he crowed.

"What do you mean?" His mother helped him out of his coat and took his hat from him.

"It's the talk of the saloon," the boy said. "They followed Jesse's trail here, so they were pretty sure they had him. But when it came time to bust in, they lost their nerve. They started talking about how he probably had a bunch of men with him, and what a good shot he was. One of the men said he didn't have anything personal against Jesse—that the James boys hadn't done anything to hurt him or his family or even this town. Another suggested they didn't even have the proper jurisdiction. They might be risking their lives, only to have to let Jesse go. Someone else said something about you being wanted in Missouri, not Kentucky. In the end, they talked themselves out of doing anything."

I stared at the boy, incredulous. Jesse laughed. Carter joined in, and clapped him on the back. "Saved by your reputation," Carter said. "If that don't beat all."

Once again, Jesse's uncanny luck had come through for him. He really did seem invincible.

But it was a long time before I slept that night. We see so much of life through a lens ground by others. The first part of my life I viewed the world my parents wanted me to see. Then Jesse had guided my vision, presenting life as he saw it—the legend of the outlaw who would never know defeat.

This day I had seen things for myself. I had faced the dark side of the legend, felt the chill of the grave, glimpsed a future draped in black. I could no longer shrug off the danger as something abstract and distant. It was a monster that sat on my doorstep, one I knew would never really leave.

The next few weeks passed in a fog of weariness and tension. When we finally moved into a little house on a quiet street in Kansas City, I slept for twelve hours, while Jesse watched the children and kept them quiet.

Jesse grew his beard long and began carrying a walking cane. He assumed the name of Jackson, which I always had trouble remembering. Thankfully, the children were too young to notice.

Annie and Frank settled nearby. Annie was happy to be near her family once more, but Frank was more unsettled than ever. He missed his farm and the friends he'd made in Nashville; he and Jesse spent long hours in our front parlor, talking and sometimes arguing.

Other men joined them—Jesse's cousins, Wood and Clarence Hite; Dick Liddil; and a new man I hadn't met before, Charley Ford. I liked Charley right away. He was young and affable, shyly polite, with rough country manners. He lacked Dick's polish and looks, but he always seemed to me to be honest and sincere. He was the first to offer to help me with a heavy package, and would chop wood or light a fire in the stove without being asked.

We lived off the money from the Muscle Shoals robbery, and what was left of the funds I'd put aside from the sale of the racehorse, Kentucky; for once Jesse resisted the impulse to gamble it away. When he wasn't riding the countryside with Frank and the others, he visited saloons, where he drank a single beer and debated politics with other men. I began to hope that we might return to the quiet life we'd known in Tennessee, before Jesse reverted to his outlaw ways.

July third, word reached Kansas City that President Garfield had been shot. The assassin, Charles Guiteau, was reportedly a madman. The idea that a lunatic would approach a man—even the president of the

United States—and shoot him for no reason, left the whole country reeling. Jesse spent the day downtown, waiting with other men in front of the newspaper office for word of the president's condition to be posted. For a little while, at least, the country had forgotten about Jesse James, and I breathed easier.

The president still lingered on July 14 when Jesse kissed me after supper and told me not to wait up. "I may be gone a few days, but don't worry," he said.

"Where are you going?" I asked.

"Don't let that concern you, sweetheart." He shrugged into his coat and reached for his hat.

"I wish you weren't always leaving," I said.

"You know I don't like to be away from you," he said. "But that's how things have to be."

Why do they have to be that way? I wanted to shout after him. But I knew my pleas and protests would have no effect on Jesse. He was a slave to his own restlessness, and I was a slave to him. As much as I had grown to hate some of the things he did, I hated the thought of life without him more.

I had just put the children to bed when knocking at the front door startled me. We rarely had visitors, and certainly not at night. Leaving the lights off, I tip-toed to the front window and looked out. I could make out only a shadowy form on the steps. The knock sounded again. "Josie, let me in, it's me, Fannie!" Annie's voice was thin with agitation.

Heart pounding, I jerked open the door. "What is it? What's wrong? Is someone hurt?"

"No. Not yet anyway." She moved past me, Rob in her arms. "Is Jesse here?" she asked.

"No. He left a little while ago." I followed her over to the sofa, where she settled Rob and wrapped him in blankets. I lit a lamp and turned it down low. "What are you doing here?" I asked. "Why do you want to see Jesse?"

"I'm here because I couldn't stand to stay in that empty house another second," she said.

"Where's Frank?"

The lamplight shadowed her eyes and cheekbones as she turned to face me. "He's gone off with Jesse," she said. "I'm sure they're up to no good. Those others—the Hite boys and Dick and Charley—were all with them."

My stomach knotted. Like Annie, I knew of only one reason such a group of men would ride out after dark. But still, I tried to deny it. "Maybe they just went for a ride," I said.

"They're going to hold up a train or rob a bank or something, I know it." She clenched her fists at her sides. "And after Frank promised me!"

That Frank would be involved surprised me. He'd seemed determined to leave his outlaw ways behind, and he'd never hidden his disdain for the Hite brothers and Charley Ford, dismissing them as feckless rubes who knew nothing about fighting. "What makes you think Frank is going to commit a crime, when he's been law abiding for so many years now?" I asked. "Even when Jesse formed a new gang, Frank never took part."

"He's been restless since we came back to Missouri," she said. "He says he doesn't have enough to do, and Jesse's over at the house all the time, talking to him. I know they've been planning something."

"Jesse hasn't managed to persuade Frank to join him thus far—why now?"

She sank into a chair. "I know he's been worried about money."

"So you think he's doing it for money? For you and Rob." If she thought Frank was doing this for their family, maybe it would be easier for her to accept.

"I don't want him to break the law for me," she protested. "What if he's shot? Or killed?"

I sat across from her. "I worry about those things, too," I said. "But there's nothing we can do."

"I should have put my foot down. I should have told him I knew what he was up to and wouldn't have it."

"I don't know, Annie. If I tried that with Jesse, it would only make him angry—and more determined than ever to do what he wanted."

She looked at me, her eyes full of misery. "How do you stand it, Zee—knowing he's out there making himself a target?"

"I don't think about it." Denial had helped me survive thus far, though since that afternoon in Kentucky it was more difficult to pretend our life was normal.

"What do we do now?" Annie asked.

"We do what we've always done," I said. "We wait and hope and pray no harm comes to them."

She nervously pleated her skirt between her fingers. "When Frank and I first married, I was so ignorant and naïve. I thought being an outlaw's wife was glamorous and exciting. The conventional life of my friends seemed boring in comparison."

I nodded. "I never wanted an ordinary life," I said. "But I never thought much about the danger."

"There's nothing glamorous or exciting about it," she said firmly. Her eyes blazed with anger and the muscles of her jaw clenched.

"The key is to stay busy." I patted her hand. "Find something else to pass the time and occupy your mind." I stood and walked to my workbasket. "You can help me wind some wool I just bought to knit Jesse a waistcoat."

So Annie held the skeins of wool while I wound the yarn into balls. "Frank tells me you and he have been reading Shakespeare," I said, hoping to take our minds off our wayward husbands. "What is your favorite story?"

"*Much Ado about Nothing*," she said. "I like the character Beatrice, who is independent and stands up to the men in her life."

As Annie had always been independent. When she'd wanted to marry Frank, she hadn't let her father's disapproval stop her; she'd run away and eloped. If Frank really was going against her wishes now, would she stand up to him as well? "Once before, you told me you'd leave Frank if he went back to being an outlaw," I said carefully.

"Yes, I said that." Her shoulders sagged. "I thought I could do it, but now . . ." She looked to where Rob had fallen asleep on the sofa. "I can't imagine living without Frank in my life."

"I know," I said. "We worry about them and wish they would consider our feelings more—but we're tied to them now." We were bound by vows and children and a web of memories and tangles of meaning that held us as tightly as any net.

On the night of July 14, a Chicago, Rock Island and Pacific train was robbed east of Winston, Missouri by five masked men who emptied the express safe. The robbery began badly, when a conductor and another man died as the results of being hit by stray bullets. Everyone agreed the men were shot accidentally and not intentionally, but the deaths of two innocent bystanders made even Jesse's supporters uneasy. In the days that followed the holdup, people were more free to criticize him, and many called for his arrest, and even demanded he be hanged.

As I clipped these articles and added them to my scrapbooks, I pondered this change from avenging hero of the people to common criminal. Jesse hadn't changed. He was still the handsome charmer who carried out his thefts with flare and daring. He still targeted the rich express companies, railroads, and banks, and he still presented himself as a champion of the South.

Jesse had not changed, but times had. Maybe the majority of people no longer saw the banks and railroads as enemies, but as the means for their own prosperity. The men interviewed in the newspapers seemed to see Jesse as stealing from *them*, and not some faceless corporation. His thefts benefitted no one but himself, and hurt the reputation of Missouri.

Though Jesse's own cunning and luck had played a part in keeping him safe over the years, he primarily owed his life to the protection of friends and neighbors. If even one of them had turned on him, he would have been imprisoned—or worse—years before. By returning to Missouri, Jesse and Frank sought refuge in the country and with the people they knew best. But I wondered if in these changing times they could truly count on the loyalty of their countrymen.

On July 28, 1881, Governor Crittenden issued a proclamation offering a $10,000 reward each for the capture and conviction of Frank and Jesse James. A man could labor twenty years and not earn such a sum. With $10,000 he could buy a fine house, a new carriage and horses, jewelry and clothes and furniture of every kind, and still have money left over.

It was the kind of money that could turn a man's head and make him question his loyalty to anyone.

While I worried about the price on Jesse's head, he dismissed the sum with a shrug. "The money just shows how desperate they all are," he said. "The railroads and the government men hate me because I make them look bad. All of them together haven't been able to stop me before now, and a dollar sign on a wanted poster isn't going to change that."

If anything, Jesse enjoyed the new spotlight focused on him. He read the best articles from the papers out loud at the breakfast table, and laughed whenever a lawman was quoted as saying the James Gang would soon be apprehended.

True to her word, Annie did not leave Frank, but she could scarcely stand to be in the same room with Jesse. She clearly held him responsible for what she saw as her husband's downfall. When she and Frank came to dinner the first week in September to celebrate Jesse's thirty-fourth birthday, she sat as far from Jesse as possible and avoided looking at him.

"Frank says he's only participating in the robberies because he's worried about Jesse," she whispered to me later, as we sat in the parlor sewing while the men smoked on the back porch. "He thinks Jesse needs his steadying hand along to prevent him from doing something foolish. I told him his brother was a grown man—let him be an idiot if he chooses. If he's going to risk his life, there's no reason Frank should do so."

"Jesse is not an idiot," I said sharply.

Her mouth tightened. "You can't say he's not being reckless," she said. "Risking more than he ought. How much longer can he flaunt the law this way before all that reward money tempts someone to turn him in? And Frank has the same reward on his head—when all along, everything has been Jesse's fault."

I gave up the pretense of sewing and laid my needlework aside. "Frank is Jesse's *older* brother," I reminded her. "He joined the guerrillas first and Jesse followed. He was with Jesse at every robbery until after Northfield. Jesse didn't lead him into anything. And wasn't it you yourself who said Frank was the one who planned the robberies—that Frank was the one really responsible for their success?"

"Jesse takes advantage of Frank's goodness," she countered. "He knows how responsible Frank is. How he has such a strong sense of duty. Jesse can be as reckless as he wants, knowing Frank will be there to clean up after him."

"That's ridiculous! If Jesse wasn't smart enough to plan everything out, there's no telling what Frank would bumble into. It was Jesse who made friends with John Edwards and got the press on their side. And it was Jesse who helped a wounded Frank get home safely after the disaster at Northfield."

"Jesse *planned* that fiasco at Northfield," she snapped. "Frank never wanted to go up there. He only did it to try to protect his brother." Her hands shook so much it took three tries to secure her knitting needles in a ball of yarn. She shoved the whole mess into her bag and stood. "I can see you're as foolish as Jesse," she said.

"I don't call it foolish for a woman to defend her husband from ridiculous accusations." I rose and faced her.

"The only thing ridiculous is how you're still so besotted with the man after all these years. I'd think you'd have grown up enough to see him for the cruel, manipulative braggart he is."

"How dare you say such things about my husband!"

"I'm only telling the truth!"

We had long since ceased whispering. Our shouts drew the men from the back steps. Frank rushed in, Jesse following. "What's going on?" Frank demanded.

"Sounds to me like we've interrupted a good, old-fashioned cat fight." Jesse leaned against the door jamb, a half-smile on his lips.

"What is this about?" Frank asked Annie.

She avoided meeting his gaze. "I'm ready to go home now," she said. Without another word, she turned and walked out the front door.

Frank looked at me. "What were you two arguing about?" he asked.

I turned away. "It doesn't matter. You'd better take her home."

When Frank and Annie had gone, Jesse pulled me close. "Were you defending my honor?" he asked.

"You heard?"

"Enough to gather that Annie blames me for leading Buck astray." He laughed. "Trust me, Buck never needed anyone to lead him into trouble. He always knows exactly what he's about."

"Do you know what you're about?" I asked. "Committing these robberies when the government is making things so hot for you?"

"Now's the perfect time to strike," he said. "The banks and railroads think this reward has made them safe—that ordinary men would be driven into hiding. They forget that we aren't ordinary men."

"Oh, you aren't, are you?"

He smoothed his hand down my backside and pulled me tight against him, pressing me into the hard ridge of his arousal. "I don't feel very ordinary when I'm with you." He kissed my temple, his lips resting over my steadily-beating pulse. "Are you still besotted with me, Zee?"

"Yes." But my infatuation was tempered by the knowledge that I had aligned myself to a man I would never fully understand or control.

I took Jesse's hand, and led him toward our bedroom. "Show me how extraordinary you are tonight," I teased.

"An invitation I can't refuse."

I smiled, even as I blinked back tears. I was no longer a blind girl who believed love would solve all our problems and erase all our differences. From the early days of our love, Jesse had fascinated and excited me. Now at times he terrified me as well.

I knew Jesse would do things to hurt me, even when he didn't mean to. I accepted that, even though I wished for a different kind of life. Loving Jesse came with a price I'd agreed to pay.

Two days later, Jesse and Frank stopped a Chicago and Alton train east of Independence Missouri, at a place called Blue Cut. They piled rocks and limbs on the track and signaled the locomotive to stop, then ransacked the express safe and robbed the passengers. According to newspaper reports, Jesse talked and joked with the passengers even as he relieved them of their valuables.

The robbery at Blue Cut took place five years to the day after the tragedy at Northfield. I wondered if this, more than concern for his brother or a desire for money, had persuaded Frank to come out of retirement. Was this Jesse and Frank's way of redeeming that date—of proclaiming to the world that they remained undefeated and uncowed?

"Did you really tell them you intended to keep robbing trains all your life?" I asked Jesse a few days later, as we pored over reports of the hold-up. "And that you would do so even if they loaded the train with soldiers?"

"I wanted to send the message that I wasn't afraid," he said. "And that I had no intention of slowing down."

But he was forced to slow down for a little while. Shortly after the Blue Cut raid, Frank and Annie announced they were moving east, to Baltimore. I don't know what exactly precipitated this move; Jesse refused to discuss it. Perhaps, having made an effort to return to his old outlaw ways, Frank found them not to his liking.

More likely, Annie had persuaded him to lay down his guns for good. Had she promised to carry out her threat to leave him? Had she forced him to choose between her and his son and the James gang?

The announcement hit Jesse hard. He and Frank had always been close. For years, they'd lived parallel lives, fighting the same enemies, working together to pull off robberies in half a dozen states, seldom living more than a few miles apart. Their public personae were also a unit: 'Frank and Jesse James', or sometimes, simply 'the James boys.' Not even I could claim to know Jesse better than his brother.

But tension between them had increased in recent months. Whether this was due to Annie's influence, or because Frank had grown more cautious with age, while Jesse had grown more reckless, I couldn't say. I don't recall a single big argument that signaled a break between them. There was no visible animosity in their interactions, but I sensed a heavy sadness between them—the grief of two people who loved each other, yet who could not be reconciled.

I believe no one was happy about the separation except Annie. I sensed her triumph when she and Frank stopped by our house to make their farewells their final morning in Kansas City. The brothers said a stiff good-bye on our front steps while Annie waited in a carriage in the street. The men's grim expressions and overly formal address said more than their words about the tension between them. "Don't bother to write; it's too dangerous," Frank said.

Jesse nodded. "You know if you ever change your mind and want to come back, you're welcome here."

Frank glanced toward the waiting carriage. "I don't think I'll do that."

"Then I wish you safe travels." They didn't shake hands, or embrace, or make any of the gestures of two men who had once been so close.

Frank straightened his hat on his head and nodded. "You take care of yourself, Dingus." Then he turned and climbed into the buggy and drove away.

Jesse watched them, the muscles of his jaw clenched, until they turned the corner and disappeared from sight. I came to stand beside him. "Do you think Annie put him up to this?" I asked.

He shook his head. "Buck hasn't been happy since we left Tennessee. I thought taking up arms again would cheer him, give him a sense of purpose, but he's lost the heart for it. And he's lost his nerve, which is dangerous for any man in our business. It's better that he go away. Better for both of us." But there was no conviction in his words.

He glanced at me. "Of course, Annie being so disapproving didn't help," he said.

"If I told you I disapproved of what you're doing, would it make any difference?" I asked.

"No. But then, you knew that before you asked." He tucked my hand into the crook of his arm. "I am what I am, and you accept that. It's the one thing I've always counted on in this world."

He was right, of course. I loved Jesse because of the man he was, and in spite of it. Nothing he could do could change that, any more than I could will myself to stop breathing.

Chapter Eighteen

Jesse left the next day, and I was sure I'd soon read in the papers about another robbery. But he returned a week later with Charley Ford, and a skinny boy who turned out to be Charley's younger brother, Bob.

"Charley and Bob are going to stay with us a while," Jesse announced. "Tell everyone they're my cousins, the Johnsons."

"Pleased to meet you, ma'am." Bob wiped his hand on his shirt front and offered it to me. "I'm more than pleased to meet the wife of the outlaw Jesse James. I've been following your husband's career since I was a tyke. Ask me anything you want to know about Jesse and I could tell you."

"Why would I want to ask you anything about my husband?" I asked. "I've known Jesse practically my whole life."

"I just want to prove to you I'm an expert on the subject of the James gang," Bob said. "Even though I just met him, I bet I know him almost as well as you."

"I'm not a gambling woman, Mr. Ford." I glanced at Jesse, who stood behind Bob, looking amused. Apparently Jesse didn't find the younger man's adoration as disturbing as I did.

"I have to figure a woman who would marry Jesse James has a more than usual inclination for risk," Bob continued. "It's not something I've spent an overly great deal of time pondering, but meeting you now, I'm sure I'm right."

Jesse put a hand on Bob's back and steered him toward the door. "Don't go picking at Zee like a sore tooth," he said. "You don't want to get her riled. She's a lady through and through, but she won't stand for any nonsense."

"Oh, I know she's a lady, Jesse. I didn't mean to imply otherwise," Bob said. "I only meant that she's an uncommon one."

"Call me Dave. And leave Zee alone. That's not a request, it's an order."

They stepped onto the back porch and shut the door behind them, so I didn't hear Bob's answer. I hoped he would leave me alone. A minute in his company and already I was wishing him gone.

"Don't let Bob upset you," Charley said.

I started; I'd forgotten Bob's brother was still here. He gave me a sad-eyed smile. "Bob has that effect on some people," he said. "But he's got a good heart. He just tries too hard to impress people sometimes, that's all."

I moved the children onto makeshift beds in the front parlor, turning their former bedroom over to these two guests who were anything but welcome. Where Charley was easy-going and affable, Bob was a bundle of nerves, jumpy and agitated. While Jesse and Charley visited the local saloons and livestock sales, or spent long evenings on the back porch, smoking and discussing little of importance, Bob trailed along, contributing to the conversations, but never really part of them.

I was hanging laundry one morning when Bob was in the side yard, fooling around with something or other. I tried my best to ignore him, though his presence alone was enough to spoil my morning. I was just stretching up to pin a shirt to the line when a loud gunshot shattered the day's peace.

I screamed, and looked around for the children. Jesse came barreling out of the house. "Zee!" he shouted. "Are you all right?"

It was the first time in memory he'd slipped and addressed me by my real name in public. "Yes. I'm fine. Just startled." I glared at Bob, who had emerged from the side yard, a still-smoking revolver dangling from his right hand.

"What do you think you're doing?" Jesse reached Bob in a few long strides and snatched the gun from him.

"I was just shooting at some targets." Bob thrust out his lower lip in a pout. "I wasn't aiming at Josie or anything."

"You want to shoot targets, you go out in the woods where there isn't anybody around," Jesse said. "A stray bullet could hit somebody, not to mention the neighbors might think it odd, a man shooting off guns in the middle of the day."

Bob hung his head. "I'm sorry J—Dave. I guess I wasn't thinking."

Jesse put his hand on the younger man's shoulders. "Just don't let it happen again." He examined the gun. "What kind of weapon is this, anyway?"

"It was my grandfather's. I know it's not much, but it's all I got right now."

"It doesn't look very reliable." Jesse sighted down the barrel. "I doubt you could hit what you were aiming at with it."

I collected my empty laundry basket and marched past them into the house, passing Charley on my way out. From the kitchen window I could see them, the three men with their heads together, deep in a discussion of weapons or horses or politics or any of the things I had no interest in, yet which occupied them for hours.

As much as I disliked Bob and even Charley's intrusion into our lives, I understood a little their attraction for Jesse. If I missed Annie, how much more did Jesse miss Frank? The two had scarcely been apart in thirty-four years. Their estrangement had left a void in his life the children and I could not fill. Maybe talking to the Ford brothers helped take up some of that emptiness.

In November, Jesse decided we should relocate from Kansas City to St. Joseph, Missouri. Charley and Bob helped us move. They loaded a rented wagon with our furniture and other belongings and drove the wagon to our new residence and unloaded things at Jesse's direction. I thought then they would leave us alone for a while, but they settled into the new house as readily as they had the old one.

"Why are they still here?" I asked Jesse. Even Dick Liddil, for all his false charm and sly looks, would be preferable to Charley, who always looked ashamed of something, and Bob, who followed after Jesse like an adoring puppy.

"I want the two of them where I can keep an eye on them," Jesse said.

I stared at him. "If you don't trust them, why do you want them in your house?" I asked.

"As long as they're with me, I know they're not out trying to stab me in the back."

In St. Joseph, Jesse abandoned the name of Jackson, and once more called himself Mr. Howard, though he changed his initials from J.D. to J.T. and introduced himself as Tom. Howard had been his alias for so many years now, I expected he felt more comfortable with it. Or maybe it was because Tim was old enough now to wonder why the family's name changed as often as its residence.

I liked the little house on the corner of Lafayette and Twenty-first streets in St. Joseph, but almost as soon as we settled into it, Jesse began looking for something better.

"I've found the perfect house for us," he announced one afternoon in late December. I was in the kitchen, rolling out pie crust for the pecan and pumpkin pies I planned to serve for our Christmas dinner.

"We already have the perfect house," I said.

"Charley and I checked it out this afternoon," Jesse continued. "It's just around the corner, so moving won't be a problem at all."

"Why move at all, if you're only going around the corner?" I asked.

"This house is on a high hill." Jesse helped himself to a handful of the pecans I'd shelled for the pie. "Off to itself."

"Nobody could sneak up on you in this house," Bob said. He reached out to take a handful of nuts as well, and I slapped his hand away.

"Four big rooms, good air circulation," Jesse said. "And the rent's only $14 a month. I told the agent we'd take it. We can start moving tomorrow."

I glared at him, but he pretended not to notice. "I'll move this time," I said. "But no more. Not for at least a year. I want us to settle for a while."

He gave me a look that passed for an apology and kissed my cheek. "No more moving, sweetheart," he said. "I promise."

The next day, Charley and Bob loaded a borrowed wagon with our furniture and other belongings and drove around the corner and up the hill to our new home. I had to admit the house was beautifully situated, with a view in all directions of the town and surrounding countryside.

The house was painted white, with green shutters, and large windows in every room promised relief from the oppressive summer heat and plenty of light even in winter. The front parlor and one bedroom faced the road, while a second bedroom and the kitchen looked out onto a neat yard.

We arranged the best furniture in the front rooms, and Jesse hung his prized painting of Skyrocket on the wall opposite the front door, so that it would be the first thing anyone saw when they entered the house. We'd had to leave the horse himself behind in Kentucky. Jesse feared the animal was too well-known and associated with Jesse James, so he'd sold him to his friend Carter. Now our stable held two new thoroughbreds, whose names I can't even recall.

The move was exhausting, but when we were done Jesse, Charley and I bathed and put on our best clothes, then took the children with us to the Christmas Eve service at the Presbyterian Church. Bob stayed behind. "I'm not of a religious mind," he said.

"I wish we had a lock on our bedroom door," I told Jesse as we walked toward the church, Charley and the children trailing behind us. "Bob might decide to go through our things while we're gone."

"That's not a very charitable thing to say at Christmas," he said.

I didn't feel Bob Ford particularly deserved my charity, but I kept my mouth shut.

"People take Bob wrong sometimes," Charley said. "Being the baby of the family, he always felt he had to try harder to be noticed."

"He'll have to do like I did," Jesse said. "Do something to make a name for himself at a young age."

I was glad enough to reach the church and turn my attention away from Bob. Jesse, too, seemed to enjoy the service. He enthusiastically sang the carols in his slightly nasal tenor and nodded in approval as he listened to the sermon. When time came for the offering, he put a dollar in the plate.

Afterwards, we walked home in the crisp night air, Tim chattering excitedly about Santa Claus coming that evening.

In spite of my misgivings about the move and taking in the Fords, we had a joyful holiday. Charley helped Jesse decorate a tree, and Bob spent hours playing with Tim and the new toy soldiers Jesse had bought him. I'd made Mary new outfits for her rag baby, and she spent hours rocking the doll and singing to it—sweet, made-up songs about birds and flowers and angels.

Jesse presented me with a jet and gold breast pin, and a length of fine Spanish lace. I gave him a new knitted waistcoat and a set of pearl and jet shirt studs. We had a dinner of cured ham and fried potatoes and creamed onions, and the pies I'd made, with fresh whipped cream. Afterwards, Charley made Bob help him do the dishes so that I could rest. That was a nice Christmas present in and of itself!

Four days after Christmas, Jesse and the Fords left again. "I haven't heard from Wood in a while," Jesse said. "That's not like him, so I think I'd better go check up on him."

The day after he left, I woke feeling sick to my stomach, and spent the morning alternately nibbling crackers and vomiting into a basin beside the bed. Tim fetched a neighbor, Mrs. Turrell, who made me tea and offered to look after the children for a few hours while I rested. "Do you think you're coming down with something?" she asked, all concerned.

"Nothing I haven't been through before," I said, nodding to Tim and Mary. I had had my suspicions that I might be pregnant again, but this bout of morning sickness confirmed it. "The first few weeks are usually the worst."

"Congratulations, then," Mrs. Turrell said, beaming. "I recommend ginger tea. It's always been a great help to me at times like this."

Whether it was the ginger tea or the knowledge that I had to keep going in Jesse's absence, the worst of the nausea passed quickly. I decided not to tell anyone else of my condition until Jesse was home. I knew he'd be thrilled, and maybe knowledge of my pregnancy would induce him to stay closer to home for the next few months.

Jesse failed to find his cousin Wood, and no one would admit to having seen him for a while. Jesse invited Dick Liddil to go with him on a tour of Kansas, but Dick was recovering from a leg injury and declined. So Jesse took Charley with him, leaving Bob behind at his family's farm. He returned at the end of the month alone, and for a brief period we enjoyed a kind of honeymoon in our little house on the hill.

A few days after Jesse returned home, it snowed. The city disappeared behind a veil of white. Snow sifted over trash heaps and toys that had been left out, and an old buggy Jesse had purchased and planned to repair. Everything old and ugly was transformed by a shroud of glittering white. All was silent as only a snow-covered landscape can be.

The children were beside themselves with joy and could hardly wait for me to dress them properly before they raced out into the yard. Jesse hurried after them, laughing and shouting as he galloped through the drifts. He tripped on some forgotten obstacle and the children doubled over with laughter at the sight of him stretched out on his back in the snow. "I meant to do that," he declared, "How else could I make a snow angel?"

He fanned his arms and legs back and forth in the snow, making the perfect outline of an angel, then rose up with a shout and swept the two giggling children into his arms. "Come out and join us, Sweetheart!" he called to me.

Safe on the porch, I shook my head. I preferred to stay relatively warm and dry, enjoying the view of the snow-covered town spread out below us.

Jesse looked at Mary, then at Tim. "Mama doesn't want to play with us," he said. "What should we do about that?"

"Hit her with a snowball!" Tim said.

"Dave, no!" I protested, but he had already set the children down and bent to scoop up a handful of snow. I turned to retreat into the house, but before I could open the door, an icy wet sphere hit me squarely in the back.

I whirled and took a second snowball in the chest. Forgetting my resolve to remain warm and dry, I charged down the steps, arming myself as I went. Soon snowballs flew between Jesse, Tim and I. Mary was content to sit in a pile of snow and watch us, laughing. Then Tim and I sided together against Jesse, pelting him mercilessly, until he held up both hands. "Uncle!" he shouted. "I surrender."

Laughing, I stepped forward to brush the snow from his hair and he pulled me into his arms. "You have pretty good aim for a girl," he said.

"You have pretty terrible aim for a man who makes his living with a gun," I teased, but softly, so that the children and the neighbors wouldn't hear.

"One more reason I've never robbed a train with a snowball." He nuzzled my cheek.

"Your nose is cold," I protested.

"What's a little cold on a day like today?"

The pure joy reflected in his smile and his eyes made my breath catch. Here was the Jesse I had fallen in love with—the bold, fun-loving young man who had seized each day with such energy. This was the Jesse before bullet wounds and grief and the burdens of wrongdoing had aged and changed him. I leaned close and pressed my mouth right up against his ear. "I love you, Jesse James," I whispered.

"I love you, Zee James," he answered. His eyes sparkled with mischief. "And I love Josie Howard and Mrs. Jackson, too."

"Scandalous!" I swatted at his shoulder, my hand scarcely making an impact in the thick bearskin of which it was fashioned. Mr. Howard and Mr. Jackson were still Jesse to me. The names were nothing more than a convenience.

"Papa, help me build a snowman!" Tim called. He was attempting to roll an irregular ball of snow across the yard, with little results.

"What about a snow woman?" I called, and started toward him.

The three of us ended up building an entire snow family—Mama, Papa, little boy and baby sister. We lined them up on the front lawn and decorated them with lumps of coal and dried tree branches. The snow woman wore a bird's nest as a hat, and the snow man had a thick twig in his mouth that passed for a cigar.

"What happens when it gets warm again?" Tim asked as we stood admiring our work.

"They'll melt," I said. "That's what snow does when it gets warm. It turns back into water."

"I don't want them to go away," he said. "I want them to always be together."

"That isn't possible," I said. "We'll just have to enjoy them now, while we can."

Jesse gathered Mary into his arms, then put a hand on Tim's shoulder and steered him toward the house. "The snow family can stand guard while we go inside and have some hot chocolate," he said.

"What are they guarding us from?" Tim asked.

"It's just an expression," I said as we climbed the steps to the porch. But the comment had destroyed the happy mood of moments earlier. It reminded me that we were not an ordinary family. We didn't live on this hill because we enjoyed the view, but because we felt safer here. Like the snow family standing vigil in our front yard, we must always be on guard, watchful for dangers hidden like obstacles in drifts of snow.

The end of February was always a hard time for us, recalling that terrible time four years previous when we'd lost our twin boys, Gould and Montgomery. I dealt with my grief by lavishing attention on Tim and Mary, spending many happy hours cuddling them, reading to them, or sitting beside their beds, watching them sleep.

At six and a half, Tim was the image of his father, with the same sandy hair and brilliant blue eyes. He never walked when he could run, and he liked nothing better than to follow in Jesse's footsteps as he worked around the yard, or to accompany him on trips into town.

Mary, a petite dark-haired princess, loved to sing and take care of her doll. But when Jesse was home, she had eyes only for him. She would launch herself at him upon his return to the house and he would swing her high. Often she sat in his lap while he read the morning papers, or played at his feet while he smoked a cigar and stared out at the town from our house on the hill.

But even our children could not comfort Jesse in his grief for the two we'd lost. The last week in February, he did what he always did when dealing with difficult emotions—he roamed, this time all the way to Nebraska, where he claimed to be searching for a farm. "We could make a fresh start out there," he told me. "Raise wheat and race horses. And children."

It was an old dream, one he'd talked about before. But I knew it was only a fantasy, never likely to come true.

I'd told Jesse about my pregnancy and as expected, he was thrilled.

"We've got a good future in front of us," he said. "It's only going to get better."

In March, a telegram arrived from Zerelda, informing us that Jesse's half brother, John, had been shot during an altercation at a party and was not expected to live. "I'd better go to her," Jesse said, as soon as he'd burned the telegram in the kitchen stove.

"Don't." I put my hand on his arm. "There's nothing you can do for John, and you know the law will be watching your mother's house."

"They've been watching the house for years and they haven't caught me yet."

"What if one of the neighbors sees you and decides to turn you in for the reward?" I asked.

He shook his head. "You worry for nothing, sweetheart." He stepped onto the back steps and called out to the children, who were playing in the shade of a tall oak. "I'm going to visit your grandmother for a few days," he told them. "I hear one of her dogs has a new litter of puppies. Should I bring you one?"

"Yes! Yes!" Tim jumped up and down, his hands in the air.

Mary also squealed with delight, though whether because of her brother's excitement, or her own anticipation of a puppy, I couldn't tell.

After Jesse left, I was restless. When Mrs. Turrell invited me for tea the next afternoon, I readily accepted.

Lydia Turrell was a plump, fair-haired woman a few years younger than myself. Her husband worked in the press room of one of the St. Joseph newspapers and they had a daughter who was very near Mary's age. While the children played with colored blocks on the floor of the parlor, my neighbor served cucumber sandwiches, little iced cakes, and dark China tea with sugar and cream. "What does your husband do, Mrs. Howard?" she asked.

"Please call my Josie," I said.

"And you must call me Lydia. I know Mr. Howard's work takes him away often. What is it he does?"

I shifted in my chair, uncomfortable with the question, even though I believed it was asked out of idle curiosity, and not because she suspected anything untoward about Jesse's occupation. "He buys and sells commodities," I said. "Wheat and corn, and also cattle and horses."

"I never realized that sort of work required so much travel."

"Yes, it does." I sipped my tea with a pretense of calm. "He also has family scattered around the country and often visits them. He's gone to see his mother, now."

"My husband thought yours might be a sporting man," Lydia said. "He always dresses so nicely, and he has a confidence about him I imagine a gambler would possess." She leaned toward me, her expression anxious. "I hope you're not offended by my saying so."

"Of course not." I relaxed a little. Her concern for my feelings was too genuine not to trust. "Tom has always enjoyed fine clothes."

"You're lucky to have a husband who takes such care with his appearance." She looked away, and I thought of Mr. Turrell, who returned each evening in ink-stained coveralls and a much-battered hat. Lydia herself favored gowns with many ruffles and elaborate bustles. I wondered if she'd been raised in a more affluent household than her current situation.

"I often see Mr. Howard playing with the children," she continued. "I saw you all together enjoying the snow earlier in the year. You looked so happy."

"I *am* fortunate," I said. "Tom is a wonderful family man."

"How did the two of you meet?" she asked. "I hope you don't think I'm prying. I've always been fascinated by stories of how couples get together."

"Tom and I have known each other since we were children," I said. "How did you and Mr. Turrell meet?"

"We met at a church social." She blushed, looking much younger than her years. "A mutual friend introduced us and I was immediately smitten." She lowered her voice and spoke in a conspiratorial tone. "The next day, my aunt read my tea leaves and told me that I had recently met the man who would be my husband, and I knew at once it was Jim."

In that instant, I was transported back to that sweltering afternoon on Mrs. Peabody's porch, when she'd read my palm and told me I would marry a handsome man who would make me the envy of many. I could almost smell the cloying scent of jasmine, almost feel the cool roughness of her hand grasping mine. And I felt anew the shiver up my spine when she'd predicted I would know hard times, and refused to look me in the eye.

All that had come true, I thought, as I sipped tea and watched the children play on the floor. Jesse was a handsome man, and I knew some women looked at me with envy. And we had known hard times—certainly the deaths of Montgomery and Gould had been wrenching, and before that those harrowing days after Northfield, when I hadn't known if Jesse lived or died. I prayed those trials were past us now, and that we'd be allowed to settle into easier days.

"Do you have any special plans for Easter?" Lydia asked. "Will your family be visiting?"

"We have no plans." I thought of Jesse's penchant for bringing home stray 'friends' such as the Fords, and passing them off as cousins. "But that could change. Tom is very hospitable."

"I was so glad when you moved in," she said. "The woman who lived in that house before was not very sociable. It's nice to have a family there. We sometimes seem very isolated up here on this hill."

"Yes. It is lonely up here sometimes." Jesse liked being above everything, with a view of the town and valley spread out below, but I missed being surrounded by people and places I knew well.

"You know if you ever have need of anything while your husband is away, you only have to ask," Lydia said. "James and I would be glad to help you."

"Thank you." I smiled. "That's very good to know." It would be good to have one friend I could count on.

Since Annie had moved away, I'd had no close female to confide in. I hadn't realized before how much I'd missed that. Only a woman could truly understand another woman's struggles to both nurture her children and encourage their independence. And only another wife could relate to the conflicted feelings a woman has for her husband—the ardent love tempered by irritation at his spending habits or his stubborn disposition or temper or some other character trait which had seemed small and insignificant during courtship, but which now rubbed her nerves like a rock lodged in her shoe. Such feelings could cripple a marriage, the way a tiny rock can cripple a walker. But my love was made of stronger stuff; I had resolved to develop callouses against the things in Jesse that disturbed me; to take these weaknesses and from them build a stronger, truer love. One that would last a lifetime.

Jesse returned home the following week, bringing with him the promised puppy, who was greeted with much enthusiasm by the children.

He also brought with him Charley and Robert Ford. "Don't scowl at me that way," Jesse said before I could utter a word. "Charley and Bob are going to help me with a little job and I need them here to help with the planning."

So once more our 'cousins' took up residence in our spare room. I grudgingly prepared their meals, though I resented their presence at the table. The second night they were with us, Charley fell into a fit of coughing just as I set a pigeon pie on the table. "What is wrong with you?" Jesse asked. "You sound near dead."

"Sorry." Charley wiped his mouth with a dirty handkerchief he'd pulled from his pocket. "I took ill this winter and it's taken me forever to get on the mend."

"I hope you don't have the consumption," I said, eyeing him warily. He'd lost weight and was decidedly pale. "I don't want the children exposed." Not to mention Jesse. With two bullet holes in his lungs, who knew how susceptible he might be?

"They won't be here that long," Jesse said.

"I knew a whore over to Hannibal who had consumption," Bob said. "She was real popular with the clientele of the house she worked for, on account of her pale, delicate complexion and—"

"I will not have such talk at my table!" I glared at Bob. To my right, Tim sat with his fork halfway to his mouth, staring at our guests in fascination.

"Bob, you ought to have better manners," Jesse said. "You apologize to Zee."

"I'm sorry, Zee. I was just trying to show that consumption isn't always an unwelcome thing."

"Well I certainly don't welcome it, or that kind of talk." I held out my plate. "Jesse, would you serve me a piece of pie?"

"My dad and I once shot forty-two pigeons in less than ten minutes," Bob said. "Do you think that's some kind of record?"

"I think it's wasteful to shoot so many pigeons if you couldn't eat them all," I said.

"Dad wanted to keep them out of the corn," Bob said. "But we ate plenty of them. My mom made a wonderful pigeon pie. Not that yours isn't delicious, too," he added.

"Charley doesn't seem to care for it," I said, watching Bob's brother push his serving of pie around his plate.

"Oh, it's good, Zee," Charley said. "I just don't have much of an appetite tonight."

"Do you think you could shoot forty-two pigeons?" Bob asked Jesse.

"I've never had occasion to want to shoot that many pigeons," Jesse said.

"What about forty-two men? If they was all after you?"

"That's not a proper topic for dinner table conversation, either," I snapped.

Bob fell mercifully silent, though his brooding presence did little to lighten my mood. He stared morosely across the table, eyes fixed on the wall behind Jesse's left ear, though the only thing to see was a section of brown figured wallpaper.

The next day, Jesse came home from town with a small wooden box under one arm. "Where's Bob?" he asked, after he'd kissed me hello.

"He and Charley are cleaning out the horse stalls, like you told them." I looked at the box. "What's in there?"

"Just a little something I picked up for Bob." He crossed the kitchen to the back door and called out, "Bob, Charley, get in here."

The Ford brothers shambled out of the barn and headed toward the house. Charley at least had the presence of mind to stop at the pump and wash up before he came inside, and he insisted Bob do likewise.

Once they were inside, Jesse led them into the room that served as their bedroom, though it was meant to be the children's room. Tim and Mary had to sleep on a cot in the front room until the Fords left, which I hoped would be soon. I stayed in the kitchen with the children, but I moved closer to the door so that I could listen in on the exchange.

"I brought you something, Bob," Jesse said.

After a brief silence, Bob exclaimed, "It's a beauty, Jesse! I never had a gun so fine."

"I don't want you getting us all killed with that relic you've been carrying. Besides, if you're going to be one of the James gang, you ought to have a decent weapon."

"Thanks, Jesse. I'll treasure it always."

"If you want to practice with it, remember to go off in the woods. I don't want you upsetting Zee or the neighbors."

The three soon emerged from the bedroom—Bob grinning, a new Colt revolver stuck in the waistband of his pants. Charlie looked pale and sicklier than ever, while I could only describe Jesse's expression as smug.

"What are you doing giving that boy a gun?" I asked that night as we readied for bed.

Jesse ran the brush through my long hair. I was vain about my thick tresses, which were still dark and wavy, though I found more and more silver strands among the mahogany these days. "The old gun he had was dangerous and unreliable," he said. "It could have blown up in his hand.

If that happened in the middle of a job, we'd be done for."

"It's too expensive a gift to be giving a boy like that," I said.

"He already thinks I'm some kind of hero," Jesse said. "There are days when he can't stop talking about all the things he's read about me. He says he's been studying me and Frank practically since he learned to read. Why not give him another reason to look up to me?"

"I don't like it." I hugged my arms across my chest, trying to ward off a sudden shiver. "I wish you'd tell him to leave. Him and Charley both. I want you all to myself."

He laid down the brush and ran his fingers through my hair, then lifted it and kissed the back of my neck. "You have me now," he said softly. "All to yourself."

We made love tenderly that night, as if with our bodies we could make up for the unintentional slights and imagined hurts of the past months. I knew I'd been impatient with Jesse, pushing him to change his life in ways that made him feel uncomfortable and trapped. And he must have been conscious of his neglect of me, regretful of the weeks he'd spent roaming in the company of men he could never completely trust, while I waited at home with our children.

With my fingers and my lips I traced the scars that marked his body—the two indentations in his chest behind which one bullet still lay, and the deep crease in his thigh where a second bullet had lodged. I stroked his bearded chin and remembered the smooth-cheeked boy who had taught me about sex and love, and kissed the lines fanning out from the corners of his mesmerizing blue eyes.

Though he'd endured many physical hardships over the years, Jesse had kept himself in fine shape. He had the body of a young man, muscular and taut, and I reveled in the feel of his corded arms and strong chest as he rolled over and lifted me on top of him. "I like to look up at you when we're making love," he said. "To watch the pleasure on your face."

Such scrutiny embarrassed me, but I soon forgot any timidity as he slid into me and began to move. The more than fifteen years we'd been together hadn't lessened my ardor for my husband, or his for me. I had heard rumors over the years of other women, but I dismissed them as lies made up by those who wanted to profit from an association with a famous outlaw. I believed Jesse had been faithful to me, as I had been to him.

We knew the benefits of a long partnership that were simply not available to more casual acquaintances. He knew just how to touch and caress me and I knew how to move and respond in order to increase his pleasure and my own. Within minutes I was biting my lip to keep from crying out, acutely aware of my children and the Ford brothers sleeping nearby.

Jesse had no such compunction. He came with a loud cry, driving hard against me, making the bed springs creak and sing. I hurried to shush him, and he laughed at my concern. "It doesn't matter if anyone hears," he said. "The children won't know what we're doing, and if Charley and Bob figure it out, they'll only be envious."

"Hush!" I said, my horror at his suggestion and the very preposterousness of it combining to make me dissolve into a fit of giggles.

I fell asleep in Jesse's arms that night, my head cradled in the hollow of his shoulder, feeling as safe and loved as I ever had.

The next day was Palm Sunday and Jesse and I took the children to church. Charley stayed behind, saying he didn't feel well. I had heard him up during the night, being sick in a basin in his room. "You should drink some ginger tea to settle your stomach," I advised.

"Charley's just suffering from nerves," Jesse said. "He'll feel better in a couple of days."

I assumed he meant after the job Jesse was planning was over but I didn't ask for details.

After dinner Jesse read the papers and I laid down to take a nap, while Bob and Charley retreated to the bluff below the house and fired off Bob's new revolver, round after round, until I put a pillow over my head to drown out the constant ringing.

At dinner that night, Charley refused to eat at all, while Bob chattered more than ever, telling some long involved story from his childhood. I pulled Jesse aside after the meal. "Those two have got to get out of my house," I said. "I can't stand them much longer."

"They'll be gone soon," he said. "I promise."

Jesse rose early the next morning, and took Tim into town with him to buy a paper. I made breakfast, which neither Bob nor Charley would eat. "What's wrong with you two?" I asked as I took away their untouched plates. "Do I need to dose you with castor oil?"

"We're just nervous about this upcoming job," Bob said. "Jesse wants us to ride with him today to Platte City, to check out the bank there. There's going to be a big murder trial there and he figures while everybody's attention is on the trial, we can go into the bank and clean it out."

"Shut up." Charley spoke more harshly than usual and glared at his brother. "Jesse never talks about such things with Zee." he said.

"Jesse always says the less I know about his activities, the better," I said. "And I believe most of the time he's right." But secretly I was pleased to know Jesse's plans. The sooner he took the Fords away from here, the better, as far as I was concerned.

Jesse and Tim returned shortly after that with the papers. Tim went into the back yard to play with Mary and their new puppy while I served Jesse his breakfast.

"What the—?" He looked up from his paper at me, his eyes flashing with anger. "It says here Dick Liddil's been arrested," he said.

I hurried to set the hot coffee pot on the table before I dropped it. "Arrested for what?" I asked.

"This doesn't say, though Dick could have done any number of things to get in trouble since I saw him last."

"Dick won't say anything about you, will he?" I asked. Dick knew where we lived and the aliases we used; he could bring the authorities right to our door. We'd had to leave Tennessee because of the arrest of one of Jesse's fellow outlaws who could have led the authorities to us. Would we have to repeat that exodus now? And where would we go?

"No, Dick won't talk." Jesse set aside his paper and picked up his fork. "At least he'd better not, if he knows what's good for him."

I reminded myself that Dick had been a bushwhacker, and Frank and Jesse both had vouched for his loyalty. Surely he wouldn't betray Jesse.

Bob and Charley said nothing; they sat like statues, not eating or talking or even moving as they waited for Jesse to finish his meal.

After breakfast, Jesse set the Fords to loading the horses for the trip to Platte City. It was a hot day for so early in spring, and he removed his fine cashmere suit coat and folded it neatly at the end of our bed.

"Are you going out with your guns showing like that?" I asked as he passed through the kitchen once more. "Mrs. Turrell will wonder why a commodities broker has to go around armed."

"Can't have her spreading gossip," he said. He returned to the bedroom and emerged a moment later without the gun belt. In all the years I'd known him, I had seldom seen Jesse without a firearm at his side, but I had no reason to believe he was in any danger in his own home.

He went back into the front room and started for the door just as the Ford brothers came in from the outside. I turned my attention once more to the breakfast dishes, though Jesse's voice from the other room carried clearly to me.

"That picture of Skyrocket looks dusty," he said. "Can't have that."

I heard the scrape of a chair being dragged across the floor, and the squeak of the wooden frame as Jesse climbed up on it.

The loud report of gunfire was so harsh and unexpected that at first I didn't recognize what had made the sound. A second shot surprised a scream from me, and I dropped the dish I'd been washing. It landed at my feet in an explosion of shattered crockery. I sank to my knees and tried to gather the fragments, then a second, louder crash shook the house, the sound of something large and solid hitting the floor.

Conclusion

I don't remember running into the front room, don't remember kneeling on the floor or cradling Jesse's head in my lap. Blood blossomed on my apron as I frantically stroked his cheeks. He stared up at me with sightless eyes, their brilliant blue already clouded. "Jesse!" I screamed, but even then I knew he was beyond hearing.

"It was an accident, Zee, I swear it was."

I looked up to see Charley standing over me, his face contorted with grief. "The gun went off by accident," he said.

"An accident!" I shrieked. "I guess it went off on purpose."

Bob had already fled the room and now Charley ran after him.

I stared at Jesse, so still and silent, his blood soaking into my apron and skirt. A high, keening wail filled the room, and it took some time to realize it came from my own throat.

A small hand on my shoulder pulled me back to my senses. Tim stared at me with frightened eyes. "Mama, what's wrong with Papa?" he asked. "Why are you crying?"

"Run across the street and fetch Mrs. Turrell," I said. "Take Mary with you and don't either of you come back into this house until I tell you."

He hesitated, his gaze shifting to his father's body. "Go!" I ordered, and turned him toward the door.

When I was sure the children were gone, I looked once more at Jesse. His blue eyes had lost their brilliance in death, and the blood seeping from his wound had slowed to a trickle now that his heart had ceased to beat.

"Oh, Jesse," I moaned. I smoothed the hair from his forehead and bent to kiss him. His skin was waxen beneath my lips. My tears splashed onto his cheeks, and ran down into his beard. Sobs shook me and pain buffeted me. I clung to Jesse, afraid to let go. For so many years he had been my anchor in stormy seas. Now I was cast adrift, the prospect of the future too bleak to bear.

I don't know how much time passed before I felt a hand at my elbow, and strong arms lifting me to my feet. I blinked, and looked around at a crowd of men that filled the small parlor of my home. Through the open windows I saw more people, pressed close about the house, everyone trying to see in.

"Madam, what is your name?" asked the man who still held my arm. He wore a dark blue suit and a grave expression.

"Mrs. Howard," I answered automatically.

"Madam, I have two men who swear the man who lies dead here is none other than Jesse James."

I looked over the man's shoulder and saw Charley and Bob standing with two other men, one of whom carried a rifle and had a badge pinned to his chest. Charley looked as if he might pass out at any moment, but Bob grinned in triumph.

"You killed him!" I shouted, and lunged for Bob. "You killed the man who was your *friend*!"

The sheriff and the man who had spoken to me had to hold me back. I don't know what I thought I could do to Bob, but more than anything, I wanted to erase that grin from his face.

The two men refused to let me go or to stop questioning me until I admitted that the man at our feet was indeed Jesse James. A murmur swept through the crowd at this news. "Mr. Howard?" someone exclaimed. "Mr. Howard was the outlaw Jesse James?"

They took away Jesse's body and his guns, his clothes and my jewelry and all of his horses. Already, the crowd outside had begun to tear pieces of siding from the house, taking the bits of wood as souvenirs. They might have picked the place as clean as a swarm of locusts if the sheriff hadn't posted guards to protect the building.

Lydia Turrell proved a true friend and helper, looking after the children and forcing me to drink cups of hot tea. She asked no questions and demanded no stories, only offered comfort and her silent support.

The Ford brothers were arrested for murder, but were soon released with a full pardon. It was some time before I realized they had both been in the pay of the governor, as had Dick Liddil. Jesse had been friend and mentor to them. He had welcomed them into his house and fed them at his table. He had made a gift to Bob of the very gun with which he was killed.

In the end, none of these kindnesses had mattered. He'd been shot in the back and left to die, assassinated for money.

Jesse had once suggested all Bob needed was to do something to make himself famous. Bob had followed that advice. Overnight, his name was trumpeted in newspapers around the world. He had his picture taken wearing a fine suit, the revolver Jesse had given him resting across his knee. In the picture, Bob held the gun with his left hand, even though he was right-handed. When a reporter asked him about it, he said Jesse was left-handed, so it seemed only fitting he should pose that way. The boy who had idolized Jesse James couldn't let go of that fascination, even after he'd murdered his hero.

If Bob thought the murder of a friend would bring him wealth and respect, he was wrong. Even people who had called for Jesse's death hated the way it had been accomplished. It wasn't long before people knew Bob Ford as 'the dirty little coward who shot Mr. Howard, and laid Jesse James in his grave.'

Word was sent to Zerelda and she came up on the next train, dressed in yards of black bombazine and surrounded by reporters. She moved like a great battleship through their midst, grief adding dignity to her six-foot frame, righteous anger lending weight to every word she spoke, all of which were dutifully reported in the newspapers.

She and I both testified at the inquest, but it was Zerelda who drew the most attention. When she shouted that Bob Ford was a murderer, and lunged for him, the room erupted with excitement. Bob cowered before her, and two strong men held Zerelda back.

I bowed my head and watched tears make damp stains on the black silk of my dress. No amount of hysterics would restore Jesse to me. No possible revenge would make up for his death. No publicity or public outcry could bring me comfort. I was utterly bereft, every breath an effort.

As I waited outside the courthouse for a ride back to the hotel where the children and I were staying, a man approached. Taking in my widow's weeds, he tipped his hat and asked. "Are you a member of the family?"

I nodded, mute. The stranger had the air of a reporter, and I'd had my fill of answering questions.

"May I ask who you are, ma'am?"

I stared at him with the detachment with which I viewed everyone and everything since Jesse had been shot. Who was I, now that Jesse was gone? I had spent my life as 'Sister' or 'Mrs. Howard' or 'Josie' or even as 'Mrs. Jesse James.' Only alone with Jesse had I been merely 'Zee.' "No one," I answered, and turned away. In losing Jesse, I felt I'd lost myself as well.

I had spent weeks alone while Jesse traveled, competently caring for house and home. But now even the smallest task—buttoning my shoes or preparing breakfast—seemed impossibly hard. I could only conclude that before I had drawn strength from the knowledge that Jesse would soon return to me. Now that promise had vanished, and with it my will. Jesse had been everything to me and nothing would ever fill this emptiness inside me.

Jesse's body was photographed and the photos sold for five dollars each as souvenirs. He was packed in ice, and displayed in the window of the local undertaker's. I shuddered when I saw him, remembering the happy morning when he had lain in the snow in front of our house, making snow angels with the children.

Local officials arranged for Jesse's body to be transported by special train to Kearney, where it was displayed at the local hotel so that people could pay their last respects. Many did so; I read later that almost as many people came to say good-bye to Jesse as did to see the body of President Garfield.

Zerelda and I rode in a special car on the train, escorted by a retinue of law officers who were properly deferential, many of whom seemed genuinely sorry for our loss. Tim and Mary stayed behind with Mrs. Turrell. I didn't want to expose them to the circus I feared the funeral would become, and doubted my own ability to keep from breaking down in front of them.

They were having a bad enough time of it, coming to terms not only with the loss of their father, but with the knowledge that he had been, not Dave Howard the commodities dealer, as they had always been told, but Jesse James the famous outlaw, about whom they had heard stories all their lives.

Mary was too young to understand much, but Tim—whom people suddenly began addressing as Jesse Junior or Little Jesse—must have felt that his whole life until now had been a lie. His father wasn't who he'd said he was and Tim's name wasn't even really Tim. The man he'd idolized simply for being his father was now a larger-than-life public figure—one revered and mourned by thousands of people, so that the boy's grief was not even his own.

Jesse was buried in the front yard of the home where he had grown up, so that Zerelda could watch over his grave. In death, she had reclaimed him, drawing the attention of the press and the public to herself. I was too heart-sick and half-crazy with grief to care. If not for the knowledge that my children needed me, I might have laid down myself and died right there.

I lost the baby I was carrying, and had to sell almost everything we owned, including the puppy Jesse had brought from his mother's for the children. Little Jesse and Mary and I went to live with my oldest brother, Robert, for a while, and then to my sister Sallie's. All those years we shared that attic bedroom in my parents' home in Kansas City, I'd never imagined she would have to take me in, but there was nothing else I could do. All the money Jesse was said to have taken in his career as an outlaw was gone. If not for John Edwards raising a subscription to support me and the children, I would have been destitute.

Not many months after Jesse was buried Frank surrendered, turning over his guns to Governor Crittenden. He was tried and acquitted, and moved into peaceful retirement. I wept at the news, thinking of what might have been.

I heard that Charley Ford took his own life two years after his brother shot Jesse. I blame Charley for not stopping Bob's rash act, but I can't help but believe Charley would have never been party to such a betrayal without Bob's encouragement. As for Bob, I don't know where he is now, though I like to think he suffers in hell, whether the one in the afterlife, or one in this life of his own making.

Zerelda guards Jesse's legacy jealously. She charges visitors who want to tour her home, and subjects them to long lectures about her famous son, who grows more virtuous with each passing year. Before they leave, she sells them stones from Jesse's grave, for twenty-five cents each. When the selection grows sparse, she replenishes it from the creek behind her house.

I care about none of this. My spirit is impoverished, if not my pocketbook. All of life is veiled in gray for me now, without Jesse to give it color. I kept the scrapbooks, and I look at them often, reliving those times when life held so many possibilities.

I never meant to fall in love with Jesse James. But I might as well have tried to stop a prairie fire or a raging tornado. He had that same wild power, both beautiful and terrible to behold, the same heat and intensity to illuminate and destroy everything in his path, both those he hated and those he loved.

Afterward

Jesse had a wife
To mourn for his life
Two children—they were brave.
But that dirty little coward
Who shot Mr. Howard
Has laid Jesse James in his grave
—American folk ballad

Zee Mimms James died November 13, 1900. She had worn widow's weeds and mourned Jesse for more than 18 years. She had raised her children, but had never recovered from the loss of Jesse. Though he had stolen hundreds of thousands of dollars in his career as an outlaw, she was left destitute. Despite her poverty, she refused numerous lucrative offers to sell her story, choosing instead to keep Jesse's secrets to her grave. Those who knew her best said she died of a broken heart.

She was buried in Mount Olivet Cemetery in Kearney, Missouri. About eighteen months later, Jesse's body was moved from the James' family farm to rest beside hers. In death, Zee and Jesse were reunited at last.

About the Author

The first books author Cindi Myers remembers loving were historical novels—The *Little House* books and *Caddie Woodlawn.* History, particularly American history, enthralled her. She began her writing career crafting historical romances, and has written nonfiction articles about American history for publications ranging from *Texas Highways* to *Civil War Illustrated* to *True West.* Her idea of a good time is spending hours reading through old journals or newspapers, and she has planned vacations around visits to historic sites and museums.

Cindi is the author of more than forty novels, both historical and contemporary. Her work has been praised for its depth of emotion and realistic characters. You can learn more about her and her work at www.CindiMyers.com or www.RomanceoftheWest.com.